S THE KALD'S
BLACK VERSE

JORDAN LOYAL SHORT

SKOLJA

Acknowledgments

No book is ever written without help. This one most of all. Thank you to everyone who made this possible. My good friends Brian Rollins, Scott Haggerty, and Lauren Gandurski, as well as my new friend Tom Riecken, who each pushed me to refine different aspects of the novel. Anne, Katherine, and Kim Munis, three brilliant sisters whose input helped shape the story and whose encouragement was like water in the desert. To Jeannie McMillan-Olson for beta-reading out of her abundant kindness. To my incomparable editor Amanda Edens for all her help polishing *The Skald's Black Verse*. To Deranged Doctor Design for their beautiful graphic design work on the cover. Thank you also to my parents Gary and Louise, and my in-laws Lorne and Linda, whose support and wisdom have gotten me this far. But most of all I want to thank my dazzling superstar of a wife, Rishelle, without whom I would be lost, despondent, and probably face-down in a ditch.

Prologue

"The mischief of the Mara and the malice of the Raag are small misfortunes next to the horror of witnessing your people conquered, the proud made to grovel, the beautiful raped, and the wise buried to the dirge of laughter."

-Bjorn Gurdsten, The Slave's Lament

Anders Nilstrom stood at his own front door as if it were the threshold of hell. He knew he was stalling, fumbling to muster the iron in his belly to do what must be done. But the deal was struck long ago. He tugged his hood down against the hail and stole a look over his shoulder, eyes darting from the well house to the tree line to the gravestones out by the road. There was no reason it would come tonight.

Just an old worry.

The Hidden was little more than a dream now. A shadow in the fog, receding into the abyss year by cursed year. Only the fear was too raw, even at the remove of decades.

And now the price was due.

If it watched him from somewhere out in the dark, what would it see? A man aged beyond his prime years. The stoop appearing in his shoulders, gray in his beard. Too many lean winters that had left him thin, scarred, and bitter, clinging to the grim hope that it would hold up its end of the bargain.

A scream within the cottage jolted Anders from his black thoughts. His shoulders crumpled, and he let out the breath he'd been holding. He whispered a prayer to the Ten Fathers, though he knew it would go unanswered. Damnation waited inside. But it was the only way to be free. Let the Fathers judge when it was done.

He opened the cabin door, the wooden hinges shrieking, a bucket of well water sloshing in his hand. The fire had dwindled to a bank of embers before which his daughter Elsa shivered under a pile of coarse blankets. Anders set down the bucket he'd fetched and knelt beside her, his knees protesting.

"What took you so long?" she asked, her voice weak.

His precious Flower. *Fjorel*, he called her, from the old tongue. She'd grown to such a beautiful girl. He couldn't tell her he'd been steeling his courage, so instead he lied. "I heard Cinder whinnying. He got out of the stall, so I had to chase him down and take him back to the barn." Anders plucked a log from the cradle by the hearth. He set the wood atop the dying fire and turned back to his daughter.

"How far apart are the pains, *Fjorel?*" he asked.

"Not long." She propped herself up, one hand on the dusty floorboard, the other on her belly. "I'm dizzy. Where is Breylin?"

Anders turned his palms up helplessly. Another lie. He had never sent for the midwife. "Let's have a look. We can manage without her."

He drew back the woolen blanket, and the pair froze, the fresh log crackling in the fireplace. A pool of darkness spread between her legs, soaking the white blankets he'd lain beneath her. They regarded this blot in shared horror, as if they'd discovered the corpse of a friend on the roadside.

Elsa wept.

He wringed his hands, groping for the words to comfort her fear. But what could he say? It was too much blood. Instead, he set his mind to the task ahead, his stomach knotting as his unease grew. His Flower cried out again, a short, sharp bark like a seal pup.

"It's all right, *Fjorel*," his finger combed the sweaty hair from her face. "Lie back."

Anders reached up to one of the rawhide chairs by the hearth and grabbed a rag and a vial of ointment. He tucked his

2

long blonde hair into the collar of his shirt. Then, he lifted the hem of his daughter's dress and bent down to have a look. "The ring is open, Elsa. It's time to push."

He held out his hand, and she took it, squeezed it as she bore down, pushing, breathing like the midwife had taught her. Another contraction came, another scream. Anders dabbed ointment on the rag and wiped blood and mucus from between her legs, the cloth soon black in the firelight.

"Keep pushing, *Fjorel.*"

"I'm trying," Elsa said. "I'm so tired. I just want to sleep."

Over and over, she pushed, and she screamed. Her grip on his hand weakened, her voice grew fainter. Her head lulled.

Anders gently slapped his Flower's cheek, rousing her. "You're almost done, Elsa. If you want the child to live, you have to keep fighting. You don't have long."

He saw his words tear the veil from her eyes, a flicker of sadness dashed by a wave of intensity.

Elsa tightened her grip on his hand, fighting with the grim determination of the doomed, a rage born of indignation that the world would dare to rob her baby of its precious, unspoiled life.

Anders whispered to the Fathers, begging for forgiveness that would not come. He would have given anything to speed her journey, but the birth drew on. Her shrieking echoed in the night, the quiet afterwards filled by ragged breaths and hail drumming on the thatch above.

At last the child's head crowned, the end of Elsa's suffering in sight. Anders mopped his Flower's brow and held her hand, spurring her when her efforts flagged. He knelt between her legs, his fingers probing for purchase to guide the baby safely. With waning strength, she heaved the child out to the shoulders. Anders hooked his fingers into its armpits and dragged it into the world.

Elsa lay back, panting. Her eyes closed.

Anders inspected the child. Its withered form a shame— and a blessing, considering his pact. One of its arms had wilted and its brow grew out of proportion to its tiny face. In the old days they would've left it in the forest. The child reached out and grabbed his thumb, its eyes crusted shut. It never cried.

It was a boy. A luckless, misshapen boy. His grandson. But doomed, he reminded himself. Doomed.

Anders turned away from his daughter, using his body to hide his crime.

"Father," Elsa asked. "Are you crying?"

Anders looped the umbilical cord around the child's neck, shielding the murder from his daughter's eyes, masking it in the form of grief.

"What's wrong?" she asked. "Why are you crying?"

When it was done, he turned to her, without meeting her eyes, and offered up its strangled corpse. "The cord was wrapped around its neck," he said.

Elsa cradled its little body, her tear-streaked eyes falling shut and snapping open. "Olek," she called him.

He could not have borne it if this were the end. But the Hidden's words had been confirmed by the midwife, and Elsa's hand went to her belly, her eyes rekindled by the movement within. A forlorn smile crept across her face.

"Breylin was right," she said.

Anders took the firstborn from her and set him by the fire. He covered the child with a clean rag, its shrouded form lurking in the corner of his eye. "Almost there, *Fjorel*. You're so strong." Anders patted Elsa on the knee. He bent down. "I can see the head already. It won't be long." He looked up, hoping for relief in her eyes, but her head fell to the side and her eyelids fluttered. Anders grabbed her wrist and jerked on it. "Elsa! Stay awake."

"I'm here," she muttered. "Still here."

"Then push, girl." He reached between her legs. "Push!"

Elsa clutched the blood-soaked blanket beneath her and cried out, the fingernails of her other hand raking the floorboards. She panted, her lips pursed, breathing, seizing a moment of tranquility before the next contraction hit.

"Good," her father said. "Again."

4

She labored on, at times losing consciousness only to awaken as pain cut through the darkness. At last, Anders wrested the child from its mother's womb. A big, black haired boy, plump and healthy. Anders blanched at the hair, the ochre skin, but he had known the boy would be a *shade*. Another legacy of the invasion, of its father's people. Yet the child had his mother's startling blue eyes. So Anders slapped him on the backside, evoking a shrill cry.

The proud grandfather held up his prize for Elsa to see. Joy lit his face. But his joy was fleeting. His Flower lay with her head turned toward the fire, its light dancing in her open eyes.

Good bye, sweet *Fjorel*.

He lay down with his head resting in the crook of her arm and wept. Anders wanted to stay there forever. He deserved no better. But the child's cries awoke him from his grief. The price was paid, but the work still undone.

Anders drew his belt knife. He picked up the baby, cradling it in one arm. With his free hand he cut the umbilical cord. "Brohr," he told the child. "That is what I'll call you."

Anders cut the cord of the other child too, his eyes averted.

He listened to little Brohr scream, the boy no doubt frightened by this strange new world, by his brother's absence. The pummeling hail gave way to pattering rain. Anders' heart galloped. He closed his eyes and began to hum, finding the rhythm of these things. His heart slowed to match the tempo. His voice rose, an otherworldly timbre, deep, grating, growing louder as he embraced the song that had cost him his soul. He twined the umbilical cords together, hands slick with gore, singing his bleak verse all the while.

Anders bound the boys with the braid, looping it around their waists, and wrapped them in a clean blanket. His head swayed, violence dancing in his mind's eye. Anders drew his knife again and cut his scarred hand, letting blood drizzle onto the twins. His song ended on a determined note, bled of joy and innocence. His Flower had gone where she could not return. His fated grandsons—one spirit, one flesh—wailed a cursed duet.

5

The Hidden had promised, he told himself. At no mean price. The invaders would pay. Every one. They'd pay a ransom of horror and defeat and pain, these pigs who'd rutted on his precious Flower.

Chapter 1

"I dreamt, as a boy, of retaking our village with song and sword. Now, as a man, my nightmares are of my brother and his family, who have found peace in the bosom of our conquerors. To what length would I stoop, I wonder, were the horns of freedom to sound again?"

–Sorin Grafstrom, Letters from the Grisben Jail

Her song drifted from the hills, lent the haunting air of a lullaby as it journeyed through the forest. Birgit's little game brought a smile to Brohr's lips. He was drawn to the echoes like a man following the lure of a Mara's voice to his doom. He quickened his step, sweating under his homespun cloak despite the chill.

Brohr's breath steamed in the morning air, though the snow had stayed in the high hills. The woods smelled of pine needles and wet soil. Finches trilled from the bare branches of the ancient, gnarled oak that marked the eastern edge of his grandfather's land. Brohr's old wolf hound, Grendie, raced beside him, a mountain of a dog with a brindle coat and muddy feet. She scouted ahead, spinning in gleeful circles as she waited for her master to catch up.

Brohr carried a goatskin knapsack stuffed with bread, blankets, and dry clothes for their trek to Pederskald. By nightfall he hoped to be far away from the judging eyes of the townsfolk and his grandfather's relentless anger. Brohr wore a hatchet and dagger tucked into his belt, and a leather pouch dangled from it, jingling with a few silver federals he'd earned chopping wood for the widows in Skolja.

As they ascended, he hummed along to Birgit's tune, straining to make out the words. The trail dwindled into nothing, a track amongst the ferns and stumps that only his dog's unerring nose could follow. When they emerged from the wood, Grendie let out a playful bark and darted ahead. He spied Birgit atop a boulder, sitting in her patchwork frock, stitched with bluebirds around the collar. Behind her rose the distant, snowcapped peaks of the the Jotunspar Mountains, framed by billowing clouds, and trimmed in golden sunlight. Brohr paused, his eyes drawn to the horizon, the hair prickling on the back of his neck.

Birgit tucked a blonde lock behind her ear and smiled when she saw Brohr and Grendie.

"Brohr Nilstrom, you're late, you oaf!" Birgit jumped down to welcome Grendie.

"*Skel*," Brohr greeted her in old Norn before switching to the conquerors' tongue. "Sorry," he said. "I got in a fight with my grandfather."

"What's new?" Birgit stood on her toes and pecked him on the lips. "And what happened to your eye? Did he do that too?"

"No." Brohr cracked his knuckles. "Just a couple of drunks trying to take their troubles out on the half-caste. It's fine. The soldiers didn't even lift a finger to help. They thought it was funny." She reached up to touch the bruise under his eye, but he brushed her hand away. "I said it's fine. You should see what they looked like when I was done with them."

Birgit frowned. "Did you bring a tin penny?"

"Yes." Brohr rolled his eyes and a smile found its way to his lips. "And I had to give Axl a silver federal for it."

"It's good luck, Brohr. You can't start a journey without a tin penny in your pocket."

"Something tells me they came up with that before the pigs invaded. Tin pennies are rarer than gold. Plus half the town probably knows we're running off after I asked everyone and their brother for it," he said. "Where are your things?"

8

Birgit's smile faltered. She reached atop the boulder to something wrapped in a handkerchief. "I brought you a treat."

Brohr had a sinking feeling in his stomach, but he accepted the little bundle. He unwrapped it, staring down at the strudel dusted with sugar and crushed almonds. She wasn't telling him something. Was this a way to soften the blow before she backed out? Brohr tore off a chunk of the pastry and stuffed it in his mouth, forcing a smile onto his face as he waited for the bad news.

Grendie sniffed the air and rested a paw on his knee to remind Brohr she was there. Her antics broke the tension. The couple laughed and Brohr fed Grendie a piece of the pastry.

"Well?" Brohr asked. "Let's hear it."

Birgit kicked a pebble down the hill. "They hadn't left for town yet. I couldn't take anything out with me. We'll have to go back."

Brohr groaned. "Is that all? You had me worried."

Birgit grasped his hand and held it in both of her own. "Are you sure this is the right thing to do? I can't stop worrying about my father."

Brohr clenched his jaw, looking down into Birgit's imploring blue eyes. "It's his fault we have to do this." He ran his hand self-consciously through his cropped black hair. "He's not going to change his mind about me. I'm getting out of this town—no matter what."

"I know." She laid her head on his arm. "I just wish there was another way."

"Are you kidding? Your father hates me. Everyone here hates me. I'm not Norn and I'm not Tyrianite. Your dad looks at me and sees one of them. Do you know what it's like to have people look at you like that? Like they want to knock your teeth out for smiling or spit in your face for all the things the pigs ever did to them?"

"It's not my father's fault that—"

"It is!" Brohr ground his teeth. "It is his fault. I never did anything to him. Everyone in this town looks at me like I'm one

9

of them. And *they* look at me like I'm a stray dog. I'm nothing. I can't be anything here. Even my grandfather…well, sometimes he tries to hide it. Sometimes not. I can't stay here anymore. I can't live in that house another day. You think your father is bad? You think he looks at me unfairly? My grandfather hates me twice as much. To him I'm just a reminder of his precious *Fjorel*, and the ones who raped her. If we're serious about making a life together, you know it can't be here."

"I know."

Brohr stared off at the mountains for a minute before he sighed and bent down to feed his dog the rest of the strudel. "Sit," he said. "There's no sense in you making a racket when you see their dogs. Lie down." Again, she obeyed. "Stay." Brohr backed away. "Stay."

With one last look back at Grendie, Birgit tugged on his hand. "Come on." She led him down the hill in the opposite direction from which he'd come.

Brohr looked up at the sun, fretting about how late in the morning it was already. A woodpecker tapped at a nearby tree trunk, and just ahead a stream burbled through the undergrowth.

Birgit gasped, grabbing Brohr by the forearm, her fingers fair against his tawny skin. "Look," she whispered.

Before them, a pair of fawns lapped from the stream. One, whose antlers had just begun to bud from its crown, raised its head, and looked right at Birgit. It poised its foreleg as if to bolt, studied the couple for a moment, then planted its hoof again and stooped back to drink once more. Birgit squeezed his arm. "It's good luck, you know." She pulled Brohr down to her so she could kiss him.

They circled around the deer and pressed on to Birgit's farm. It wasn't long before they reached the clearing. A low stone wall ringed the homestead. The Gelstroms' log farmhouse, with its thatched roof, stood in the center of a reaped field beside the barn.

"Good," said Birgit. "They've gone."

10

She took his hand and led him into the clearing toward her house. A pair of hounds barked and ran up with tails wagging. Brohr scoped around for any sign of her father, but the wagon was gone, so he followed her into the open.

"I feel a little guilty," she admitted.

"Why?"

"Well, I just don't want them to worry."

"I talked to Vili," said Brohr. "He'll tell them tonight."

Her pace faltered when Brohr mentioned his best friend.

"What?" He asked.

"Nothing."

When they reached the front door, a round-topped portal with a brass knocker, Birgit looked over her shoulder and blew a kiss at Brohr. He smiled at her and squeezed her hand. The latch clicked, and the joy vanished from her face as the door opened from within.

Arni Gelstrom folded his arms, bare to the elbow beneath his tunic and tattooed with fading blackbirds. He was tall, and blonde, and wore a long beard that couldn't mask his anger.

"My own daughter. About to run off with a damned half-blood." He spat at her feet. "We'll have no shades in my line."

Brohr squirmed as Arni's eyes tallied the hints of his Tyrianite side: Brohr's black hair, his darker skin. A wisp of a smile crossed Arni's lips as he took in Brohr's aquiline nose, broken by his grandfather years ago and never set properly. Birgit's father noticed they were holding hands.

"Get your filthy hand off my daughter. *Svik!*" Arni cursed him in the old tongue. "Pig!"

"Master Gelstrom—"

"Quiet!" Arni roared. He took a step towards them, backing the couple away from the house. "Just going to run off, were you? Off to Pederskald to live like a whore with this lout?"

"Father, I'm sorry." She held up her hands in surrender. "Please, you're not being fair to Brohr."

"Fair?" The farmer shook his fist in his child's face. "Was it fair when a horde of these murderers dropped out of the sky and burned everything to the ground? Fair? They killed your grandparents! All four of them! They killed two of your uncles. And now you're all cozy with this—"

"I was born right down the way." Brohr pointed back toward his farm. "Skolja is my home. I didn't come from anywhere but here."

"You shut up, pig." He stormed Brohr as if to tackle him, but Brohr stood his ground and Arni pulled up short at the last second, face-to-face with his daughter's suitor. A nasty smile crept onto Arni's lips.

"It's a good thing," said Arni Gelstrom, "that your friend came to warn me. Come out here, boy." Brohr ground his teeth, shaking his head. His best friend, Vili Olsten, appeared in the doorway, head hung, golden curls veiling his face, hands clasped before him. "Come on out, boy," said Arni. "I owe you my thanks."

Vili took a few steps out of the doorway. He looked up at Birgit with pleading eyes. Arni kept gloating, close enough that Brohr could smell the onions on his breath, but the man's words were lost to the roar of Brohr's blood in his ears. He felt that other presence, angry, full of childish rage.

Vili looked up with shame in his—

★★★★★

Brohr's fist cracked Vili's jaw.

"Stop!" Birgit wailed. "No more."

He threw her aside, bending over Vili, snatching the knife from his belt. Vili looked up through his good eye, the other a mess, a mass of bruise and blood.

"No," Birgit pled.

Brohr hesitated, dizzy, disoriented. He wiped drool from the corner of his mouth. He stood by the big oak tree on the west side of the clearing. He had been... over there. Brohr looked back at the house across the field. His ire retreated, that familiar, frightening presence receding, turning over into slumber.

That anger had always been with him, always clawing toward the surface. Railing against his grandfather's unfairness, the taunts of a few bullies. But nothing like this. It had never broken free. Never taken over. Until now.

"Son," Arni sounded wary. "That's enough."

Birgit's father stood twenty paces away. He ran his finger down his cheek from the corner of his eye, a ward against evil spirits. Blood dripped from his torn earlobe into his beard.

Brohr stood up, dropped his friend and backed away, sheathing his knife. Birgit rushed over to Vili, cradling his head.

"Are you okay?" she asked.

Vili mumbled something unintelligible.

Birgit flinched as Brohr reached out to her. "Stay back," she said. "What *was* that?"

"I," Brohr hesitated. "Sometimes…" He couldn't explain. How could he put words to a curse, a mystery that lurked in the dim corners of his life?

"Go." She kept her eyes on the ground. "Please. Just go."

He looked from Birgit to Vili to her father. Brohr backed away. "I'm sorry. It was an accident."

She picked up a rock and threw it at him. "Just go!"

A final plea died on Brohr's lips. He hung his head, turned on his heel, and started the long walk home.

★★★★★

Prefect Brasca Quoll stood looking out the porthole as their ship flew over the hamlet of Skolja. Short and umber-skinned, a whisper-thin mustache on his upper lip, the prefect spied a sleepy seaside village below, a backwater of log and thatch and muddy streets. North of town, a crude fort dominated a large plateau—his new command. To the east, another hill dotted with a large house and a statue of the local saint at the top.

13

Beyond that, the choppy waters of the Selvig Sea stretched toward the horizon.

What a disgrace, to find oneself here at the edge of civilization, lording over a den of pale savages. He'd only left Tyria a week ago, but the homeworld seemed a distant memory, a half-dream. Once, he had hoped to be raised to the Electorate, even to be anointed a Judge. But that was all ashes now. He supposed he was lucky; if his father wasn't an Elector, he'd probably have been burned at the stake, or at the very least excommunicated. The idea did little to cheer him. He was marooned here on Heimir, this insignificant planet, so far removed from the real seat of power, a victim of his own conscience, his own stupidity.

Brasca grabbed the rail behind him and gripped it tight as the ship circled around to land. Its ancient engines screeched, the vessel lurched, and the arcane machinery geared down, settling into a hum. They touched down beside the fort, the iron hull groaning from the strain.

He choked down the acid rising in the back of his throat and quelled the revolt in his stomach. Void travel had always unnerved him. Not just the discomfort—the cold, the weightlessness—but the very idea of it. Something about the age of most ships, relics of the bright era, patched together with suppositions and salvage by the lesser binders of today.

He stood on a grated catwalk, overlooking the cargo bay, which comprised the interior of the cylindrical transport ship. To his left, the three pilots of the void craft awoke from their trance, removed their elaborate helms, and unbuckled themselves from their seats. The devices allowed them to communicate with other helms across the vast emptiness above, to receive orders from Trond, the provincial capital on the other side of the mountains, and to navigate the ship through the cold and merciless abyss. Below, the crewmen raced about, preparing to unload.

The captain, a wisp of a man with thinning black hair and ashy skin, strode over to him and threw up his right arm, hailing his superior officer. Brasca gave him a slight nod.

"Prefect," said the captain. "We have reached Skolja."

This was obvious, but he saw no reason to scold the man. Instead, he donned his tricorn hat, which he had laid on his seat while looking out the window. "Very good, Captain. Once your men have unloaded the supplies, you can be on your way."

The captain hailed him again and began issuing orders to the crew. The eldritch engines ceased their hum, the silence filled by boots on metal and then the whirring motor of the bay door opening.

Brasca strapped on his short sword and descended the stairway to the cargo bay, waiting at the rear of the ship as the ramp unfolded. A delegation of two men stood at the foot of the ramp, their breath steamy in the morning chill. The first was an officer of the federal legion: in his thirties, muscular, with the brown skin, straight black hair, and the shorter stature of a Tyrianite. He too wore a tricorn hat, an etched breastplate, and an ornately stitched leather skirt with woolen leggings for the cold. The other man was a provincial—a Norn—the locals called themselves. Old and pale and portly. He wore a leather suit trimmed in fur and green felt, and eyeglasses, quite an extravagance. The pair couldn't have been more different.

The Tyrianite officer doffed his hat and hailed Brasca as he approached. "Welcome, Prefect. It's an honor to have you here."

Prefect Brasca Quoll returned his subordinate's salute. "Thank you, Ordinal." He turned next to the older man. "And you are?"

"Olen Torvald, Mayor of Skolja, at your service." The provincial forced a smile. "But please, call me Olen." He hailed him as a soldier might, and Brasca frowned at him, turning back to the officer.

"It's Carthalo, right?"

"Yes, sir."

Brasca waved off the provincial and said, "Thank you. Ordinal Carthalo and I have much to discuss. That will be all for now, Mayor Torvald." The man didn't seem to realize he'd been dismissed at first. "Goodbye," Brasca added.

"Of course," said the Mayor, muttering something else as he walked away.

An honor guard of Federal legionaries bearing round wooden shields ringed them, beyond which many of the locals had turned out to watch the ship's arrival. The Tyrianites were all clean-shaven, wearing leather skirts, black-iron breastplates, and conical helmets while the Norn locals favored drab woolen cloaks, leather breeches, and unkempt beards.

"Perhaps," said Ordinal Carthalo, "you would like a tour of the fort or the town. We could even inspect the mine if you are up for another journey so soon."

"That can wait, for now," said Brasca. "I'd like to talk about the nature of my mission."

Carthalo looked away.

"I see you've heard the rumors," said the prefect.

Ordinal Carthalo nodded. "Yes, about your lapse. After your son, well, it's understandable you balked at putting the torch to Crassa."

Brasca shouldn't have been surprised that his embarrassment had reached the Ordinal's ears. His father was an Elector of the synod after all. "That is only half of the reason I'm here," he said.

Carthalo looked far off toward the hills. "Every man has doubts, sir. There is of course the matter of the rite of command. Will that be... a problem for you?"

Brasca started walking toward the nearby fort, a rude palisade of tarred logs. "There is no need for any awkwardness, Ordinal. This is a temporary command. The rite is unnecessary. Though I would like you to step in at offerings."

A pair of Tyrianite legionaries carried a crate of cold iron bars up the ramp and onto the transport ship. Overhead, a trio of gulls wheeled on the sea breeze, keening at the new arrivals.

16

Carthalo nodded. "The men will notice, of course."

Brasca knew he was shirking his responsibility. Every Tyrianite officer, from the lowliest Ordinal to the deified Pontiff himself, was a link in the holy chain of command. The rites were as much a part of his duties as the soldiering. Even if it was all a hill of dung.

"I really don't care," said Brasca. "If they didn't burn me at home, it doesn't matter what the men whisper out here."

"Permission to speak frankly, sir?"

The prefect stopped and turned to face his subordinate. "Very well."

"Things are not as, shall we say, *liberal*, here. This isn't Trond or Tyria. This sort of…unorthodoxy… will not sit well with the men."

Brasca smiled. "Spoken like a true believer. Don't worry, Carthalo; this exile won't last long. As I said, the nature of my mission is temporary. In the meantime, you fret about the men's souls, and I'll worry about the rest. Just see that they follow orders."

"Yes, sir."

"Good." The prefect resumed his course to the fort. "I'm told you've been in command here for six months. Any trouble I should know about?"

"A few outlaws in the back country now and then. Nothing major. Drunken brawls, locals speaking their old tongue once in a while. We put them in the stocks or give them a beating. A few repeat offenders we've sent up to the mines. As long as the tithes flow and the mine runs smoothly, I don't push too hard."

"What happened to the last prefect?" Brasca asked.

"A pox, sir. He died early this spring. They haven't bothered to send anyone to replace him."

"Well, I'm told you kept the mine running smoothly, kept the prisoners there in check. The cold iron met quota every month. Most ordinals would've been content just avoiding a rebellion, but you've done well, a credit to your command. And there is no binder stationed here?"

"No, sir," said Carthalo. "But the Mayor—the man you just met—and his son are both binders."

"Really," Brasca marveled. "I've never even heard of provincials teaching themselves proper magic. It seems…inappropriate."

Carthalo nodded. "Will you have a legion binder transferred here?"

Brasca shook his head. "We likely won't be here much longer. I'm to prepare for a possible evacuation."

Carthalo stopped. "Sir?"

"A situation has arisen in Trond, which may require these troops in the provincial capital. We're to make ready and await orders." Brasca clasped his hands behind his back. "I want a report on the disposition of our men and the state of our supplies in one hour. Understood?"

Ordinal Carthalo shot out his arm in salute. "Yes, sir."

"Good," said the prefect. "One last thing. I want you to draw me up a list of potential troublemakers."

Chapter 2

"Bormian's attempt to establish a timeline of metaphorical events demonstrates a strong lack of discernment in his otherwise laudable character. Let us instead begin with what is actually supported by the material culture of the Norn: chiefly, their arrival upon the world of Heimir."

-Mago Tibrus, *Archeological Foundations of the Myth of the Ten Fathers*

His grandfather snored in the back room. Brohr sat before the fire, listening to the grating sound, and imagining what it might be like to smother the mean old bastard once and for all. If he didn't get out of this town, sooner or later Anders would drag him into his nonsense, into the hopeless, bitter war that his grandfather had lost long before Brohr had been born. Brohr had heard all of his stories a hundred times, heard all of the bile that spilled from his lips when he threw back a horn of mead. Skolja didn't feel like home anymore. Neither did the cabin. He imagined walking out into the starry night while his grandfather slept and never coming back. Something out there called to him. But he didn't want to go alone. Birgit had finally seen the side of him he tried to keep hidden. He had to find a way to show her he could control it, to remind her that there was more to him.

The hour was late, and Brohr would find no mercy in the morning. Chores at first light. But he couldn't help himself. Sleep just wouldn't come. He set a fresh log in the fireplace and sat back down in one of the rawhide chairs before the hearth.

In one hand, he held his great-grandfather's dagger, the bone hilt carved with the faces of elder generations, and in the

19

other, the figurine he was whittling. The young man was pleased with his work, hopeful in a desperate way. Already he had captured the essence of the fawn, foreleg frozen in the air, head cocked to listen.

He knew she would remember it. The moment was etched so clearly in his own mind. Birgit had her hair in two long braids, her freckled face alight with wonder. He'd held her hand, emerging from the wood, the fawn lapping water from the stream. It heard them, raised its leg, ready to run, and tilted its head warily. The little creature looked right at them, then, untroubled, it bent back down to drink.

Maybe if she could remember this moment, like he did, she would forget the rest. Even if her parents hated him, even if she thought of Vili laying broken in his bed, she could push it all aside and see him as he was. Or at least as he wanted to be.

He shaved away a bit from beneath the fawn's leg, careful not to apply too much pressure, gently revealing the moment trapped in the wood. Brohr changed his grip on the piece then held his knife like a quill, scraping at the eyes until he was satisfied that he could see a hint of curiosity there.

He'd been working on the deer for a few days, careful to keep it hidden from his grandfather. He didn't want the old man's scorn to mar it. When he finished, he blew away the last grains of sawdust, polished the warm wood with his calloused thumb, and held it up to the flickering light.

Nodding to himself, Brohr stood up from the chair, licked his thumb, and snuffed the candles on the table. From the hook beside the front door, he gathered his cloak, threw it over his shoulders, and tucked the carving into one of its pockets.

He listened to Anders's snoring for a moment, reassuring himself that his grandfather wouldn't wake. If he did, there would be hell to pay, especially for leaving the fire unattended. But he was resolved, and if he could get through to Birgit, the old grump's ire was worth it.

Brohr unbarred the door and opened it, grimacing as the hinges creaked. He was afraid that Grendie might bark, but the hound stood at the foot of the steps, wagging her tail. It was crisp and starry out, the tiny crescent of Otho moon a green sliver above the western horizon. To the south, Quaya moon waxed three quarters full, casting the night in crimson and shadows.

"Good girl," Brohr cooed, shutting the door behind him.

He tiptoed down the stairs and scratched Grendie behind the ear. She pressed her head against his hip, relishing the attention.

"Ready for an adventure?" he whispered.

The Gelstroms' farm was miles away. It would take most of the night to get there and back. So he set out at a trot, eager as he was. Brohr hadn't seen Birgit in nearly a month and only once since the fight with Vili. She wouldn't even talk to him, wouldn't hear his apologies. She'd hardly looked him in the eye. With shame, he remembered her fear.

Brohr left his farm behind, Grendie heeling, delighted by the spontaneous excursion. Quaya's moonlight filtered through the pines, slashing the forest floor into stripes of red and black. A faint trail that he'd worn with his own steps led to the Gelstroms' farm. He daydreamed as he climbed the gradual rise to the west, thinking of the moment when Birgit would find his gift. He knew her routine. Like him, she'd be awake at dawn. After her mother boiled her an egg, she'd head out to the barn to milk the cow. That's where she'd find it. In the milk pail. She'd be startled at first, like the fawn; perhaps she'd look around, ready to bolt, but then she'd stoop back to the pail and hold the figurine aloft.

He smiled, sweating as he jogged up the hill. He'd see her again soon. Maybe in town. Saint Olaf's Day was tomorrow. He pictured their rendezvous. Maybe he'd steal a kiss. He'd need a better apology though. He could even try to explain his episodes.

The thought robbed his daydream of its luster.

Brohr crested the rise and slowed to a walk. Grendie dashed ahead, emitting a playful woof as she disappeared into the night. Brohr pressed on after her, but Grendie didn't return for almost an hour. He knew she must be close, though. She wouldn't leave him undefended. He circled around the Bergen's farm, not wanting to disturb them. That's when Grendie, big as a wolf, burst from the brush ahead, startling him. He laughed, embarrassed despite his solitude, and gave her a playful swat on the rump.

When they reached the stream, he detoured to the place where they'd spied the fawn. He relived the moment, though his thoughts inevitably turned to Vili. The worm. He pushed away the anger, the betrayal, and the shame. It's not a night for dark thoughts, he resolved.

Brohr turned to his dog, who looked at him expectantly, her tail swishing back and forth.

"Sit," he said.

She did. Brohr knelt and rubbed her ears, kissed her on top of the head.

"Stay," he commanded.

Grendie looked a little disappointed, but she obeyed.

Brohr stood up and turned toward the Gelstroms' farm. He forced himself to walk, though he wanted to run, because he knew that Grendie wouldn't be able to help herself if he did. The Gelstroms' had hounds of their own. He knew them well enough, so he hoped they'd tolerate him, even after his last visit, but another dog might cause a fight.

Brohr vaulted the stone fence, slick with the first hints of the season's ice. Somewhere on the other side of the clearing, an owl hooted its warning note. He crouched, skulking to the edge of the Gelstroms' home where he paused a moment, trying to imagine Birgit asleep inside. He'd never been allowed in, of course. The barn was built about thirty paces north of the house, the smell of its new coat of white paint still lingering in the air. It was small too, just room enough for a couple of stalls, one for the horse and one for the cow, with a chicken coup out back.

Brohr crept closer, taking careful, quiet steps, his eyes on his feet, hoping he wouldn't wake the chickens or the dogs. He assumed that their hounds slept outside of the barn, but he couldn't see any sort of shelter for them.

When he reached the edge of the house, he headed past, the night still silent, save a frog somewhere that didn't seem to realize it was nearly winter. As Brohr approached, a bark startled

22

him and he whirled around. The hair on the back of his neck prickled, and that haunting sensation reared up over his shoulder, like someone looming behind him with a hatchet.

The Gelstroms' wolfhounds, each waist high and more than half his weight, yelped. One of them turned and bolted, disappearing around the house. The other froze, tucked its tail between its trembling legs, and peed. Brohr cursed. He breathed, clenched his fists, and pushed that presence away. When he opened them the other dog had fled too.

Someone would wake with all that racket. They'd probably come out to investigate. Brohr pivoted toward the barn and ran to the door, sliding it open as quietly as he could. The Gelstroms' draft horse, Flint, whinnied in the darkness. Brohr cast around in the dim light for the milk pail and found it beside the stall door at the back. He dashed over, plucked the fawn from his cloak pocket and set it in the pail. As he ran out, he whispered to his mother, his great-grandfather, and ancient Father Freyan that his gift would find Birgit, and that she would see he was not a monster, not a brute. That he loved her.

Brohr closed the barn door behind him, grimacing at the noise it made and took off across the clearing at a sprint. With luck, they wouldn't see him even if they came out; with a little more luck, her father wouldn't see the fawn, even if he looked in the barn. Once he cleared the fence and reached the forest edge, Brohr ducked behind the trunk of an elm and watched Birgit's father emerge from the far side of the house, carrying a lantern.

Brohr turned back to the forest and trotted a few strides up the trail before he froze. At first, he wasn't sure why he had. A strange fear for which he had no explanation came over him. His eyes scoured the darkened woods, searching for the source of his sudden apprehension. Just a few yards off the trail was... something. He squinted into the forest, his gaze drawn to a patch of deeper darkness at the foot of a great willow tree. His eyes ached to make sense of it, to confirm it was real and not his imagination. But it was too dark to sort out whether someone was hidden there or if his mind was playing a trick on him.

"Hello?" Brohr asked, his breath steaming in the cold. "Is someone there?"

Brohr waited for an answer, his heart pounding. He could swear someone was there. A stranger. Lurking. A thing. Not like the familiar rage that sometimes stole over him. He felt that presence too. Simmering below the surface. Watchful. Wary.

"Hello?" Brohr shivered. "Hello? I know you're there."

Behind him, the Gelstroms' dogs started barking again. Brohr steeled himself. Not daring to take his eyes off the patch of darkness, he made his way past the foreboding gloom, chiding himself for jumping at shadows, and finally broke into a dead run.

★★★★★

"Up!" A boot dug into Brohr's ribs.

He was almost grateful to be roused from the nightmare— old men watching Brohr try to hide his grandfather's body beneath the floorboards.

Brohr saw his breath as he looked up at the candle Anders held. He rubbed his eyes. His grandfather stooped over and tore the blanket off of him, the icy clutch of an early winter morning sending a shiver right through him. Anders Nilstrom glared down, scratching at his short, white beard.

"Damn you!" Brohr shouted.

A gust of wind guttered the candle his grandfather held. It went out.

"*Skolta vekt tu tram, Brohr.*" Anders spoke old Norn, as he often did when they were alone. "Guard that blasted temper of yours." The old man wasn't afraid of federal rules *or* his grandson's ire. In fact, he delighted in coaxing Brohr's anger to the surface and then drawing back from the precipice at the last moment. "I had a nightmare about you last night, Brohr. And now I wake to find your temper has followed me from my dream."

With his scarred hands, the gray-haired Norn relit the candle and set it on the altar at the back wall of their little cabin.

24

Figurines carved of wood and alabaster, the bearded faces of their ancestors, lay behind the candles, a cup of salt, and a handful of wilted wildflowers. The largest idol was Father Freyan of the Ten Fathers, those ancient scions of the Norn clans sent by the Shining Ones to conquer this world.

Brohr stood up, walked to the cupboard, put on a flannel, and took his boots over to the bench beside the table.

"It's dawn already," Anders said. He made his way to the front door of the cabin. "If you didn't stay up all night staring at the fire, I wouldn't have to roust you out of bed."

"What bed?"

His grandfather snorted. "Get to chopping. I expect to see some work done when I return." With that, Anders opened the door, its wooden hinges creaking and a patch of morning light spilling in. He stepped outside and slammed it behind him.

"Good riddance." Brohr slipped his boots on and buckled them. His cloak hung by the hearth. It smelled of mildew and woodsmoke. He threw it over his shoulder and was about to leave when he remembered his bedroll. If grandfather tripped over it, no doubt there'd be no end to his carping. Brohr bent over and bundled it up, tucking it on the floor beside the cupboard. He fetched the wood axe from the corner and headed outside.

The sun was up and would soon burn off the fog that had rolled in from the hills. Brohr squinted up as an eagle soared south toward the sea. Their cabin perched by the edge of the forest in a large clearing full of withered corn stalks.

Brohr had felled a tree the day before and sawed the trunk into manageable chunks. He heaved a section onto the chopping block, hefted his axe, and split the log with a single swing. At nineteen, he was as big as any man in the village, but the wood was still wet and it was hard work.

An hour later, he had stacked a waist-high row of firewood beneath the shed. He wondered how much of the wood the old man would expect chopped when he returned. It didn't matter, he'd be unhappy even if Brohr finished it all.

He combed the sweaty forelock of his black hair out of his eye. Brohr kept the top a little longer, and shaved the sides every few mornings, halfway between a Tyrianite's neat grooming and a Norn's lack of it.

It was Saint Olaf's Day. In town, they were already feasting on pancakes and lingonberries. They'd be tapping the kegs soon and eating roasted elk. Brohr's stomach rumbled in dismay. He'd be lucky to get a pinch of salt and a rabbit haunch to gnaw on. Brohr wondered if his grandfather would let him walk to town. Unlikely. His grandfather hated Saint Olaf. Braggart, he called him. More of his self-righteous nonsense.

Brohr decided to go into town. He didn't care what the old man said. Birgit would probably be there. He hoped she'd found his gift. He hoped she could forgive him. It was his best chance to mend things with her—maybe his last.

Brohr marched back into the cabin. Why bother asking for permission when he knew what the answer would be? He set the axe in the corner and put on his other shirt. He knelt down and slid his hand into the gap between the cupboard and the floor, pulling out the pouch with his silver.

His grandfather would be back soon with the game he'd snared, so Brohr wasted no time. He jogged out of the cabin, stopping only to tell Grendie to stay behind, and headed south toward Skolja, glancing back now and then to see that his grandfather hadn't followed.

Chapter 3

"The Norn, who dwell in the north of the Trondian continent, on the world of Heimir, trace their lineage from ten patriarchal figures whom they venerate as deities. Each clan is organized based on the scion from which they descend despite a complete lack of genealogical records, and common intermarriage practices. The Norn worship their ancestors, seeing them as intermediaries, capable of interceding with the Ten Fathers on their behalf."

–Acerbas Eidolinus, The Faith of Nornlund

Henrik watched his father transform in the presence of the newly arrived prefect. He actually ducked his head, hunching shorter, a fawning smile splayed across his lips. Pathetic.

"Prefect Quoll! Please come in." The mayor performed an awkward bow and stepped back from the doorway to allow the federal to enter his mansion. Prefect Brasca Quoll wore his dress uniform, a red tunic with a proliferation of emblems and badges adorning the chest, a fine leather skirt, doe hide boots, and an elaborate tricorn hat with a rakish plume that was tucked under his arm. A thin, waxed mustache twirled above a grim smile, his skin a little darker than most Tyrianites, something of a status symbol amongst them.

"Thank you for the invitation, Mayor Torvald," said the prefect.

He stepped through the vaulted doorway into the Torvalds' foyer. An amateurish painting of Henrik's grandfather dominated the southern wall, an elegant sofa beneath it. Above them hung a chandelier crafted from elk horn, glass orbs glowing from the cardinal points of its three tiers.

27

"Spirit lamps?" The prefect didn't wait for an answer. "A bit ostentatious don't you think? Are you skimming off the tithes? It would be quite disappointing to discover the mine's bounty had gone astray."

Mayor Torvald forced a chuckle. "Of course, you know I created it myself. One of my hobbies." He was a homely man, round face, pocked skin, hairline receding. He wore homemade eye glasses, his hair cut short and his face clean shaven in the Tyrianite mode. He was always imminently practical, adhering to federal fashion even more than Henrik. "It's one of the simplest bindings but terribly interesting. Only the oldest trees will suffice. The animus is drawn in, and—via a sort of inversion of the effect by which they convert sunlight into nutrition—there is light!"

"Do they use cold iron?" the prefect asked, his face serious.

"No, sir," said the mayor. "It isn't necessary for this sort of binding."

The prefect's polite smile returned. He marveled up at the chandelier. "My adjutant told me you were a binder, but I didn't quite believe it. It's an embarrassment not to have one of our own at the fort. Something I hope to remedy soon. However did you manage that out here?"

"Books, sir. I have a weakness for them." His father finally gestured to Henrik. "This is my son, Henrik."

Henrik had half a mind to say something rude so that he could get back to his book, but instead, he gave the federal a perfunctory bow. The prefect, in turn, studied Henrik's groomed mustache and long, flaxen curls, his high cheek bones and dimpled chin. The Tyrianite's scrutiny unnerved him a little. He wondered if the prefect had already heard that Henrik could bind spirits too, if the man would feel threatened by a pair of provincials capable of magic. With a winsome smile, Henrik held up his goblet, as if to toast. "A pleasure to meet you."

"I hear you share your father's hobbies," said the prefect, confirming Henrik's suspicion. "Wonderful. I would never have imagined it possible, so far from civilization." The mayor blanched. "We'll have to get the pair of you over to the fort one

28

of these days. There are a few things that could use a binder's touch."

"We'd be honored," the mayor said. "We're always happy to help." Mayor Torvald fussed with the buttons of his shirt, at a loss for what to say next.

"My mother is just finishing up breakfast." Henrik took a sip of his brandy. "Where are my manners? Let me get you a drink. It's a holiday after all."

"No, thank you."

"It's tradition," said Henrik.

His father shot him an angry glance. "Young man, I have matters to attend to after this," said the prefect. "I'll need a clear head."

Henrik shrugged, turning his father a deeper shade of red. "Of course."

The mayor broke in, hoping to repair the moment. "Quite admirable, sir. I'm inclined to agree. Just because it's an occasion is no reason to waste the day."

The prefect acknowledged him with a grunt.

"Please," the mayor continued. "Join us in the dining room." He gestured to a door in the north wall.

Mayor Torvald led them into the cloakroom, taking the prefect's flamboyant hat and hanging it on a peg amidst the stoles and boots arrayed neatly around the little room. He then proceeded them into the dining room, where the ceiling reached twice as high, with two chandeliers identical to the one in the foyer hanging over a long table carved with embellishments and surrounded by upholstered chairs. At the back of the room, the scent of oven-fresh pastries wafted in from the doorway leading to the kitchen. The table was set with glassware and silver cutlery, garish by local standards, but Henrik noted a look of disappointment on the prefect's face.

The mayor gestured to one of the settings and waited for the prefect to sit before he followed suit.

"Hildur," the mayor called. "Hildur, the prefect has arrived!"

Henrik rolled his eyes at his father's social lapse.

"Coming love!" his mother answered from the kitchen.

A heavyset woman with graying hair pinned up in a bun entered the dining room, carrying a tray piled with sausages and pancakes. Though the years had added wrinkles and pounds to her, Hildur's eyes still sparkled, and she carried herself with the grace of a beautiful, happy woman. She set the tray in the center of the table and sat beside her husband, opposite Henrik and the prefect. Smiling at her guest, she picked a decanter off of the table and poured brandy into each of their goblets.

"The prefect was just telling us he must abstain from drinking this morning," said the mayor. "A busy day."

"Pity." Hildur grinned at the prefect. "But more for us, I suppose."

Brasca laughed, his first genuine smile appearing.

An awkward silence ensued.

Hildur's eyes went from the prefect, to her son, and back again. "Did you know that Henrik is a painter?"

"Mother." Henrik blushed.

She waved away his embarrassment. "It's true. He's very talented. Did you see the portrait in the foyer? He should paint you sometime. I'm sure he'd be honored."

Henrik loosened his collar. "I'm sure the prefect is very busy. Besides, I haven't painted anything in over a year. You know that."

She shook her head. "I know. It's such a shame."

Mayor Torvald cleared his throat. "Let him be, Hildur. It's good that he's devoting more time to his studies."

The prefect watched the exchange, an amused look growing with every word.

"A toast perhaps?" Hildur held up her glass, waiting until her husband gave her a little nod. "To Saint Olaf, who may or may not be coming back soon."

The prefect chuckled and picked up his glass. "How can I say no to such a charming woman? To our absent friend, Saint Olaf."

The quartet toasted the martyr, and Mrs. Torvald served breakfast, beginning with the prefect and ending with herself.

"I've always wondered," asked Henrik, "why you allow us Saint Olaf's Day. I mean, the whole point is that when he returns, he'll lead a rebellion. It doesn't seem the sort of thing you'd encourage."

The mayor stepped on his son's foot under the table. "Forgive my son, Brasca. May I call you Brasca?"

The prefect's smile vanished. He sat up straighter. "No, too familiar."

"Of course." The mayor picked up his goblet, thought the better of it, and set it back down. "I think Henrik has had too much brandy before breakfast. Ignore him."

The prefect nodded, all levity gone from the room. "I think you're right, Mayor. He forgets himself."

The table grew quiet, waiting for the prefect to pardon Henrik.

"Forgive me," Henrik said. He propped a smile onto his face, deciding the only thing he liked about the man was his hat which Henrik would have looked rather dashing in. "I hadn't meant to be impertinent. I was genuinely curious. Forget I asked."

"Not at all." The apology seemed to rekindle the man's good humor. "I suppose all three of you have taken the rite?"

The mayor nodded. "We have all embraced the Pontiff's light."

Tyrianites split the world into five castes. The more provincials assimilated, the higher they rose. Outlaws still spoke the old tongue, while most Norn had let it go, and were subjects, with limited rights. Henrik and his family had taken the rite of submission, renouncing the worship of their ancestors, and elevating themselves to the ally caste.

"I suppose I can let you in on the secret then." The prefect was of course a step above them, a citizen, above him only the Electors, the true elite of the Tyrianite Federation. "In fact, I believe it's a shame that Saint Olaf's Day is merely a local tradition. Ride a fortnight in any direction, and they won't have heard of it. In fact, since I arrived, I have discussed how we

31

might encourage more pilgrimage to the shrine. Good for business, of course, but compliance as well."

The mayor raised a bushy eyebrow. "I'm afraid I don't follow."

The prefect nodded. "As I've heard it, old Saint Olaf was burned at the stake just over there." He pointed out the window, toward where the shrine stood atop the hill. "When he returns, we'll happily give Skolja back."

"I see," Henrik interrupted. He glanced from his mother to his father. The prefect obviously didn't know that Olaf was his great-great-uncle. That his idol sat atop his mother's secret altar as big as Father Tristan's. It was part of the reason their family had received the Mayorship. "Instead of doing something about it, the folk are forever waiting for Olaf to do it for them."

"Correct." The prefect bit off the end of a sausage. "And in the meantime, I'm blessed to run the most docile corner of Nornlund. You should count yourselves just as lucky. In most places, a local mayor doesn't get to grow old and fat. They find themselves in bogs with their heads chopped off." The prefect grinned, causing the mayor to squirm. "In the Pontiff's light, such superstition looks pathetic. But for us, it's truly a blessing."

The Torvald's had publicly embraced the federal scriptures, a necessary sacrifice to maintain their favored position in Skolja. In theory, they would make simple offerings to the Pontiff on auspicious occasions, observe the federal holidays, and reject the worship of the Ten Fathers and their ancestors. In practice, they were not so pious. It was merely an expedient.

"Yes," Henrik smirked. "I've always found superstition pathetic."

The mayor choked on a bit of pancake and had a coughing fit. He used it to cover the sharp kick he delivered to his son's shin. When his fit subsided, he apologized. He held his glass aloft, glaring at his son. "To the divine Pontiff, in His light may we reign."

The prefect held up his brandy, looking oddly sad, despite Henrik's insult. "In His light may we reign," he said, draining his glass.

32

★★★★★

Lyssa tucked the key into the pocket of her trousers. By the sun, it was already midmorning, and she was due at the tavern by noon. Most days, she'd wake to the sound of the smith's hammer. Even the nights when she'd kick old Rogan out to close the tavern, he'd still be up, making a racket with the dawn. But today was a holiday.

The smith was probably downstairs at her father's pub already, playing Six Pins, tipping a horn of mead. Lyssa dreaded celebration days. While everyone else in town played games and drank until they were green, Lyssa would be running herself ragged, dodging sots like the blacksmith who'd had enough drink to forget they were old enough to be her uncles. Rogan wasn't so bad, she supposed, as drunks go. He was a widower, more sad than anything, when he was in his cups. More likely to tell her she had a pretty smile than to get handsy. She'd seen him blubbering like a baby when he thought no one was watching. He wasn't the worst by far.

Her father mostly ignored men who got too friendly, though he kept a cudgel under the bar just in case. Even used it on a pilgrim once. As a matter fact, that had been Saint Olaf's Day too. If she never had to work another damned holiday, it would be too soon.

Besides, Breylin always said it was bullshit, a story for the fools. Olaf the Skald led the fight after the pigs invaded. Olaf lost. He said he would come back one day and win. The pigs burned Olaf. The end. So, naturally, everybody got drunk once a year to celebrate it. And Lyssa got to pick up the mess.

If she was going to slave all night, Lyssa was at least going to poke around town a bit before going in. Her father would just have to make do without her a while longer. With playful stealth, Lyssa descended the steps from their rooms above the tavern, pressing her slender frame to the outside of the stairs so they wouldn't creak. Instead of going into the tavern, she turned up the alley between their bar and Ivar's market. A pair of watchful rats skulked along, hunting for anything tossed out. Ivar and her father bickered incessantly about who was to blame for the rat epidemic in the alley they shared. At times it got a little nasty. Since Ivar was their landlord, there had been more than a few threats of eviction. It seemed her father was always behind on rent.

Lyssa continued her stroll, emerging from the alley next to the smithy, where a muddy road from the west ran into the cobbles of the town square. A group of boys played catch the pig, tackling each other and squealing with delight until a man's voice scolded them from somewhere around the corner. They darted behind the jail into the maze of clotheslines and shanties.

Lyssa hugged the side of the market and peeked her freckled face around the corner, her auburn locks pinned up in braids. Ivar stood on the covered porch, stacking a pile of tomatoes the boys had disturbed with their roughhousing.

Watching the old prick brought a scowl to her face. He was irritated that the boys had upset his precious display and muttered to himself, scratching his bald head. In the summertime, he'd open the shutters of his office to cool off, and she'd sometimes crouch in the alley and listen to his monologues about young folk, paying tithes, and whatever else was stuck in his craw that day.

Once he had arranged the tomatoes to his satisfaction, Ivar went back inside his store, and Lyssa sauntered out into the square. The last thing she wanted was to be hassled about rent.

Most of the town was busy celebrating, and most of the shops were closed.

Breylin's apothecary tottered on the southeast side of the square, moldering logs and a sagging roof, charms of feather and bone dangling from the eaves. Lyssa considered visiting the old woman, but she was late already, and if they got to talking shop, she'd be in there forever.

"Looking for me?"

Lyssa jumped. The voice in her ear was followed by a good-natured cackle. Lyssa whirled on the crone. She shook her head in disbelief. "How in damnation do you do that?"

The little old woman smiled up at her, an impish glint shining through the cataracts in her eyes. She shrugged. "It's a gift."

"Scaring the shit out of me is no gift!" Lyssa traced a line down from the corner of her eye as if she were warding against evil.

Breylin pinched her forearm. "Fun, though."

Lyssa hugged the old woman and kissed her on top of the head. "It's good to see you out of the shop."

Breylin grinned. "I brought some dahlias to Axl."

"Breylin." Lyssa swatted her on the shoulder. "He's a married man."

Breylin shrugged. "Hetta stole him first."

Lyssa folded her arms. "I love Hetta. She's so nice. Don't you think it would crush her to find out about this?"

"Oh, it's harmless. We're old now."

Lyssa cocked her head. "You don't have a tonic for that?"

Breylin snickered and reached out to pinch Lyssa, but she scooted away.

"I have a new recipe I want you to try," said Lyssa. "Are you coming to the tavern today?"

"Ten Fathers, no!" Breylin made a spitting sound. "On Saint Olaf's Day?" She waved off the suggestion. "You know my father knew Olaf."

"Yes, Breylin."

The apothecary turned toward her shop. "I'll come try the new ale in a few days, honey. Once all that white ribbon foolishness is over."

"Fair enough," said Lyssa. "Do you need any more firewood?"

"Not for a few days yet."

"Want me to fetch you a bucket of water?"

"I'm not completely helpless, young lady." Breylin turned back and patted Lyssa on the cheek. "Don't you worry about me."

Lyssa watched her shuffle back to her shop, marveling at how she could still sneak up on her when she wanted a laugh.

Once Breylin had made it into the apothecary, Lyssa crossed the square, ignoring a dirty look from Ingrid Alsten who stood at the well with her sister, Nora. Lyssa had braided her hair up today in hopes of appeasing her father. She preferred wearing it under a hat, but he always complained. She would've cut it off if busybodies like Ingrid would ever have shut up about it. Maybe if Ingrid wasn't such a prude, her husband wouldn't be sneaking kisses with Nora. She'd seen it once when they thought no one was looking.

Lyssa headed east toward the far end of the square where the old stone steps ran up High Hill. The mayor's mansion perched atop the hill to her left and the statue of Saint Olaf crowned the apex to her right.

She thought about heading down to the docks to see if a new ship had moored. Skolja didn't have much to offer passing vessels, but from time to time one would drop anchor in the hamlet to resupply and spend a night ashore. Lyssa never missed a chance to chat up the sailors, plying them with endless questions about the world beyond Skolja. In the back of her head, she always hoped that her mother would be aboard one of them, but with every passing year that seemed more and more unlikely.

An angry voice echoed down from the crest of the hill. Lyssa looked up just as the new prefect and another soldier came into view, descending the stairs. She glanced over her shoulder to see that she was alone, and Lyssa ducked behind one of the boulders littering the foot of the hill. The prefect's voice grew quieter as he grew cautious, nearing the town, but as he reached the bottom of the stone steps, she began to pick out some of his words.

"Regardless, I want those men recalled. If we evacuate, it'll be in a hurry."

"Yes, sir," replied the other soldier.

Lyssa crouched tight against the boulder, holding her breath to hear as much as possible. As the federals passed her hiding spot and continued into town, a mischievous grin stole across her face. "Ten Fathers," she whispered. "I'm starting to like Saint Olaf's Day."

Chapter 4

"The skalds were largely purged during the rule of Procambian. The title, once descended along hereditary lines, has passed into history. The skalds were at once the stewards of Norn culture, their rulers, priests, and practitioners of a vile magic that has since been expunged from provincial society."

-Annocar, A History of Norn Mysticism

Brohr had never been inside Mads's Tavern without his grandfather. It was cheerier than he remembered, but of course today was a holiday. White candles—purchased for the occasion—flickered from every table, along the bar, and from wall sconces. Around the candles lay fresh-cut pine boughs tied with white ribbons. Atop the boughs rested wicker poppets, their hands bound in white string. A crackling fire added the waft of wood smoke to the stink of sweat and sour ale.

At just past noon, the place was already packed with bachelors and a few women who'd joined the festivities. In the back of the tavern, a small crowd watched a game of Six Pins.

Brohr pushed his way up to the bar, admiring the tavern keeper's daughter while he waited to order. She had dark ginger hair, bright green eyes, and a little swagger that made him smile. She was a strange one, no doubt, going around in breeches, but he had to credit her—she did as she pleased.

The girl handed a flagon to the man beside him and asked Brohr, "What'll it be? If you're hungry, we've got cakes and berries or morel and mincemeat stew."

"An ale," he said.

"Dark or light?"

"Which is your favorite?" he asked.

She smiled. "Well, I brewed them both myself. But the dark is my favorite. It's got more hops than a bunny." She winked.

"Dark then. Those berry cakes sound pretty good. I'd better have two helpings." Brohr held up two fingers.

He traded her a silver federal, and she gave back a copper from her apron. Brohr tucked it in his pouch, noticing her cheer evaporate. Puzzled, he gulped some brew from the dented tin mug. It had a crisp bite and a funny aftertaste, sort of like skunk cabbage. He stood at the bar and wolfed down the sweet cakes, dotted with overripe berries, trying not to stare while she waited on the next patron.

The only empty table in the place faced across from where the veteran, Torin, sat. The ex-legionary glanced up, his hair greasy and black, his skin a little darker than Brohr's own. The drunk scowled and looked away. Brohr could see why the seat was vacant. Even though they were the only shades in town, Torin had never shown any sort of camaraderie.

The first generation after the conquest had drowned the sons of the federal invaders, until they made it a hanging crime like carrying a long bow or a double-bladed axe. Most folk still did it, but it was a secret now. He wondered what had moved Torin's mother to spare him. According to Tyrianite law, Torin was a caste above the rest of them like the mayor's family. Like Brohr could be if he took the rite of submission. Of course, he'd never gotten so much as a kindly look from the veteran or the mayor's family, so what was the point? Brohr couldn't imagine why Torin had moved to Skolja after his service here. It must be better for shades in Pederskald. At least, Brohr hoped it was, but maybe they didn't like him there either.

Instead of taking the open table, Brohr joined the men playing Six Pins in the back.

"Can I take the winner?" he asked.

A skinny man with pox scars under his beard spat on Brohr's boot. "Piss off, shade."

The scarred man stepped up to the scuffed line painted on the floor boards. He held his dagger by the blade and took aim at

39

a piece of firewood standing on end across the room. A hush fell over the crowd, and he hurled his dagger, lodging it into the log and knocking it over. A fat man in a stained brown tunic on the far side of the room cursed and stomped back over to the group.

The pockmarked winner sneered at Brohr. "All right, piglet." He lowered his voice. "You can play. But it's five silver a game."

The man behind Brohr gasped at the hefty wager. "Johan, is that wise?"

"You can piss off too, Sven." He smiled, unveiling a row of snaggle teeth. "Five silvers. You in or out, piglet?"

"Fine," Brohr said.

Johan thumped the hilt of his dagger on the nearest table. "Drinks on me, boys." He waggled his blade at Brohr. "Set them up, shade."

Brohr felt his haunt squirm. The hair on his forearms stood up, his stomach muscles clenched. He shared a longing to send this loud mouth's teeth skittering across the floor, an eerie feeling not entirely his own. Brohr breathed, practicing calm, and strutted across the room to select his pins.

The game was a simple one: each player selected six logs from the pile of firewood and set them on end, a row of three, a row of two, and one up front, forming a triangle. Players took turns tossing their knives at their opponent's pins. Knock one over, it's a point. If your blade sticks, it's two. High score after six throws wins.

The second he took his hand off of the last piece of wood, Johan stuck his knife in the log from across the room. Brohr leapt back, startled.

"Two points!" Johan called, eliciting cheers from his friends.

Brohr glared at him and stepped to the line. "You're pretty good."

Johan laughed, relishing the moment. "It's too late to back out now."

Brohr nodded. "I was thinking the opposite," he said. "What if we added a little spice to the pot? Something more

40

important than a few coins." Though, of course, five silver was all he had. "I'll stake my dagger against yours."

The men fell silent.

Their knives were generations old, usually heirlooms, a mark of their manhood. To lose one was beyond shameful, to wager one unheard of. Johan had nothing to say.

One of his friends gave him a shove. "Come on, Johan. You haven't lost all day."

"If you're afraid," Brohr said. "We can pretend I never asked."

"I'm not afraid!" Johan snatched his flagon of ale off the table, guzzled the last of it, and wiped the froth from his beard on his sleeve. He slammed the mug down and belched. "Daggers and silver! I'm going to melt that thing into slag when I—"

Brohr's dagger sunk deep into the back-right log, sending it careening into the wall. "Two to two," he called, grinning.

Strangers sensed the tension and began to crowd around—some jeering him, others, acquainted with Johan, needling the man with unsolicited advice and playful gibes. The players retrieved their knives and stepped back to the lines.

Johan threw again, knocking over a pin but failing to stick his blade.

"One point," Brohr added helpfully as he buried his own knife. "4 to 3."

Johan's next round was better, but Brohr scored two again. He noticed coins changing hands as spectators wagered on the outcome. The following round they both lodged their blades. "Eight to seven. That second round may come back to haunt you," said Brohr. "Lucky for me, I practice every day in the barn. Not much else to do on the farm." He smiled. "This is fun. What should we wager next game?"

Johan rushed him, but Sven grabbed him by the arm. "Look at the size of him," he warned his friend. "Don't be stupid."

"There are six of us, you chicken shit." Johan looked at his friends.

"Oh no." Sven held up his hands. "This is your mess. Just finish the game."

Johan tore his arm free and stepped to the line. His hand trembled. "Look," he pleaded. "I'm sorry about earlier. Too much ale I think. Let's—"

"Take your shot," Brohr interrupted.

Johan gritted his teeth and hurled his dagger. It sailed wide of the pins. Brohr scooted out of the way just in time to avoid it hitting his shin.

The crowd erupted in whispers and laughter.

"If you do that again," said Brohr. "I'm going to shove that dagger down your throat." Then he thumped his own knife into another log. "Ten to seven."

If everything went wrong, they could still tie if Johan stuck his blade and managed to somehow knock over the other pin. It was a tough throw, though. Vili had pulled off a throw like that once. He'd been so excited that he had leapt on Brohr's shoulders. Despite everything, Brohr chuckled to himself.

Everyone quieted as Johan concentrated on the remaining pins. He practiced the motion, releasing the blade on the third go. It flew through the air, sticking in the edge of the front pin, spinning it in a wobbly circle until the knife handle swatted the other log, and they both crashed to the ground. Johan clapped his hands and cheered, as did many of the onlookers, but Brohr waved his dagger in the air, and they sobered.

He held it by the blade, looked over at Johan, spat on the floor, and flipped the knife in the air. Snatching it by the handle as it came down, he threw with a fluid motion. The pommel struck the log with a loud knock. It toppled over, and the crowd went wild.

"Eleven to ten," Brohr called. "Close one."

Some of the crowd booed, others, delighting in Johan's defeat, applauded. A man Brohr didn't know clapped him on the back. Brohr picked up Johan's dagger and crossed to his adversary. Johan shoved his friend aside, picked up Brohr's blade, and scurried over to meet him.

"Here," he said. Fishing in his coin purse he held out a handful of silver. "A bet's a bet. I get it. And I was an ass. I know. I'll do whatever you want. But that knife has been through four generations. It was made before the pigs came. No offense!" he corrected himself. "The Tyrianites."

"You really think I'm one of them?" Brohr asked.

Johan looked flabbergasted. "Well, you're not one of us."

Brohr came very close to hitting him. It was only the thought of coming to, bewildered, that stayed his hand.

"Right now, I'm closer to stabbing you with this knife than giving it back." Brohr folded his arms. "If you want it, you'll have to do better than that."

"I'm really sorry." Johan clasped his hands together. "If you keep it…" He opened his mouth but couldn't think of what else to say.

"I'll tell you what," said Brohr. "If you just get the hell out of here, I'll let you have it back."

Johan's mouth closed, and he nodded.

Brohr dropped the dagger in front of him. Johan bent over and scooped it up.

"Piggy." Johan spat on the floor.

Brohr feinted toward Johan, taking a quick step at him and cocking his fist. The pox-scarred bully flinched and tripped over his own feet, trying to get away. Mads's Tavern burst out laughing. Even Johan's supposed friends had a good chuckle. Humiliated, Johan picked himself up and shoved his way through the crowd, looking back over his shoulder with murder in his eyes. Some of the folk looked disappointed, some kept laughing. The barmaid, Lyssa, brought him a horn of mead.

"Here," she said. "This one's on the house."

"Thanks," he said, smiling.

"Don't go getting a big head. Everyone hates Johan. That's nothing special."

Brohr thanked her again and played another round with the next challenger. He won again and again, had a few more horns of mead, and was having a grand time—until the crowd gathered around the match parted just enough for him to glimpse Vili and Birgit seated across the bar. She laughed at something Vili said, and he leaned closer, tucking a lock of her hair behind her ear.

Brohr heard the distant sound of glass breaking and found himself looming over their table. Someone cursed behind him. The corners of his vision darkened and the hair on his neck stood up. He gripped their table, gnashing his teeth as he struggled not to be dragged down into a rage. The lovers stared up at him with eyes that saw the murder in his heart.

"Brohr." It was Birgit's plea.

He looked down at her, anger threatening to swamp his reason, that familiar presence roiling with contempt, yearning to lash out. Vili started to speak.

"Quiet," said Brohr. "If you say a word..."

"Brohr." Birgit stood up, her chair tipping to the floor. "Brohr." She tugged on his sleeve. "I got the fawn you carved me. It's beautiful, but it doesn't change anything."

"Why?" he asked. "What about our life?"

"Look at yourself," she said. "I'm sorry, Brohr Nilstrom, but you're scary. I never saw that until..." She looked over at Vili. "How can I run away with you after that? What would become of me?"

She was right. But it didn't salve the wound. Brohr recited the names of the Fathers in his head and exhaled. Repeated them and inhaled. "And suddenly," he said. "The two of you are sweethearts?" Brohr flicked his eyes at Vili, whose bruises hadn't quite healed yet.

"I'm sorry," Birgit said. "I didn't mean to hurt you. It wasn't until after..."

The tavern girl strutted up. "Is there a problem here?" She looked at each of them in turn, landing on Brohr.

"No," said Birgit, pulling Vili to his feet. "We were just leaving."

"Off you go then," said Lyssa, folding her arms.

Vili never even met his eyes on the way out, but Birgit flashed him an apologetic look that tore at his stricken heart.

"You need some stew," Lyssa said.

Brohr watched them go, his anger fading into sadness. "Mead."

Lyssa thumbed her chest. "This is my bar. I can see an angry drunk coming a mile away. I won't have you spoiling the night with a brawl." She switched to a friendlier tone. "I'll bring you a bowl of stew and an ale. How does that sound?"

"Fine."

"Good," she said. "You'd better tip this time too, or it's out on your ass."

Brohr sat at the table Birgit and Vili had fled. Lyssa hadn't taken away their half-empty flagons, so Brohr gulped down the abandoned drinks and brooded until Lyssa returned.

A bowl of steaming red stew plopped in front of him. It smelled of rosemary and pepper. Lyssa set a mug of beer beside it. Noticing the empty flagons, she narrowed her eyes at Brohr. He stared back, shoveling a spoonful of stew into his mouth.

She held out her hand.

A little good humor returning, he pressed a federal into her palm. "Keep the change."

She nodded, snatched the empty mugs off the table, and hustled off toward the bar.

Chapter 5

"When Moriigo fell in the last great battle to purge the primeval horrors, his brother Tyrus was overcome with sorrow. Breaching the deep magics, he pulled Moriigo back from the other side. But when Tyrus looked upon his brother, he saw that the crossing had changed him."

-Hannibal Bomilcar, The Shining Ones at Twilight

Henrik's father pried the goblet from his hand and set it on the end table beside the divan. "Son." Mayor Torvald clapped his hands in front of Henrik's face. "Are you listening to me? This is important."

Henrik yawned, crossed his legs, and folded his hands over his knee. "I'm listening, Father."

The mayor studied him for a moment, his chin quivering. "Something is happening. Something very big. Very dangerous."

"Oh?"

Old Torvald turned toward the door and beckoned for Henrik to follow. "It's better that you see for yourself. Come here." After a pause, he added, "Please."

Henrik sighed and tottered to his feet. He smiled at his father's consternation and followed him out onto the veranda. It was late afternoon and cold outside. The sky was free of clouds, and Quaya moon was already out. A faint red orb, nearly full. His father had his telescope trained on it. The elaborate device, wrought from brass and exorbitant lenses, was his father's prized possession. At least *it* didn't drink, Henrik mused.

"Well?" Henrik prodded. "I've seen your mistress before, Father. She's quite a piece."

"Just look."

"It's daytime. What's to see?"

"Please," the mayor asked. "Just do as I say for once."

"Anything for you." Henrik smiled and bent to the eyepiece. "What am I looking at?"

"The federal city of Mora. Or rather the ships coming and going from it."

"It's a blur. Just a jumble of motion."

"Yes."

"Is it always like that?" Henrik knew that his father spent every free moment with his eye glued to that telescope or toiling away in Rogan's smithy on his ridiculous ship that would never fly. He was in love with the heavens.

"No," the mayor said. "Not at all. In fact, every city is like this."

"Every city? What do you mean, 'every city'?"

Mayor Torvald produced a pipe from his jacket, another trinket he'd created. Without striking a match, he inhaled, and the pipe ignited. The mayor exhaled a thick cloud of smoke.

"Father," Henrik demanded. "What does it mean?"

"I believe it means that the Federation is evacuating Quaya moon."

Henrik laughed. "You're joking."

"No, my son." He puffed, his expression grave. "I'm afraid not. And the fact that the prefect didn't mention it this morning should give us great cause for concern. The town is going to need us. Both of us."

Henrik scoffed and headed back inside.

"Where are you going?" The mayor asked.

"I'm getting a drink. Perhaps you'd better get to work on that toy of yours. If you can make it work maybe I won't have to die in this pit."

The mayor reached out and grabbed his son by the elbow, turning him back around. "This is serious, Henrik. You need to sober up."

"Why?" Henrik pulled his arm free. "Why should I bother? Do you think anything that happens in this town really matters?"

47

"Of course it matters."

"It doesn't! This place is nothing. I could be the best mayor in the town's history, and no one outside of Skolja would ever know, or ever care. We could all die tomorrow and it wouldn't matter. Why do you think I hate it here? I could have been on Tyria, studying at one of the academies, or at least in Trond." It was humiliating, to be rejected, even if it was because he was Norn. In a way, it was even more humiliating that he had actually expected them to make an exception for him. "Instead I'm stuck in Skolja, on the outside of nowhere. I don't want to be the mayor. Don't you see. I don't care." Henrik spun away from his father, marching inside.

"Sober up!" The mayor called after him. "This isn't a joke, Henrik. Skolja needs us."

★★★★★

Brohr discovered that his Six Pins game did not improve with mead in his belly. He'd lost his spot, worked his way through the line twice, and was up next. Rogan, the blacksmith, had just beaten Mjoller, a tired old man with a wiry beard and a lazy eye. Rogan picked some food out from between his teeth. Satisfied, he motioned Brohr to the back wall of the tavern where they were playing.

"Set up your pins, son."

Brohr slugged down the last of his mead and shuffled over to the stack of firewood. He grabbed an armload and set up his pins, but he was getting sloppy, and Rogan dispatched him handily. Brohr's last throw went high and clattered off of the back wall, falling to the ground. He found himself staring at the pin he'd missed.

"Hey." Rogan shook him by the shoulder. "It's time for you to head on back to the farm, son. It's a long walk." Brohr shrugged out of the blacksmith's grasp, bumping into a patron behind him. They dropped their horn and spilled mead on their

48

shirt, cursing. Brohr turned around to find himself face to face with Torin, his shirt soaked, his brown eyes bloodshot and angry. The veteran socked him in the stomach, a deft shot that knocked the wind out of Brohr and doubled him over onto the floor.

Torin reached for the blade on his belt, and a scuffle broke out as Rogan and another man grabbed the veteran by the arms and struggled to keep him from drawing iron. A few of the surlier patrons traded insults and shoves, trying to inflame a fight between the shades. Torin struggled to get his arms free. He growled at Rogan like a mountain lion, unable to break the smith's burly grip.

Mads burst into the melee, hollering at the top of his lungs. "Half-priced drinks at the bar for one minute! One minute! First in line gets a free shot of the private stock." This cleared out most of the rabble rousers. Mads slapped a lingerer on the backside. "Go on Nils or you'll be paying double. Get."

Mads planted a kiss on Brohr's cheek, which was so unexpected it broke him out of his fighting mood. Brohr turned to the bartender, shocked. Mads took the opportunity to drag him by the elbow toward the door. Brohr planted his feet and tried to pull free, but Mads pivoted, waggling his finger in Brohr's face. "Listen son, I don't want to have to call the constable, but I will. Do you want to spend the night in jail? Answer me that. Do you want to spend the night in jail?"

"No," Brohr admitted.

A cold wind tore through the tavern as Mads opened the front door, guttering the candles inside. He herded Brohr out into the street.

"Now go on home before you get yourself killed." Mads slammed the door shut, leaving Brohr confused and a little nauseous.

Dusk settled upon Skolja. The streets were empty, save a few celebrants singing somewhere over by the mill. Brohr wandered around for a while until he realized he was going the wrong way. He stopped and took in his surroundings. He'd stumbled south into the low market. The stalls were empty this time of night, just weathered wooden tables and walls of moldy canvas lashed together with black rope. Brohr heard the waves breaking against the shore and emerged from the second row of stalls to see the docks jutting out into the sea.

Quaya, nearly full, dangled, almost touching its own reflection in the choppy water. Higher up and to the west, the little moon, Otho, waned to an emerald sliver. It was dusk, the stars still faint, but a comet blazed in the east, a blue spike suspended just above the horizon.

He blinked. Brohr had never seen a comet. It took him a moment to associate the light in the sky with the stories his grandfather told. Anders claimed they were messengers. Some nonsense like that. They were pretty, though.

Goosebumps prickled on his forearms. Looking up at the celestial visitor, he felt wonder, childlike, pleasant—until he realized it was not his own. The feeling unnerved him. Brohr pushed the sensation back into the darkness.

A wind picked up, but the mead kept him from shivering. He turned around, meaning to head back through town toward the farm, but found himself looking into Torin's bloodshot eyes once again.

"You little worm," Torin said. His finger jabbed Brohr in the chest as he painstakingly enunciated. "You… little… worm."

Brohr tried to step back, but Torin seized the collar of his shirt, the reek of his rotten teeth curdling Brohr's stomach. Torin pulled Brohr's shirt over his face and punched him in the ear. The ground tilted, and Brohr found himself looking up at the unshaven veteran as he leaned over him and spat in Brohr's face before kicking him in the belly. The kick was low enough that it didn't wind him, but it hurt like hell.

"Don't," Brohr held up his hand. "You'll—"

Torin kicked him again, but the feeling in his gut wasn't pain. It was fire. The sensation of someone looking over his shoulder was unbearable, like he was hollow, filling up with acrid smoke. He looked up at Torin, light-headed, as if he'd stood up too fast. As if he'd taken another blow to the head.

★★★★★

50

Brohr came to on the docks, stirring to the rhythmic crash of waves against the pier. Someone behind him was shouting, a woman. Brohr discovered one of Torin's boots in his hand. Torin himself lay in the fetal position at the end of the dock, just a few feet away. His face was swollen, there were some teeth and a pool of blood on the planks by his head, but he was breathing.

Brohr was in trouble. The federals would never let an attack on a legionary slide. He'd be lucky to get the skin lashed off his back. *Ten Fathers,* he thought, they might even hang him. Brohr stumbled and sat down on the dock. He dropped the boot. It had blood on the heel. The woman behind him ran past and bent over Torin. She must be brave, he thought, or not very bright, to put him between herself and the shore.

Someone on the other dock found their voice and started shouting for the constable. Brohr couldn't make out who it was, the night had come. He looked up at the stars, hoping Torin would live, but the mead in him dulled his worry. The comet burned blue in the sky. It was pretty.

"What happened? Hey!" Lyssa snapped her fingers in his face. Brohr realized she was holding his cloak. He'd left it in the tavern. "Is that you?"

"Must be," Brohr said.

"You," she hesitated. "You were crazy." She ran her finger down from the corner of her eye like a tear sliding down her cheek. A ward.

Brohr nodded.

"It's happened before?"

He nodded again.

The man at the other dock shouted. "Stay right there. The constable is coming." He made his way back to land and then to the base of the dock they were on, careful to leave himself enough room to run. It was the mayor's son, Henrik.

The air grew cold and still. Brohr exhaled, marveling at the steam from his breath. The Mayor's son retreated a few steps. He emitted a high-pitched, aborted word. Brohr and Lyssa

51

turned in unison as much toward the source of their own unease as to see what Henrik was gawking at.

A gloom stood at the end of the pier. It had the shape of a man, but the light of the moons didn't diminish its darkness whatsoever. It was just the outline, a deeper blackness etched against the night sky. Whatever it was, it moved with disturbing grace, taking a few steps closer. The malformed silhouette betrayed a hint of the inhuman, too tall to be a man, its skull oblong.

It waited for a moment, regarding him. Brohr felt his haunt stir, coiling within him, and for once, he was glad. His mouth went dry. He tried to speak, but only a stammer emerged. As if the spell were broken, the thing stooped over Torin and clutched his throat. Lyssa broke free of her terror enough to retreat a few steps. The drunkard's legs flailed as he struggled. But he was helpless. It choked him without any hint of passion, the sot clutching uselessly at the creature's hands until, finally, he flopped to the pier, still. The horror looked over its shoulder at the trio of witnesses, put its finger to where its lips would be as if to shush them, and dissolved through the beams of the quay into the water below.

Chapter 6

"Moriigo; thy name is pain to the ears, thy countenance a sore upon the eye, and thy return a blot upon the scripture's page."

—Tolbero Aquina, The Endless Shadow

The fort stood alone atop a plateau north of town, overlooking Skolja and the sea beyond. A simple log palisade surrounded it, a perfect square with watch platforms at the corners and above each gate. Prefect Brasca Quoll and his ordinal, bearing a torch, marched inside.

As federal practice dictated, each wall measured precisely 300 paces. Within, an interval of open space hugged the wall, surrounding the barracks and camp buildings. In the very center, an expanse of mud served as the parade ground. Even at that late hour, legionaries trotted back and forth, preparing provisions and relaying orders.

Brasca turned toward the command building and was hailed by the guard on duty before he entered. Inside, the air was warm though the building itself was crude. Federal officers were afforded many of the comforts of home, including the rune-scribbled brass cube in the corner, which radiated a pleasant heat. A hand-painted map of the continent was nailed to the wall behind a simple oak desk which his adjutant, Carthalo, leaned over, studying a scroll.

"Any orders that make sense yet?" Brasca asked.

Carthalo rose and hailed him. "No, sir. None that make much sense, anyway." After the prefect nodded, Carthalo sat back down and continued. "We received a dispatch just a few moments ago ordering us to withdraw inland to Pederskald.

Almost immediately it was rescinded. We are to make ready for extraction. Disclose nothing to the locals."

"Who is wearing the helm?" the prefect asked.

"Belizar, sir." Brasca turned to head for the communications room, but Carthalo stood up. "Sir?" Carthalo asked.

"What is it?"

"I was hoping for your permission to use the helm for personal reasons. Just for a few minutes." Carthalo walked around the desk to stand face to face with the prefect. "It's my brother, sir. He is stationed on Quaya. I was hoping to speak to him."

Brasca smoothed his mustache, fidgeting while he considered the request. He thought of his son, fretting about what would happen to the boy if he didn't return. Not for the first time, he wondered if it was pride or principle that had marooned him on Heimir. "I'm afraid not," he finally said. "We need the helm open in case of incoming orders."

Ordinal Carthalo bristled, but he said, "Yes, sir."

Brasca stepped around him, opened the door to the communications room, and without looking back, closed it after him.

A flickering candelabra on the table beside the cot lit the windowless room. A husky Ordinal with a mole on his chin lay motionless on the bed, an ornate silver helm strapped to his head. It was ringed with inset stones: basalt and quartz, granite and limestone, each gouged with a symbol and linked by cold iron wiring. On the table, beside the candelabra, an inkpot, quill, and roll of parchment awaited new orders.

"Belizar," Brasca bent over and shook the messenger. "Belizar, rouse yourself."

The Ordinal sat up. "Sir?"

"I need to speak with Prefect Arabo by noon. You can reach one of his men at the relay in Trond. I will speak with him myself. Do you understand?"

"Yes, sir." The officer lay back down and closed his eyes.

The prefect considered offering a prayer, but dismissed it as a false, forced sentiment. The Pontiff would be no help, but perhaps his old friend Arabo could be.

★★★★★

The mayor's son found his voice and started yelling for the constable again. "Murder!" he cried from the foot of the dock.

Torin lay on his back, staring up at the abyss.

Lyssa scurried back to Brohr. She shook her head over and over, her hands clasped to her chest.

"What was that?" he asked.

Torin's boot lay beside Brohr. A bloody handprint marred the corpse's face. Over at the foot of the dock, Henrik cupped his hands to his mouth, shouting back toward town. Waves crashed upon the shore, a sudden surge drowning out his calls.

Henrik produced something small from one of the pouches on his belt. His eyes closed and his lips moved. Glowing symbols whirled around his hands and the shimmering image of a pine tree with writhing roots flared before him. Its light coalesced into a ball that shone above his head.

A binding.

Lyssa turned to Brohr. "You'd better run." She held out his cloak for him, but he didn't take it.

Brohr squinted at the beacon over Henrik's head. Why should he run? It was that thing that killed the old drunk, not him. There were witnesses.

Lyssa grabbed him by the wrists and turned his hands so that he could see the blood on them. Brohr snatched his cloak back and wiped his hands on it.

From the foot of the dock, Henrik resumed his cry. "Murder!"

Brohr stood, took one last look at the body, and bolted into the night.

★★★★★

His grandfather sat by the fire, waiting to pounce when Brohr returned. As he opened the door, the old man glared up at him with eyes like pitted iron. He hadn't lit any candles. The room was dark, only the flickering hearth burned. Anders slammed his fist on the arm of the chair. "Where the hell have you been?"

"I'm sorry," said Brohr, blinking back tears. "I'm so sorry, grandfather."

He stepped into the firelight, and Anders froze, cruel words arrested by the blood smeared on Brohr's face.

"What is that?" He pointed.

"I had a fight," said Brohr.

Anders considered this a moment. "Your temper?"

He nodded.

The old man rose from his chair with a creak and came over to inspect his grandson. "You aren't hurt. That's good. And you came home. That's good too."

Brohr squinted in the darkness, unsure if he was reading the old man right. He seemed pleased.

"You've seen the comet?" Anders asked him.

"Yes, but—"

"But nothing." He smiled. "It's no coincidence you drew blood tonight. I thought that the herald would appear when both moons were new. No matter."

"Grandfather," Brohr interjected. "You're rambling. You need to listen. A man is dead. That old vet, the drunk Torin."

Anders tried to hide his smile by turning away. "You killed him?"

"No," said Brohr. "I didn't. That's what I've been trying to tell you. There was some sort of... thing. It choked him."

The old man seized Brohr's wrist. "You saw?"

"Let go."

"Tell me!"

56

Brohr jerked his wrist free, and his grandfather tried to snatch it back. He shoved the old man away, knocking him to the floor. "Don't touch me!" Brohr shouted. "What's wrong with you? Everyone in town is going to think I'm a murderer. There's some sort of creature on the loose, and you're happy. You're happy! Wipe that smile off your face. What's wrong with you?"

Anders laughed at Brohr's rage. "You should be afraid of me. I should be unhappy. Tonight everything begins to change."

"Are you a lunatic?" Brohr paced before the fire. "Why are you acting like this?"

Anders rose to his feet, his knees crackling. "You're right of course. It's all happening so fast. So suddenly. Sit down."

"I'll stand."

"Sit. Down." The old man ground his teeth. He walked over to the hearth and put another log on the fire. Brohr sat. "Now tell me what happened."

Brohr took a deep breath of the smoky air, still cold despite the fire, and recounted the night's events to his eager audience. Anders nodded throughout the story as if it confirmed what he had long suspected.

"In the oldest sagas," Anders began, "the Shining Ones ruled every world in the system, every moon. They gave birth to man, even called back the dead to serve." He held up his scarred hand to forestall Brohr's interruption. "For all their beauty and wisdom though, they were but slave masters, every living thing bent to their will. The Tyrianites claim that the Shining Ones are gone, but that is another of their lies. The Hidden's appearance is a sign. More ominous than the comet." Anders set his hand on Brohr's forearm and shook it. "Our time has come!"

"What are you talking about?" He pulled his arm away. "You realize they're going to hang me? I don't care about fairytales. This is serious, Grandfather." Brohr shot to his feet. "I need to leave right now. They're going to blame me for this." He started toward the kitchen. "I'm such an idiot! I should have left without Birgit. I'm taking some food. I'm really going this time."

"Brohr!" Anders grabbed his shoulder and spun him around. "Listen to me. None of that will matter soon. Everything is about to change. One dead drunk is nothing compared to what comes next."

"Is that what you are going to tell the constable when he gets here?"

"I can handle the constable."

Brohr took up his pacing again.

Anders sucked in a deep breath. "There is more."

"Go on." Brohr folded his arms.

"It's time you know about your brother."

Brohr squeezed his eyes shut and shook his head, as if to clear water from his ears. "What do you mean?"

"Your brother. He was stillborn." Anders gave him a moment to absorb the revelation. "Your haunt, your temper, that's your twin brother."

Brohr sat, staring into the fire. "My brother?" He asked.

Anders nodded, studying his grandson's face.

"How do you know?" Brohr asked.

Anders stood up and walked across the cabin. He opened the pantry door, took out a bottle, and uncorked it. With his back to Brohr, Anders smelled the wine to see if it had gone to vinegar. He pulled his belt knife, slyly cut his thumb, and let a few drops fall into the bottle.

"I know it's a lot to take in. Especially given everything else that happened tonight. It makes sense though. You can feel it's true. Can't you?"

"I had a brother?"

"Here." Anders offered the wine to Brohr. "Have a little wine. It will help."

Brohr took a swig. "What are you muttering?"

"Nothing," said Anders. "Feel better?"

Brohr shrugged. "Tired, I guess."

His grandfather smiled. "Go ahead, boy. You can finish it off."

★★★★★

"Brohr." His grandfather shook him by the shoulder. "Brohr, wake up. It's nearly dawn. The constable will be along soon. Up!"

Brohr groaned and sat up, bracing his throbbing head with the palm of his hand. A vicious chill hung in the cabin; the hearth was unlit. A single candle that his grandfather had set on the kitchen table outlined the old man's gaunt face.

"Do you remember last night?" he asked.

The question horrified Brohr. For just a second, he could not. He'd gone to town, he was playing Six Pins at Mads's. How had he gotten home?

"The fight?" Anders prodded.

The first detail surfaced: the mayor's son screaming. Holding the bloody boot. Torin's teeth on the planks of the quay. The rage. His brother. Ten Fathers. His brother. And that thing. That thing on the docks. He looked up at his grandfather, eyes wide.

"It was real?"

"Yes, boy."

"The constable is coming?" Brohr cast around in the darkness for his boots, his hands groping over the dusty floorboards.

"A man is dead."

"What should I tell him? Will they believe me?"

Anders held out his hand and hauled Brohr to his feet with a grunt. "I can make them believe you. But we'll need a more palatable story for him. There is a chance that the girl and the Mayor's son both told about the Hidden One." Another recollection bubbled into Brohr's mind, his grandfather's strange excitement the night before.

"The Hidden? Are you serious?"

"Don't interrupt. If they both say they saw it, then you can say so too, but probably not. You tell the constable the girl did it. That'll at least buy us the time we need."

Brohr rolled up his bed and tucked it in the corner of the room.

"I'm not blaming Lyssa. Besides, who would believe a girl could strangle Torin?" Brohr unlatched the front door. "I'm leaving. No one's going to believe some shadow thing or some girl killed Torin. Vili's parents will tell the constable what happened to him and no one will need to hear anything else."

"Listen!" Anders shouted, slamming the door closed. Brohr flinched. "It doesn't matter that you roughed up that little rat. Your friend had it coming."

"Yes," Brohr agreed. "Just like Torin."

His grandfather sighed and set his hand on Brohr's shoulder, changing tact. "Look, my boy, I know you're scared, but you have to trust me."

"Trust you? Trust you?" Brohr shrugged away from Anders' grip. "You *hate* me. You think I can't tell you hate me?"

Anders looked away. "I...don't hate you, Brohr. You're my only kin. I..."

"You hate me. Because I look like them."

Anders folded his arms. "I hate them. I don't hate you."

Brohr turned his back to his grandfather. "You do."

A sneer grew on Anders' face. "Fine," he said. "Just do as I say. I will keep you from hanging. You can't run far enough once the federals want you to swing."

Brohr's shoulders sagged. It was true of course. Torin was a veteran. If they decided he was guilty, they'd find him.

"Sit," Anders commanded, pointing to a chair by the kitchen table. Brohr sat, still poised to bolt. "Good," his grandfather said. "Roll up your sleeve." His grandson looked skeptical. "Just do it. You may not understand the folk ways, but you'll do as I say."

Brohr bit his lip and waited as his grandfather continued. "Before the federals learned to bind spirits, our people worked the blood." Anders drew his knife. "It's old magic, from the time when all men were slaves."

"What are you doing?" Brohr pushed the dagger away. "Have you lost your mind? I'm not going to let you cut me."

Anders waved the blade in Brohr's face. "Do as I say!"

Brohr flinched at the old man's manic eyes. He'd always been mean, but the froth in the corners of his mouth made him look unhinged. Anders grabbed a clay jar off the kitchen table. "Brohr, you must accept right now that the world is full of secrets and you know almost none of them. You must see already that the folk in town fear me." Brohr nodded. "Why do you think that is? I have a gift." Anders tapped his own chest with the dagger. "Just like my father. Just like you. Listen and you might learn something. There is music in our blood." He made a small cut on Brohr's forearm and held the jar below to collect the trickle.

This was black magic. Skald lore. Outlawed by the federals after the invasion, after they had wiped out the skalds. The old folk all believed in it, whispered about it, just like they spat over the side of a bridge before crossing or fasted the morning of a hunt. It didn't make it real. It was just the mutterings of the old folk, trying to fit the world back into the shape it had once been in. But Brohr's mind drifted to his brother, to the thing he had seen on the dock, and his certainty ebbed away.

"You're crazy," said Brohr. "The constable is coming. I need real help, not this horse shit."

His grandfather waved his blade before Brohr's eyes and pressed it on his cheek with firmness just shy of breaking the skin. "I understand your skepticism. I've kept things from you. Many things. And you're scared. That's natural. But if you don't shut your mouth and listen, this may not be done in time." He waited a moment and smiled at the silence. "Good," he said. "Put some pressure on that cut." Anders pulled up his own sleeve, revealing rows of scars. The familiar marks took on a sinister aspect this morning. Anders pricked his own arm, and their blood mingled in the jar.

"The crown of innocence I call it. A simple song. The blood will make you innocent, at least to the constable's eye."

"I am innocent."

"Hardly," Anders said. "When the constable comes, blame the girl. Don't worry, nothing bad will happen to her. Now, go, build a fire. We'll have a guest soon."

Brohr did as he was told, picking a log from the cradle and setting it in the hearth. He laid another atop it and stuffed wood shavings from the tinderbox into the lea. Brohr paused, groping inwardly for that familiar presence that was his brother, but it was remote, unresponsive. Brohr struck flint and steel a few times until a spark caught then blew on the little flame until the kindling flared and fire curled around the logs.

Brohr could count the folks in Skolja who had been kind to him on one hand. He saw the looks that the other villagers gave him, he heard the jokes the soldiers made. Lyssa smiled at him, teased him like a real person, not a stranger, not a shade. Kindness was too rare. He wasn't about to shit on it. To the hells with what his grandfather thought.

Outside, Grendie barked.

Anders sat at the kitchen table holding the jar of blood in both hands, his eyes closed, humming under his breath. Brohr cocked his head, his ears tickled by the impossible sound. Grendie's barking grew frantic.

Someone pounded on the door. "Hello? It's Constable Gunnar. Are you up?" He pounded again. "I need to speak with Brohr Nilstrom about last night."

Brohr looked back at his grandfather, who was already on his feet.

"Just a moment!" Anders walked over to Brohr, dumped the contents of the jar over his head, then opened the door.

Shocked, Brohr wiped blood out of his eyes.

"Shut up, Grendie!" Anders flung open the door and feigned a kick at the dog, who retreated a few steps, growling. "Come on in, Constable Gunnar. What seems to be the problem?"

The Constable nodded to each of them, eyes narrowed, but no sign that he registered the macabre spectacle. He wore a new red coat made of good felt that hung to his knees. It was a stark contrast to his stained tunic and frayed trousers.

"Have a seat, Constable." Anders motioned to one of the chairs beside the fire.

Constable Gunnar sat down and pointed at the other chair. "Young man, take a seat." The constable was middle aged and fat, bald and weak chinned, with a broken nose, like Brohr's, but far worse. It whistled with every breath.

Drenched in gore, Brohr sat opposite the constable.

"What do you want?" Brohr asked.

Anders stood beside Brohr and clamped a hand on his shoulder. "Let Constable Gunnar ask the questions," he coached.

"Quite right, young man. Now then, did you have an altercation with Torin Granstrom last night?"

Anders cleared his throat. "Has someone made an accusation against Brohr?"

"Well, yes, in fact. The mayor's boy, Henrik, has said he saw you beat him to death."

Anders squeezed Brohr's shoulder and asked, "And Henrik was the only person to see this?"

"Lyssa Pedersten may have seen it. But she seems confused. Drunk, I'd say."

Anders patted Brohr's shoulder. "Go ahead, Brohr. Tell him what you saw."

Brohr wiped his mouth on the back of his hand to keep the blood out when he spoke. "It wasn't me, sir." The constable started nodding. Brohr continued. "I was at Mads', and when I left, I went out to the dock for some fresh air. Torin came out and started arguing with Henrik." His grandfather dug his fingers

63

into his shoulder, but Brohr pressed on. "It was Henrik who killed him."

The constable had been nodding the whole time. "Yes," he said. "That makes perfect sense, now that I hear your side of it. There were some... inconsistencies in Henrik and Lyssa's accounts."

Anders glared at his grandson. "Well," he said at last. "Do you have any other questions?"

The constable sat there for quite a while. He was still nodding.

"Constable?" Anders prodded.

"Yes?"

"Will that be all?"

"Oh." He stood up. "Yes, of course. Thank you." He shook Brohr's hand. "Thank you for telling me the truth."

Anders shook his hand as well and opened the door for him.

Before he left, the constable turned back. "With all the slander against you over the years, I just knew there would be more to it. I'm sorry to bother you again."

Anders forced a smile, shutting the door behind the constable. He glared back at Brohr, still seated before the fire. "Damn you, boy." He shook his head. "There'll be trouble now."

Chapter 7

"Whence from outer dark, his Brightness raised the blot of ages, did He sum that dire cost, that coin struck with ugly likeness, that rend, that shadow pierced of deepest breach?"

-Oren Redfoil, *The Ancient's Folly*

Henrik sat in an upholstered chair by the fire in the drawing room. A leather-bound volume lay open in his lap, an old favorite: Bormian's *Historical Examination of the Binder's Art*. Others might find it pedantic, needlessly and exhaustively reiterating the mechanics of binding to an audience well versed in the minutiae. But Henrik found subtlety in his explanation of how to harness the animus that others overlooked. Bormian wrote at length about the three categories of runes: the archetypes, essences, and intentions. He waxed eloquent about the ear and the voice, the sound which was not sound. Even Caden's Axioms were given their due inspection. And throughout, Henrik detected a deeper current of thought, hints of heretical assertions deeply veiled in analogy and syllogism.

Bormian went on to recount the transmission of that knowledge from the Shining Ones to the ancient Tyrianites. The way Bormian spoke of the first human binders, as slaves, was not strictly speaking heretical, but it was unquestionably bold. In those bygone days, when the solar system was wracked by civil strife, the Shining Ones had at last turned to their chattel, mankind, to fill their depleted ranks and taught them the secret lore of binding. The ancients were a musical race, graceful, terrible, and mellifluous. They discovered magic through the lens of that musicality, coaxing the animus of the creatures they bound into physical objects where they could be stored until their loosing. Bormian's dense prose cloaked the dangerous confession that he had understood more than they had meant to convey to mankind. The bindings of today paled beside those ancient works of arcane might, the runes a mere construct that the Shining Ones had fashioned to vulgarize the art for human comprehension.

He set the book down and stretched, then dropped to his knees to check the spirit trap beneath the end table. A mouse had lately found its way into the mansion, and Henrik hoped to lure and bind it before the pest chewed up one of his books. Henrik had hidden the chalked runes beneath a buttered crust of bread, a simple dormant binding that would trap the vermin's spirt within a rock. But the rodent had evaded the trap for nearly a week.

Henrik settled back to his reading, but a line from the book conjured an image of the night before, and his mind wandered instead to the episode at the docks.

Henrik had drunk rather a lot after his father's revelation. While the mayor had busied himself with calculations, Henrik, already affected by a touch of brandy, let intuition confirm the connection between the comet and the evacuation. It was too much of a coincidence that a new player would appear in the heavenly circuit just as a sudden exodus of Quaya moon spelled ever nearing disaster.

So Henrik had gone to the High Tavern and polished off a bottle of Quayan red to toast the vineyard's doom. No doubt his father would be outraged by the extravagance. But with such black news on his mind, no indulgence could cheer him.

He had wandered up to the shrine with a bottle of more modest vintage, but the flock of pilgrims and local celebrants gathered around the statue of Saint Olaf and its moss-covered stone altar made for poor company. That was how he found himself witness to the strange murder on the dock. Thinking he'd at last found a little solace, Henrik had drained the last of his bottle, tossing it in the sea, gazing up at Quaya and the gleaming comet.

It was the farm boy's bizarre shrieking that had drawn his attention. At first, he thought it was a man crying as if in unspeakable pain. It was only after he saw the veteran scurrying onto the dock, his hands warding off his attacker's blows, that Henrik registered it as a sort of battle cry. It was even more shocking to discover that it was the man's own boot with which the farm boy had nearly bludgeoned him. Drunk as he was, Henrik had almost walked off the dock, instinctively backing away from the savage brawl. It was like watching a Raag maul a child.

Just as he imagined that shadow appearing on the scene, someone knocked on the front door of the mansion. He set his book on the end table and walked out into the hallway. His mother reached the foyer first, and he heard her welcome the constable inside.

Henrik froze. All night he had dreaded this moment. The constable would inform them that the culprit was apprehended. He'd thank Henrik for bearing witness. The farm boy would hang by week's end. But what could Henrik say? A shadow killed Torin? A Raag? Even the girl had balked at sharing the unpalatable truth. They would think him mad to speak a story like that. The prefect might even decide he was unfit to inherit the mayorship.

On the other hand, it could return. A catastrophe that would cast him in quite an unfavorable light. Henrik realized he was biting his thumbnail and chided himself for it. He had chosen his course, so he donned a look approximating grim satisfaction and rounded the corner.

"My good man." He shook the constable's hand. "I trust the miscreant has found his way into your jail."

The constable stood there a moment in his bright red coat, looking uncomfortable, his broken nose whistling. "Where's the mayor? I think we three should discuss this together."

"Of course." Henrik fought to keep the panic off his face. He should have just told the truth. *Damn!* What had Brohr said?

Or had the girl changed her story? Henrik wondered if it was to late to amend his own account. Alarmed, he realized he was blushing, and turned down the hallway to hide his face. "He's in his work room. Follow me."

The mayor sat hunched over his desk, which was piled with innumerable sheets of calculations and figures, oddities, tools, broken quills and reference books. He took one look at the constable and removed his eyeglasses. "I'm afraid I really haven't got time for this. I trust the boy is in your custody. I'll leave it to the federals to arrange his hanging." He went back to his work until the constable cleared his throat. The mayor rubbed his eyes. "What, Gunnar?"

The constable sucked in his gut and clasped his hands behind his back. "According to the Nilstrom boy," the constable began, "it was your son that killed Torin." He glanced around shyly, his voice growing quiet. "And I believe him."

The mayor shot to his feet. "Have you taken leave of your senses?"

"There are some inconsistencies in Henrik's testimony. Nilstrom's story makes more sense."

"In what way?" Henrik demanded. He was a little surprised that the constable realized he was lying, but he surely had not expected this level of bungling.

"Well..." Constable Gunnar took a moment to ponder this question. "It was mostly his bearing. He didn't seem like someone who had just committed murder. I'm a fine judge of character, you know."

The mayor shook his head. "I'm hardly surprised that the murderer tried to accuse the witness. I am *shocked*, however, that you would believe him." He looked back and forth between his son and the constable, astonished. "Think very carefully now." He dropped his voice as if admonishing a child. "What specifically about his account makes you believe him over my son?"

Gunnar bit his lip. "Well," he said. But no further explanation seemed forthcoming. He began again. "It was quite clear to me earlier. Give me a moment."

"Perhaps a sleepless night has clouded your judgment," Henrik suggested.

"No disrespect to your father, but I'm afraid the evidence points to you."

The mayor pounded on his desk. "What evidence?"

Again, the constable paused to consider this. He gestured as if the movement of his hands would dislodge a word he couldn't quite recall. "It's odd." He blushed. "I begin to doubt myself."

"Rightly so!" The mayor's cheeks burned. "What are you thinking? Why didn't you arrest him? That young man is a murderer."

"I'll pay him another visit."

"Gunnar?"

"Yes, sir?"

"If you persist with this strange misunderstanding, or even discuss it outside of this room, I'll see you in the stocks."

"Yes, sir."

★★★★★

After the constable left their cabin, Brohr and his grandfather sat before the fire, listening to the damp wood hiss and pop. The blood covering Brohr dried and began to itch. He clutched the arms of his chair, gripping it as if he might fall out.

He realized that his grandfather was staring at him. Still, he neither moved nor spoke. At last, Anders stood and walked over to the hearth. He picked the kettle up off its hook by the mantle and hung it on the one over the fire.

"Let's get you cleaned up," said Anders. "That must be itchy by now."

"It's a strange day," said Brohr, "when you discover that your grandfather knows exactly what it feels like to be drenched in blood."

Anders laughed and went to the cupboard to fetch a rag. When he returned, the smile had left his face. "I'm trying to decide how much to coddle you. I know this has all been frightening and confusing. But I have a feeling that things will get much worse over the next few days."

"Great," Brohr said. "You must be very excited."

Anders smiled again, teeth gritted. "I am, my boy. I truly am." He used the rag to pull the kettle off of the fire. The spout jetted steam, but it wasn't whistling yet. "You shouldn't be afraid though. Great things lie ahead for you."

Brohr snorted. "Yeah, I look forward to being burned alive with my grandfather, the skald." He shouldn't have come home. He should run. Temper or no, he couldn't take on the federals. He should have just run.

Anders kicked Brohr hard in the shin. When he doubled over in pain, the old man cupped his hand and cuffed him on the ear. Brohr crashed to the floor, reeling. Anders set the kettle down by his grandson's face, and, groaning, knelt beside him.

"I see that I've been too kind to you." His grandfather wiped a bead of sweat from his brow. "Joke all you want, boy. You'll be grateful for my secrets before long. My power. The pigs who rule us may forbid the old songs, but I don't care about their laws. Before they came, I would've ruled this village. We are going to take back our world, Brohr. Imagine it. No price is too high."

Brohr pushed himself to his feet, and his grandfather followed suit, knees popping from the strain.

Anders shrugged and gestured for him to sit. "I'm old, Brohr. Too old to fight the federals and my own blood, too. Trust me when I say that you can't even imagine the changes to come. Finding out your grandfather is a skald is the least of them. You can be certain of it." He gestured to the chair again. "Please, sit. We'll get that mess off you."

Brohr relented, collapsing into the cowhide armchair. His grandfather patted him on the shoulder and picked the kettle up off the floor. He wet the rag with steaming water and wiped the crusty blood, first from Brohr's eyes, and then his mouth. He poured more water on the rag and wrung it out over the fire, the drops sizzling in the awkward quiet. Anders returned to his grandson and began cleaning the blood out of his hair. "For once," he joked, "I'm glad you wear your hair short like a federal." After a moment, he added, "Not really of course."

"Of course," Brohr echoed.

Anders rinsed the rag again and dabbed at the mess collected in Brohr's ear.

"Can I do that, please?" Brohr asked. "Tell me about that thing on the dock."

Anders handed over the rag. "I've told you most of what I know already."

Brohr doubted that. His grandfather was angling at something. "You seem like you expected it? How?"

Anders sunk into the other chair and stared at the dwindling fire. "It's hard to explain. When you work the blood, you become sensitive to certain things. The whole world is a song, and you can pick out strange notes. Do you understand?"

Brohr shook his head, mopping the blood from his face.

"Well," said Anders. "There are echoes in the blood. Secrets of others, ancient memories and new. It opens you up, you're awake to things that others are not. I hear whispers. They foretold the coming of the comet. The uprising."

"And that thing… was it a Raag?"

Anders shook his head. He opened his mouth to say something but snapped it shut instead, pausing. "This is something worse. Moriigo was the first to rebel, you understand? It's sympathetic to our plight."

"Moriigo?" Brohr asked. It seemed like every time his grandfather opened his mouth, a lie spilled out. Anders loved his secrets. He loved to poke and prod Brohr in one direction or another, but Brohr had glimpsed the truth enough times to take his words with a grain of salt.

"Moriigo." His grandfather nodded. "The Hidden."

Brohr didn't want to argue about it, even if his grandfather was lying. Sometimes when Brohr called him out, he got nasty. "Did I get it all?"

"No," said Anders. "Around your neck there's more blood. Here too." He pointed at his own cheekbone.

Brohr finished cleaning himself up. "I didn't like that thing. Whatever it was. It was wrong. Scary. I don't want its help, damn it. I don't want to ever see it again."

Anders nodded. "Quite scary. Especially for our enemies."

"I don't have any enemies!" Brohr threw the rag on the floor.

"Oh yes you do. And you always have." Anders peered into the embers. "You were born from the rape of our people, the rape of my sweet *Fjorel.*" He paused. "She died bearing the fruit of their crime."

Brohr blanched. "And what about my brother? How did you know it was him? Have you known all of this all along? Why are you keeping secrets from me?"

"I am a skald after all." Anders grinned. "I'm sorry, Brohr. You just weren't ready. These things I'm telling you could get you killed, after all." Anders sighed, looking down at his scarred hands. "His name was Olek. Your mother named him."

"I don't care what his name is. I wish he would go to the dead place where he belongs." Brohr stared into the fire. "None of this would have happened if it wasn't for him."

"You should be grateful," the old man said. "His rage is a gift."

"A gift?" Brohr stood up. "You really are twisted. I'm leaving. This time I mean it."

"If you run now, they'll just blame that tavern wench for everything."

★★★★★

72

Lyssa sat at the granite foot of Saint Olaf's statue, watching the mayor's mansion. A river rock wainscoting wrapped around the first of its two stories, moss collecting here and there along the mortared seams and beneath the open-shuttered windows. A few of the shops in town had windows too, but none so many. Lyssa loved windows. She sat here often, looking in.

But this visit had a purpose; it was no idle lark. She'd seen a horror on the docks. The sort of thing whispered of to naughty children. Raag or Mara or something else entirely, whatever it was, it was very real. Its pitch-black hand had reached down and choked the life from Torin's bull neck.

When the constable arrived at the docks, he'd questioned Henrik. She supposed it was unfair to hate him for omitting that *thing* from his account. But he had glared when it was her turn, a petulant look that warned her not to drag fairytales into the simple case of one drunk murdering another.

Looking back on it, she wanted to slap herself. *Speak up!* But of course, she hadn't. She just pretended to be confused so she wouldn't have to lie. She should have said there was a fifth person on the docks. It didn't have to be a monster. Just someone else.

A frigid sea breeze carried the briny scent of the water inland. Lyssa squinted down the hill toward town. From her vantage, she could see her father's tavern, a squat longhouse with a sagging roof and a haphazard second story room. Lyssa turned farther to look at the docks. Her stomach roiled, and she pulled her fur stole tight around her. That thing might still be under the waters. Did it live under the dock like a Mara under a bridge?

Lyssa forced her attention back to the mansion. She knew that the mayor, his son, and the constable were in the reading room on the bottom floor. From her position, she could see inside, but other than the constable pacing, her view showed her little else.

Still, she was cheered by the fact that the constable had returned to town without Brohr. Perhaps he'd told him about the thing on the dock and the constable had believed him. No, that thought didn't carry water. It was too much to hope that Henrik would confess that his first version of events was incomplete, but perhaps he would. The family owned more books than the rest of the town combined, maybe they even knew what it was.

Lyssa stood. Scoping around to be certain she was unobserved, she surveyed the hilltop. A few bottles and a leather glove that one of last night's revelers had lost lay near the well, but there was no other sign of life. She was alone on High Hill, at least outside. She made her way down the steps to the well, halfway between the shrine and the mansion. Lyssa spied about again and crept to the back side of the mayor's home where a patio faced the forest and sea. She knew the mayor's wife was somewhere inside too, so she crouched past the windows on her way to the back door. It was a stout portal, hewn from oak with a brass peep hole up top. Naturally, it was locked.

Lyssa took off her cap and produced a pair of hairpins which she kept twisted into shape for such occasions. She pressed her ear to the door so she wouldn't be surprised on the off chance someone opened it. Then Lyssa slid the first hairpin into the lock and explored its tumblers. A smile settled onto her face as she set to work. The mayor's stern voice rose from the drawing room. She paused to listen, but it was too muffled to make out his words. With a soft click, the tumblers fell into place. Lyssa turned the second hairpin to rotate the lock. The door opened without a sound. Grateful that the hinges were well-oiled, Lyssa slipped in and shut it behind her before a draft could betray her entrance.

She stood in the dining room. A long, darkly varnished table was set with an embroidered cloth runner and two unlit silver candelabras. Lyssa leaned across the table and picked up one of the candlesticks, admiring its heft, trying to appraise the quantity of silver in it. She could keep Ivar off her back for another month, maybe two. Her father had lost most of the coin he'd made on Saint Olaf's Day at dice. With that much silver, Lyssa might even secure passage on the next ship that docked in the harbor and sail away from the likes of Ivar and Arius forever. She looked back at the door she'd just entered through, wondering if she could get away with it, if it was worth it.

She set the candelabra back on the table with a sigh and scanned the rest of the room. A pair of hutches, for displaying the family's finest dishes, lined the opposite wall, full of imported boneware from Old Hemmings far to the south. Arched doorways led out of the room to either side. The smell of roasting, extravagantly seasoned meat wafted from the door to the right.

To her left, the mayor's voice echoed from another room. "If you persist with this strange misunderstanding, or even discuss it outside this room, I'll see you in the stocks."

Lyssa crept to the doorway to hear better. The men were not in the next room but somewhere deeper in the house. She tip-toed through the arch into an elaborate closet. Damask and mahogany chairs sat against one wall; around the others hung soft cloaks, rare furs, and an assortment of fancy hats. There was even a mirror over an open trunk full of fine leather boots.

The figure in the reflection startled her. Lyssa's heart fluttered. Breaking into the mayor's house was bolder than any of the watch work she'd dared before. For just an instant, she thought she had been caught. She studied the young woman wrapped in a fur mantel, her hair up under a knit cap. She wore a loose tunic and leather breaches. It could have been a boy staring back. Lyssa stared at the mirror for a moment until a frown appeared on the face regarding her.

She tiptoed to the next doorway. On the other side, the mansion featured an open area by the front door, where guests were greeted. An expensive sofa and a pair of chairs flanking a small table hugged the opposite wall. Bright light streamed down from a chandelier fashioned from elk antlers, its spirit lamps glowing in three tiers. She almost whistled, then smiled at the thought of where that would have led.

A chair in the next room creaked as someone stood, then footfalls on hardwood echoed through the foyer. Lyssa retreated towards the dining room and listened from there, throwing glances over her shoulder. All three men walked to the front door and the mayor said, "Check back with me in the morning. I expect you to have him in hand by then."

"Yes, of course," the constable replied.

Lyssa heard the front door open and close. She cursed herself for waiting too long. All that sneaking for nothing! She'd missed the meat of the conversation.

Behind her a woman's voice called from the other side of the house. "Dinner!"

Lyssa's stomach lurched.

"Coming," Henrik called.

Lyssa darted back into the dining room, shocked to find a platter of steaming ribs on the table. Henrik and his father were already in the coat room. There was no time to get out the door without being seen, or at least without them seeing someone fleeing the house. She could make a break for it, try to scramble down the hill, and disappear into the woods. Henrik was tall and long-legged, though; if he gave chase, he would catch her.

Of course, both men were also binders. The Fathers only knew what sort of magic they could unleash on her.

She dropped to her knees and rolled beneath the table, closing her eyes and fighting to slow her breathing. Her heart still made it impossible to hear what they were saying, but the chair beside her head was pulled out and Henrik's glossy boots appeared. Ever so carefully, she shied away so that if he stretched his legs he wouldn't kick her.

The thought of hiding beneath an ordinary family's dinner table popped into her head and she stifled a giggle, imagining that she'd have to set her head in somebody's lap. Not the case here; the Torvald's table could accommodate a dozen guests and left plenty of room for Lyssa to keep out from under foot. The idea calmed her, and she managed to slow her anxious heartbeat enough to eavesdrop. They obviously didn't know she was there. With a little luck, they would eat dinner and leave the room. Then she could slip out.

Lyssa marveled at the exotic aromas of vanilla and rose oil. Hildur's house-slippers shuffled across the paisley rug, and her perfume mingled with the scents of stale pipe smoke and roasted garlic. Hildur served her husband first, then her son, and finally sat down to load up her own plate.

The Torvalds dined without a blessing, silver forks chiming against their fine dishes. Silence lingered.

At last, Hildur called across the table, "Did the Nilstrom boy cause any trouble?"

Henrik made a fist and kneaded his thigh with it.

"Gunnar hasn't fetched him yet," the mayor answered.

"What a time for such a senseless death," said Hildur. "What with... the comet and all. Do you think they will hang him, dear? He's so young."

"I don't think we should let that happen," said Henrik. "You know what I saw. There has to be an explanation."

Someone pounded their fist on the table, dishes and silverware jumped up and landed with a clatter. Lyssa rolled to her knees and crouched on the balls of her feet.

The mayor shouted. "Enough! We've enough to worry about without this... this... this fable you've concocted to absolve that ruffian. You were drunk and upset, and it was dark. So your mind conjured this fantasy. I don't want to hear another word of it."

"Father," Henrik said. "Even the federals admit the truth of the ancients."

"As an allegory!" The mayor insisted. "Don't try to use an argument you don't even believe yourself."

"Well, I saw something," Henrik said. "I have to believe what my own eyes told me."

"You were drunk."

"Father, have you ever seen something that wasn't there at all? Drink doesn't cause that. Perhaps it was a spirit."

"Shaped like a man? That choked that fool to death? That's even less likely."

"A Raag then."

The mayor scoffed. "Absurd!"

Henrik wiped his sweaty hands in his lap and took a deep breath. "It was you, Father, who taught me to trust only my own senses and experiences, to judge for myself what is true or false. Well, I do trust my senses, and I do believe I saw something that I cannot quite explain. That means to me that something we *cannot* dismiss is happening. To pretend otherwise would make us no better than the folk in town waiting for Saint Olaf and hanging fetishes by their doors to ward off the Mara."

A long silence ensued. "Hildur, my dear," the mayor said, at last. "Would you mind clearing away these dishes while I talk to our son?"

"Of course." She stood up and went around the table, collecting their plates. "I'll get the rest later."

When she had gone, the Mayor tamped the bowl of his pipe full before continuing their conversation. He puffed a moment, contemplating his words, the savory smell of roasted meat soon overpowered by the sweet smoke. "We have no way of knowing how bad it will get," he said at last. "But if they are evacuating Quaya altogether, it will be very bad indeed. A catastrophe. We can ill afford to be distracted by this. The safety of every man and woman in town is in our hands."

Lyssa had thought the prefect meant they were evacuating the village. She wondered if she could have been mistaken. A dread settled over her as she huddled beneath the table. All of Quaya?

"I know what I saw, Father," said Henrik. "There is more going on here than we can see right now. Do you think you can get that toy of yours working in time?"

"It's been working for years, Henrik. But that should be an absolute last resort." The mayor folded his hands in his lap for a moment before a bout of coughing seized him. Lyssa heard him tapping out the ash from his pipe.

"I'll see what I can do for this boy, but don't tell anyone what you saw. We can't lose face in the coming days. I fear the worst."

Henrik stood up and walked over to his father. He paused there, and then Lyssa watched him exit through the coat room. The mayor sat at the dining room table for a moment before he began cleaning his pipe. Lyssa stuck out her middle finger at him, cursing him for not leaving with the others. After a few minutes, she heard a faint sound she couldn't place. She studied the mayor's lower half until, finally, she realized that he was crying. He wept for about a minute more before venting a loud sigh. Then he packed a fresh bowl into his pipe and lit it. Beneath the table, Lyssa made shooing motions, but oblivious to these, the mayor lingered at the head of the table until he finished his smoke. At last he pushed his chair back and followed his wife into the kitchen.

Lyssa rolled out from under the table, took one last look at the Torvald's dining room, and slipped out of the back door, grinning like a Mara.

Chapter 8

"The path of priesthood is a lifelong act of sacrifice. Officers give their time, their blood, and their innocence for the Pontiff. What incense could smell sweeter?"

-Avocar Shineius Bara, The Martial Offering

Brasca's father had taught him that nine times out of ten, you could guess a man's house by his skin, his eyes, a few facial features. It was typical of the sort of uncritical, arrogant assumptions that the old man passed off as wisdom.

Brasca studied his ordinal who lay on the cot, noting skin as dark as roasted coffee, a flat nose, straight black hair. Likely one of the older houses by his father's way of reckoning. Carthalo's wide-set, hazel eyes snapped open and roamed the dimly lit room until settling on Brasca seated in his chair. The junior officer sat up and doffed the elaborate helmet he wore.

"He's waiting, sir," said Ordinal Carthalo.

Brasca Quoll stood up and backed away from the cot, giving his subordinate room to get up. The young man stood, keeping both hands on the precious helm, and moved aside for the prefect to lie down.

"Can I help you out of your armor, sir?"

"That won't be necessary."

Brasca wore a practical leather skirt and a breastplate, but his tricorn hat already lay on the bedside table. He sat on the cot and kicked his legs up, leaving on his muddy boots. The prefect held out his hands for the helm.

Carthalo obliged, carefully handing his officer the device.

"Has it been very long since you've used one, sir?"

Brasca donned the ungainly helmet and buckled its leather strap beneath his chin. "It's been a few years." He wiggled around until he was comfortable. "But I was a caller at your age myself."

"Of course." Carthalo bowed his head.

"Have you ever been across the mountains?"

The ordinal clasped his hands behind his back. "Yes, sir. I was stationed in Trond when I first arrived on Heimir."

"Good." Brasca smiled. "Then you can remind me which are the sending stones for Trond?"

"Of course, sir." Carthalo beamed at the opportunity. "It can be found where *Absalon, Darmuz,* and *Ashtara* meet."

Brasca closed his eyes, envisioning the runes orbiting his head. Each one corresponded to one of the stones fashioned to the outside of the helmet. Beginning with the first circuit, Brasca listened to one rune after another until he came to *Absalon, the Rampant Warleader,* a constellation of simple lines, heavy with meaning. Anchoring the rune in his mind, its frequency resonated in the back of his head. He hummed quietly until he had matched pitch. His awareness climbed to the second tier of stones. Again, he groped from one to another, a bit chagrined at his ineptitude, until at last he located *Darmuz, the Dancing Fool.* He pictured the runes side by side until a tenuous filament of light connected them. Brasca found the second note and hummed them both. Finally, the prefect ascended the highest tier, where only three stones crowned the helm, and tethered the first two runes to *Ashtara, the Angel of Accord,* intoning the triplet. His mind hurtled through the darkness, billowing gas and spinning rocks careening past at dizzying speeds, until a spinning blue light sucked him back into its orbit.

"Brasca?" A familiar voice reached out, a shimmering figure coalescing in the astral veil between this world and the next. "Is that you stumbling around out there?"

"Arabo, you halfwit! Are you too drunk to recognize an old friend?"

"Of course not," Arabo quipped. "Just drunk enough to tolerate an old braggart preying on my kindness for a favor."

81

"Fair enough, Arabo." Brasca oriented himself toward the familiar presence, readjusting to the starscape surrounding him. "I suppose since you still owe me all those racing debts, you'll be looking for a way out. I shudder at what the interest has done to feed them."

"Ha!" Arabo replied. "I'm filthy rich now, you usurer."

"Yes," Brasca grew serious. "I heard about your father."

"Don't gush, Brasca. We didn't get along any better than you and your father."

"Still."

"Yes," Arabo sighed. "Are you regretting your little bout of conscience yet?"

Brasca groaned. "No, I suppose not. What's the point of serving if you serve a lie?"

Arabo laughed. "Stubborn as ever. Just say the words and get it done with. What does it matter if you aren't the most pious officer in the legion? At least you wouldn't have to live out there in the mud. I know that the offering was especially difficult, given how Silvano died, but you have another son to look after."

"It's complicated, Arabo. I don't want to live a lie—"

"Anyway," Arabo interrupted. "I really don't give a fig about your little doubts. Everyone has doubts. That's between you and the Pontiff. Stop being so proud, I'd say." A silence followed. "Have you spoken with Sabina since you left?"

"No," said Brasca. "There's nothing else to say."

"You can't afford another scandal back on Tyria. Call your wife, old friend. I heard a rumor that she made a scene at one of Elector Rodan's parties. She'd been drinking again. She's embarrassing you, Brasca."

"Leave it, Arabo." Another silence. "Anyway, I'm afraid I don't have much time to reminisce. Things are chaotic here. That's why I called. I've had a series of orders issued and retracted. Bishop Adrychaeus must be as senile as the rumors say."

"Don't be too harsh on the old boy. The astronomers keep revising their predictions. The one thing they are certain of is a total disaster on Quaya."

82

"I can practically look up and see that," Brasca replied.

"Full-scale evacuation is impossible before the comet hits. It's a mess down here on Heimir; imagine the anarchy up there. Naturally, the slaves are being left behind. But with no one to mind them, they're causing all sorts of havoc trying to get off."

"Wouldn't you?" Brasca asked.

"If I was a slave I'd fall on my own sword."

"If you were a slave, no one would give you a sword, Arabo."

"Fair enough."

"Why the flip-flop on orders?"

"Well, at first the idea was to bring everyone from Quaya here to Heimir. Since it was the closest planet, it was the easiest. We have considerable stores set aside here in Trond. Not enough for all of Quaya but at least the citizens."

"And then?"

Arabo scoffed. "And then some scholar flicked the beads of his abacus a few more times and..."

"And?"

"I know you're not one for prayer these days," Arabo said. "But, my friend, you should pray."

★★★★★

Brohr pulled hand over hand on the old rope until the bucket rested on the stone rim of the well. He lifted it over the edge and dumped the contents into the cooking pot that he ferried back and forth every day in a handcart. Sweat ran into his eye, and he wiped his face on his forearm before dropping the bucket back down the well and hauling it up again. He brooded while he worked, tension building in his gut like cramps. With so much happening so quickly, he'd been slow to absorb everything his grandfather had said. It also occurred to him that the old man might be spinning lies, but the trick with the blood meant some of it must be true. But why was he holding back?

When the pot was full, Brohr set the bucket down beside the well. He grasped the rough handles of the handcart and dug in, careful not to slip in the mud, until he got the cart rolling. It was about a hundred paces from the well to the cabin. The gentle rise made pushing the cart hard work. He wore his cloak still and was regretting it by the time he set the handles down.

Brohr brought the full pot inside and set it on the table where his grandfather was dicing onions with a cleaver. Brohr waited, his hands still resting on the pot, until his elder looked up.

"Something on your mind?" His grandfather asked.

"Yes." Brohr folded his hands before him. "I can't seem to think of anything else."

"All right then. Ask your question."

"You said…" Brohr pinched the bridge of his nose. "You said the soldiers raped my mother."

"This again?

"Well?" Brohr asked.

"Well what?"

"You know what!" Brohr said through gritted teeth.

A gust of wind rattled the front door, and outside Grendie started barking. Anders cocked his head to listen.

"Answer me!" Brohr insisted. "Which one of them is my father?"

Someone knocked on the door. They both flinched, standing there like imbeciles until there was another knock. Anders moved to the door, but Brohr snatched the old man's wrist.

"Was Torin one of them?"

Anders pulled free of his grandson's grip with surprising strength. "We'll speak of this later."

Grendie howled. Another knock sounded, this time followed by the constable's voice. "Master Nilstrom. It's Constable Gunnar again. Open the door. I have soldiers with me."

Brohr and his grandfather met eyes.

"They're going to arrest you, I'm afraid."

Brohr looked at the shuttered window at the back of the cabin. "They'll hang me," he said. "I should have run."

His grandfather held up his hands, palms out. "Stay calm, boy. Stay calm. It's too late to run now. I won't let them hang you. Hey! Are you listening?" Anders reached out with both hands to cradle his grandson's worried face. He craned his neck up and stood on his toes to kiss Brohr on the forehead. "I won't let them hurt you."

The constable rapped on the door with the butt of his cudgel. "Open up in there. I don't want to have to knock this door down. Be reasonable now. You'll have your say."

Brohr jerked his head free of Anders' embrace. He slid the dagger from his belt, looking around the room for another weapon. His eyes settled on the kitchen cleaver lying on the table beside a pile of onions. He felt the bile rising in his gut, that first twitch of his brother's ire. Like someone deadly stood behind him.

He felt thankful. For the first time he was not afraid of his brother. But he was still afraid. The light seemed to dim from the room. Brohr felt a hand on his arm; it stroked his skin soothingly. His grandfather spoke in a gentle voice, but for some reason he couldn't understand. Another knock on the door jolted Brohr from his trance.

Grendie's barking grew more aggressive. "Back!" shouted the constable. "If this dog bites there'll be more trouble. Open up in there!"

Anders pried open Brohr's grip on the dagger. "I'll keep it safe."

Brohr nodded to his grandfather, who tucked the knife in his belt, and turned to unbar the door. "Grendie be quiet!" Anders shouted. The dog barked again. "I said quiet!"

The constable made no move to enter, his eyes darting from Anders to Grendie and back. He stood flanked by two federal soldiers with their swords drawn, their shields high. Gunnar leaned forward and peeked inside. "What was the delay, Nilstrom?"

Anders held up his hands again. "Peace, Constable. The boy is frightened. Do you blame him?"

"It's time for him to come out."

Anders eyed the legionaries' swords. "Will you put those away?"

The Constable turned to the soldiers and nodded. As they sheathed their blades, Gunnar rested his cudgel on his shoulder. "Come on out, young man. Our patience has its limits."

Anders turned to Brohr and embraced him, whispering in his ear. "Keep that temper in check until the moment is right."

Chapter 9

"The ruins of Grisben stand as a dire testament—a scar upon Heimir's face that will never heal. Though today the Norn speak our tongue and pay our tithes, we can never turn our backs to them, lest they find the courage to bare their barbaric resentments."

-Adriano Sychaeus, The Tramp of Boots: A Federal History of Tyrianite Conquest

Skolja's jail squatted on the northwest corner of the town square. The moss-shrouded log building looked due for some fresh thatching. It had no windows and a single oaken door, banded in iron and capped by a lintel painted with a red star.

Lyssa stood across the cobblestone square, having just left the apothecary. A morning fog lingered, obscuring the hills beyond the heart of the village. Axl and Hetta, who owned the clothier next to the jail, had stopped off at the tavern on their way home yesterday. While most of the talk that evening centered around the comet, there was no shortage of gossip about Brohr and Torin.

She loved Hetta, a conspiratorial old woman always in a mischievous mood. Hetta still liked to drink, crediting her nightly ale or three with the steady hands that stitched half the clothes in town. Axl, on the other hand, patiently quaffed his brew, content to daydream or pick up a game of Six Pins.

Hetta had told her about seeing Brohr Nilstrom escorted to the jail by soldiers. All night, Lyssa had soothed her guilty conscience with nips of mead. But the consequences of her silence were all too obvious now. She almost told Hetta about Breylin and the dahlia's she'd brought to Axl, just to unburden herself of the tiniest shred of guilt, but after Hetta mused that they'd hang Brohr, Lyssa couldn't bring herself to stir up any more trouble.

Lyssa wiped her sweaty hands on her pant legs and started across the square. She looked around to see who was watching and realized no one was paying any attention to her in the slightest. The women waiting at the well stared at the sky, transfixed as the fog parted to reveal the comet. Lyssa stopped to marvel at the path of the Wanderer, now bright enough to be seen in the daytime sky. When her wonder wore off, she turned back to the jail and marched up to the door. She banged upon it with the heel of her hand, and hearing a muffled voice reply within, she entered.

An oil lamp shone atop the constable's desk. He sat behind it, wheezing as he waited for her to state her business. The damp stink of mildew hung in the air. It was cold enough for her to see her breath, but the constable's body odor still vied with the stench of rotting thatch. At the back of the room, behind a set of bars, Brohr looked up from the cot he sat on.

"Good morning, dear." Constable Gunnar hiked his thumb toward Brohr. "Is this about the murderer?" He laced his fingers together over his paunch.

"It's about Brohr," she said.

Brohr stood up and walked to the bars.

"Well?" The constable prodded. "What have you got to say?"

Lyssa folded her hands behind her back. "I was a bit shaken when I talked to you the other night. There was something I should've mentioned but I was frightened." She paused. "When Henrik didn't mention it, I… Well, I was afraid to."

"Out with it." Gunnar leaned forward.

"There was someone else on the dock." Lyssa held her breath, but he took his time considering this, his own breath whistling through his broken nose.

"It's true," said Brohr, pressing his face between the rusty bars.

88

"Quiet, you." The constable frowned back at Brohr. Satisfied he'd made his point, Gunnar turned back to Lyssa. "Who?"

"I don't know," she said. "But it wasn't Brohr who killed Torin. Whoever it was choked Torin after the fight was over."

The constable scratched inside his ear. "This seems very unlikely. You'd never seen this man before?"

Lyssa shook her head. "It was dark."

"Where did he go after he killed Torin? No one else seems to have seen him."

Lyssa considered what to say. She knew that her story sounded far-fetched. Mentioning that it melted through the pier seemed a tad too honest. Still, as much of the truth as the constable could stomach was probably best.

"It dove off the dock."

"It?" The constable cocked his head, as if he'd misheard her.

She glanced at Brohr, who shook his head. "He." Lyssa recanted.

"Was he there on the dock before the fight started? Why kill Torin?"

"Yes," she said. "He was already on the dock. And I don't know why. All I know is that Brohr didn't kill Torin. By the Fathers, I swear it."

The constable shook his head as she concluded her tale, a doubtful frown appearing. "Who would dive into that sea? They'd freeze to death. Besides, not even the prisoner mentioned this fifth person. He said that Henrik did it. And another witness has come forward."

"Who?" Brohr asked.

"Keep your moth shut, shade. It was Johan Thorsten. He said he saw you running away covered in blood."

"You can't listen to Johan," said Lyssa. "He's just an ornery drunk. He got into it with Brohr at the tavern. I'm telling you the truth, there was someone else on the docks."

"It's true," Brohr said. "I only said Henrik did it because I didn't think you'd believe me!"

"I said quiet!" The constable rose from his chair, snatched his cudgel off the desk, and banged on the cell bars where Brohr's face had just been. "Prisoners are not to speak when visitors are in the jail."

Brohr stepped back and held up his hands. "Please believe me."

Gunnar walloped the bars again. "Another word and you'll get no supper!" The constable paused to scowl at Brohr before nodding to himself and taking his seat.

"I know this all sounds a bit strange," Lyssa pleaded. "But it's true. You can't let them punish him for this. He's innocent."

The constable set down his cudgel and put his hands back on his belly, digesting her testimony. Eventually he began to shake his head. "In any case, it's up to the prefect, and I'm afraid it's more of a question of whether they'll hang him as a common outlaw or burn him at the stake."

★★★★★

"I'm told you have a surprisingly well-stocked wine cellar." Brasca pulled a stool out and sat at the bar of the High Tavern. "What's your best vintage? I want the best bottle you've got."

The boy set down a glass he'd been polishing, leaned back against the shelves, and folded his arms. "Easy," he said. "I've got a forty-year-old Shineian spice wine, bottled at the Keffi Oasis. My grandfather bought it off of Prefect Flaucus. It's sort of an heirloom. But I could let it go for five bright ones." The boy held his breath.

Brasca glanced around the High Tavern. Lanterns in wall sconces beamed merrily, and the mixed clientele of off-duty legionaries and well-to-do provincials chatted on blithely, unaware of the looming disaster. If the wine really was bottled at the Keffi Oasis, it was worth five golden federals, but this kid would never be able to sell it.

"I'll give you one gold federal for it."

The tavern keep licked his lips. "I couldn't take less than three," he said.

Brasca rooted in his coin purse and slapped two coins on the bar. "Fetch it."

Without looking Brasca in the eye, the young man scooped the gold off the bar and headed into the back room.

Brasca leaned back, tipping his stool onto two legs. He glanced around the bar again and had to admit the place was nicer than he would have expected for this backwater. With its wainscoting, its mounted boar heads, and its fire roaring in the great stone fireplace, it had the feel of a nobleman's hunting lodge. Just rustic enough for a change of pace.

In the stairwell that led up to the rooms on the top floor, he noticed a buxom Norn girl with long hair in golden braids. She turned her back to him, gesturing angrily to someone around the corner. The young woman cocked back to slap whoever she was arguing with, and a dark hand appeared, snatching her wrist. It wasn't, strictly speaking, against regulations for the men to fraternize with provincials, but it had caused no end of trouble since the occupation had begun. And rumor had it that the Norn did not take it lightly, ostracizing and occasionally beating or even killing women who chose to warm a Tyrianite's bed.

The girl pulled away from her lover, tears streaming down her cheeks, and stormed through the tap room on her way for the door. She looked up and met Brasca's eyes. The color drained from her lovely face as she put her head down and strode right past him.

Brasca ogled her as she fled the inn. When he turned back, he was surprised to discover Ordinal Carthalo standing in the stairwell, looking quite surprised himself. Brasca arched an eyebrow and waved his subordinate over to the bar. Carthalo looked as if he'd just been caught skimming from the tithes. Grimacing, he made his way over to the prefect and hailed him.

"Lady troubles?" Brasca asked.

The ordinal managed a tense laugh. "To say the least."

"Join me." Brasca pulled out the stool next to him and patted the seat. "I've got an excellent bottle of wine on the way. And I could use the company."

The ordinal nodded, taking his seat. "It's an honor, sir."

Brasca's nostrils flared. "You only have to kiss my ass when you're on duty, Ordinal."

Carthalo smiled. "Yes, sir."

The young innkeeper returned with a green bottle wrapped in dusty gold foil. He presented it to Brasca, who held it up for Carthalo to see.

"Ever had spice wine?" Brasca asked. "I've heard it's delicious."

"Yes, sir. I had an aunt who drank it by the barrel. Wonderful wine. It can make for a nasty habit though."

Brasca bobbed his head. The Shineians added a mild narcotic to the wine. It was all part of its charm. He handed the bottle back across the bar. "Two glasses." As the boy uncorked the bottle, Carthalo squirmed in his chair, looking around the tap room. "You aren't in any trouble, you know," said Brasca. "It's not against regulations to bed provincials. Troublesome, perhaps, but permissible."

"Yes, sir. Of course."

"So, why do you look so glum? Exquisite wine, peerless companionship," Brasca smirked at his own joke. "What's the trouble? The girl looked upset."

The tavern keep plucked a pair of crystal goblets off the top shelf, polished them with the rag that had been flung over his shoulder, and set one in front of each of them. He poured a dram into the prefect's glass and waited. Brasca held it up, inspecting its amber hue flecked with ground herbs, in the lamplight. He swirled it before his nose, inhaling the pungent bouquet: cinnamon, noble root, and something sweet that he couldn't put his finger on. The narcotic, perhaps. He sipped, exhaling through his mouth to savor the subtler parts of the body. Brasca set his glass down and twirled his finger, indicating that the boy should pour.

"It's Astrid," Carthalo confessed.

Brasca sipped his wine, enjoying the warmth spreading in his belly. "I assume that's the one that just ran out crying. What about her?"

"Well..." Carthalo drained his glass—much to Brasca's amusement. "She's pregnant."

"Ah," said Brasca. "I see."

"She hoped, I think, that I would welcome it."

Brasca stared at Carthalo until the ordinal grew uncomfortable, then the prefect lifted the bottle of spice wine and refilled his companion's glass.

"A child is quite a responsibility," said Brasca.

"It's not what you think," said Carthalo. "I'd be lucky to have her. But she doesn't understand how it really is. I couldn't take her back to Tyria. And here they have no love for half-breeds. They call them shades because their skin is a shade darker. The kid would be doomed from the start. They kill the babies, you know; that's why there are so few of them. Sometimes the mothers too."

"I can't tell if you're concerned or inconvenienced."

Carthalo held his wine to his mouth, paused for a breath, then sipped.

Brasca waited a few moments, but Carthalo merely finished his wine and poured a third glass. "Go on," said Brasca, ignoring the presumption. "You might as well tell the rest."

"I told her she should get rid of it." He looked at the prefect from the corner of his eye. "We'll all be better off."

Brasca leaned back on his stool. "Have you ever played a game called Black Bones?"

Carthalo furrowed his brow, puzzled. "No, sir."

"I wouldn't expect you had. It's all the rage at home. Among the children, anyway. It's a game they're all playing. It seems simple at first; you have a few stones and you arrange them this way or that trying to get more. Anyway, I'm getting off track.

"Silvano, my son, loved it. Little Silly, his mother called him." A smile crept onto Brasca's face. "He absolutely obsessed over that game, as boys are apt to do. But he was the best at it. I was always complaining that he didn't practice his wrestling or swordplay enough, but he absolutely trounced all of his little friends at this stupid game they all loved." Brasca's smile crumpled.

"I lost my temper once and knocked the gameboard on the floor. We were late to go riding with the bishop and his son."

Brasca stared down at his hands for a moment. "It was a big day. If Silvano had made friends with the other boy, it could have paved the way for an alliance between our houses. At least, that's what I hoped. But he was mooning over that damned Black Bones board instead of getting ready. That was the day Silvano died. The pieces were still on the floor when I came home."

Carthalo set his wine down. "If you could spare yourself all that pain, spare him, wouldn't you?"

"Of course not!" Brasca hadn't meant to snap. Patrons turned around to stare, but Brasca ignored them. "When I saw the game stones on the floor, I could have retched. I could have stabbed my own eyes out. I'd wanted to impress the bishop, of course. It was important, I thought. Do you want to know what the last words I ever spoke to my son in private were?"

Carthalo shook his head.

"As we were riding up to the Bishop's stable, I turned to him and I said, 'Don't embarrass me.' When I came home and saw the game stones on the floor, I fell down and wept. Everything that I thought was so full of meaning—piety, patriotism, power—they were all less than shit compared to my son. I would have done anything—committed any crime, any sacrilege—just to take those words back. When the ride was nearly over, we sent the boys ahead so that the bishop and I could talk alone. There was a fire in the stable, one of the grooms had locked the gate for some reason. A million little chances conspired to trap the boys there. But if I hadn't been scheming with the bishop, things would have been different. The only thing I can tell you is that you can't go back. Whatever you choose, you can't ever go back."

94

Carthalo sipped his wine, glancing over his shoulder toward the door.

★★★★★

Henrik was forced to admit that he had underestimated his father. In fairness, he still had to take his father's word that it would fly, but Henrik's father, for all of his failings, was no liar.

The design borrowed much from the writings of Zaracas, whose ancient curiosity had delved the secrets of the Shining Ones' relics. More contemporary works on the subject, those with practical void lore, were not available to members of the indigenous castes. At least, not at a cost a simple mayor could afford. The Torvalds might be wealthy by Norn standards, but such books demanded an astronomical price. Even if he had access to those, binders capable of this work were beyond rare. To build something like this from the metaphysical musings of a long dead philosopher was impressive, almost unbelievable. In a way, it irked him.

The vessel dominated the back half of Rogan's workshop, which was separated by a leather curtain. It looked, to Henrik's eye, like a giant disk, like a pair of dinner plates—one upside down atop the other, big enough to serve a wagon on. The iron vessel featured thick glass portholes around the rim of the top bubble and a ring of rune-laden stones joined by copper bracings. The bindings of it gave him vertigo. That, more than anything, provided strong evidence of its power. He set a hand on one of the brass plates joining the two halves of the saucer.

A marvel like this required an incredible amount of cold iron. And the mystic ore was staggeringly valuable in the right markets. If used to hold a bound spirit, the metal could maintain the enchantment indefinitely. It was the basis of all the magical technology the Tyrianites had used to cross the void and the fuel that the ancients had used to conquer the heavens. Henrik assumed that cold iron was the reason the Tyrianites had come. He saw little else in Nornlund to justify an interplanetary invasion.

There was just no way his father had come by it legally. Most of the ship was constructed from mundane materials. Still, a device like this would require ten, maybe twenty, pounds of it, carefully poured veins of cold iron conducting spiritual energy to power the intricate bindings. He couldn't say how much ore it used but certainly enough for it to be a dangerous secret.

His father absolutely beamed at him, but Henrik ignored him for the time being. Rogan stood by the forge, a ring of metal cooling in his tongs as he stared through the gap in the curtain. Henrik tried to focus on the bindings, to isolate them into individual works, but their intricacy baffled his ear, made him dizzy when he tried to make sense of the silent cacophony. He removed his hand from the craft, struggling to soothe his nausea.

"You'll get used to that," his father said.

"I'm fine," said Henrik. He hiked his chin at Rogan, who was eavesdropping.

The mayor turned around and shooed the smith back to his own work.

"Are you insane?" Henrik asked. "How did you get the cold iron?"

A smile like none Henrik had ever seen appeared on his father's face. "I had a longstanding arrangement with the former prefect."

Henrik's mouth fell open. He shook his head. "How do you even know it works if you haven't flown it? Testing this seems incredibly dangerous."

Henrik felt like he was the parent here. He wasn't just worried about the federals finding out either. At times, his father glossed over the appropriate methodologies when he was excited. The void would forgive no such omissions.

"I have been testing it for years, Henrik. Years."

Henrik's eyebrows arched.

"It's true," the mayor continued. "I've checked and rechecked every seam and every binding ten times. More. It's as sound as a Hemmish coffer."

"And yet you haven't flown it."

96

The mayor held out his hand for patience. "To be quite honest, I never really intended to fly it. I was only interested in the theory, you see. To wander the avenues of thought that Zaracas himself meandered. Imagine!"

Henrik scoffed. Something here didn't add up. He snapped his fingers. "You're afraid."

The mayor's shoulders collapsed. He studied the sheen of his new boots. At length, he sighed. It was as good as a confession. "As the proverb goes, 'what we lack in courage we must make up for in wisdom.'"

Henrik put his hands on his hips. "And vice versa," Henrik said. "But you do believe it works?"

"Oh yes," his father assured him. "Of that I'm quite certain. As I said, I have scrupulously verified the functionality of every system. I simply can't seem to find the time," he made eye contact, "or admittedly the nerve to take her up."

Henrik glanced at Rogan, who immediately started hammering the lukewarm metal on his anvil. Despite his inclination to downplay his father's achievement, Henrik found himself smiling, a rare look these past few days. Perhaps this contraption would prove to be his coffin. Whatever amount of faith his father had for his own work, they would not know if it flew until it did. Given their calculations about the impact of the comet, it was well worth the risk.

"Tell me everything, Father. I'll fly it."

The mayor scowled. "Oh, no, my son. It's too dangerous now. If the prefect were to discover this at such a time, there's no telling what he would do. Normally I think a bribe would smooth over any trouble. But we don't know him well enough. With everything going on, I can't imagine the discovery going well for us. We'll have to watch him, mark my words. If things get nasty, we need to look to ourselves and our town. To hell with the federals."

"Father," Henrik smiled. "I never imagined you harbored such a treasonous heart."

"You jest, son," the mayor replied. "But a very ugly week lies ahead." He glanced back at Rogan, who was finally at work and ran his fingers over his thinning hair. "So very ugly."

"As you've said."

"My son." The mayor set one hand on each of Henrik's shoulders and looked him in the eye. "Don't forget that this family has a responsibility to the people of Skolja. I hope that one day, many years from now, you will be mayor after me. But we have to keep the herd alive if you ever want to be its shepherd."

Henrik nodded, admiring the ship. "What's her name?"

★★★★★

A gust of wind flickered the candles on the bar as Ivar entered Mads' Tavern. The balding grocier squinted around at the sawyers playing Six Pins in back and the blacksmith, Rogan, who sat at the bar complaining to Lyssa.

She sighed, shared an exasperated look with Rogan, and put her hands on her hips. "Come for a pint?"

Ivar leaned on the counter. "You know perfectly well why I'm here. Where is your father?"

She shrugged. "Could be anywhere."

"I'm getting awfully tired of chasing your father all over town. I've had it!" Ivar pounded his fist on the bar and then pointed at Lyssa. "You tell your father that I'm sick of his mess attracting rats, and I'm sick of him dicing away *my* rent." Ivar jabbed his thumb into his own chest. "If he doesn't pay up by week's end he's out. You're both out!"

Lyssa folded her arms. "Fine," she said. "I'll be sure he knows."

Without another word, Ivar spun on his heel and stormed out of the tavern.

Rogan shook his head. "Never liked him. I'd love another ale though. That speech made me thirsty."

Lyssa filled Rogan's horn with dark ale, poured out some foam, and topped it off again. She had a silver necklace shaped like a crescent moon that had belonged to her mother. She could sell that to cover the rent if need be. Lyssa had been telling herself to get rid of it for years anyway. She never wore it, and it made her sad to look at. When she handed back Rogan's ale horn, his fingers lingered over her own. She snatched her hand away and socked him in the shoulder. The old smith spilled beer in his lap and looked up at Lyssa, shocked.

"What in the hells?" he demanded.

"I'm not in the mood for that dung, Rogan. As if I don't have enough trouble with Ivar's nonsense. Don't start getting handsy already. The sun's barely down. You need some stew?"

Rogan blushed. "Honestly, what did I do?"

Lyssa put a hand on her hip. "Did you skip supper?"

He winked at her. "Yes, mother."

She held out her hand. "A set of coppers then."

Rogan laid one hand on his chest. "Apologies. Bowl of stew sounds wonderful, my sweet." He fished a few coins from his purse.

"Cut that crap out. You know I don't like it when you talk like that. What's gotten into you?"

"Can't a guy have an off day?" he asked. "Bronnar Helstrom said his cousin said there was a riot in Pederskald. On account of the comet. Think that's true?"

"Who cares," said Lyssa. "You ever been to Pederskald?"

"No," Rogan admitted.

"Me neither. Can't make much difference to us then. Can it?"

Rogan gulped his ale. "Makes a difference if the whole world is going to shit. Mayor's even desperate enough to try to fly that infernal machine of his."

"What's this about the mayor?"

Rogan waved her off. "Oh, nothing. I probably spoke too far as is." Lyssa took Rogan's horn with a smile. "Let me top you off there." She handed it back and said, "To your health." Rogan held up his horn and drained it.

"How about that stew then?" Rogan asked.

Lyssa smiled and reached out for his horn. "Won't be ready for a bit. Another horn while you wait?"

Chapter 10

"I have done it. For the coin of my soul. I have done it."

-Hessiana's Grimoire

The wind gusted just as Anders tried to light the first candle. Cupping his hand around the next match, he struck it on a rock and carefully brought the flickering flame to the candlewick. Anders used the burning candle to light the other two and set the first back down. Then he dug into the pouch on his belt and produced a dried strip of Briarwood bark. Its scent was pungent in the night air, but it was sweet to the one he called. Before him, a clay chalice half-filled with shea oil and a horn-handled iron dagger lay set out for the ritual. Anders picked up the cold knife and held it out before him.

"Hidden of the ancient folk," he incanted. "I call, a supplicant in search of wisdom. May the spirits of my forefathers guide you to this circle."

Anders slid the dagger across his palm and squeezed blood from his fist until the chalice was full. He blew into his hand, and the wound clotted and scabbed over.

"This blood is a bridge, a blade, and a whisper." The old man stirred the cup of blood and oil with his knife.

"If it pleases you, I bid you come, Hidden of the ancient folk." Anders poured the libation counterclockwise in a circle around himself. He set the blade and cup beside the smoldering twig of Briarwood.

Nothing happened.

He peered around him in the darkened wood. Trees and ferns, the moons glowing through the canopy, even the comet peeked out from behind the clouds. The candles burned low. He

began to shiver. Doubt crept into his heart. Perhaps the boy had
lied? But how could he have hit upon such a perfect scapegoat?
No, perhaps his incantation was flawed. With renewed fervor he
picked up the dagger again.

"Moriigo!"" He cried. "Hidden of the ancient folk!"

Though the air was still, the candles flickered out. Behind
him, he felt a profound cold and heard a rasping voice.

"Cease this inane pageantry," it said, its voice a chorus of
noise and terror. "I have come." Anders struggled with the urge
to bolt. He feared the thing's nearness but was unable to look
over his shoulder. His ears pricked for any hint that it would
strike. "Your pact is nearly concluded," it said.

"Yes." Anders pushed the word from his throat like
vomit.

"You will obey."

"Yes."

"You know the one called Torvald? The puppet. The
collaborator."

"Yes." Anders bowed, pressing his forehead to the frozen
ground. "The Mayor."

"Go and kill him. Lest his mercy make your grandchild
weak. The boy is the sacrifice that will free us all."

Anders did not understand. More than that, what was this
all for if the boy was lost?

The thing stalked around the circle until it stood before
him. Anders kept his head down and gritted his teeth. "I will not
sacrifice him."

"If it is death you fear, calm your trembling." The
creature reached out and dragged a finger across the line of blood
and oil, breaking the circle. "Have you lost the iron in your
blood? Now? When at last the hour draws near to end our
slavery? To turn the order of things on its head?"

Anders folded his arms, shivering. He kept his face planted
on the earth.

"Speak."

"I will not leave Brohr to the mercy of the federals."

"Still stubborn after all of these years." It drew closer, radiating icy malevolence. "Do as I say and you will reap the fruits of your pact. Disobey and I will kill the boy myself. All of your sacrifice for naught. So which will it be: submit or suffer?"

Anders held out for a few seconds, his teeth chattering. It was the only defiance he could muster. "S-S-Submit."

"Good," Moriigo whispered in his ear, its voice an ache. "Quiet your fears. Death is not the only sacrifice that pleases me. The boy's part is far from over. Have a little faith. Even now the Wanderer hurtles toward Quaya, bearing the sum of our hopes, the weight of my resolve. We will free our people from bondage and death. A bleak age dawns for those who would rule us."

★★★★★

Anders dismounted Rebel, glad to get his feet on solid ground again. His thighs burned, his back ached, and his hands throbbed from holding the reins. It was his first time on horseback in years, but hurting as he was, he took only a few seconds to stretch before hitching his horse to the rail outside of the Pilgrim's Inn. Though no one was awake this time of night, it would certainly raise an eyebrow if someone saw him out at this hour.

Anders walked through the alley beside the inn, ducking under the charms and wind chimes hanging from the eaves of the neighboring apothecary. He knocked on the back door of the old woman's shop, hoping it would be loud enough to rouse her without drawing anyone else's attention. After a moment he knocked again, this time rewarded by a lamp lit behind the shutters.

"Who is it?" the old woman demanded, far too loudly for Anders' purpose.

"Hush!" he hissed. "It's Nilstrom. Let me in."

The door cracked open, spilling light into the alley. The old witch stuck her head out, her myopic gaze studying Anders and then the alley to the left and right.

"Quickly," he whispered. "Before someone sees."

Grumbling, the ancient midwife turned back into the bedroom behind her shop, leaving the door open for Anders. The pungent smells of pickling agents and ammonia salts assailed his nose. Anders' eyes itched, and his sinuses burned. Shelves lined the walls of her room behind the shop, crammed with a dizzying array of oddments and curios: drying herbs, ratty old books, vials and tinctures, jars with hogs' heads and baby goats floating in brine.

"Ten Fathers, woman! How do you sleep in here?" He shut the door behind him.

"Don't insult my home." She slapped his shoulder. "You're uninvited. What mischief brings you at this shameful hour?"

"I've orders," he lied. "Urgent ones."

"Orders?" She held the lamp up to his face so that she might inspect it. "From Gareth? Have you been to the outlaws' camp?"

"No Breylin, the Hidden One told me to do it." A perverse smile twisted across his face. "Of course it was Gareth. Who else? It's beginning, Breylin. Can you believe it?"

The old woman sat back on her straw mattress and set the lamp on the stool next to it. A boot lay beside the stool, and she busied herself with getting it onto her gnarled blue foot. "Why now?" Excitement had wiped the suspicion from her face.

Anders bent over and tossed her her other boot. "The comet, of course."

She nodded and stopped fussing with her boots to absorb this. "Just an omen then."

Anders plopped down beside her and rubbed his aching legs.

"Not just an omen, Breylin. Chaos." He smiled. "Unimaginable chaos. The federals will be desperate just to survive. The perfect time to strike."

She squinted over at him. "I hate riddles, you mean old shit. What sort of chaos?"

"Forgive me, Breylin," he said with an acid smile. "The comet will strike Quaya. There will be devastation and strife unlike they've ever faced. It's now or never."

She nodded. "You said you had orders. I didn't think you took orders from Gareth. Has he finally grown a spine? Have you two repaired things? What about Marta? Is she well? I'd heard she was ill."

"Peace, woman. I can recognize friend from foe. He asked for help, and I accepted. Let's let the ghosts rest, eh?"

Breylin leaned forward. Putting one hand on the stool and the other on the floor, she rocked to her feet. "Get off my bed and tell me what we're up to."

Anders rose with difficulty, his joints aching. "I need witch fire. Gareth wants the mayor gone. We don't need that collaborator muddying the water. When the comet strikes, it should be us against them. No turncoats playing peacemaker."

"That's bold," she said. "Especially for Gareth. But I see the logic of it." Breylin took a deep, rattling breath and let it out slowly. "I've been having bad dreams…a forest fire…a stag drenched in blood. I never used to dream. But it's every night now. I suppose it's the witchfire. Hungry, nasty stuff. I'll be glad to be rid of it."

★★★★★

Henrik sat in his reading chair beside his bed, studying the rather dry specifications his father had furnished him for *The Muse.* He sipped his port and set it back on the cherrywood end table. A spirit lamp hummed beside the goblet, bright enough to read without tiring his eyes but giving no warmth. A thick quilt covered his legs. Henrik set a few pages on the table and picked up another stack. When he'd finished memorizing the enchantments that navigated the craft, he laid those pages down too and yawned.

It was late, even for him. He tossed the quilt on the floor and stood up, stretching. Henrik kicked off his boots, walked past a pile of painted canvases leaning against the wall, and climbed into bed. With a curse, he realized he'd forgotten to turn off the lamp, so he threw off the blankets, sighed dramatically, and shuffled over to press his thumb against the metal plate that turned it off. He shivered in the dark and dove back into bed, pulling the covers up to his chin.

He lay there for some time, imagining both the experience of taking *The Muse* out into the void, and also what sort of turmoil it would take for it to actually happen. On paper, *The Muse* was quite convincing. He had demurred when offered the copious notes on his father's years of testing. It should work. Unless there had been the tiniest error or omission. In that case, he would no doubt die screaming.

What an opportunity.

These thoughts kept him awake. At length, he resorted to some old tricks to calm his restless mind. He began to recite Caden's Axioms of Spirit Binding, those esoteric pillars of the craft whose commentaries nearly managed to make magic tedious.

By his third trip through the axioms, his mental recitation had become sluggish, and he began to drift off into sleep when a torrent of sound and light threw him from his bed.

He reeled on the verge of unconsciousness, discovering himself on the floor by the window. Shattered glass and splinters of flaming timber lay all about him. Motes of light swam in the corners of his eyes.

Somewhere, someone was screaming. Henrik lay facedown atop one of his paintings, an unfinished landscape of Skolja's waterfront, now sizzling with droplets of azure fire. From the hallway came the sound of cracking wood as if a Raag were breaking tree trunks over its knee. Disoriented by the concussion, he couldn't puzzle out what had happened. The comet had struck, he decided with befuddled certainty. The comet had struck... and it had hit Skolja. But that wasn't right.

Over the ringing in his ears, the whoosh and crackle of fire brought him to his feet. The impact must've happened near his parents' room; he could see in the eerie blue flames that his door had blown open, clean off of its hinges in fact. It lay across the room, aglow with licks of indigo.

It seemed that the house itself chose this moment to stagger from the blow. For a second, the straining creak of the support beams outmatched the roaring blaze, and then the floor buckled, sagging away toward the far corner of the house where the blast originated.

Henrik stumbled around his bed toward the glowing doorway. Once out of his bedroom, he stood on the landing, stupefied by the conflagration around him. The stairs down were clear, but where the staircase wrapped around the wall toward the opposite landing, the blaze had already devoured the bannister, its flaming remnants dropping one post at a time to the ground floor. A thought arrested him completely at that moment, and as if that fear had conjured him, his father opened the bedroom door across the landing in the fieriest corner of the mansion. With a preternatural hush, the flames dashed into the open doorway, and the instant of silence was shattered by screaming. Aghast, Henrik watched in the space of a few frantic breaths as the inferno consumed his father, sucking him dry and leaving a smoldering husk.

Witch fire.

This was not the comet. It was murder. A scream rose above the crackling roar. *Mother!* Amidst the flames Henrik froze, his heart shaming him for his failure to save his father, his mind urging him to flee before he too was consumed. The caustic smoke seared his lungs and burned his eyes, drawing out tears. He couldn't see her, only hear her frantic sobs. She called his name, stumbled through the doorway, and fell to the floor, hair and nightgown ablaze, reaching out toward him. There was no way to save her, fire roared between them, the way impassable. And once witch fire tasted flesh, there was no quenching it, no hope. He turned away. "I'm sorry!" he cried, unsure if she could hear him.

Henrik ran down the staircase to the front door, his mother's haunting cries drowned out by the frenzied blaze and

106

the pounding of his heart. Behind him, the very bones of the house splintered and groaned.

He slid the massive bolt, unlocking the entrance to the mansion, and ran out into the cool air, rapturously free of the choking fumes.

A trumpet resounded somewhere in the night. He looked north to the fort and saw a squad of soldiers sprinting over with torches in hand. He looked down the hill where groggy villagers emerged from the inn and the townhouses to investigate. A pang of loneliness struck as he realized that organizing a bucket brigade would have been his father's duty. Henrik dropped to his knees and pummeled the earth beneath him. Though he had survived the fire, he could not escape the look on his father's face or the terror in his mother's voice. And he had run. When they needed him, he had run.

Chapter 11

"There are three basic categories of runes in a standard binding. The archetype *is an abstraction of the spirit itself, to distract it from crossing over. The* essence *distills the transfixed animus into those energies useful to the binding's purpose. And finally, the* intention *provides that purpose, shaping the effect to suit the binder's will."*

–Hamilcar Drausus, Fundamentals of Binding Lore

Most of the townsfolk had gone back to bed. Dawn would soon rise over the wilderness. The fire had finally gone out, but the fumes still hung thick in the air, eliciting unhealthy coughs from the soldiers sifting through the collapsed mansion.

Prefect Brasca Quoll cupped his hands to his mouth. "Fall back from the house!" He made eye contact with a nearby ordinal and waved him over. "See that the men clear out. The mayor is dead."

"Yes, sir." The ordinal trotted off, shouting orders.

The mansion had collapsed; only the stairwell and the western wall were more or less intact. The fire had spread quickly, its voracious alchemy devouring the house and its owners and burning itself out in about an hour. The coming dawn shed just enough light to make out the shell of the mansion, tiny pockets of mundane embers smoldering around the edges. Brasca stood by the wreckage, his mind drifting back to the fire that had claimed his son.

"Sir!" One of his ordinals hailed him. "We've questioned the crowd, but everyone claims to have been sleeping, no witnesses.

"Where's the constable?" the prefect asked.

One of his hovering officers spotted the constable questioning a pilgrim in from Pederskald.

"Ordinal, if we've already questioned that man, tell that bungler to do something productive, for once."

"Yes, sir," the ordinal hailed him. "What shall I tell him to do, sir?"

"Tell him to show some damn initiative," the prefect commanded. "Three murders in two days. Tell him to—"

"Prefect!" Henrik leapt up from the boulder he'd been grieving on. "You're going about this all wrong."

Brasca scowled at the mayor's son. "I understand what you're going through, young man, but we've got—"

"Don't you see? You're wasting your time here."

"Henrik." Brasca clamped a hand on his shoulder. "You need to let us handle this."

"Then handle it. Get down there!"

"I know that you're upset, Henrik. I can sympathize. My own son was killed in a fire but—"

"I don't care about your brat!" Henrik shouted. "The apothecary. She has to be part of this. Who else?" Henrik pointed down the hill toward the town square where the folk were up early today.

Brasca snatched the collar of Henrik's shirt, dragging him face to face. "Because you are grieving, I will forgive your insolence. Once. If you ever speak to me that way again, I will have *you* burned alive. Are we perfectly clear?"

Henrik eyed the prefect up and down. Finally, he nodded. "Yes, yes, of course. I'm sorry. I shouldn't have said that."

Brasca released his collar, still entertaining what it might feel like to break the arrogant shit's nose. "Good," he said.

He supposed he hadn't liked Henrik in the first place. Drunk and disrespectful and smug as could be. On top of his insult, Brasca was irritated he hadn't thought of the apothecary himself. Doubly irritated that the constable hadn't thought of her either. He hadn't the faintest idea how one made witch fire—it was too volatile for military use—but he supposed the old woman was as good a bet as anyone. Add to that the fact that she was ancient enough to have been around during the conquest, and she seemed a very likely suspect.

"Constable!" Brasca shouted. "Get down there and interrogate that hag. I want arrests and I want them today."

★★★★★

Brohr paced his cell, straining to hear the dwindling commotion outside. He wore a tattered blanket around his shoulders. Without a fire, it had been a cold and sleepless night. The room reeked of the chamber pot, which he'd pushed into the corner for fear of tripping over it in the dark. It had been a long time since the shouting had awoken him. But that was his only clue. The cell had no windows, and there was no light within. So he brooded in the dark, endlessly retracing his route, seven steps from the head of the bed, seven steps back. His mind groped for an explanation of the panic, producing a host of unlikely possibilities.

An argument broke out just in front of the jail. Brohr cocked his ear, trying to make out the muted voices.

The front door of the jail opened. A man stood in the doorway as if to block it, his silhouette trimmed in the red light of the moon.

"… care if she's a hundred!" Henrik shouted. "I want to know why!"

"We've been over this ten times." The constable pushed past Henrik, dragging an old woman into his office behind him. "She won't say more. And I won't be roughing up an old woman. It's not right. She'll be swinging soon enough. Let that satisfy you."

"He was a collaborator!" cried the crone, turning on Henrik and pointing her finger at him. "Serves him right, getting fat off our woe!"

Henrik lunged at her, and Gunnar stepped between them, fending him off with a one-armed shove. "Soldier!" he shouted. "Soldier, get him out of here."

110

A Tyrinate rushed into the jail and scuffled with the mayor's son for a moment before Henrik relented. "Fine!" he said, ceasing his struggle. Henrik started to leave but stopped in the doorway and turned back to say something. Whatever jibe it was died on his lips as he noticed Brohr, standing in the darkness at the bars of his cell. The legionary shoved him out the door and closed it behind them.

Breylin thanked the constable in a feeble voice.

"Don't you thank me!" he railed at her. "You old hag! Don't you dare thank me." His voice quieted. "Honestly, Breylin, why would you do this? I never would've pegged you as a murderer."

"Ain't murder," she said. "It's war. And you're on the wrong side of it, Gunnar."

"The war is long over, Breylin. We lost before I was even born."

"It ain't over while I'm alive," she said.

Gunnar laughed. "How long do you think that'll last now, dear?"

Brohr waited for her to reply, but after a moment's quiet, Gunnar unlocked the cell door and ushered her inside. He stood in the doorway, studying his prisoners.

"Boy," Gunnar said. "You'd best make peace with your ancestors. I expect the prefect will be in no mood for mercy. You'll hang today. No mistake. They're already fetching timber for the gallows." He slammed shut the cell bars, turned, and left the jail, locking the front door, and leaving them in the pitch black.

"What did you do?" Brohr asked after a moment.

"Help me sit down. I'm tired." Brohr led her by the arm to the cot and eased her trembling body onto it. He unwrapped the blanket from his shoulders and put it around her, then sat beside her.

"You're Anders's kin, right?"

"Yes," said Brohr. "What's happening?"

The old woman patted him on the knee. "It's finally happening. I didn't think I'd live to see it."

111

"What's happening?"

"No more groveling to those pigs. The fight," she said. "The fight's begun."

"Please," he asked. "What's happening?"

"Your grandfather killed the mayor. His wife too. I lent him some witch fire and he burned them up in their fancy house."

"Did they kill him?"

"No," she said. "They don't know he did it. But I'd guess the mayor's boy is smart enough to see I can't have done it myself."

Brohr stood up, pacing in the dark again. "They're really going to hang us then."

"Oh yes," she said. "I'm afraid so. Not much of a bother for me. Shame about you though. At least you gave that shade Torin his due, no offense. After what he did to your ma. She was a sweet girl."

Brohr leaned back against the far wall, his eyes straining to pick out the outline of the old woman as dawn light crept through the cracks in the cell.

"What do you know about it? No one will ever give me a straight answer."

The old woman clucked her tongue. "I suppose you deserve the truth. Won't be another time for it." Breylin shooed away a fly that buzzed around her face and sat for a moment, catching her breath. She coughed, a wet, wheezing rattle. "Things were rougher in those days. Your ma wasn't the only one. More than a few of the girls got that treatment. Barracks girls they called them. The pigs would just pick a pretty girl and drag her up to the fort. No warning. Keep them there for a night or two. Some of the girls died there. Some of them came back pregnant. Elsa was one of them. She came back with you. The rest of the girls saw one of the skalds to be rid of… the children. But your grandfather wouldn't have it. I always thought that was so strange. Him being him."

112

Brohr slid down the wall and slumped onto the floor. He was sitting next to the chamber pot, but the stink hardly seemed to matter.

"And Torin was one of them?"

"Oh yes," she said. "You know he's not from around here. Pederskald, they say. One of your lot doesn't have much chance in these parts, I suppose. Look at you now. Course that doesn't excuse that ornery bastard. Still a traitor in my book."

"I didn't kill him."

"Well," Breylin said. "I wouldn't blame you if you did."

They sat in the dark for a while. Brohr couldn't help brooding, blaming his grandfather. He'd always talked like the war had never ended, and for Anders, Brohr supposed it hadn't. But if his grandfather could just have let go of all of his rage, things might have been different for Brohr. Anders might have been able to let Brohr go. But instead he was here, waiting to be hanged.

"Young man." Breylin waited for him to answer.

"Yes?"

"I remember your mother well. I was to midwife for her. But your grandfather never sent for me on the night she went into labor. Strange, no?"

"What are you getting at?"

"Just a regret. One of many. I might have helped her." Breylin sighed. "Anyway, I'm not going to let them hang me. I'm too old to suffer for them anymore." She was moving around, searching for something. "I have an herb. I hid it in my unders as soon as your grandfather left. I knew they'd come for me. We can take it together if you'd like."

"No," Brohr said. "I'm not dead yet."

"I understand," she said. "I'll leave some in case you change your mind. It's in my hand. Good luck, boy. If...if you see Axl Norvald...tell him I was thinking of him."

"I will." Brohr squinted at her outline as she lay down. He listened to her chew and swallow.

"No surprise," she chuckled. "It's bitter. Good night."

"Good night."

Breylin's wheezing grew into a ragged cough. She spat on the wall beside her. A little moan escaped her lips. She coughed again, drew in a deep, wet breath, and let it out.

Brohr hugged his knees to his chest. He sat there in the cell with the old woman's corpse, feeling very alone. He wondered what it would be like to hang. He supposed it wasn't such a bad way to die. Faster than most.

There was nothing he could do. No way for him to fight back. At noon they'd march him out into the square, loop a rope around his neck, and string him up. And no one would care. His grandfather had all but turned him in, Vili and Birgit hated him. He was alone.

Brohr blinked back tears. He wiped his nose on his sleeve. In the dark cell, he shivered, but it felt wrong to take the blanket back from Breylin. Goose bumps stood up on his neck and his forearms. But not from the cold. It was his brother. And that macabre comfort tipped him over the edge, and he sobbed, and sobbed, abandoned, doomed, but not alone.

★★★★★

Sunlight crested over High Hill, over the smoking shell of his ruined home, mercifully cloaking it in silhouette. Henrik pushed away the image of his father smoking his pipe, pressing his eye to his telescope. If he could only go back to yesterday. Just to make a show of marveling at *The Muse*. Just to give his father a little pride. Just to show him…

Henrik was headed north from the town square up to Federal Hill. Absorbed in his grief, he almost ran into a woman carrying a bucket of water. She dodged out of his way, her face switching from annoyance to pity. Henrik turned away, compiling a list of what must be done.

The cobbles of the town road ended, replaced with soft dirt rutted by wagon wheels. Storm clouds loomed beyond the fort, pushing the smell of cookfires out against the sea breeze.

The federal flag flapped above the gate, a crimson band at top and bottom with a golden sunrise dawning in the center.

Henrik marched past the sentries and through the open gate, struck by the bustling activity within. It would be no surprise to see them on alert, especially after last night, but this was more. A row of wagons lined the interval separating the palisade from the camp buildings. There were six of them, loaded to capacity with water barrels, sacks of grain, and boxes of who knew what. Obviously, they were making ready to leave. Would they really abandon Skolja? That spelled doom.

Henrik made it past another guard and entered the command building. He studied the enormous map behind the adjutant's desk as he waited for the prefect. The minutes stretched, and Henrik's irritation grew, until finally the door on the back wall opened, and Brasca Quoll stepped out.

The prefect waved him in. "Henrik." There was no warmth in his voice, no pity. He struck Henrik as rather impatient, feigning a hint of civility. "Join me."

Henrik followed Brasca into his office. As he shut the door, the prefect took his seat, motioning at the chair opposite him.

"I'm sorry, Henrik," he said. "Sorry about your parents, and sorry that I don't have time for pleasantries today."

Henrik nodded. "I would find them distasteful in any case. Still, there is much to discuss." Henrik sat down, exhausted.

"Agreed." Brasca folded his fingers together, tapping them on his chin. "Dark days are ahead, Henrik. Darker than you probably realize."

"We know about the comet. About Quaya." He corrected himself. "I know."

Brasca arched an eyebrow. "Really? Your father was a clever man. Truly."

Henrik cleared his throat, nodding.

"And I think," the prefect continued, "that you are also a clever man. The loyal subjects of Skolja will need one of their own to look to. I'd like you to replace your father as mayor."

"Of course."

"Good." Brasca leaned back in his chair. "Even without the impact, these are difficult times."

"Yes," said Henrik. "Superstition naturally aggrandizes the comet. Makes it the harbinger of sedition. Once the strike happens, Uncle Olaf may as well have risen."

"Uncle?"

"Oh." Henrik wished he hadn't said that. "I thought you knew. He was my great-great-uncle. That's why the Torvalds became mayors. We're a compromise. Anyway, it's irrelevant now. What is important is that we are ready. After the impact, there will be disorder, bloodshed. Best to meet it head on and mitigate the trouble."

"I'm glad to see that your tragedy hasn't dulled your judgment." Brasca picked a stack of parchment off of his desk as if he were about to read it, then set it down. "Perhaps, once we get this unpleasantness out of the way, and things settle down, we can even sit for that portait. I'm sure your mother would be pleased by it."

Henrik stared down at the planks of the floor. "I was a mediocre painter, sir. I wish my mother hadn't mentioned it." Henrik bit his fingernail. He looked up, saw the distaste on Brasca's face, and wringed his hands. "She always thought too highly of me. I don't think I could stand to put brush to canvas again."

Brasca nodded. "To business then. I've dispatched soldiers to the homes of a few troublemakers in town. One of them will be Anders Nilstrom. I believe he is the one who set last night's fire."

Henrik swung forward in his chair. "How do you know this?"

"We found a horse wandering around the foot of High Hill. One of the townsfolk identified it as Nilstrom's horse."

"Anders Nilstrom."

"Don't worry," the prefect said. "We're going to hang the lot of them. Today. We'll hobble this pathetic little insurrection before it gets off the ground."

"You're not going to burn them, then?" Henrik asked.

The prefect scooted around to get comfortable in his chair. "I've decided not to make an offering of them." Brasca straightened some of the papers on his desk. "Anders Nilstrom will be just as dead."

Henrik sat for a moment, absorbing this information, trying to catalog what he knew of Anders Nilstrom. He could picture him, a surly old wraith of a man. He knew he was a farmer a few miles from town. He had always seemed like an old storm cloud drifting around Skolja. Everyone tried to keep out of his way. Realization struck. Nilstrom was the grandfather of the one from the dock, Brohr Nilstrom. Was this payback for his silence?

"I have a list here of the men I intend to execute," the prefect said. "Perhaps you could take a look and see if there was anyone we have overlooked." He handed a sheet of parchment across the desk.

Twelve names were written on the page in the prefect's elegant handwriting. Anders Nilstrom concluded the list, just below his grandson's name.

Henrik sat in silence as the prefect watched him. He knew the Tyrianite was judging his reaction, gauging his loyalty, his pliability. Henrik's wrath and guilt warred in his gut for a fleeting instant before he crushed them. Nilstrom could swing, should swing, but most of these men hadn't done anything wrong. He looked up at the federal. "This is a bit... excessive. Don't you think?"

Brasca cocked his head to one side. "I want to stamp out any treason quickly."

"That's perfectly reasonable." Henrik crossed his leg and folded his hands over his knee. "But I know these people. Most of the names on this list are just loud mouths. If you go and hang everybody who can't mind their tongue, everyone will worry that they're next. It won't go over well. It'll cause more trouble. Trust me. Maybe we can pare that down a little. Get the real trouble makers. Folks will stomach it better."

"Fine, I'll spare a few." The prefect stood and gestured toward the door. "Thank you for coming to see me, Henrik. I'm afraid I have to get back to work. Please come to see me again after the hangings. They'll be at noon. We need to discuss how to handle the comet strike. As you said, disorder is a certainty, I'm afraid."

"I have a question."

"Of course."

"Are you preparing to evacuate Skolja?"

The prefect dropped back in his chair again, steepling his fingers as he considered his response. "We're preparing for the worst, Henrik. Whatever that may be."

Chapter 12

"The cutthroats who roam the outer dark style themselves free spirits who have cast off the chains of governance. In truth, there are no civic minds among them, no noble ideals, none of the fierce virtues which popular fancies ascribe to them. They are a crass lot, animated by the spirit of anarchy. Only a federal yoke can bring any semblance of society to the giants and the outer folk, and only the hangman can sway a fool who dares to fly the black flag."

—Cruscio Iovani, Civilizing the Stars

Lyssa stood over her snoring father, holding a candle. Their apartment above the tavern was cramped and smelled faintly like unwashed clothing. They shared the same room for sleeping, two straw mattresses separated by a simple wooden shelf bearing their clean clothes and the family idols: a collection of carved stone figurines, each about the size of a thumb, and one, a little larger, carved from bone.

Mads lay on his side, his knees hugged to his chest. He mumbled something.

"Papa." Lyssa nudged him with her foot. It was just after dawn, far earlier than they would normally wake. An ale horn lay beside his bed, speckled with fruit flies.

She tried again, a little more insistently this time. "Papa! Get up!" Lyssa clapped her hands. "Hey!"

Mads squinted up at his daughter. "Was I talking in my sleep again?

"No." She shook her head. "You're probably the only person in town who slept through last night."

He sat up. "What time is it?"

She held a candle up to her face so that he could see how serious she was. "Dawn."

"Ten Fathers, girl! Go to bed." He lay back and pulled the blanket over his head.

"Listen to me." She kicked his mattress.

"Have you no respect for your elders? What?"

"The mayor is dead," she said. "Murdered. I've just seen them arrest Breylin."

"Damn," he whispered.

"It was a fire. They're saying it was witch fire."

"Light another candle." Mads stood up and stripped off his nightshirt. "Get your things together, Lyssa. We need to go."

She lit the other candle and set them both on the shelf. "Do you think they'll arrest me too? Just for knowing her?"

"Never underestimate the pigs. They'd hang you for smelling funny." He leveled his gaze at her. "But…"

Lyssa shoved a pair of woolen breeches into her knapsack. "But what?"

"They're just as likely to come for me." He winked at her. "I've been passing letters for the outlaws for years. Ever since your mother left. It just seemed wrong that they could be so close to their families and never get to speak with them."

Lyssa nodded. She knew this, of course. She'd seen the clandestine exchanges. As a little girl it had puzzled her. A glorius mystery that brought excitement to the muddy streets of Skolja. Her first foray into what she liked to call watchwork. She had even imagined that her mother was herself an outlaw, wanted by the federals for some sort of daring defiance. It had made discovering the truth all the harder.

All the secrecy over the letters seemed a bit dramatic, in the end. As if anyone cared. The outlaws didn't pay tithes, sure, maybe they'd gotten into a brawl or two with the soldiers, but tracking them through the wilderness was too much bother for a bunch of no goods. They had been living in the hills for years. Everybody knew about it and the federals did nothing. Didn't seem to care. "Did the outlaws have something to do with the mayor's house?"

Mads shrugged, lacing up his boots. "I don't know, probably. Folks have been talking ever since the comet."

Someone pounded on the front door. A soldier's voice filtered through to the sleeping room. "Open up in there! Mads Pedersten? Open up on the orders of Prefect Quoll!"

Lyssa and Mads locked eyes.

"Under the mattress," he whispered. "Hide!"

She started to argue but her father grabbed her by the arm and picked up the edge of the mattress, a massive burlap sack stitched together with twine and stuffed with straw.

Lyssa kissed her father on the cheek and dropped to the floor, rolling beneath the mattress. He covered her with it and worked the straw to either side of where she lay until he obscured the lump she made. Another thump sounded out front. It was claustrophobic beneath the mattress, but she could breathe. She heard her father open the shutters and then the soldiers out front kicked in the door. Footfalls thundered in from the front room.

A soldier shouted. "He's going out the window!"

There was a scuffle, shouts and curses. Her family idols clattered to the floor as her father was thrown into the shelf. He yelped when someone clubbed him over the head. Lyssa struggled to control her breathing, fearful that the soldiers would see the mattress rise and fall.

"Glad we don't have to chase this sot all over Skolja."

"It stinks in here."

"Grab his legs. I'll get his arms."

The front door slammed. Lyssa waited until they were long gone. She mastered her breathing and strained to hear if anyone remained. At last she pushed the mattress off herself and crawled out. She looked around the devastated room, careful to stay away from the open window.

On the floor beside her bed, amidst the scattered idols of her clan, her father had dropped his dagger. Lyssa knelt before it, admired the fine scrollwork, how keen her father kept the blade. She stood up, shivered at the frigid breeze drifting in the open window, and tucked the dagger into her belt.

121

★★★★★

There was no time for sleep though he longed for it. Henrik was exhausted, of course, but more than that, he couldn't get the image of his father opening the bedroom door out of his mind, his mother reaching out for him. The flash of blue flame. The screams. What had his mother thought in that moment? Had she expected, against all hope, that her son would save her, only to watch Henrik flee down the steps to save his own life?

Logically, he knew that his mother would have wanted him to save himself. His father too. But that was a cold comfort. As he walked through the town square, ignoring the stares and unwelcome commiserations from the townsfolk, he considered getting blind drunk and letting the chaos unfold, while he was blissfully unaware. But he returned to the notion that his survival might be a consolation to the spirits of his parents. He could give them that, at least. He could fight.

So Henrik secured the largest room at the High Tavern. He was homeless after all. The next logical step was to purchase provisions. Ivar's general store occupied the entire southwest corner of the town square. But like a lodestone, the hunched little apothecary, with its superstitious wards and fetishes, drew his eye. It stood across the street from the market, a shack in disrepair, moss and mold lining the cracks between its timbers, black rot spotting the thatch.

He turned away from it, forcing himself to ignore the wretched hovel and see to the necessities of survival. Henrik stepped up onto the covered wooden porch of Ivar's general store, where baskets of leeks, potatoes, and tomatoes were set at an angle atop barrels to attract business from the square. A metal stove kept the place warm even with the double doors propped open. Sacks of wheat and flour and seeds lined the walls along with shelves full of tools, casks of ale and butter, and just about anything else the townsfolk might need.

Ivar was an excellent shopkeeper, the place was always clean, the tables heaped with goods to catch the eye. He seemed to always be rearranging his merchandise. Henrik supposed he must have an unhappy wife, to be so obsessed with the shop. Still, Henrik respected his diligence and knew from his father's collections that he was the wealthiest merchant in town.

Henrik walked to the back counter where Ivar and his shop girl were each serving customers. Ivar immediately apologized to the woman he was helping and walked around the counter to greet Henrik.

"Master Torvald." He took Henrik's hand in both of his own. "My deepest regrets at the loss of your parents. Your father was an excellent mayor, and, if I may say, one of my dearest friends."

Henrik let the statement pass though he knew it to be a lie. As two of the more prominent loyalists in town, they invited each other to dinner perhaps once a year. They were polite allies, he supposed, but far too different in character to be friends.

"Thank you, Ivar. As you seem to have guessed, the prefect has asked me to succeed my father as mayor."

"A wise choice, of course." Ivar cleared his throat. "Who else could take the reins?"

Henrik nodded. "I have temporarily taken a room at the High Tavern. I'd like to purchase some supplies, but embarrassingly, I find myself suddenly without funds. Everything was in the house, you see."

"Think nothing of it," Ivar swiped a hand through the air as if to dash Henrik's embarrassment. "There is no trouble to extend you credit. I want to help in any way I can."

"Thank you, Ivar."

"It is the least I can do."

"Well then... I'd like a barrel of salted beef. Three full sacks of lentils. A cask of butter. A sack of flour—"

"Henrik." Ivar set his hand on Henrik's shoulder. "Forgive me, but of course you have no way to know it. This is far more than you need. Besides, won't you be taking your meals at the tavern? This sort of stock is for cooks. I can't imagine you'll be cooking much." He smiled.

"I'll be hiring men to rebuild the mansion," Henrik lied. "The supplies are for them."

"Of course. Foolish of me not to have considered that."

Henrik dictated a long list of groceries and tools. A hint of worry crept over the shopkeeper's face as the tally grew and grew. Noting his dismay, Henrik said, "Of course, to compensate you for this generosity, I'll exempt you from the next tithe season. In addition to paying for the goods themselves, naturally."

Ivar's face lit up.

"I'll need the goods delivered right away. I'll need them today. All of them delivered to my room at the High Tavern."

The grocer nodded. It was an odd request, but to skip a season of tithes was a great deal of coin.

"One last thing. This one is a bit strange. I'd like to take the rats you've trapped today. For bindings, you see."

Ivar managed an unconvincing smile. "Please," he said. "Take them."

They shook hands and Ivar drew up a bill of sale and a note of credit. Once he'd signed it, Ivar shouted for his delivery boy in back and set him to work. Henrik excused himself and exited the store.

Standing on the porch, he was again confronted by the apothecary across the street. He closed his eyes and imagined the dilapidated shack on fire. He opened them and looked left where the jailhouse sat beside the clothier. The bitterest part of him had hoped he would get to beat the truth out of the old woman. He felt cheated that the discovery of Nilstrom's horse had made her interrogation moot.

There was much to do before noon. He didn't want to miss the hanging. A pang of guilt surprised him—the farm boy would hang too. *Be reasonable,* he thought, *you can't save him now.* Besides, it was his kin that had killed Henrik's parents whether the old man did it because Henrik had kept silent or not. A dread settled upon him as he was reminded of the creature on the docks. For the first time, he allowed himself a moment of fancy. Could this be the end of the world? Folklore spoke of a time when the ancients would return. But even the religion of the federals dismissed this as nonsense. It must've been a man he'd seen. The light was poor. He'd been drunk. In that moment, he resolved never to drink again. It had muddied his senses to the point that he'd entertained pure superstition. No, the dangers ahead were very real. He needed *reason* to survive them, not intuition, not foolishness.

The rain picked up again, though he was shielded by the porch. An accompanying wind set the apothecary's chimes to tinkling; feather and bone, driftwood and iron, spinning in the breeze.

★★★★★

Lyssa set the jar back on the shelf after reading its witch marks. Though she loved books, Breylin could hardly read, so she used the old symbols to label her vast collection of ointments, reagents, potions, and poisons. The crowded shop, no bigger than her sleeping room, had a U-shaped countertop of burnt, stained, and gouged oak boards, behind which were floor-to-ceiling shelves overflowing with various bottled elixirs, rare herbs, and strange talismans.

The talismans were the only things Lyssa and Breylin had ever fought over. Although the shop had just about every tincture and remedy in the world, Breylin made most of her coin selling charms. Poppets to keep the Mara out of your garden. Chimes to frighten away angry Raag. But Lyssa didn't believe in that sort of thing; Breylin was selling the townsfolk a load of manure.

Eventually they'd settled into an uneasy peace, never speaking of that part of her business. Breylin had no children, and she wanted to pass something on after she was gone. At the thought, Lyssa turned to the altar Breylin kept behind the counter. Breylin's family had died in the invasion and the first few years of occupation. Every last one.

Lyssa studied the largest idol. Carved from a soapstone found in the hills near the mine, it was the bust of a stern, bearded man wearing a conical helmet: Freyan, the Father that Breylin and Lyssa's clan descended from, that most folk in town did. Around his idol gathered a collection of smaller figurines, representing the notable figures of more recent generations. Lyssa had no idea who they were. That knowledge would die with Breylin. The thought made her uneasy. To be forgotten by your descendants was akin to damnation among the Norn. She wondered what happened when your line was utterly annihilated. Whatever it was, she didn't accept that fate for Breylin. She was like a dear old aunt to her. More than that: a mentor. Lyssa realized that she had tears running down her cheeks. She wiped them away, still staring at the nameless idols.

After a moment's reflection, Lyssa returned to her task, collecting the most useful and valuable elixirs and components. Her hide knapsack lay on the counter, already almost full of healing drafts, vials of quicksilver, gold dust, and other things she could sell. It was uncertain what would happen to the shop now, but whatever did, it wouldn't go to Lyssa with Breylin and her father both arrested. Her stomach turned. She wanted to be on the road as soon as possible. She'd head for Pederskald. Try to start over. But part of her insisted she stay to watch the hangings. It was as if bearing witness would give them a measure of peace. But she couldn't go. The risk of being arrested was too high.

A loud crash startled her. The front door shuddered from a second blow as someone outside tried to kick it in. Lyssa snatched her knapsack off the counter and ducked through the doorway that led into Breylin's back room. She looked around, but the tiny room offered nowhere to hide. More shelves filled with Breylin's odd collection of pickled animal parts and books she could hardly read. There was a mattress on the floor, a table next to it, and a chair by the back door. Lyssa fumbled with the latches, hoping to disappear into the alley, but before she could undo them, the front door crashed open and the mayor's son stormed in.

Henrik saw Lyssa in the back room and ran toward her, planting his hands on the intervening counter and vaulting over it. He charged through the inner doorway and tackled Lyssa. She

126

struggled to fight her way out from under him, but Henrik pinned her wrists behind her head.

"Get off me!" she shouted.

"You're not going anywhere!" he screamed, spit flying in her face. "Did you help murder my parents too? Did you?" He picked up her hands and slammed them down against the floor for emphasis.

"No," she pleaded. "You're hurting me. Get off."

"You're part of all of this. Why else would you be in this witch's house? Your father is already under arrest. Admit it." Froth collected in the corners of his mouth. "Why did Nilstrom murder my father? Tell me!"

"I don't know! I don't know!" Lyssa screamed. "I didn't have anything to do with it. I swear it." Henrik loomed over her, studying her face for hints of deception. Lyssa said, "Maybe he was after you. Did you ever think of that? After all, his grandson is about to hang because we lied."

"Don't you dare blame me!" Henrik clamped one hand on her throat. "My parents didn't deserve what happened to them—no matter what!"

"I know." Lyssa gagged. "I didn't have anything to do with it."

"Swear it by your Father," said Henrik, easing his grip enough to let her speak.

"By Father Freyan, I swear." She squirmed beneath him. "Now get off me!"

"Why should I believe you?" Henrik's eye twitched. He swallowed noisily, adjusting his grip on her throat.

The first pang of real fear hit her. Henrik's face twisted into a mask of anger and grief. "Henrik, please. I'm not a killer. I wouldn't."

His wild eyes darted back and forth over every detail of her expression, scouring her for any hint of a lie, until he saw that she was pleading for her life. And the fire went out of him. He broke eye contact, disgusted with himself, and at a loss for what to say. Finally, he rolled off and lay beside her.

"Do you think that's true?" he asked.

"What?" Lyssa rubbed her throat.

Henrik expelled a long, slow breath. "That my parents are dead because I didn't tell the truth about what happened at the docks."

Lyssa turned her head toward him. "I don't know. Anders Nilstrom is a mean old bastard. It wouldn't surprise me. We should have told everyone. That thing is still out there."

Henrik didn't respond.

"I'm leaving Skolja," Lyssa said. "This town got ugly. Just let me leave, okay? I didn't have anything to do with what happened to your family. I'm sorry."

After a while he nodded. "What do you think it was?" he asked. "I keep telling myself I was drunk. That it was just a man and I imagined the rest."

Lyssa shook her head. "I don't know. But whatever it was, it wasn't just a person on the docks. It was blacker than the sky behind it. Cold too. The air all around it was as cold as I've ever felt. It was almost like it turned to mist at the end." She shuddered. "I want to get away from here."

Henrik sat up and turned to her. "Something very bad is about to happen."

Chapter 13

"Witness! Harken to this tale of woe, of pride brought low, this saga of shame and dishonor and sacrilege, the severing of that sacred bond which lashes one generation to the next—the end of Breyga's line."

-Brig Olsten, *The Skald's Tale*

When the constable opened the outer door, Brohr saw the old woman's face in the light for the first time. It was a wrinkled horror of broken blood vessels and wide, rheumy eyes.

Legionaries took away Breylin's body and left Brohr alone in the gloomy cell, with only a fly buzzing around the chamber pot and his brother's restless spirit for company. It seemed a long time, waiting, straining to hear the muffled voices of passersby in the square. Brohr cupped his hands over his mouth and exhaled, trying to get some warmth back into his fingers. He tucked his hands in his armpits and rocked back and forth on the cot while he waited.

Constable Gunnar returned with a pair of soldiers and the miller, Sten, a burly redhead with an unkempt beard. They shoved the miller into the cell and shut the gate. The man fretted, ignoring Brohr completely as if he too were already a ghost. Sten stuck his face between the bars, pleaded his case to the constable until the constable finally lost his temper and jabbed at him through the bars with his cudgel. After that Sten sat on the bed muttering to himself and clawing at his beard.

They brought Mads in next. The pale, lanky barkeep kept quiet, more resigned to his fate. He looked hungover. Sten asked Mads why he thought he'd been arrested. Mads shrugged. Sten protested his innocence again, but no one seemed to care.

"We'll be hanged, Sten." Mads nodded. "Didn't you see them building the gallows?"

As Sten began to panic, trying to shake the bars loose, Brohr considered his future. Perhaps his grandfather would help them escape. He was a skald after all; he could find a way. But his grandfather didn't inspire hope. Just the opposite. Brohr had wanted to run, but Anders had talked him out of it. He could have been in Pederskald by now. His trust had led him here. There were so many other paths he could've taken. How had he ended up here, about to hang for a murder committed by some fairytale horror?

They dragged in Soren by the ankles. The fisherman was unconscious and barefoot, a nasty purple eye swollen shut. Two federals dumped him on the floor of the cell and waited for Constable Gunnar to lock it again before they left.

Mads and Brohr lifted the fisherman onto the cot, and he stirred but did not wake. Not long after, a soldier brought a rolled sheet of parchment and presented it to the constable. He read it, looked up at Brohr, then reread it. He rolled it back up and returned it to the soldier.

"I'll be ready," he said. "One of the prisoners is still unconscious. He should've woken up by now." Gunnar turned to the prisoners. "Is he still breathing?"

Mads held his hand over the fisherman's mouth. "Yes."

The constable shrugged and turned back to the soldier. "It's been a long time since we had a hanging, and of course I've never hung anyone who was knocked out before. Can we do that?"

The soldier shrugged. "That's up to the prefect. Just wait for me to come back."

Gunnar nodded and shut the jail door behind the soldier, angry shouts from outside punctuating the dim roar of the crowd gathered in the square. Gunnar turned gravely to the prisoners. "I won't have it said that I denied a man his proper right to beseech his elders before they welcomed him. Now is the time. Course if any of you would like to embrace the Pontiff's light, now is the time for that as well." He blushed. "I can help you with the rite of submission."

Mads laughed at him. "I'd rather not die with the Pontiff's cock in my mouth."

Sten stepped up to the bars and spit through them at Gunnar's feet. The constable turned to Brohr, waiting for his answer.

"Will they still hang me?" Brohr asked.

Gunnar paused, deciding whether to lie, Brohr thought. "Yes," said the constable.

Brohr puffed out his chest. He looked over at Mads, who inclined his head. "Guess I'll pass," Brohr said.

"So be it." Gunnar looked at each of them. "Make your peace."

The Constable went back to his desk as Mads and Sten knelt and began to whisper to their ancestors. Brohr supposed he should do the same but couldn't quite manage to believe it would help. His grandfather had only made his situation worse; what could he expect from the kin he'd never met? He closed his eyes, groping for his brother, the only family who seemed to care. He tried to steer his racing thoughts, but they gathered inevitably around the noose awaiting him.

The front door of the jail opened and a squad of legionaries strode in. They wore leather skirts and iron breastplates with round shields on their arms and short swords dangling from their hips.

"It's time," said the unshaven squad leader. He had light skin for a federal, almost as light as a shade.

Gunnar nodded and produced a key from his desk drawer. He unlocked the cell and stepped out of the way. The squad leader drew his sword and the others followed suit.

"Cassian!" He bellowed.

One of the soldiers stepped forward, a shield on one arm, a load of chains and manacles in the other. He leaned his shield against the wall and dropped all but a pair of manacles to the floor with a crash. Each set was joined by the chain and could be fastened with a wingnut. Once he'd unscrewed the first of these, the squad leader pointed his sword at Sten.

"You," he barked. "Step forward. I'll have no foolishness. Die with dignity, and there should be no reason to punish your families. Move it, prisoner."

Sten shuffled forward and held out his hands. The soldier clamped the manacles shut and tightened the nut holding them together. He nodded to the squad leader.

"You." The man leveled his sword at Mads. "Come out."

While the federals were busy chaining Mads, Brohr charged the squad leader. He'd hoped that the danger would rouse his brother, that rage might overwhelm him and he could at least have a chance at escape. But the squad leader lunged forward and bloodied Brohr's nose with the hilt of his sword. The jail spun around him, and a soldier shoved him to the floor. One man sat on his head as another pinned his arms behind his back and locked him down with the others.

Fear clenched his gut. Brohr's mouth went dry. He was really going to hang. In the back of his head, he realized he was expecting his rage to save him. But when he had reached for it, it was gone. He wondered if his neck would break or if he'd strangle.

"What about him?" Gunnar asked, pointing at the fisherman who lay unconscious on the cot.

Without hesitation, the squad leader marched into the cell and slid his sword across the prisoner's throat. They all watched, fascinated by the red gash, pumping blood onto the woolen blanket until his heart stopped. He never even stirred. The squad leader wiped his blade on the lower half of the man's filthy shirt.

"Move out!" he commanded.

They hauled Brohr to his feet, his eyes still locked on the gory spectacle, and led the condemned outside, into the town square. The chain jerked tight and pulled Brohr off balance; he looked to the constable in panic, but Gunnar turned away. The line of dead men dragged Brohr out backwards, his hands shackled behind him. He squinted at the sudden light, dazed by the burst of jeers and cries of sympathy. Soldiers and townsfolk

132

jostled one another, cursing and shouting. The air smelled of sweat and sea brine. It seemed that everyone in the world was there.

Walking backwards, Brohr looked over his shoulder toward the well at the center of the square. Townsfolk crowded a simple platform of fresh-cut timber on every side, more people than he had ever seen in one place during his life.

Blood ran from the cut on the bridge of his nose into his eye. He tried to wipe it with his shoulder, but it only made it worse, and he stumbled as the line lurched forward.

A chant started up in the crowd near the gallows.

"*Het Alta Drood! Het Alta Drood! Het Alta Drood!*" It was a line from the Tale of the Ten Fathers, shouted in the old tongue right in front of the federals. It meant "here is our doom". Father Freyan's final line of the saga, his declaration that it was better to die than to cower. But as defiant as the sentiment was, the chanting was soon quelled, more disorganized cries erupting in its place. Brohr looked back over his shoulder in the direction he was being led. Soldiers beat a group of townsfolk ruthlessly. He saw the federal prefect point out one of the rabble-rousers. His soldiers snatched the man from the crowd and dragged him up onto the gallows by his long hair.

Someone shouted Brohr's name. A woman. Brohr looked up, squinting through the blood to see his old friend Vili's mother, Inga. She spat on him and shouted "Brute!" before the crowd swallowed her up again.

Brohr tripped over a step he hadn't seen. Two soldiers grabbed him by the arms and hauled him onto the gallows. Someone detached his shackles from the chain linking him to the other prisoners. Each of them was led to a wooden box beneath a noose by a pair of legionaries. The prefect shouted to the crowd, but Brohr wasn't listening. He looked over at the other men as he mounted the wooden box. He realized the troublemaker who had been added to the execution was Sten's brother. The siblings looked at one another, saying something, but he couldn't tell what. His ears were roaring. He looked out over the crowd; they shook their fists, their lips curled back, teeth bare, snarling.

One of the soldiers looped the noose over his head and cinched it tight around his neck.

Birgit stood at the far end of the square, holding Vili's hand, shoulders trembling as she sobbed. Brohr's face flushed, his ears burned. He felt naked, humiliated that they should be here together, that they should see him like this. A sudden panic seized him that he should say something, should think something, somehow find a way to make sense of it all, maybe even to make it better before they—

"For Torin." The legionary whispered in Brohr's ear and kicked the box out from under him.

The first sharp pain shot through his body as his fall snapped the noose taught. It was unfair that they had manacled his arms behind his back. What chance did he have now? He struggled against his own suffocating weight, his feet desperately seeking the edge of the box, just out of reach.

The rope constricted around his neck. With every strain, every second, it strangled the retreating light, set panic like a wildfire. His hands were behind his back, he couldn't reach his throat. It was around his neck, choking tighter and tighter. He couldn't breathe.

The cord was around his neck. All warmth and safety vanished. He kicked and wailed, an infant cry. Where was his brother? Why didn't he help? The cord was around his neck, the man weeping, pulling it tighter, whispering apologies. Rage flared like the pressure of a strangler's hands.

"Not again!" they cried, their voice a croak, a chorus of grinding metal, a sound which was not sound.

An ocean of violence swelled in him like a damn full to bursting with hate, with vicious blows, with outrage. It was bottled only by the noose, the strange umbilical noose that bound the brothers in a knot of twisted love and regret and fury. Brohr tucked his legs up and looped his manacled hands beneath them, getting them in front. The weight on his neck was terrible, bursting the vessels in his face, in his eyes. Fear drove him like a

134

whip, becoming a giddy strength as if he could sweep Skolja into the sea with a wave of his arm. His mind was a jumble of drool and blood, of dying fresh from the womb and here on the gallows. He reached up and grabbed the rope between his neck and the beam above. Brohr hauled himself up, slack enough to breathe, and swung upside down to brace his feet on the beam. He yanked on the rope as if it were looped around his grandfather's neck, heaved on it as if it would snap the spine of this unfair world. He opened his eyes, and through the blood, he saw soldiers shying back.

And then the beam split.

Brohr fell to the gallows floor. The lumber that supported the nooses had cracked, and the prisoners fallen with him. The others were still tied to the board, but Brohr's noose had snapped the beam, and Brohr was free. He rushed to the nearest soldier, his brother held his arms high and brought the manacles crashing into the man's face again and again, the wingnut that bound him slashing the man's eyes to pulp.

"Not again!" Brohr shrieked at the dead man as he pummeled his corpse.

The metallic ring of a sword clearing its scabbard drew Brohr's attention to his right. He elbowed the man in the nose, snatched the sword from his hand, and noted a delightful flash of panic cross his face as Brohr drove the blade into his guts.

★★★★★

From her vantage atop the apothecary, Lyssa looked out over the crowd around the gallows. They had carried Breylin's body out of the jail a few minutes ago and taken it off toward the fort. She wiped her eyes and her nose on her sleeve, wondering what the federals would do with Breylin's remains. Not the proper things, she was sure.

The cobblestone square below stretched a hundred paces to a side, surrounded by timber and river rock buildings with thatched roofs. Villagers packed the square shoulder to shoulder, waiting for the executions in a kind of anxious frenzy. Federal

135

soldiers waited too, a squad stationed by each of the four roads leading into the square, a few roving the crowd, a few atop the newly constructed platform.

The nearest squad was just to her left but out of sight. She lay behind the apex of the straw roof, the point of the A-frame running parallel to the nearest side of the square. Her plan felt more foolish now that she was up here. It would be difficult to aim her throw from this distance, and if she was spotted, the squad guarding the road next to the apothecary could easily trap her on the roof.

Across the square, the jailhouse door swung open, and another squad led out the condemned. The square erupted into shouting and shoving. Some of the soldiers drew their swords, but the squad leaders ordered them to sheath their blades and instead draw the truncheons they carried on their belts.

Her father was second in the line of prisoners, his hands chained before him. He held his head up, looking around at the faces in the crowd. Calm. The thought brought tears to her eyes, but she quashed the tide of emotion before it could distract her.

Lyssa took a deep breath and bent to the knapsack she had pinned to the roof with her knee so it wouldn't slide off. She reached in and pulled out the vial of Wood Wraith. Keeping one hand on the lip of the roof, she arranged the other contents so that the jars of Raag Breath were on top, within easy reach.

Some of the townsfolk up by the gallows started chanting. *"Het Alta Drood!"* Lyssa took heart. All she could really do was stir up trouble. It was up to the crowd to do the rest. The prefect began shouting orders, and his soldiers rushed to break up those who dared to raise their voices. He singled out one of them, and the soldiers dragged the hapless man up onto the gallows.

The line of prisoners mounted the steps. She noticed that Brohr was at the end of the procession, chained backwards. Each of them was led to one of the nooses by a pair of soldiers and forced up onto a wooden box.

Her father remained calm. He looked from face to face in the crowd, nodding at a few men. A woman in the crowd threw a red scarf at his feet. Lyssa smiled.

136

She held onto the rim of the roof, pinning one of the knapsack straps with the same hand. With her right hand, she practiced the throwing motion. She readjusted her legs, glancing down at the green bottle peeking out of her knapsack. Breylin had taught her to distill Wood Wraith from tanner's acid steamed over a hazelwood fire. When a small rodent, in this case a rat, was drowned in the solution, the preparation was complete. If the Wood Wraith burst on the platform, it might eat away enough to collapse it. Ideally, she would hit the beam the nooses were tied to. Lyssa visualized the throw. She thought about where to hurl the Raag Breath after, in order to maximize the effect of the caustic smoke. Lyssa would have to make all five throws in rapid succession. The federals would almost certainly see her, but she had her escape route carefully planned. With the apothecary between them, the squad nearest her was the biggest threat, though on the other side of the building, they were least likely to spot her.

The prefect stood on the gallows behind the prisoners. He was giving some kind of speech, but it was drowned out by the crowd. He turned to the soldiers posted behind the condemned and nodded. One of them kicked the box out from beneath her father. He dropped a foot and flailed at the end of the noose.

Lyssa popped up to a standing position, the town square, the crowd, and the federals spread out below her. She locked her eyes on the beam just above Mads's head and hurled the vial of Wood Wraith. Before it struck, she reached into the knapsack and plucked out a jar of Raag Breath. She couldn't help herself; her eyes darted over to the gallows, joy erupting in her heart at the telltale wisp of smoke atop the beam. She threw the jar in her hand at the platform too, and it burst almost at the prefect's feet. A cloud of reeking vapor erupted as the contents mixed with the briny air.

Lyssa almost lost her rhythm, noticing Brohr hanging upside down, his feet above him, braced on the beam. He jerked frantically on the noose, straining the beam. It snapped, sparking pandemonium below. The soldiers were already reacting, but when the beam gave, the crowd surged towards the gallows. Her

137

hope swelled, but she forced herself back into motion, throwing jar after jar of the foul smoke into the crowd as near the groups of soldiers as she could get. The last jar she tossed over the side of the apothecary where she knew the nearest squad lurked.

Lyssa took one last look at the gallows just in time to see Brohr bludgeoning a soldier with his manacles. Her father knelt on the platform, struggling with his noose. Lyssa looked at her footing and crawled back down to the edge of the roof. When she was as low as she could get, she dropped into the alley, careful not to get tangled in the wind chimes and fetishes hanging from the eaves. She looked up to see a soldier leaning against the shop wall, vomiting. Acrid fumes curled around from the other side of the building. Another one rounded the corner. Red faced, he coughed and gagged. Hand over his mouth, he swallowed, noticed Lyssa watching, and called out, "There!"

Lyssa spun on the ball of her foot and sprinted down the alley. A pair of legionaries ran after her, shouting lewd threats and curses as they gave chase.

★★★★★

Brasca staggered backwards out of the noxious cloud. He dropped to one knee, his eyes and lungs burning from the fumes, and hacked phlegm onto the freshly hewn platform. Around him, the shouting and panic escalated as the vapors filled the town square.

He'd seen the young man who killed the veteran in the tavern brawl go mad, the crowd surge with rebellious hope. He couldn't catch his breath. His lungs ached for fresh air, and he crouched, gasping, until the sickening thickness in his lungs eased. A breeze pulled the fog south toward the fighting around the boy and began to defuse it. Before he found the wind to shout orders, a fleeing soldier ran into him, tripped, and fell a few feet off the side of the gallows into the irate crowd.

Brasca could see that this was about to devolve into a massacre, one way or the other. He needed to get things under control—and fast. The prefect stood straight and sucked in a deep breath.

"Put those prisoners to the sword!" he shouted.

As soon as he'd finished, a coughing fit seized him. Brasca dry heaved, acid searing the back of his throat. The prefect looked around the platform for Carthalo just as the raging prisoner killed one of his soldiers with the fool's own blade. The young half-Norn was shrieking as he twisted the sword in the poor man's belly and shoved him into the stunned crowd below. Brasca discovered Carthalo crouching on the stairs over a puddle of vomit.

"Get up!" The prefect kicked his subordinate in the backside. "Sound the call to clear the square! Now!"

Brasca surveyed the scene, assessing the disposition of his troops. Clouds of gas had spread over most of the square, thinning out but leaving the whole area trapped in a caustic fog. As Carthalo blew three sharp notes on the brass horn he carried, Brasca gave up on trying to command the legionaries he couldn't see and turned back to the situation on the gallows. Three of his men were already dead. The rest were hacking at the prisoners still bound by their nooses.

One of the soldiers pulled his blade free of the tavern keeper's back but hadn't bothered to watch his own. Behind him, the enraged half-Norn prisoner rushed forward and windmill-slammed his stolen short sword down through the distracted legionary's collarbone. The wound cleaved almost a foot into his torso and sent an explosion of blood spraying in the faces of the nearest men. Shocked, the soldier looked down at the blade as it disappeared from his mangled chest and then up at another of his stunned comrades before he collapsed.

"To me!" Brasca drew his own sword as terrified soldiers backed away from the rampaging Norn. One of them scrambled off of the platform and fled into the crowd. The rest formed up around him, falling back on their training, regaining their discipline. Roiling vapors obscured most of the square, but Brasca heard squad leaders calling out orders, organizing, asserting control. Brasca looked beside him where Carthalo had drawn his blade and joined the ranks.

"Call the reserve squads," the prefect ordered.

His officer shouted, "Yes, sir," and blew a message on his horn.

The half-caste prisoner cocked his head at the blast of the horn. He looked around at the carnage, making for a bizarre figure, blood and a baffled look on his face, a sword in his manacled hands, a noose still wrapped around his neck. He seemed suddenly startled and jumped back a step. Then without warning, he turned, hopped off the platform, and disappeared into the mob.

"After him!" the prefect bellowed. He didn't want to lose the outlaw in the fog hanging over the square. "After him!" He pointed his sword into the crowd. "We stay together. No unnecessary killing, but suffer no foolishness. Do you hail me?"

As one, the group of soldiers shouted. "Hail Tyria!"

Brasca continued the chant as the squad pressed forward, hopping off the gallows. "Do you hail me?"

The next line was picked up by soldiers hidden in the fog all over the square. "Hail Tyria!"

"Double-time!" Brasca shouted.

Chapter 14

"Cognates of old Tyrianite can be found in the tribal dialects of Burning Shinei, Heimir, and the outer giants, further evincing that the dominion of the old ones encompassed the entire system."

-Varo Braga, The Shining Tongue

The road snaked up into the hills. Lowland fields of poplar first gave way to choking briar and pale birch, then to virgin fir and elder pine. Anders stopped to catch his breath. It was cold, a light rain falling. Still, he sweated under his woolen cloak, his knees throbbed. Last time he'd made this journey, he'd been a younger man, he'd had a horse, and it was summer then. The witch fire had spooked Rebel, and she'd run off, leaving the old man to make this miserable trip on foot.

Another hour or so up the road, a twig snapped behind him. One hand reached instinctively for his dagger, though he was so tired he doubted he'd be able to accomplish much with it. In any case, it wasn't likely to be a federal patrol; they marched down the road, they didn't skulk in the bushes.

"*Skel,*" Anders called out. "Aren't you going to greet an old friend?"

Rain drops pattered on the last leaves clinging to the trees. A jaybird landed on a nearby branch, craning its head toward him. Then, back the way he'd come, someone stepped out onto the road. Anders turned to see a bedraggled young man in a leather cloak. He carried a longbow with an arrow knocked but not drawn.

"What are you doing here?" the man asked.

"As I said," Anders began. "I'm an old friend. It's been some time since I've made it up this way. I don't recognize you, but Gareth knows me. I have news he'll want to hear. Good news. And grave news as well."

"Nilstrom? Anders Nilstrom?" Another voice called out from the trees. A lean-looking man with long brown hair starting to gray emerged from hiding and limped up to the trespasser. He slid an arrow fletched with raven feathers back into its quiver as he approached.

Anders didn't recognize him. "Yes," he said. "That's right."

The outlaw motioned to his comrade to put away his arrow, a scowl on his face. "It's Nels," he said. "Nels Bergen. My mother was Marta Bergen."

Anders gulped, turning fast to hide his watery eyes. "Was?" he asked, hoping somehow he had misheard the man.

Nels nodded. "Just this summer. She'd been ill for some time."

Anders blinked back tears. *Don't be foolish,* he told himself. *You haven't seen her in years.* But it was not so simple as telling himself to tuck away that heartache for another time. Anders faked a coughing fit so that he could compose himself. *How?* He wondered. *Did she suffer?* Finally, he looked up. "I trust Gareth is well."

Nels studied the skald, folding his arms. "Fit as ever."

Anders gnashed his teeth, embarrassed that Nels had seen his weakness. "Let's be on our way. There is much to speak of."

Another pair of outlaws trotted into the clearing. Nels waved everyone after him and turned west, heading off the road toward their camp. "This way, Nilstrom," he said. "It was a mistake to come here. My father won't be happy to see you."

★★★★★

Henrik needed sleep. He needed time to prepare bindings. But he couldn't shirk his first day as mayor, not at a time like this. After the riot, he helped to mediate the crisis, urging townsfolk to return to their homes.

With a pair of soldiers in tow, Henrik made the rounds, informing the loyal citizens of the night ahead and reminding them, as the prefect had insisted, that federal scholars had divined the comet's impact with their calculations. He wanted to cut off the inevitable superstitious rumblings by staking a claim to it.

Henrik entered the High Tavern, flanked by his official bodyguards. The tap room smelled of lemon oil and wood smoke, a cozy fire crackling in the great stone hearth at the back of the room. Lantern sconces behind the bar lit the parlor, casting warm light through shelves of wine and liquor bottles. A ring of mounted heads, elk and wolf and bear, adorned the cedar walls above the wainscoting. Unlike Mads's Tavern in the low quarter, federals and the upper crust of the provincials frequented the place.

The tavern keeper stood behind the burnished counter, a kid really, who'd recently taken over for his doddering father. He held a quill in one hand and was counting casks on the other. When Henrik cleared his throat, the boy spun around.

The tavern keep's voice cracked. "Is it true?"

"The comet?" Henrik asked. The boy covered his mouth, marring his cheek with the quill. Henrik nodded. "Yes," he said. "I'm afraid so. I need to rest, sorry. Send someone up to wake me at nightfall."

Imported rugs from Old Hemmings covered the second-floor landing. Henrik fished the key from his pocket, and unlocked the door to his finely appointed room. Opposite the front door were two shuttered windows and an elaborate mahogany desk with a cage full of rats atop it. To his right stood a four-poster featherbed with a canopy draped in Sonderlund lace. On his left, a fireplace flanked by piles of supplies: burlap sacks and oaken barrels, tools and rope. Henrik locked the door behind him, eyeing the bed longingly, and went to sit before the desk.

A twinge of guilt made him bite his fingernail as he bent over the cage, studying the rats. "Sorry, gentlemen."

143

He looked at the rodents, trying not to imagine their fate, trying not to let it conjure images of his parents' demise. After a moment he envisioned Anders Nilstrom, and the thought of what he might do to the murderer with these bindings gave him the resolve to go through with it. Nodding, Henrik stooped to the cradle beside the fireplace and plucked out a thick log. He laid it in the hearth, then leaned two spindlier ones against it. A tinderbox with a scrimshaw lid lay on the mantle—Father Freyan opening Grenja's belly. It was a scene from *the Tale*. He stuffed some tinder beneath the logs and struck flint to steel until it caught.

He needed something else to hold the fire while he worked the binding; he didn't want to set the room ablaze. From his pile of provisions, he recovered a large iron pot with a lid. Henrik sat back down and began to meditate on his anger. As Caden's first axiom stated, "The binder's will shapes most the binding."

When the fire was good and hot, he used the tongs to transfer the logs into the pot. Henrik produced a skipping stone from his pocket, inspected it, and set it on the floor beside him. He picked the cage up off the desk and set it down near the pot full of burning logs. He needed to hurry, the smoke was getting thick.

He opened the top of the cage and used the tongs to take out one of the squealing rats. Then with his free hand, he grabbed the lid off the pot, and froze. He berated himself for thinking about his parents, about what he was doing to the rat.

"It's just a rat," he said.

But the justification didn't mak him feel any better. He pictured Nilstrom again, dropped the vermin in the fire, and covered it.

Henrik cocked his ear, listening for the precise moment the rat perished. As Caden's second axiom stated, "The time since death is inversely proportional to a binding's relative power." When the charred little beast struggled no more, Henrik pictured the first of the three runes, the archetype. To snare the rodent, Henrik had chosen *the Scavenger*. As Bormian noted, an archetype should match the departed as closely as is possible, for in the end, all creatures are most interested in themselves. Henrik smiled at the philosopher's wit. Once he had visualized the sigil, he sounded the note, his voice seeding the rune with the taste of power it needed to transfix the spirit and keep it from crossing to the dead place. In the air before him, the symbol flared to life, painting the room in viridian light.

The second rune would dictate which of the ten essences suffused the binding, and after what had happened to his parents, only *Fire* would do. He envisioned the rune and intoned the next note. It flared red before his eyes, refining what was left of the little spirit until only *Fire* remained. Finally, Henrik meditated on the purpose of the binding, forming the image of the intention rune, *Destruction*—a circle slashed by a diagonal rend. He sang the last note, and the third rune blazed beside the others, each taking on the crimson hue of the fiery essence. Henrik held up the stone he had prepared, and the runes began to orbit it, the animus of the rat spiraling inward until, with a searing flash, the rat was bound and the symbols gone.

Only then did he notice the thick smoke and the vile stench of burnt rat. He went to the shutters and opened both windows. Again, he stared at the bed with longing. But no, there was still plenty to be done before this accursed day was over. He examined the rock. The binding was sound. It screeched in his ear. Henrik closed his eyes, picturing that old murderer Nilstrom, stumbling down the streets of Skolja, in flames.

★★★★★

Brohr barreled over the open ground, the shouts of legionaries echoing through the trees behind him. His feet churned dead leaves and mud in his wake, an easy path for his pursuers to follow. He crested the hill west of town and scrambled down the scree cliffside, an avalanche of dirt and gravel erupting around him. At the bottom, Brohr turned back but the soldiers chasing him still hadn't reached the top of the hill. He sprinted across the stone bridge that spanned the south fork of the Ormt. On the other side, Brohr plunged into the dense woods, the call and response of the Tyrianites drowned out by the babbling river.

After climbing to the top of the next hill, Brohr slowed to a jog, his lungs burning and his throat raw from the cold and the strangling noose. He kept pace as long as he could, but eventually he stopped, knelt, and dropped the sword to the bed of pine needles and maple leaves covering the forest floor. With his teeth, he tried to loosen the wingnut that kept his manacles in place. It wouldn't budge. Brohr was afraid he might crack a tooth, but he tried again to no avail.

He supposed he was heading home though he had no real plan. Brohr was a doomed man. For the first time it really sunk in; he was a killer. An outlaw. What choices did he have left? Perhaps he'd finally see Pederskald. Brohr had heard it said that the town was big enough that not everyone knew each other. The thought buoyed his spirits.

But if he walked into Pederskald manacled and soaked in blood, he obviously wouldn't escape notice. His only hope was that his grandfather was home, that he could help him unshackle himself and clean off the blood. He hated looking to his grandfather for help. Anders practically turned him over to the federals—and certainly left him to die. He hadn't even bothered to come to the hanging. Brohr relented a bit; of course he didn't come, not after what he'd done to the mayor. He couldn't. Still, the bitterness was there, and excuses wouldn't sweeten it any.

He set off at a jog again. They'd send legionaries to the farm to look for him. Staying off the road might keep him out of sight, but if the prefect dispatched soldiers straightaway, they would beat him there.

Brohr was stunned to discover that he was not afraid of soldiers. For the first time, he had stayed while his brother raged. They fought together. It was… incredible. Brohr was proud. And dangerous. The soldiers on the gallows had looked ready to piss themselves. And the ones who'd fought were like children: slow and clumsy and weak.

As he cleared the trees at the north fork of the river's edge, he felt an unexpected pang of guilt, a moment of loss. Birgit had been right to fear him. He would never hurt her of course, but he was a freak. He couldn't control his anger. Sooner or later he would get himself killed, and where would that leave her?

He pushed the unwelcome realization out of his mind, crossed the rocky shore, and waded into the frigid river. The ford was knee-high in the summertime but now was over his waist, the treacherous water rushing by with drowning force. Brohr crossed deliberately, feet probing for solid footing with each step. When he reached the shallows on the far bank, Brohr chucked the sword up onto the shore, and it clanked onto the rocks. He sat in the knee-deep water, teeth chattering, and dunked his head, scrubbing the blood from his face. With the manacles, though, he couldn't scrub his hands very well, so he stood up, collected the blade, and headed home.

A couple of miles from his farm, he paused in a little glen surrounded by barren oak trees. A pair of crows squabbled overhead, fluttering from one branch to the next, cawing and pecking at one another. Brohr sat on a boulder in the center and a shaft of afternoon sun warmed him while he caught his breath.

Curiosity.

It was a strange and sudden feeling, a sensation that was not entirely his own. He looked back the way he'd come as if he had missed something interesting. The crows flapped their black-feathered wings and flew off toward the south. Brohr's intuition grew unaccountably. He couldn't see anything odd, couldn't quite explain why he felt this way, until understanding finally dawned on him. He smiled to himself and marveled to share the sensation with his brother.

"Is someone there?" he called.

Brohr waited a moment until someone leaned out from behind a tree and waved. Clad in a pair of leather trousers and a matching vest with a dagger at the hip, she came closer. Brohr marveled at the novelty of a woman wearing a dagger on her belt. It was the tavern keeper's daughter, Lyssa. Brohr smiled.

She wore a heavy-looking knapsack on her back. When she drew near enough to speak, she instead bent over, hands on her knees, and gasped for breath.

She held up her hand. "I'm glad you stopped. I was about to die."

"Why are you following me?"

Lyssa flopped onto the ground, face up. She didn't say anything for a moment. Brohr thought she was just exhausted until he noticed Lyssa biting her lip.

"My father," she said at last. "Did he escape?"

Brohr shook his head.

A tear streaked from the corner of Lyssa's eye. She cleared her throat, about to say something, but instead a whine emerged. She rolled over, burying her face, and pounded the patch of clovers she lay upon, over and over, as if sounding a drum to tell the world of her father's passing. Brohr wanted to reach out and touch her but didn't. He kept silent, waiting, not wanting to interrupt her grief.

After the worst had, for the moment, passed, Lyssa wiped her nose.

"I'm sorry about your father," Brohr said. "We had better go. There might still be soldiers following us."

"Thank you," she said, looking up with bleary eyes.

"For what?" He surveyed the clearing, anxious to be on his way.

"For hurting them. I know it won't help my father, but they deserved it. How do you fight like that? It's... I've never. You're a big guy, but you throttled Torin like he was a puppy. And today..."

His temper had always been an embarrassment, his haunting a shame that grew darker every year. But at least it made sense now. And suddenly it was the only reason he was in trouble—and the only reason he was alive. What did it matter after everything else? He wasn't sure if he could trust her, but everyone could see that he was a freak. What use was trying to pretend anymore?

"I guess I'm haunted," he said. Lyssa cocked her head, waiting for more. "I always have been," he continued. "My brother. He was stillborn. I never understood until that night, after I ran away from the dock. Grandfather says he protects me." Brohr shrugged. "It feels like a curse most of the time. He's so angry. But today I'm glad for it."

Brohr mulled over the paradox. His brother had always felt like a pall hanging over his shoulder, an inexplicable looming storm that he could forget for a while, but which was always brooding just over the horizon. It had cost him his only friend, and Birgit too.

Brohr held up his shackled, bloody hands. "Can you help me get these off?"

"Sure." Lyssa stood up and edged toward him. "The whites of your eyes are bloody. It's a little intimidating." Brohr noticed her wariness as she fumbled with the manacles, tearing away a snarl of hair caught in the threads of the nut, her eyes flicking up at him for signs of sudden violence.

"Doesn't just happen for no reason," he said. "Like grandfather says, he protects me. Though sometimes he goes too far."

Lyssa nodded. Grimacing, she finally loosened the gore-encrusted wingnut and twisted until it came free. Brohr shook off the manacles, rubbing his bruised wrists.

"Are you going home?" she asked.

Brohr nodded.

"You know they're going to send soldiers to look for you there, right?"

"I need to see if my grandfather is there. I have no idea what else to do."

Lyssa hooked her thumbs in her belt and leaned back against an elm tree. "I guess we're both outlaws now. I think the smartest thing we can do is get far away from here. As far as we can."

"Yeah." Brohr smiled. "I think I'll go to Pederskald. I've been on my way there, it seems like forever. You can come if you want. I need to check on my grandfather and pick up Grendie first."

"Grendie?"

"My dog."

"Pederskald isn't far enough away. Not even close. You killed legionaries." Lyssa folded her arms. "They won't stop looking for you."

Brohr shrugged and turned deeper into the forest, trotting out of the glen. "Coming?" He looked back over his shoulder to find Lyssa following, her knapsack bouncing on her back. Brohr stopped, remembering his manners. "I can carry that."

She jogged past him. "No thanks."

Brohr caught the first hint of smoke in the air not long after. Lyssa called out to him, warning him, as he sprinted home, but he ignored her. He knew. He knew what the smoke meant, but he ran headlong, unafraid. If there were soldiers... His anger flared, grim imaginings fueling his temper.

He burst from the trees onto the farm, coming out near the graves where the idols of his mother and grandmother were buried. The cabin smoldered, the damage done. They hadn't bothered to fire the shed. Brohr ran across the field, nearly tripping onto his sword as he hurtled through the high grass.

It wasn't until he passed the well house that he saw the body laying not far from the burning home. "No!" The cry startled a nearby crow which fled into the sky. Brohr fell to his knees before Grendie's corpse.

Two crossbow bolts protruded from her side. A gash yawned across her snout. Blood clotted in her open eye. Flies scattered. Brohr scoured the clearing, looking for someone to vent his loss upon. But the soldiers had gone, and Lyssa kept out of sight.

His rage cooled. He looked back down at Grendie, pressed his head against her hip where there was no blood, and he wept. Her sudden absence shocked him in a way that even his trip to the gallows hadn't. He could barely remember a time before her. She had been the runt of the litter, her eyes still crusted shut when his grandfather had plucked her from her

150

mother's teat and brought her home. Brohr had fed her milk squeezed from a rag, taught her how to sit, to heel, to hunt, to explore. They'd huddled by the fire in the deep winter, content, a pack of two.

And she was dead because of him. Though he knew she would gladly have died a thousand times to keep him safe, it only made her loss all the more bitter.

The back wall of the crackling cottage gave way, crashing to the ground and rousing him from his sorrow. He looked up, discovering that Lyssa sat nearby, her pack unslung, eating a piece of bread. With a sympathetic look, she held the crust out to him. His belly rumbled.

He smiled halfheartedly, grateful but still stricken. She stood up and brought him the bread.

"Thank you," said Brohr. Chewing, staring off, he stood and walked nearer his smoking house. The heat kept him from going inside, but the thatch was long gone, and with the western wall collapsed, he could see inside. It was a mess of burnt logs and swirling ash; he recognized the skeleton of one of their rawhide chairs, but there was no sign of his grandfather. The smoke started him coughing, and he backed away.

Brohr walked over to the shed. There was no sign of Rebel either. Her tack was missing. It made sense. A horse was too valuable to kill for no reason.

"What now?" Lyssa asked.

Brohr shook his head. "I don't know. Part of me just wants to run. But..." He looked over at the smoking ruin, then his gaze drifted to Grendie's mangled body.

Chapter 15

"The aftermath of the Shining Empire's collapse is shrouded in discrepancy. Federal dogma names Tyrus and Cassian as contempories, but historical records cast doubt on the period of chaos that followed the old ones' civil war. Is it not possible that He placed these accounts to test our faith?"

-Anysus Darian, A True and Orthodoxical
History of the Divine Advent

A speckling of canvas tents dotted the clearing beneath a ring of ancient hemlocks. Anders had hoped to find the encampment full of fighting men, ready to avenge the conquest of their homeland. Instead, he had discovered women, children, and a few bedraggled outlaws eeking a grim existence from the deep woods.

He had expected as much. They'd had a Hemmishman in charge. It was time to change that.

The outlaws lived in a little valley deep within the hills, close enough to reach the road and the mine in less than a day's travel but far enough that the federals wouldn't stumble across it. Judging by the number of tents, there must have been twenty or thirty men and their families here.

Nels nudged him, indicating one of the larger tents with his bow. "My father is this way."

Nels was right. Gareth hardly seemed to have changed at all. Crows feet gathered in the corners of his eyes. His long brown hair hid a few strands of gray at the temple. His beard was trimmed, more gray on the chin. Though short, he stood straight and lean, showing little evidence that so many years had passed.

Gareth and Anders appraised one another. They had been friends once, but there was no warmth in the look they shared.

At last, Gareth turned to his son. "Perhaps," he said. "You should give us some privacy."

At about ten paces to a side, Gareth's tent was large enough to accommodate the three of them without crowding. A wicker chair was pushed up beside a wicker table with a pair of woolen stockings draped over it to dry. An apple core lay on the far side of Gareth's bedroll.

Nels scowled, but he headed out. "I'll be nearby." He gave Anders a warning look.

The skald smiled at Gareth. "I see you've been telling horror stories about me."

Gareth folded his arms. "That's not it. He hasn't gotten over the death of his mother yet. He doesn't want us picking at the scab."

"I was sorry to hear about Marta," Anders said. "I didn't know until today."

"I know how you felt about her," Gareth said.

Another silence lingered.

Anders broke it. "You've seen the comet?"

Gareth threw up his hands and turned away. "After all these years, you haven't changed a bit. Why have you come here?"

"It's time, Gareth!"

"Please." The outlaw puffed out his cheeks. "Hasn't that zeal done enough damage? What new madness is it this time?"

"Just listen!" Anders stepped closer, his eyes intense. "The comet will strike tonight. It'll hit Quaya moon. You can't imagine the chaos. This is our time. Our only chance!"

Gareth did not retreat. He leaned forward, glaring up into the skald's eyes. "She saw what you were, you know?"

"What?" Anders asked.

"She saw you. Even though she loved you. She saw. And she rejected you."

Anders cast his eyes away, mumbling. "You don't understand." He raised his voice. "Just wait until tonight. You'll see. This time their throats really are bare."

★★★★★

Despite the hour, the square teamed with soldiers and anxious Nornfolk. The various groups mixed uneasily, the merchants eyeing the farmers, the fractious crowd watching the legionaries, all of them looking up at Henrik. He stood atop the gallows, pacing. At the far end, a squad of federals hovered around the seated prefect.

Henrik quieted the unease rising in his gut. What a fool he would look if nothing happened. Of course, that was ridiculous. He had every confidence in his father's prediction, not to mention the federal astronomers' confirmation.

Tonight, the maelstrom began.

As much as he imagined that everyone was looking at him, knives close to hand, he was forced to dismiss this as fantasy. For in truth, their eyes had drifted toward the sky. Though the storm clouds missed Skolja, it was a blustery night, clear and cold. To the east, a brooding mass of thunderheads obscured the stars, but up over the water, pendulous Quaya awaited her doom. The Wanderer's tail seemed to poke out of the side of the moon, evidence of the imminent collision. But for all of their expectation, it remained, as yet, a night like any other.

Some of the folk had gone back to bed, scoffing at the dire mood and the unholy hour. Yet most of the townspeople ingested the atmosphere of alarm, fed by the sour taste of the morning's executions and riot.

Henrik looked down at the worried faces, the whispering women, and the doleful, bearded Norn, arms folded, gravely patient. The prefect sat at the far end of the platform in a chair someone had fetched for him. The officer spoke orders in the ears of his men, pointing here and there.

Henrik's opinion of the prefect was evolving. Before his father's murder, he'd disliked the prefect as a bland representative

154

of that distant power that had devastated his people. Another rival to trade insults with, perhaps. Another arrogant federal. But he didn't hate their might, he respected it; he hated their ridiculous culture. Their ridiculous religion that deified a politician, that mercantilized superstition, with offerings of coin or blood or flowers that bought happiness in the afterlife.

Henrik had lacked insight into the man, dismissing him as another prop in that farce. But Henrik was beginning to glimpse the violent humors that stirred him, the fatalistic resolve, the rejection of simple morality. The prefect was a strange mix of pragmatism and idealism. He realized that if he did not prove useful in the coming ordeal, Brasca Quoll would happily cut his throat and forgo diplomacy. If it came to rebellion, Henrik would not survive. Regardless of the outcome.

He needed to salve the wound inflicted on Skolja today. Unless Henrik could find a way to keep the town from devouring itself, the federals and the Norn would turn on each other before long, and he entertained no illusions about what either side thought of him.

Henrik looked about the square, then up at crimson Quaya. His father's instrumentation had been destroyed in the fire, but he could estimate, by the angle of the moon and the little green sliver of Otho, that it was nearly time. He held up his hand.

"Skolja!" he shouted. "Heed me!"

Some of the curious townsfolk turned to him while others continued to gossip or gawk at the heavens. The prefect scooted his chair around to face Henrik and crossed one leg over the other.

"Skolja!" Henrik bellowed. The murmuring and scuffing of feet grew quiet as all eyes turned to the fledgling mayor. "Tonight," he began, "you will see something of astonishing beauty." He paused for effect. "And it will fill you with absolute terror. You will see something so... otherworldly, something so strange and fascinating, that many will call it an omen."

Henrik noted the prefect sitting up straight out of the corner of his eye. The man was worried he'd put these notions

155

into their heads, but of course they would think this. It was inevitable. Better to refute it now and steal its power over them.

"Someone will say this is the sign of which our grandfathers spoke. And you'll think to yourself, well... not exactly. They spoke of my great-great-uncle, Saint Olaf, rising from the dead to break his bonds." Henrik pointed up the hill where the shrine overlooked Skolja and the Selvig Sea.

"A part of you will want it to be true, so perhaps you will nod instead of saying, 'no, that's not quite right. I've never heard any prophecy about a comet.'

"And if you let that little lie pass, you may even start to believe that it's a sign. You'll say, 'Of course it is' it's so incredible, so big. We have to give it meaning.'

"Do you remember the story of the pig and the apple? Of course you do, we've all heard the *Tale of the Ten Fathers* a thousand times. The pig is so fiercely greedy that when it tries to bite the apple, it shoots out of his mouth and up into the sky. That's Quaya. We used to call it *Omska*. Apple."

Henrik pointed up and studied it along with most of the crowd. "Of course, that was before we knew it was an entire world with its own nations. We thought the meaning of the story was that the pig had shot an apple into the sky."

Henrik chuckled. "But what I think the story really meant was that we should not be greedy. Don't try to hold something so hard that it shoots off into the sky."

Henrik looked pointedly at the prefect who leaned back in his chair and waited for him to continue. "I'll tell you what this means." Henrik again pointed at Quaya. "It means we're in danger. It's a whole world up there, not an apple. And a gigantic rock hurtling through the void is about to collide with it. Imagine one mountain dropping on another above our heads.

"I can't say what sort of trouble it will bring. Perhaps the ground will shake or the sky will burn. That part won't happen tonight. Tonight we will only bear witness. It's tomorrow that we'll have to sort out what it means. Can we convince ourselves that our grandfathers warned us of this? Will we believe the apple

156

is falling from the sky? Or will we look up and see the wondrous and terrible truth?

"It means that we are in trouble. Whether it is fire or flood or any other calamity, the simple truth is that we must work together to survive it. If we warp this into an omen of rebellion, we will find ourselves fighting the Tyrianites," he gestured to the prefect and then up at the moon, "as well as the heavens themselves.

"Many of you chafe at the rule of the federals. Especially after a morning like this. It is not lost on me that I'm speaking from the gallows." Brasca began to rise, but Henrik held out his hands for forbearance, and the prefect sank back into his chair, signaling his men to wait.

"The simple truth," said Henrik, "is that the federals want us to survive. They want us to survive so that they can continue to tithe us, to take prisoners to mine the hills. They want to keep us alive because we are valuable servants."

A grumble swept through the crowd, but Henrik shouted over it. "Heed me, Skolja! You may not like the sound of it, but it is true. Remember that the meaning of this terrible collision is danger. Pure danger. Danger unlike anything else. Danger in proportion to the awe you will feel tonight.

"You may chafe to be counted as a servant, but now, the only glory will be found in survival. For many will not survive this calamity. Meaning will not survive. Cities will not survive. Rebellions will not survive. Only the strong and the wise will survive. Only together will we survive."

The crowd regarded him in shock. They had been warned of the event but not prepared for its magnitude. Henrik worried that he had gone too far; both the locals and federals looked dumbfounded. Perhaps that was good. Perhaps he could even shake them all loose from their prejudices and misconceptions.

He had hoped, too, that the collision would start about now. But overhead, nothing had changed.

The prefect applauded from his chair. He stood, looked up at the moon, and adjusted his sword belt. At last he turned to Henrik and doffed his tricorn.

"A noble sentiment," he said. "And quite true. It has been an eventful week. A sad one. Good Mayor Torvald and his wife have been murdered. Now perhaps," he waggled his finger at the crowd, "you disliked the man. Even called him nasty words like 'collaborator.' But he was an honest man. He did not cheat you. He did not force himself on your wives or make unfair laws. Most people in his position would be greedy." He smiled at Henrik. "Like the pig from your quaint little story.

"Perhaps he was a bit too kind. As I have been. You are a conquered people, and yet you live as free men. The laws of the federation allow me to arrest whomever I choose, to take your property if it pleases me. But I have been lenient despite your ingratitude.

"Many of you remember what it was like in Skolja under my predecessors, Prefect Flaucus in particular."

Brasca swept his gaze over the crowd, lingering here and there to make eye contact with the older townsfolk. "Rape and murder and cruelty. That was the way of it. The slave tithe taking one in ten. But to be fair to Flaucus, this town had a rebellious spirit in those days. Rough justice was necessary to maintain order.

"Each of you must understand this: there is no victory against the federation. It stretches to the heavens. There are ten thousand soldiers for each of you. More. There is a never-ending flow of us, like the source of a river.

"So accept the peace I offer you or you will remember what it is like to defy us. You should be grateful for the tolerance we have shown you. I don't want to reinstate the slave tithe, but if you force my hand—"

A woman in the crowd screamed. Gasps and cries of alarm echoed through the square. His speech forgotten, the prefect dropped his hat, his eyes fixed on Quaya. Without thinking, he fell to one knee to pray, then, chiding himself, he rose again, and started issuing orders.

★★★★★

Brohr recognized the stretch where they rejoined the road. It was the first steep rise heading up into the hills, a place wagons often became mired in the mud. The trees thinned out here, but a stout oak perched beside the road. Long ago, the federals had installed a winch on its trunk, but the contraption was useless now; it had been vandalized too many times and fallen into disrepair.

The light began to fail. As the sun set back the way they'd come, it cast long shadows, slashing perpendicular to the road. Trimmed in burnt orange and purple, the clouds were so beautiful that Brohr and Lyssa stopped to admire the scene.

"Do you think it's safe to use the road?" Lyssa asked. "It's getting dark."

Brohr shrugged. "It's probably fine. I can't imagine they have patrols this far out. Probably another half day or more to get to the mine and at least twice that far to Pederskald."

Lyssa un-slung her pack, set it down, and stretched. "Have you ever been there?"

"To Pederskald?" he asked.

She nodded.

"No." Brohr sighed. "I've always wanted to go. I always imagined I'd just pick up and leave one day. I want to see Pederskald. Trond too. I want to see the ruins of Grisben. Everything there is to see." Brohr chuckled. "Maybe this is just the kick in the seat I needed. At least now I won't die in Skolja."

Lyssa looked at him oddly.

"What?"

"You're shivering," she said.

"It's cold, and I'm wet."

Lyssa smiled and bent over her knapsack. She rummaged through it, tossing him a red sweater.

He held it up, seeing if it would fit. "Good," he said. "The blood stains won't even show."

Her smile faltered.

159

"Sorry," he said, pulling the sweater over his head. "Just a joke." It was tight, and the sleeves a little short.

"Freyan's ghost." She shook her head.

"It was just a joke. Sometimes you've got to laugh, or you'll just go crazy." This did not seem to comfort her at all. Brohr shrugged. "Anyway, we should get going."

They headed north on the wagon tracks toward the crossroads. As the sun set, Quaya rose, its orbit dragging the moon inexorably toward its collision with the Wanderer.

"What about you?" Brohr finally asked. "Have you been to Pederskald?"

She shook her head. "This is the farthest I've ever been too."

A silence followed, Brohr brooding on the burnt-out cabin he'd once called home. "My grandfather is probably with the outlaws," he said at last.

Lyssa turned to him, studying his expression in the red light of the moon. "We won't pass them if we take the road to Pederskald."

He nodded. "Good. I don't miss him. If that's what you're thinking. I feel a little guilty. He's kin after all. But he usually didn't treat me any better than our plow horse. I feel like I escaped him as much as I did the hanging."

"I've met him," said Lyssa. "I think he liked you a little better than the horse, course he never had a nice word for me. A lousy tipper too." She winked.

Brohr smiled. "He taught me everything I know. Guess what he gave me for my last birthday?" She shrugged. "A new saw. And then of course he expected me to cut twice as much wood. The prick."

Lyssa laughed. "Well, don't be too harsh. At least he's around. My mom signed on as a cook on a merchant ship and never came back. I'll probably never know what happened to her. At least your grandfather stuck around."

"Trust me, it would be better if he hadn't."

Lyssa turned to Brohr, a reply arrested on her lips as she froze. She grabbed his forearm. Crickets chirped in the twilight.

160

Lyssa cocked her head to listen, and so did he. Back the way they'd come, the percussion of galloping horse hooves echoed along the road.

Lyssa darted to one side of the path and Brohr to the other. They crouched in the gloom, waiting for the rider. The figure rounded the last bend. Whatever his errand, it must have been urgent to risk the horse stumbling in the dark.

Brohr felt around at his feet until he found a stone a little bigger than his fist. He cocked back and waited for the courier to pass. When the horse was twenty paces away, Brohr sprung up and hurled the stone at the soldier, striking him on the shoulder. The horse startled and bucked the man from the saddle.

Brohr dashed across the road, raised his short sword, and hacked at the rider. His first blow struck the legionary's helm, dazing him. The second cut deep in his neck, a ribbon of hot blood splashing up in Brohr's face. The horse whinnied and faltered. The stumble frightened it even more, but it didn't lame the beast. When the smell of death reached its nose, it laid its ears back and bolted up the road at a gallop, disappearing into the night.

Brohr turned back to the fallen rider, realizing for the first time that he alone, and not his brother, had killed this man. His stomach churned, and a hot flash brought sweat to his brow. The moment of violence echoed in his mind's eye, and he shuddered, reliving the wounds, horrified at how fragile a man could be. Lyssa emerged from her hiding place. She squinted down at the soldier's corpse and then at Brohr.

"Why did you do that? Why didn't you just let him ride past?"

Brohr squinted down the road in the direction the horse had disappeared. He closed his eyes, wiped the soldier's cooling blood from his face. "It couldn't be helped. Why?" He gritted his teeth. "Do you feel sorry for him?" Brohr pointed at the body. "Do you think he'd feel sorry for you? Or me?"

"That's not what I mean," said Lyssa. "It's dangerous."

He'd already been hanged today. What was left to fear? Brohr looked down at the corpse. He forced himself to stare, to see it.

"I killed the soldier who murdered your father." Brohr held up his bloody sword in the moonlight. "I cut right through his shoulder with this, and he looked down at it like an idiot. A lot of it is fuzzy, but I remember him looking down at the sword point."

"Good," she said. Lyssa knelt beside the legionary, her mouth drawn in a grim line. "I do feel bad for him." She fixed Brohr with a glare, her eyes bright amidst the shadowy contours of her face. "But I'm glad he's dead. Better him than us."

The soldier wore a satchel over his shoulder, and Brohr's attack had cut the strap. It lay beside the corpse.

"I think he must've had an important message." She opened the satchel and found a scroll sealed with wax inside. She un-slung her pack again and sorted through its contents until she found a candle and matches. Careful not to tear the parchment, she broke the seal and handed the message to Brohr.

"Hold this open for me." Lyssa bent down, struck a match against the stone, and lit the candle.

Brohr crouched beside her and held the dispatch up to the light. The markings were gibberish to him. He was embarrassed to admit he couldn't read, but when she gasped, he couldn't help himself.

"Well," Brohr asked. "What does it say?"

Lyssa turned to him, watching his expression in the candlelight.

"It says," she began. "Ordinal Ennio— Disorder in Skolja. Execute the mine's prisoners. Return with all refined ore immediately. -Prefect Brasca Quoll."

"Fathers," Brohr cursed.

"How many people do you think that is?" Lyssa asked.

"How should I know?" he said. "A lot."

Brohr reached down and grabbed the soldier under the armpits, dragging him out of the road and hiding his body in a briar patch. When he returned, Lyssa had extinguished the candle and stood waiting.

"The outlaws are up near the mine somewhere. I read some letters my father had that said so."

Brohr looked down the path toward Pederskald. "I should have left Skolja years ago. But I let one thing after another drag me back. They're on their own. We all are."

Lyssa laughed at him, shaking her head. "Well aren't you just a heart of stone?"

"Do you think they'd stick their necks out for some half-caste stranger?" Brohr thumped his chest. "Cause I don't."

"You think it makes you strong to be so cold?" Lyssa spat over her shoulder. "I don't know, maybe they wouldn't help you. So now you're just like them, aren't you?"

Brohr tugged at his collar where the rope burn had scabbed over. She stared at him and he looked away, squinting down the road. Pederskald was there, waiting a day or two's hike. And he wanted it to be a different world there, but he knew it wasn't. He was always one step away from leaving. Always so close until something brought him back. What was it about this place that wouldn't let him go? He wanted to run. Just to break into a sprint and leave it all behind him. He wanted to get as far away from his grandfather and all the others who had scorned and hated him his whole life. But in the pit of his stomach, he knew that Pedskald would have a whole new batch of folks to hate him, and that he would have lost the closest thing to a friend that he had left in this world.

Brohr let out a long sigh and nodded. "Alright, Pederskald will have to wait. You're right, we can't let them hang all those men."

Lyssa set her hand on his shoulder and nodded. She smiled, and Brohr felt a tightness in his chest, a strange pride that he had pleased her.

"I know what it's like to put your dreams on hold," she said. "After my mother left, I daydreamed non-stop about stowing away on a ship. About finding her on the high seas. I wanted to captain a ship some day. But if I'd left too, I don't think my pa could have taken it. After what my mother did."

They headed up the road in silence as Quaya and the Wanderer drew closer to one another. Before they reached the crossroads, the two seemed almost to touch. Lyssa was first to notice the strange new nimbus of light surrounding the side of the moon behind which the comet had disappeared. At first it was a simple curiosity. But his grandfather's ramblings sounded in his ears as they trudged on toward the crossroads. He watched as the hue of the moon faded, the impacted quadrant bleeding from red to gray. Lyssa noticed his intensity. "What's wrong?"

He pointed up at Quaya. "My grandfather was right," he said.

"What did he say?" she asked. An owl hooted somewhere ahead.

"Disaster," said Brohr.

A sliver of blackness crept through the center of the red moon. The surreal fissure widened as the minutes passed, a crack in the sanity of all who beheld it. Brohr and Lyssa stopped to gape at the vein of darkness that cut through Quaya's heart. Wolves howled their lament in the hills. A ruby halo ringed the horror, a crown of ruin to frame the glinting pieces of the shattered moon. Lyssa knelt and whispered prayers to Father Freyan. The top half of Quaya drifted apart from the rest, the fractures spreading with agonizing lethargy. Brohr felt lightheaded and realized he had been holding his breath.

The moon was broken.

Hair stood up on Brohr's forearms, his brother's wonder made manifest. They stood in awe of the majestic nightmare, lost in the luster of their doom. He had never imagined that the end of the world could be so beautiful.

Chapter 16

"When the apple falls, the tree will shake. When the pigs cry out, a slaughter make. When a man's in your way, cut the knave. And when the world grows old, dig her a grave.

-Jonas Wulfrick, The Dire Hour

The clearing above the outlaw encampment afforded a spectacular view, but as the night drew on, many wandered the woods in search of solitude. Alarm receded to foreboding, a rich broth of wonder and dread in which they stewed, each looking up, struggling to come to terms with the enormity of their peril.

Some of the men whimpered. Some wept. One gathered his family and fled into the forest. But Anders was content to let the outlaws steep in their fear. Gareth seemed as dumbstruck as the rest. Soon, Anders would offer them a hope to which they might cleave.

He emerged into another glen, his eyes drawn up to the shattered moon, wreathed in a corona of crimson dust. When at last he dragged his eyes back to the forest, Anders discovered he was not alone. Gareth's boy. Lost in thought. He stared up at the deadly sky, his mouth open, shifting his weight back and forth to spare his bad leg.

Perhaps it was time to begin his work. Anders approached, hands clasped behind his back. Though he closed to within a few feet, Nels still startled when he spoke. "Terrifying, isn't it?"

Nels turned away for a moment, dabbing at his eyes. "Yes," he said. "Only a fool would pretend it wasn't."

Anders nodded as if this was wisdom. "Nothing like this has ever happened." The skald looked up at the grim augury above. "Our horror should be absolute." He let his words sink in, but Nels seemed hardly to notice them. "Unless," Anders said, "there is a dire sort of hope here."

"What sort of horse shit is that?" Nels pointed at Quaya. "Look!"

Anders nodded. "Do you believe in the old stories?"

Nels studied the old man by the light of the dying moon. "What sort of game are you playing? My father warned me you were a cunning old snake."

Anders shrugged. "Your father has always been cautious. Some would say timid. Your mother propped up his courage. Without her, he seems... lost. Little doubt he will counsel that caution now. Hide under the blanket until it's all over." Nels did not defend his father, Anders noted. Good. "Perhaps we're all doomed to perish. In that case, what do we risk by fighting? The pigs will never be as vulnerable as they are now."

Nels stiffened. "My father rules here." He slid the dagger from his belt. "Not you."

Anders spit. "I don't care who rules this wretched band. Besides, what of your mother? That's where your strength comes from. Her people came from Grisben. Have you ever seen the bones of that city? I have." Anders looked up at the carnage. "Did your mother ever tell you stories about it?" Nels didn't reply. "I suppose I can't blame her if she didn't. It was a... a bad time to be alive. The things they did. The things we did." Anders shook his head. "I just want you to help make your father see some sense. You've been cowering out here for a generation. Waiting like sheep for precious Olaf to wake and fight your battles for you. Look up! Either we'll be damned or be free. What use is hiding now?"

Nels watched him for a moment before looking back at the sky. His eyes teared up again, and this time he didn't bother hiding it. Gareth's son tucked the blade back in his belt.

Did he really need this whinging half-Hemmish cripple? Anders prayed to Father Freyan for patience. He must wield the tool at hand. Had he not felt fear when the Hidden came? Surely he had. But he had mastered his heart. Anders glanced over his

166

shoulder as if the creature might be lurking even now. The path of greatness followed a dark route. The price of freedom was pain and death. He would not let his suffering steer him from it, nor the suffering of anyone else. He laid it all upon the altar.

★★★★★

"How in damnation are we supposed to sleep with that up there?" Lyssa asked.

Brohr rolled over to face her. They were wet and miserable already; add the heavens exploding overhead, and it seemed impossible to him too. In truth, he had been thinking of Birgit, thinking of Vili holding her hand in the square as they came to watch him hang. He rolled over and looked up through the forest canopy where the clouds had covered the horror. Still, it was up there.

"I can't sleep either," he said.

She laughed at him. "No kidding." Lyssa rolled on her back, staring up through the pines at the ruddy patch of clouds concealing Quaya. "I feel like the whole world could catch fire any second. I'd almost rather it was over. At least that way I wouldn't have to worry about it."

"My grandfather doesn't drink often," Brohr said. "But once in a while, when he does, he recites the black verses. It always baffled me that he would know the forbidden parts of the sagas. Usually I thought he was making them up." Brohr laced his fingers behind his head for a pillow. The clouds parted, and he glimpsed the wreck of Quaya. "Once he told me a different version of Father Freyan's victory over Grenja. And how the moon was not always red but once as white as bone."

Lyssa ran her finger from the corner of her eye and winked at him. "Just in case."

Brohr shook his head, fighting a grin. "Grenja grew in darkness. She came from the void, the mother of horrors, a great, starry serpent with three heads and three crowns upon those heads. And on each crown was written a terrible curse.

167

"Freyan and his brothers surrounded her, raising their voices, a harmony of war. But Freyan's eldest brother read the curse writ across Grenja's first crown and was filled with the knowledge that he would be forgotten, that he would be devoured without striking a blow. A terrible sadness overwhelmed him, and in that instant, one of Grenja's maws snapped him up and swallowed him to the dead place.

"Freyan's second brother charged the horror, but just before his blow landed, his eye chanced upon the second crown and the curse there scrawled. In that instant, he understood all of Grenja's strangeness, and he staid his blow, feeling a hint of kinship for the thing. But Grenja had no such mercy in her, and she devoured him too.

"Seeking to follow his brothers to the dead place, Freyan cast his gaze upon the final crown. But Freyan was ignorant of letters—he disdained the lies trapped inside them—and so he was safe from Grenja's final curse.

"But he was alone then and could not abide the loss of his brothers. Always they had been together whether in the field, in the mead hall, or the shield wall. Great Freyan could no longer bear the pain of being a man. And so he cut himself that the pain might drown the thoughts of all that had gone where it could not return. His mighty song became a howl, and Freyan made a beast of himself to slip free the knowledge of his loss. His fury made him powerful, and he joined Grenja in the sky, biting and thrashing and clawing. He split open her belly, the torrent of blood so vast it stained the moon forever red that when men should look up at it, they remember how all things end."

Lyssa socked him in the shoulder. "Well that was cheerful," she said. "Can't wait to hear the rest of those."

Brohr shrugged, fighting off a shiver. The ground was damp beneath him, and the night could almost pass for winter. Brohr didn't want to look weak in front of Lyssa, but he was too cold to care any longer, so he tucked his legs up into a ball and cradled them.

She looked over at him, adjusted her blanket, and growled in frustration. "Are you cold?" she asked.

"A little."

She didn't say anything, but he could guess at the wheels turning in her head.

"Fine," said Lyssa, holding up the blanket on his side. "I'm cold too." She had concealed a knife, which she beckoned him with. "Don't get any ideas," she said.

Brohr scooted over and let her cover him with part of the blanket. "Too cold for any of that."

Lyssa tucked the dagger away. "Well, even if you warm up, just don't get your prick sliced off. It's been a rough night already. Okay?" She waited a tick. "Okay?"

"Yeah," said Brohr. "Okay."

Satisfied, she nestled up to him. "You'd better be the front spoon."

"What?"

"Roll over, you big lug. I don't want you shoving that thing against me all night."

"Oh," he said. "Yeah, okay." He rolled over, facing away from her.

She cozied up behind him, her body pressing against his back. Lyssa threw one arm around him, and Brohr held his breath.

"Ten Fathers," she whispered. "Breathe, Brohr. It's just cold. Nothing is going to happen. No matter what."

Brohr exhaled. He was glad she couldn't see his embarrassment. A minute ago, he'd been pining for Birgit. And suddenly this. He shook his head.

"What?" she asked.

"Nothing."

"What? Come on."

"Do you know Birgit Gelstrom?"

"The one who came to the bar," she said. "Pretty."

"I was just thinking of her."

Lyssa laughed. "Don't think too hard."

"That's not what I meant." Brohr pictured Birgit and Vili holding hands again. "We were going to run away together."

Lyssa sat up. "What happened?"

169

"My brother. He's like a black cloud, always hovering in the back of my mind. It was like the square or with Torin. Except it was my best friend. After he stabbed me in the back. I lost my temper, and I hurt him. Now she's with Vili."

"Well," she said. "Remind me not to piss you off. Is your brother always angry? Is he evil?"

Brohr bit his lip. "For a long time, I thought so. I didn't know it was my brother, it was just the thing that always haunted me. A ball of anger. That ruined things. That hurt people. But lately... like tonight... we looked up at the moon. He felt like I did. He was amazed."

"So he's not evil."

Brohr shrugged. "Tell that to Torin."

"You didn't kill Torin, remember? That thing did. Besides, Torin was a man-sized piece of shit. He needed a good whooping."

"It's just... I just wish I could be alone once. I just want to get away from my brother, just for a minute. So I could just be alone."

"Uh," Lyssa squinted around the woods. "Is he here now?"

"He's always here. He's just, it's hard to explain. Sometimes he's more here. Does that make sense?"

"Nope."

Brohr rolled onto his back to look at her. "It's like he's always half-asleep. And sometimes a thing will wake him up."

"That's when people get killed."

"Not always," said Brohr. "Sometimes he's just excited or even sad. But yeah, seems like all of a sudden that's when people get killed."

Lyssa laid back down. "I think you're lucky."

"Lucky?" he asked. "Me and Birgit were going to leave this place. We were going to go to Pederskald, where they don't care if you're a shade. Then my damned brother lost his mind when I got in a fight with Vili. Now Birgit thinks I'm a monster, and she's with him. And she won't talk to me."

"Ten Cocks!" Lyssa poked him in the ribs. "Sounds like one of the sagas. Besides, if she's already locking legs with your best friend, she was probably a tramp anyway." Brohr brooded on that until she poked him again. "Hey," she said. "Are you about to go berserk again? Say something."

"No," he said. "Just wishing is all."

"Wish in one hand and you know what in the other."

Brohr growled. "And now we're going to the outlaws, and my grandfather will be there. Damn! Every time I try to get away from here, something worse drags me back."

"To Skolja or to him?"

Brohr pondered the distinction. "Him," he concluded.

"Maybe you just need to—"

"Enough! Can we just try to sleep?" Brohr hadn't meant to shout. He wiped spit off his chin. "I'm sorry. It's just been the worst day of my life is all. I was hanged today, remember?"

She edged away, taking the blanket with her. "Yeah," she said. "You weren't the only one."

Brohr grabbed the corner of the blanket and rolled away from her. He lay there, shivering, searching for the courage to apologize, but before he found it, Lyssa began to snore.

Chapter 17

"The overarching framework of Cassianism is essentially intact in the various religions of the system. Even barbaric cultures such as the Norn and Shinei, who venerate their dead in place of the divine Pontiff, effectively subscribe to the cosmological narrative of the Federal Scriptures; the Shining Ones created mankind, were destroyed by filial discord, and bequeathed the world of the living to their mortal creations before departing to govern the afterlife."

-Ariano Erebin, Tyranny of the Elders

The knock freed Henrik from his nightmare, pulling him up from his burning home into his bed at the High Tavern. Whoever was pounding on the door was relentless. A soldier, no doubt. The air on his face was cold, but beneath the down comforter, he was delightfully snug.

"Mayor Henrik?" The knocking resumed.

He resisted the urge to throw the bedside lamp at the door, instead kicking off the covers and rising to his feet. "A moment!" Henrik snapped.

He pulled his shirt on and buttoned it as he went to the door. *Thus begins another glorious day in office,* he thought. When he opened the door, it was not a soldier knocking, though a pair of them stood in the hallway looking anxious. Henrik didn't know the fellow by name, but his knuckles bore the concentric triangle tattoos fishermen employed to ward off the Mara. He smelled of the sea and his feet were bare and filthy.

"Ten Fathers, man!" Henrik berated him. "I've only just gone to bed. What is it now?"

"Beg your pardon, sir, but it's morning."

Henrik looked over his shoulder where light seeped through the shutters.

"Get on with it," Henrik said.

The fisherman took off his stocking cap and scratched his beard. "It's the tide, sir. The tide is all wrong."

Henrik's stomach clenched. "What do you mean?"

"I've never seen the tides this high, sir. It's a foot higher than I ever seen it, and it shouldn't be high tide for a while yet."

"Damn." Henrik retreated into his room and sat on the bed. There was no sense in trying to avoid it now. He pulled on his boots and then buckled them, muttering. Whatever awaited them had begun. First, Henrik addressed the senior soldier in the hallway. "You should run up to the fort and inform the prefect." He turned to the fisherman before receiving a reply. "Show me."

With Henrik and the remaining soldier in tow, the fisherman hustled down the stairs two at a time, turning back to the mayor with obvious impatience. They hurried through the deserted taproom and out into the morning air. Henrik paused to survey the sleepy town, crouched at the foot of the hill beside the sea. To his left rose Skolja's other hilltop, upon which lay the ruins of his house and Olaf's shrine, backlit by the sun rising over the distant mountains.

The fisherman called back to him, already halfway down the stone steps to the square. Henrik hurried after him. From up high, nothing looked amiss. Even as he crossed the square though, alarm registered on the faces of the folk he passed. The sky showed no trace at all of last night's spectacle. The pieces of Quaya had set a few hours ago. It wasn't until they passed the low market that Henrik spied the crowd gathered at the beach.

Normally, at high tide the water rose to a few feet below the docks and left a stretch of rocky shoreline. He saw why the man was so alarmed; the docks were nearly swamped already, waves breaking over their planks. At most there was a few feet of shore before the bushes and trees took root.

Henrik observed Skolja's shoreline carefully, calculating the distance from the seaward foot of High Hill to the rocky outcropping over by the mill at the opposite edge of town.

"What does it mean?" the fisherman asked.

Henrik ordered his thoughts. He ignored the fisherman, prioritizing a list of actions before turning to the remaining soldier.

"I need you to go and wake Ivar at the general store. Send him here at once. Suffer no excuses. Then return to the fort and wake the prefect if he is not already up. He must come as well."

The soldier folded his arms. "You don't command me. My orders are to guard you. I can't leave you alone."

"This is an emergency. Do as I say." The legionary took note of the crowd watching and puffed up a bit, resting one hand on his sword. Henrik looked him squarely in the eye. He reached into the pouch on his belt and held up a binding stone. "Do you know what this is?" The soldier nodded, taking a step back. "Good. If you do not do as I say this instant, I will loose it right up your stubborn ass."

The federal shrank further back, hesitating. Henrik closed his eyes and bluffed the beginnings of a loosing. That was enough for the legionary, who spun about in such haste that he stumbled, scurrying off to the fort. The effect was so comical that the crowd forgot for a moment the reason they had gathered and basked in their tiny victory.

"What is your name?" Henrik asked the fisherman.

He seemed offended. "Glenyl, young master. You don't know me?"

Henrik patted him on the shoulder. "Of course, Glenyl. It has been difficult to sleep these last nights."

The fisherman nodded even as the others gathered around.

"First," said Henrik. "No one goes to sea today. Prepare for a tempest. So anyone with a boat, drag it well ashore before the tide steals it." They nodded, hungry for answers. "Who has a wagon?" Henrik asked. No one responded. "Who knows someone nearby with a wagon then?"

"Rogan, the smith, has one." A dowdy woman carrying a wicker laundry basket offered. "And so does old Axl."

"Good," said Henrik, nodding to her. "Go and wake them. Get those wagons down here right away. Be sure to tell them it's an emergency. Go on." She set her basket down and shuffled off into town. "Now," said Henrik, turning to a scrawny teenage boy. "You run to the mill and bring back every empty sack there. Every one."

The spindly boy nodded.

"Off you go then. Everyone else start knocking on doors. I want every man in town here within the hour. Skolja is in danger of flooding. We've got work to do. Get!"

★★★★★

The outlaws intercepted Brohr and Lyssa not far past the crossroads. A squad of woodsmen reeking of sweat and campfire emerged from the forest surrounding them. Their leader hobbled forward, broad shouldered but back twisted to favor his left leg. Hints of gray flecked his dark beard.

"*Skel!*" The limping man called to them in old Norn. He carried a longbow, an arrow knocked and drawn, the black fletching just below his eye.

Brohr held up his hands, sword still tucked in his belt. Lyssa took a step forward and held up her hands as well.

"*Skel,*" she returned the greeting. "We're friends. We've come from Skolja. Brohr killed a federal messenger last night. Before…"

"You saw?" asked the leader.

Another of the outlaws stepped forward. He had bad teeth and a torn cloak. Brohr caught the hint of a tattoo on his neck. "Now that's a stupid question, Nels! How in damnation could they miss it?"

Still, the man, Nels, waited for an answer.

"We saw," she said. "What's it mean?"

"It means we fight!" The man in the torn cloak lowered his bow and raised his fist like he was grabbing a federal by the collar. He stomped up to Brohr, his breath so foul that it led him by a few paces. "You got black hair!" He narrowed his eyes.

"Skins muddy too." He looked meaningfully at the other outlaws. "I wouldn't trust this one."

Brohr leaned away from him, waving away the stink. "You have to get that close to get a good look?" Brohr shoved him back a step.

He laughed, leaning forward again and intentionally exhaling in Brohr's face. "What's your business here, piggy?"

"Like she said. The message."

Their leader stepped up, pushing the bully aside. He held out his hand. "Let's see it."

Lyssa set her pack down and dug out the dispatch, handing it to the outlaw. He took a few steps back and unrolled the scrap of parchment.

The man with the horrid breath crowded in and stared over his shoulder. "What's it say?" he asked.

The leader elbowed him back. "Kriega's balls, Lar! You been eating dead fish again? Get away!"

The others chuckled. Brohr got the feeling it wasn't a new joke. The man, Lar, turned to despise them all, one by one.

"Well, what's it say?" Lar insisted.

The squad leader rolled up the note but didn't return it. "They're closing up the mine. Going to kill the miners too. My father will want to see this."

"Yes," Lar agreed. "But will he do anything?"

★★★★★

"Blood of my Fathers!" Anders spat in the fire. "You are a coward. A total coward."

"Lower your voice." Gareth looked around the camp at the staring womenfolk.

"Do you want to die in your cursed tent?"

The old outlaw paced the opposite side of the campfire. He folded his arms and huffed. He was coming around, Anders decided.

"Keeping my people safe is no joke," said Gareth. "We're not just a pack of vagabonds. As you see, we have families. If I let you take a few men, you could endanger the entire camp."

Anders held out his hands to warm them. "I see I've misjudged you. I hoped that despite our past you would be an ally. You've raided the mine before after all. Or was that Marta's idea? When did you lose your last shred of nerve?"

Gareth stopped pacing. He clasped his hands behind his back and straightened his spine. "You would do well to have a little fear, Anders Nilstrom. I am a dangerous man."

Anders laughed in pure delight. Shaking his head, he casually took the knife from his belt and ran the blade across his finger. He flicked a little blood into the fire and returned the blade to his belt.

The motion was so unthreatening that the terror didn't touch Gareth's face until the knife was put away and the blood hissing in the fire. Anders sucked on his cut fingertip as Gareth crumpled to the ground. The outlaw threw up a hand to protect himself from a phantasm only he could see. He scurried backwards through the dirt and pine needles until he ran into a stump and yelped like a kicked dog. The sound broke the enchantment, and Gareth looked up with horror, wide-eyed at the mirth on his old rival's face.

"Get up, Gareth. You're embarrassing the women."

Anders waited for Gareth to regain his feet and dust himself off. The outlaw glanced around the camp, blushing at the number of people staring.

"You have some pine needles in your hair, Gareth." Anders pointed at his own gray locks.

"Monster," Gareth hissed. "You won't control us with your black magic. We are free people."

Anders shook his head. "Hardly. Is this freedom?" He indicated the camp. "And besides, it was just a reminder not to muck around with me. *I* am the dangerous one." His tone softened. "But I don't want to fight you, old friend. I want to fight *beside* you."

Gareth put his hands on his hips. "What happens if we fight? What happens if we rise up and kill every federal from Skolja to Pederskald? What happens then?"

Anders examined the cut on his fingertip. He blew on it, and it scabbed over. "Then we win, obviously."

"Fool! Don't you think there are more of them out there? More than you can imagine. You think about Skolja as if it was the whole world. Well I've seen the rest of the world, and it's all federals. From here to Old Hemmings, and out there, there are even more of them." He gestured toward the sky.

"The blood is strong, Gareth. I know you don't hear it pounding in your ears. You're not a Norn." Anders shrugged. "But we feel it. That's why your men will fight. They know that the blood calls for battle. So that is what happens if we kill them all from here to Pederskald. We'll meet our cousins there, and they'll be soaked in Tyrianite blood too. We'll drink to the Fathers then and sing songs. Even your son feels the call. It's no shame that he's a shade. His mother's blood is stronger. He's Norn too."

Gareth grasped the hilt of his sword, but Anders didn't mind. They were past the moment of violence, and after all, it was true that Gareth was a coward. A moment later, Gareth wilted, taking his hand from his blade. "My son is no shade. He's got no pig blood in his veins. Unlike that whelp of yours."

Anders hated him. Hated this pathetic last thrash of defiance. He was already beaten. He might look strong and healthy outside, but within, Gareth was withered, weak, Hemmish.

"Old friend," Anders said. "Let's put this squabble behind us. We are on the same side, after all. This is your camp. I make no claim on it. These are your people. But they are Norn. Their hour has come. Let them fight."

Gareth fussed with a button on his vest, eyes downcast. "We shall have a council tonight. That is our way. We shall discuss it, and I'll decide then."

Anders nodded, satisfied. Good, he was beaten but not completely broken.

Anders left Gareth to stare into the fire and enlisted one of the wives to help him erect the tent they had given him. After it was set up, Anders lay down for a short rest, but just as he was closing his eyes, a horn blew.

Anders hadn't any idea what the signal meant, but obviously he wouldn't be getting any sleep. With a curse, he pushed himself to his feet, his knees cracking as he rose. Outside the tent, he realized that the horn blast was coming from the south side of camp. A crowd had gathered there.

One of the patrols had returned. He gasped, nearly dropped to his knees before mastering himself, willing the tears not to shame his eyes. Brohr. Brohr was there. Alive.

The old man hustled across the camp to the group forming around his grandson. Faith was a fickle thing. He'd wagered everything on him and been promised, but the Hidden was always cryptic. Always wrapping the truth in lies and riddles. Its desires and predictions circumspect. Mercy would make him weak, it had said. Submit or suffer. So he had left the boy to fate. And here he was.

As Anders burst into the group, the others parted for him, and he wrapped the boy in a bear hug, only to find himself sprawled on his ass, his happiness vanished. Brohr glared down, so angry that Anders felt his brother rear up.

"Don't touch me!" Brohr shouted, his voice making the hair on Anders' neck stand up.

Anders held up his hands in surrender. "Wait! Wait!" he pleaded. "What could I do? I knew you were strong enough." He jumped to his feet, defiant, lying. "I knew. Here." Anders pulled Brohr's dagger from his belt and held it out to him. "I knew I'd see you again."

Brohr cocked back his fist. "Bull!" He snatched the knife from his grandfather's hand. "How could you know? You left me to die. You convinced me not to run, and then you left me for dead. They hanged me." Brohr pulled his collar down to show the bruise ringing his neck.

"But you're not dead. You had your brother looking out for you." Anders bared his teeth. "And who do you think gave

179

you that advantage, boy? I did that." Anders thumped his chest. "I did what everyone said was impossible. I did it. Damn the Fathers! I bound you together!"

They all recoiled at his blasphemy. Confusion and suspicion darkened Brohr's face.

"You?" Brohr asked.

The question hung in the air. At least he wasn't enraged. But it still might come. Every word the old man uttered now risked the ire of little Olek. What did he remember? Could he share his secret?

Finally, Anders nodded. "You have greatness in your fury. I gave it to you because I loved your mother and they ruined her. They beat her and raped her and tormented my Flower. They ruined her!" He grabbed Brohr by the elbows. "They sweated and grunted and knocked her teeth out when she spat on them. But they never broke her. Do you see? I bound you together so that you could *murder them!*"

The hair on the back of Anders' neck prickled as Olek wrestled for control of the boy. The old man's heart thundered, reminded of his old crime, his old shame. Olek knew. And it hated him. If he could only steer that hate, perhaps all was not yet lost. Brohr growled, a fell utterance full of eldritch noise that pushed the onlookers back a step. He turned away from his grandfather, hunched there for a moment, grappling for himself. Lyssa lay a hand on his arm, but he tore free, shaking, and stormed off into the night before he lost control.

Chapter 18

"Few accounts exist of men elevating themselves to the Electorate, but the life of Drussa perfectly illustrates the permeability of the caste system. Interested scholars are quick to tarnish the reputations of risen men with words like scoundrel and butcher, but greatness rises, just as the ancients intended."

-Cruscio Iovani, Distinction of the Classes

The sawyers had already felled three tall fir trees, hacked their limbs off, and were busy carving them into lumber. Another team loaded the planks into a dilapidated wagon which was harnessed to an ornery mule. The woodcutters laughed when the mule nipped at one of the men who came too close. Even after everything they had seen last night, the townsfolk didn't realize how much danger they were in. Still, Henrik surveyed their progress, encouraged by how far they had come.

Rocky hills wrapped around Skolja like a horseshoe, leaving the beach unprotected. He was going to build a dike along the shoreline to shield Skolja from the sea, but at the rate the water was rising, it would take the whole town working together to finish it in time.

Henrik left the forest on the far side of High Hill and ran back between the cliff and the sea, across the dwindling stretch of beach, to Skolja's waterfront. When he came around the corner, the sight of all the villagers toiling together heartened him. Two squads of soldiers had arrived, finally, but they milled about, not deigning to help. As he approached, many of the townsfolk took a break to listen for news. One of the soldiers waved him over.

Henrik cupped his hands to his mouth. "Back to work, everyone. All is well."

"Hey!" The soldier who had waved him over scowled. "Get over here."

Gritting his teeth, Henrik trudged across the shore, noting that the workers were about half finished with the first course of sandbags.

"Let's go!" the soldier shouted.

Annoyed but determined to get through the delay as quickly as possible, Henrik hustled over, his wet feet aching from the cold.

"Well?" he asked. "What is it?"

The soldier folded his arms. "The prefect needs to see you in the square immediately."

Henrik scoffed. "Impossible. I have too much to do here. There's no time."

"It isn't a request. You're coming with me. Now."

"Ridiculous, I'm trying to save the town at the moment. The prefect will have to wait."

Henrik turned to leave but the soldier caught him by the arm. "Now," he demanded.

Harsh words gathered in Henrik's throat like bile, but over the soldier's shoulder, he saw the miller's apprentice stop shoveling. The whole beach watched them.

Henrik nodded to the soldier, though he bristled, wanting to pluck a stone from his belt and burn the fool where he stood.

"Keep working!" Henrik shouted. "I'll return shortly."

The remaining soldiers formed up around the mayor, and they all filed off toward the town square, passing the low market, every stall empty, as the townsfolk strove to raise the makeshift dike.

When they reached the heart of Skolja, it was similarly deserted, except for a group of soldiers standing on the porch of the general store and a few pilgrims watching from the opposite side of the square. The squad leader headed inside Ivar's and nodded to the soldiers guarding the entrance.

Henrik cursed. The store was in shambles. The fastidious displays of dry goods and tools had been ransacked. Beans and broken glass crunched beneath his feet. The prefect stood behind

182

the counter, speaking to the weeping shopgirl. When the federal noticed Henrik's arrival, his eyes grew stern.

"Five men wearing masks. They threatened to burn the place down and locked her in the store room. You should have gotten permission before you emptied half the town for your little project." The prefect swiped a hand through the air to indicate the mess. "Look at this. This looting could've been avoided."

"Excuse me, sir," said Henrik. "I've been marshalling the town to defend itself against the sea for hours now. I sent word to you at first light. Was I supposed to wait until you could be bothered to help?"

The prefect shook his head. "You arrogant little shit. Don't think for a second that I can't manage this backwater without you. That shop-keep, Ivar, would lick my boot for a chance to be mayor. Especially now."

Be cold, Henrik told himself. He inhaled and exhaled, considering his next words. "Ivar might lick your boot, but he's not a leader. Which one do you need right now: a leader or a bootlicker?"

The prefect leaned forward until his hat nearly poked Henrik in the face. "I don't need anything."

Again, Henrik wrestled his emotions into stillness. "Don't you see I am trying to help?" Henrik winced at his defiant tone. He held up his hands in apology. "Really, I am. Perhaps I should have considered this." He needed to save face. "Where was Constable Gunnar?"

"At the waterfront with everyone else."

"Well," Henrik said. "I certainly didn't know that. I would've told the twit to see to his duty if I had."

The prefect looked him up and down. "Mmm hmm. No doubt that bungler still has no idea this happened."

"I'll see that he returns at once."

"Wait," said the prefect. "I doubt the good Constable is up to the task of catching the looters. This is a delicate situation, Mayor Torvald. This sort of thing needs to stop before it consumes Skolja. If I have the soldiers tear the town apart

183

looking for the missing goods, it will only increase the tension. Skolja needs its good citizens to act." He set his hand on Henrik's shoulder. "Find me the culprits, and I will take care of it from there."

Henrik thought about the unfinished dike. "I can't abandon the work at the shore. The whole town may flood."

"I'll send Belizar to oversee the project. He's quite capable."

"All right," said Henrik. "What will happen to the looters?"

"They'll be hanged, of course."

Henrik shook his head. "That will only cause more trouble. Can you send them to the mine?"

The prefect started to speak then stopped himself, mulling something over. "Yes," he said. "I'll send them to the mine. But you have to find them today."

★★★★★

Anders folded his arms as he waited for the outlaws to cease their chatter. The last of the patrols had just returned to camp. Already it was late afternoon. The day was nearly wasted. Inaction seemed the weapon of choice for these so-called outlaws. Even now they stood in a large circle, gossiping like fish wives.

"Ten Fathers!" he shouted. "You would think this was harvest festival. Be quiet."

Every head whipped toward Anders. His grandson folded his arms, and Gareth stomped over trying to look tough. It took the Hemmishman a moment to muster the courage to say something.

"That's enough out of you," he said. "I'll tell you when it's your time to speak." Satisfied that Anders would be quiet, he held up his hands and turned to his men. "All right now, gentlemen, we've much to discuss."

Anders grumbled under his breath at the outlander but didn't interrupt.

"As you may have already heard," said Gareth. "We've intercepted a message. This shade killed a federal courier riding out to the mine." Despite Gareth's insult, many of the men nodded to Brohr, a few pumped their fists approvingly. "The message was sent by the prefect himself. It ordered the execution of every prisoner at the mine. Also that the soldiers there return to Skolja."

A chorus of fresh outrage and speculation broke out. As Gareth quieted the furor, Anders scanned about until he found Lar, the vile-breathed lout he'd groomed for this moment. He nodded, and Lar nodded back, a nasty smirk growing on his face.

"Well, why in damnation are we standing around again?" Lar shouted. "Let's go save them."

Gareth glanced from Lar to Anders. "Now hold on," he said.

"Ain't that what we're always doing, Gareth?" Lar asked. "Holding onto our cocks while the world goes to shit."

Before Gareth could respond, Anders jumped in.

"He's right, Gareth. Everyone knows you've kept this band alive by being cautious, but if we don't do something, everyone at that mine is as good as dead. Isn't it time to fight back?"

Nels cut in. "What do you mean 'we,' Nilstrom? You've been here for one day."

"I mean *we*, the Norn folk!" he countered. "The heavens themselves break above our heads and your father wants us to skulk around the hills doing nothing. Nothing! Well if you do nothing, you are nothing. It's now or never. Keep hiding or fight like men."

A silence settled over the outlaws as they weighed the choice he offered.

Gareth wringed his hands. "We've survived for years while other bands were cornered and slaughtered by the pigs. Because we're careful. Because I don't let my pride make my decisions for me. Now more than ever we need to be cautious." Lar and a few others jeered him. "I'm not saying we do nothing. We plan. We do things right. This fool will have us charge up and die to a man rather than wait a few days to strike at the right moment."

Anders cackled. They all turned, waiting for his reply. "How many federals are at the mine?"

Gareth sensed the trap but had to answer anyway. "Twenty, maybe twenty-five."

Anders began to count the men present on his fingers.

Lar took the cue. "There's more of us than them! Ain't it time we fight back? Some of our own are up there."

They nodded to one another, voicing their approval.

A short fellow with stout shoulders stepped up. "It's time, Gareth."

Another outlaw followed suit. Nels put his hand on his father's shoulder, and Gareth sagged. He turned a look of pure venom on Anders, who smiled back. "All right." Gareth said. "But we need to scout first and make a plan. We'll send Nels and a few others out tomorrow, and we can hit them at nightfall next."

The man who had first stepped forward waved off this proposal. "Most of us have seen the mine, Gareth. What use is scouting? Let's get on with it!"

"Today!" Anders shouted.

A few others assented, and Gareth was forced to concede. He had a haunted look in his eyes as he stared at his battle-hungry men.

Anders could hardly wait to kill the coward.

Chapter 19

"The first principle of truth must be to trust the evidence of our senses lest all wisdom be cast into the pit of superstition."

-Zaracas, The Pillars of Knowledge

"We'll need a couple more men," said Henrik.

Ivar dropped an already broken jar on the floor and ran his fingers through his thinning hair. "Well, I don't think I should go." He walked behind the counter as if it would shield him from the responsibility. "I'm not constable or mayor. You two should sort it out."

"Don't be a child," Gunnar said. "If we don't find these men, it will happen again."

"Yes, but I'm no good for this sort of thing. I've never been in a fight in my life."

Henrik knelt to inspect a footprint that one of the culprits had left in some spilt flour. It was small, small enough to be a child's, or perhaps a woman's.

"Ivar," Henrik looked up at him. "If you're too afraid, go fetch your son. He can take your place."

The shopkeeper blushed. He tried to hide it, but it was too late. "Yes, that's a fine idea. I'll go get him."

"We'll need more men than that. There are five looters. At minimum we should outnumber them. Send Rogan too; I know we can trust him at least. But if you can't recruit a couple of others, you'll have to come with us."

Ivar paled. "I'll pick a few men and send them up."

Henrik waved him on his way, still studying the boot print. "Hurry."

"In the meantime," said Constable Gunnar, "let's have a chat with the gawkers in the square. Perhaps one of them saw something useful."

Ivar headed back to the waterfront to find some deputies, while Gunnar and Henrik walked out onto the porch and marched across the square toward some of the onlookers. More townsfolk had gathered since he'd been inside. They stood in little knots, gossiping. Henrik stopped and turned to the constable.

"Gunnar," he said. "Run down to the waterfront and look around. Try to make note of anyone who is down there so we don't waste our time searching their homes."

"Yes, Mayor."

Henrik strutted over to the travelers who'd been watching since he first arrived. The three men stood in the southwest corner of the square, out front of the Pilgrim's Inn, High Hill behind them.

Each of them wore white ribbons tied around their wrists. Two looked like father and son with stout jaws and matching blue stocking caps. The son was a husky young teenager, and his father just getting the first flecks of gray in his beard. The third man stooped a bit, his white hair and beard snarled and greasy. He wore a shabby tunic and woolen hose, patched at the knees, and carried a walking stick that trembled in his hand.

"Greetings," said Henrik.

The father and son lit up at his approach, enjoying the eventful morning. The old man barely seemed to register his arrival.

"Hello there!" The young man, a little taller than Henrik, lit his meerschaum pipe, puffed a few times, and passed it to his father.

"Good morning." The father stepped forward and held out his hand. "Gurnswald Olfrick," he said. "This is my son, Thoril."

Henrik shook hands with each of them. They smelled like sour ale and stale smoke.

"You can call me Gurnsie," the father said. "Everybody does."

Henrik nodded, turning to the old man. He offered his hand, but the hermit didn't take it.

"Did any of you see the robbers?" Henrik asked.

"I saw them." Thoril smiled at his sudden importance. "There were five." He held up five fingers to clarify.

"And you two?"

"I was abed," Gurnsie admitted. He passed the pipe back to his son. "We were celebrating last night, you see."

The old man didn't volunteer anything. "What did you see?" Henrik asked him directly.

"I have nothing to say to a man who abandoned his ancestors to damnation for the chance to feed at the federal trough. Father Tristen would spit on you. Your uncle Olaf would spit on you. I spit on you." The Pilgrim did not, in fact, spit on him. But he turned his head and spat on the ground beside him. The old man cringed, as if Henrik were about to strike him.

Young Thoril broke the tension. "Are you really related to Saint Olaf?"

Gurnsie stepped up and put his hand on his son's shoulder. "This is Mayor Torvald, if I wager, Olaf's great-grandson."

"Grand nephew," Henrik corrected. "Olaf's sons were pressed into slavery. Were the looters on foot or horseback?"

Thoril stepped in front of the old man, eager to answer. "They had horses all right. They rode out of here in a hurry, whooping like old reavers." Thoril pointed west with the stem of his pipe, down the road that led past the smithy and the jail on its way out of town.

"They took the road out into the wood?" Henrik asked. Thoril nodded. "What did they look like? What did their horses look like?"

Thoril scratched his chin, struggling to unearth something useful. He shrugged. "They had axes, I guess. One of the horses

189

was a paint. Had a big spot. A big black spot on its backside. Right here." He cupped his hand on his buttock, laughing.

"Anything else?"

Thoril snapped his fingers. "They were all redheads."

Great, Henrik thought. *Kriegans.*

★★★★★

Lyssa nibbled a loaf of bread that she'd packed while the men kissed their wives and sharpened their axes. Brohr sat beside her on a fallen log, whittling, brooding. While he carved, his lips mouthed angry words, as if he was rehearsing a confrontation in his head. He had blood dried around his collar and behind his ear. A thick bruise ringed his neck. Brohr still wore the red sweater she'd given him, and with a wicked smile, she noted that you really couldn't tell where it had been splattered with the courier's blood.

The outlaws were already forming up, looking for someone to tell them it was time to go. It surprised her that the old man hadn't come to talk to Brohr, he was in the Hemmishman's tent still.

"Brohr," she said. His scowl remained. He ignored her. "Brohr," she tried again.

At last, he pried himself from his thoughts and turned to her. Somehow it reminded Lyssa of drawing a bucket of water up from a deep well. "What?" he said.

"Trying to figure out what to get me for my birthday? It's coming up soon." She hoped to nettle him out of his mood, but Brohr grunted and covered his face with his scab-knuckled hands, blood caked beneath his fingernails. "Out with it," she prodded.

"You ever wonder if the old stories are true?"

That wasn't quite what she had expected. "Were you thinking about that thing on the dock?"

He looked off into the forest. "In a way," he said.

She waited for him to elaborate, but he was content in silence. "I suppose," Lyssa said, "I've always figured that they're stories for children. A little truth maybe."

"And if they are just stories to scare little boys into doing their chores and keeping up the family altar? What of the rest of it?"

"The rest?"

His eyes flared. "Did the Shining Ones promise this land to the Fathers? We conquered this place once. What makes us any better than the Tyrianites?"

She nodded, at last seeing the drift of his thoughts. "Is there any reason to fight, you mean? With everything... why bother?"

"Yes," he stared at her, as if her answer could explain all the bloodshed.

She hadn't meant to sway him, only to draw him out, but the answer came unbidden to her lips. "They murdered my father."

He looked away, his head bobbing. "Yes," he said. "I suppose you're right."

Chapter 20

"Breyga, for all of his glory, did not treat his daughter as a father should. She kept this secret for all of her tender years, a wound festering in her heart, until the day of her brother's wedding feast, when many horns of mead were raised to toast the succession of their proud line."

-Peder the Skald, A Song of Hateful Cups

The rain drenched their search party, but it hadn't yet obscured the hoof prints left by the galloping brigands. They trudged along on foot, cloaks pulled tight against the downpour. The trail led a mile or so up the road and out of town, dwindling out into the hinterland to the haunts of Clan Kriega—the Henstens, the Dorvalds, and the Grafstroms. The Kriegans kept to themselves, occasionally causing trouble at tithe time but not so much as would tighten the federals' noose. They were a clan of hill folk apart from the village, sowing spuds in the rocky soil, marrying one to another—natural suspects. Henrik likely would've come this way, even without the trail to draw him here.

He did not expect a warm welcome.

The rest of the posse lagged behind. Ivar's son, Arius, wore a fine cloak trimmed in ermine. Already, he complained about the weather, but he was young and ambitious, probably good in a fight. Henrik suspected that one day the shopkeep's son would be after his job. For now, he was glad to have him. His friends seemed less imposing. Dirk looked as if he'd drop his axe and run at the first angry word while Orel was stout and dim, one pinky finger habitually rooting in his ear. Rogan, the blacksmith, could cleave a man's skull with those forge-strong arms. Still, he was old. Finally, there was Constable Gunnar. He'd been in plenty of scrapes, true enough, but his experience inspired little confidence.

The tracks grew fainter as the bandits had slowed from their mad gallop, the downpour eroding the hoofprints into a muddy mess. Still, it didn't take a woodsman to follow five horses through the mud. Dark clouds gathered overhead, and thunder growled in the east. Henrik peered into the gloomy woods. This was their country. If the Kriegans ambushed them, they would know just the spot to do it.

The prints split in two directions. One set continued up the road while the other turned off toward Erk Grafstrom's farm. Just after harvest, Henrik had been out this way collecting tithes with his father, and he remembered the place. Erk was young, his wife pregnant.

Gunnar peered ahead. "I have a bad feeling about—"

Henrik cut him off. "Keep your mouth shut and your eyes open. They might be waiting to ambush us." The posse traded worried looks.

Up ahead, the road opened up onto the Grafstrom farm. Henrik and the others squatted just outside the clearing, watching Erk dig in the mud. Grafstrom labored beside a stout barrel, burying his share of the loot. Henrik motioned for his men to huddle around him and whispered, "Arius, take Dirk and Orel around the back. Stay out of sight and don't make any noise. When you get there, fan out and get as close as you can without him seeing. We'll do the same from over here. There may be others in the house, so keep an eye on it. But don't let him get away no matter what. The last thing we need is Grafstrom rounding up his kin." Henrik eyed them one by one. "Do you understand the plan?"

They nodded, and the trio of Arius and his friends went creeping off around the perimeter of the farmstead. Branches cracked under their feet, and they skirted the farm too closely, but the rain picked up, and the sound masked their bungling.

Rogan and Gunnar spread out too, and each crouched at the edge of the wood, peering at the tree line on the opposite

193

side of the farm. Over by the house, a dog barked and Grafstrom's head shot up, scanning the field for trouble. The dog barked on, its nose in the air as it trotted out toward Gunnar's hiding spot.

Arius and his friends broke from cover before they had circled all the way around.

Henrik plucked a stone from the pouch on his belt and shot to his feet. He sang three dour notes, a trio of argent runes erupting around his fist, circling, the scintillating figure of a rat floating from the stone as a swirling smoke. Henrik willed the animus into a shield, and it spun around him like a whirlwind, the flash of magic catching Grafstrom's eye.

Henrik charged, and Rogan and Gunnar followed him into the open, bellowing war cries.

Erk Graftstrom dropped his shovel and scooped up his bow, snatching an arrow from his quiver, nocking it and drawing in one fluid motion. He let fly, and the arrow sailed across the clearing, caroming off Henrik's ward with another flash. Grafstrom's jaw dropped. He backpedaled and slipped in the mud, but before they could close on him, he popped back up with his bow in hand, nocking another arrow.

Henrik gripped a second stone in his fist. He sounded the notes of his cant and cracked the mystic cage which bound the spirit. Runes blazed around his fist and loosed the molten rat within. Flame darted from Henrik's hand to the looter's neck. Grafstrom screamed. Panicked, he dropped his bow and clutched at the ravenous spirit gnawing and searing his jugular. He tried to run and fell into the hole he'd been digging.

By the time Henrik reached the edge, he looked down at the man writhing in his open grave. The posse gathered around the hole, watching Erk Grafstrom's death throes, covering their noses at the smell of burning flesh.

Henrik had never killed a man before. Erk Grafstrom seemed so pathetic and overmatched as the rain doused his smoldering corpse. He wondered if these men would talk of this, if word would get back to the prefect. It was perfectly legal for a man of the ally caste to practice, and Brasca knew that he was a

194

binder, but a wary voice told him it was best to hide how far he'd come.

Yet the deed was done. They'd only whisper all the louder if he told them it was a secret.

"Arius," he said. "Lead those two around to the back of the house."

Arius nodded, taking one last look in the hole before heading behind the cottage. After retreating to the edge of the wood, Grafstrom's dog bayed at the men who had killed its master, keeping a leery distance. Henrik jogged up to the front porch, flanked by the smith and the constable. Once they were in position, he tried the door, but it was bolted. So, he pounded on it.

"Open up in there, in the name of the law. This is Mayor Torvald."

After a moment, a woman's voice answered. "Where is my husband?"

"Your husband is dead. He committed robbery and tried to murder me. Open this door right now."

Inside, the baby shrieked. "I'm not coming out," the widow said. "You killed my husband! You'll just kill me too."

Henrik pounded on the door again. "If you do not open this door, I will be forced to burn you out. Think of your child."

The rain pattered on the thatched roof, poured off it in spouts as they all strained to listen to her response. The dog whined behind them, dusk approaching. At last the bolt slid open.

Henrik motioned for Gunnar to go in first. The constable entered with his axe high, backing the widow into a corner. She clutched her wailing child in one arm, her ragged blue dress wet at the nipple from which she'd been nursing.

"Arius!" Henrik shouted. "Get in here."

The men ransacked the little cottage as the widow tried to quiet her baby, finding a small sack of beans, some butter, and a keg of beer that had come from Ivar's.

"Dirk," Henrik snapped his fingers. "Take the child."

"No!" The woman screamed, tucking the infant away from Dirk's grasp. "No!"

"Don't make us get rough." Henrik said. "We won't harm the child. Is it a boy or girl?"

"A girl."

"And what is her name?"

"Elise."

Henrik did not smile, but his voice was gentle. "Give Elise to Dirk here. He won't hurt her. Otherwise he'll have to wrestle her from you."

The widow kissed her baby on the forehead and handed her to Dirk with trembling hands. Her posture grew rigid, and she looked at Henrik like something foul she had discovered on her boot.

Henrik nodded. "Good," he said. "I think we understand one another."

Predictably, she spat on him. In a way, he admired her. Even if she was a backwater fool, at least she had some iron in her veins.

"You're going to tell me who rode into town with your husband." Henrik glanced pointedly at her daughter. "Think of your poor child."

She lunged at him, but Rogan and Arius held her by the elbows. The widow swore tearful oaths against him and spat once more at his feet. She whispered prayers to Father Kriega. But to her credit, that was all she'd say.

★★★★★

"New orders, sir?" Ordinal Belizar stood beside the dike, looking back at the prefect.

Brasca shook his head. "Still nothing," he said. "The helm is useless. Too much noise."

The water beyond the dike had risen just above the first course of sandbags. Norns splashed around, setting logs about a man's height to hold the bags in place. The third layer was

196

already laid across the length of the beachhead. It seemed the work would be done well before nightfall.

"The water is still rising," noted the prefect.

Amusement flashed across the ordinal's pudgy face, but he hid it at once. "Yes, sir," he said.

Of course, they'd been racing it all day. Perhaps Belizar thought it was an obvious, asinine comment. He hoped it was not a hint of insubordination. The Prefect waved for him to follow and walked far enough from the workers that they would not be heard.

"I didn't just come to inspect your progress." Brasca took his hat off and looked out at the angry sea. "Nothing yet from the mine. Not even the courier has returned." Belizar stood at attention, holding his breath. Brasca continued, "At the very least, the courier has been waylaid."

"We should send a detachment to investigate at once."

Brasca shook his head. He gestured at the dike then looked back at the town. "Things are tense enough here already. Violence could erupt in an eyeblink. We can't afford to send a significant number of men. Further dividing our forces will only weaken us."

Belizar turned toward him, his posture coiling.

"You may speak," said the prefect.

"To hell with this town," said the ordinal. "We're here for cold iron aren't we? Why waste it? We should march out to the mine and unite our forces. Then we can march back and retake the town if need be. Our soldiers and the ore should be our concern. Not this worthless town."

"Enough." Brasca stared his ordinal down. "Have you forgotten Quaya? Are we to abandon all of our food cache, the wagons?" He kneaded his temples, grimacing at the sudden headache. "What if a transport ship comes? Do you want to be on the road when catastrophe strikes? What if the village moves into the fort while we're gone?" He clasped his hands behind his back and began to pace. "I'm afraid those men are on their own. It would be unwise to send them reinforcements when they've already been recalled to reinforce *us*. As for the ore, my superiors may find it a convenient excuse to burn me at the stake, but I'd rather face that than get my command wiped out hunting for trade goods."

Belizar clenched his jaw. "Of course, sir." He clasped his hands behind his back. "Perhaps we should raze the town?"

"It hasn't come to that," said Brasca.

"And the looting? Has Torvald returned?"

"Not yet." Brasca put his tricorn back on.

"Do you trust him?"

"I trust him to follow his own interests. He's too tangled up with us to break free now. His own people think of him as a collaborator. What can he do but serve?"

Chapter 21

"The slave tithe has proven more effective as the proverbial stick in the southern region of Trondia. The Hemmishmen quickly assimilated the lesson that organized disobedience would garner only the decimation of their population. Though our proffered carrot, elevation to the ally class, has effectively brought the nobility into the fold, the lower orders still kneel to their Hero. Never-the-less, they no longer gather en masse to provoke discord. And thus the stick proves its worth."

-Ollian Barca, The Metrics of Civilization

The mining encampment hunkered at the base of a tiny vale. Several shafts had been cut into the surrounding hills, but only one remained in operation. A palisade of logs, tarred black, with red ivy creeping up the sides, enclosed the outpost. The fortification was just big enough to house a few simple cabins and a one-room smeltery, their thatched roofs and smoking chimneys peeking over the wall. The gate was barred, a watchman standing atop a platform at each corner of the little fortress.

Brohr crouched beside Lyssa, both of them watching the whispered argument between Anders and Gareth. He wondered if the old Hem had it in him to kill his grandfather. He doubted it.

After several minutes of heated discussion, the old men came to an agreement. Anders slipped back into the trees, circling around to the road. He lingered over the corpse of the soldier they'd found guarding the approach. Brohr watched as his grandfather drew a knife and cut the dead man on the forehead. Singing softly, the skald rubbed the blood around his own face, painting it on like a mask. The song buzzed in Brohr's belly like an earthquake; he felt it humming in his teeth. Brohr looked around, but no one else seemed to notice. He felt a twinge of disgust and anger and was surprised to discover that it was his brother. But as soon as the sensation appeared, it was gone again. Once Anders had finished smearing his face with the man's blood, Gareth gave a few hand signals to his men, and they formed up on the lip of the hill, making ready to charge the gate. At the end of his strange song, Anders stood up and ran down the hill toward the mine as fast as his rickety old legs would carry him.

"Open up! Open up!" he cried, running to the foot of the gate.

A sentry looked down from one of the corner platforms. "Malchus? You okay?"

"A message from the prefect!" Anders held up a scrap of the dead man's shirt. "It's urgent. Let me in. The ordinal needs to see this."

The soldier climbed down the ladder which leaned against his platform and jogged over to the gate. One of the other guards called down to him. "Hold on! Astegal, you twit. Get the challenge word. Wait!"

But the entranced soldier didn't hear him. Anders looked back over his shoulder and nodded to where the rest of the outlaws lay in wait. When the ensorcelled legionary unbarred and pushed open the gate, the rest cried alarm.

Brohr broke from cover, dashing down the hill and crossing the open ground to the blackened gate. A thrill washed over him as he fell into a rhythm, feet pounding over the field. His grandfather back-peddled away from the fighting, retreating to a safe distance. Lar slashed the guard who had opened the gate across the belly with his axe. The man dropped to his knees, fumbling with his entrails in the heartbeats before Lar took his head off. Brohr drew his sword, forming up with the other outlaws as they closed in on the federals.

The remaining sentries hurried down the ladders from their platforms and fell back in good order with the rest of their comrades beside the barracks. They lined up shoulder to shoulder, shields up, and braced for the outlaws' charge. Crossbows twanged, wrenching Brohr from his excitement. Beside him, one of the bolts found Lar's gut and the foul man fell over, screaming.

"Brother!" Brohr shouted. His mouth was dry, his ears ringing. Swords clashed, and men cried out around him. He wanted the rage to drown his fear.

Federals threw open the doors and rushed out of the barracks. Some of them wore their armor, but a few were bare chested, looking comical in their leather skirts and conical helms. Each of them carried a short sword and a round wooden shield with a metal boss. Despite the success of the outlaws' ruse, the federals fell into ranks with practiced discipline, forming two tight lines between the barracks and the slave quarters. A naked ordinal emerged from the far side of the building, deeper within the fort, half of his face still covered in shaving cream. He clutched a sword belt in one hand and his hat in the other. Bellowing orders, he ran up behind the line and took his place, completing the formation.

The outlaw charge crashed into the ordered defense, the line holding. Brohr slashed at the nearest Tyrianite, an older man a full head shorter than he was, skinny and fast. He felt his brother stir, drawn in by the fear and danger. The man hefted his shield just in time to deflect the attack and jabbed at Brohr's belly with his sword. Brohr sucked in his gut and scooted back to avoid the thrust, but the legionary to his left caught him on the temple with the rim of his shield.

The blow staggered Brohr, and he stumbled back a pace, cocking his head at the sound of a wailing infant. Keeping discipline, the little legionary didn't break ranks to finish him. The naked officer shouted fresh orders, and a squad of men detached from the back line, tromping off through the mud and disappearing behind one of the nearby buildings.

Brohr shook his head, fighting off the dizziness, stoking the fire of his brother's wrath with bloody thoughts. It felt different this time, not a cacophony that would drown him out while at its grisly work but a tune he could dance to. He smiled, delighted despite the carnage, at the sudden note of fraternal accord. His eyes flicked to his little adversary, and the smile fell away. Brohr felt his bowels quail. He almost stabbed himself, so sudden his eagerness to let blood. The runt took a step back, and his ordinal barked at him to form up.

Brohr slashed down at the soldier, a stroke that was easily blocked by a raised shield, but as the legionary cocked back to retaliate, Brohr's foot lashed out and caught him between legs. The kick lifted him clean off the ground. He landed on his heels and disappeared behind the line as a second kick caved in his chest. Brohr darted through the opening, his blade biting into the back of another soldier's head as he passed.

"Quarrels!" The nude ordinal commanded. He leveled his sword at Brohr, but the berserker closed the distance between them with a stride, swatting aside his clumsy parry and slashing the ordinal's throat with the back stroke.

Brohr unleashed a battle cry of impossible volume. The Tyrianite line wavered. A pair of crossbowmen swiveled toward him, one was still winding his bow, but the other shot his bolt. It lodged deep in Brohr's chest, halfway between his solar plexus and his shoulder. Brohr looked down at the quarrel, shocked. Blood crept up the back of his throat.

He glared up at the crossbowman who had shot him, and the gaze was enough to break the man. The federal turned on his heel to flee, but with a curse, Brohr flung his sword at him. It struck hilt first on the back of the legionary's helmet with enough force to stagger him. Brohr tackled him from behind, heedless of the rest of the battle. It was a distant thing, the desperation, the killing, a furious backdrop to a slower tempo— something building.

The crossbowman tried to turn over beneath him. In a flash, Brohr saw the quarrels sticking out of Grendie's corpse, the gash on her snout. He ripped the bolt from his own wound, the pain merely a flourish to the rising tune. Gritting his teeth nearly to the breaking point, he jammed the bolt into the man's side and wiggled it around in the federal's guts as he screamed for mercy. Brohr only twisted it more, reveling in the man's suffering.

Brohr snatched up his sword and shot to his feet. The line was broken, Tyrianites fighting in little clusters now, back to back, desperate and undone. But the group the officer had dispatched came around the far side of the barracks and unleashed a volley of crossbow fire. Nels dropped his axe, a startled look on his face. He reached over his shoulder, turning in a circle as he tried to pull the quarrel from his back.

Brohr flung himself at the nearest legionary, batting the sword out of his hand and tackling him to the ground. Brohr caught the Tyrianite's fierce expression, a gap-toothed snarl, just before he slammed his forehead into the man's nose. The rim of the federal's helm cut Brohr just above the eyebrow. He flung it away and butted him again. Brohr reared up, noting that the defiance was gone from the soldier's eyes and crashed his forehead down again and again and again and again.

Brohr reached out to brace himself with a hand to the earth. The world spun. He was so tired. Around him the battle continued, but he couldn't focus. He couldn't think and the ground reeled when he tried to stand. It was so cold. Blood dribbled from his chest wound. Bile rose in his throat. His eyes rolled back.

★★★★★

The clouds overhead veiled the grisly scene above, but the red light of Quaya spread behind them in a disturbing spatter. Henrik led the procession back toward Skolja. They saddled Grafstrom's horse and fashioned a skid to drag the stolen supplies. Dirk led the beast along, whistling a few bars of an old sea shanty over and over, the lilt of the tune grinding on Henrik's nerves with every note. Grafstrom's widow cooed at her babe, her left eye swollen shut, a fresh limp slowing her down.

Henrik looked over his shoulder at her. He was embarrassed by her resolve. He'd seen her boot print, he knew it was her, but she wouldn't relent, wouldn't confess, wouldn't inform on her accomplices. They'd fled deeper into Hensten Wood. Into Kriegan country. He'd need soldiers to go in after them and hope to come out alive. What a mess. He wished this woman was a prize he was bringing home, an outlaw queen, but she was just a widow with the temerity to call his bluff.

Once they saw the light from town, Henrik steered them north, circling the group behind the plateau atop which the fort perched. He didn't want the townsfolk seeing a beaten woman clutching an infant tied behind a horse. It was a recipe for more rioting. The road climbing up the back side of the hills was wide and well traveled, but at nightfall it was deserted. By the time they crested the rise, Henrik called a short rest.

He stood, hands on his hips, watching as the widow untucked one of her breasts and offered it to the hungry child. Backlit by the sanguine clouds, it would have made a beautiful painting, not that his clumsy strokes could ever have captured it.

"You're a tough woman," Henrik admitted. She ignored him. "Even if you're right about me, though," he said, "I have to hand you over to the prefect. I doubt he is as tender."

"Do you?" she asked, a sneer on her lips. "Do you have to? Poor Henrik Torvald. Forced to be a traitor on the eve of the end. Such a pity you only get a few days as mayor before it's off to damnation."

He scoffed. "You think that nonsense scares me? Forget all of that. It's time to face the truth and save yourself." She pointed up at the red clouds behind him, saying nothing. Henrik looked over his shoulder, shrugging. "Fine," he said. "I tried. I tried to help you save yourself. Remember that."

She pulled her daughter away from her breast and covered it again. "Oh, I will remember. Henrik Torvald tried to help me, but was too busy sucking the prefect's cock. Too busy murdering my husband, dooming my little Elise."

"I should. I really should. But I'm not a vindictive man. Give the child to Gunnar here."

Gunnar looked surprised. "What?"

The widowed clutched her babe tighter.

"Your actions have damned you, woman." Henrik folded his arms. "The federals will probably hang you. Or at least they'll send you to the mine. And you deserve it. You broke the law. You robbed Arius's family. But the girl isn't to blame. And if I turn her over to the prefect along with you, who knows what will happen to her? Certainly, they can't take care of her. Maybe they'll damn her alongside her mother. It might just be easier to suffocate her than to find a nursemaid. So I'll do you a kindness. I'll pass her on to one of the women in town."

The widow didn't speak. A tear ran down her cheek and fell from her chin onto the baby's face. She wiped it away and sniffled.

"It's time," said Henrik. She kissed the child, froze. "Now," he insisted.

At last, she handed her to Gunnar, her hands shaking, her nose running. She glowered at Henrik, minding her tongue for her daughter's sake.

They were challenged by the outer sentry a hundred yards from the rear gate. Passing the stench of outhouses, the sentry led them within the palisade. Torches and campfires burned all around. Even at night the business of the camp kept men hurrying to and fro. Once they neared the front gate, Henrik instructed Arius to head into town and scout the situation at the waterfront, Gunnar to find a woman to mind the baby.

Henrik grabbed the widow Grafstrom by her elbow and ushered her to the command building. The guard demanded his business, and after hearing Henrik's report, disappeared within. Henrik waited outside with the widow, ignoring her baleful looks until the soldier returned to his post and hiked his thumb over his shoulder.

"The prefect is waiting."

Inside, a scribe sat behind the desk sorting through a pile of parchment. Brasca stood, studying the giant map with his hands clasped behind his back. Without turning around, he said, "You've brought a friend."

"This is Erk Grafstrom's widow. We followed some tracks up into clan country. Some led to Grafstrom's farm, but more led deeper into Hensten wood."

"Go on."

"We found Grafstrom trying to hide some of the loot. He drew his bow, and we killed him." Henrik considered what else to say. "We questioned his wife here about who else went on the raid, but she wouldn't talk. I saw a boot print the size of a woman's foot at Ivar's. It's likely hers."

The prefect finally turned around to examine the woman. "You couldn't manage to break this little thing?" He clucked his tongue. "I guess I'll have to get Carthalo to clean up this mess. My ordinals will get tired soon of following you around fixing your mistakes."

Henrik stiffened. He was especially embarrassed when the widow gave him a snide grin. He took a deep breath, about to argue, but the prefect cut him off.

"Perhaps I was too harsh," he said. "Things are worse than any of us expected. I shouldn't blame you. You're doing your best."

"Thank you, sir."

"Take this woman to the brig," Brasca told the guard. "We'll have to deal with her later."

As the soldier led her out, the widow Grafstrom spat on the floor, gave the prefect a lewd look and said to Henrik, "Don't choke on it."

He ignored her. When she was gone, the prefect gathered his hat off the desk and told his scribe, "I'll be in the square if any messages arrive. If there's word from Trond, you must find me immediately."

"Yes, sir," said the scribe, watching them go.

The prefect led him out of the command building and through the front gate. Henrik gazed out over the torch-lit town, noting activity at the waterfront and a fair-sized crowd gathering in the square. Above them, the clouds obscured the shattered moon. Below, the ocean heaved against the dike they had erected.

Many of the townsfolk stood around in the square, gossiping with each other and jeering the Tyrianites who were loading up wagons with goods from the shops around the square.

"What's happening?" Henrik asked.

"We're securing supplies. The water is still rising. I'm afraid the dike we built may yet break."

Henrik squinted at the torches in the distance, but it was impossible to see much detail around the waterfront.

"You need to calm the shopkeeper down," Brasca said.

"Ivar? Why?"

"He is panicked that we're taking his merchandise. Assure him that we are merely keeping it safe."

Henrik eyed the federal. "Is that true?"

He didn't hesitate. "Of course. We're just being careful. Get him to see reason."

The light caught the edge of the prefect's face, one intense eye staring, the other lost in shadow. It was a grim portrait, but as the prefect turned away, Henrik followed. He had little faith in the man's sincerity, but saw no other choice at the moment.

They entered the square, ignoring the townsfolk clamoring for an explanation as they waded into the crowd. The rebellious air of the previous night seemed to have given way to fear. They had been watching the water rise all day long. *Finally*, Henrik thought, *they see that we can't afford a fight.*

Ivar had already seen them descending the steps, and he pushed through the throng with Arius at his side.

"Henrik!" he cried. "Henrik, they're taking my property!"

"Lower your voice," he said. "It's for your own good. Don't cause a scene."

"A scene?" Ivar knitted his hands as if praying. "I'll be ruined. They're taking everything."

Henrik grabbed him by the collar of his fine shirt. "I told you to keep your voice down."

"You have to help me," Ivar hissed. "They're worse than the looters."

Henrik looked around at their audience. The folk of Skolja jostled one another to close within earshot, holding their torches and lanterns aloft to see the faces of the town's most prominent citizens.

"They aren't confiscating anything." Henrik dared not look over to the prefect for confirmation. "We're just concerned about the town flooding. It would be a disaster to waste all that fodder at a time like this."

The prefect chose this moment to join the conversation. "The water is only a half foot below the top of the dike. At this rate, it will spill over into the low quarter in a few hours." Henrik swung his head toward the prefect, judging his face. This was news to him. Brasca turned to him and added. "It's true."

Henrik cursed. "Ivar, you need to be a leader now. I'm making you deputy mayor." There was no such office, but he hoped it would placate him.

Ivar looked from Henrik to the prefect and back. "I have your word? My property is still my own?"

Henrik fought to keep any hint of doubt from his face. "Yes, Ivar." He feigned an indignant look. "Now will you help me or not?"

Ivar bowed, a facile grin spreading across his face. "Your deputy mayor is at your service."

"Good," said Henrik. "Stay close. We'll talk more in a moment." Henrik climbed up the wheel of a wagon and stood in the bed.

"Skolja!" he cried. "Citizens of Skolja!" He immediately regretted his choice of words, for of course they were not citizens, but the crowd did not seem to notice the distinction, so he plunged on. "The town is in danger of flooding despite the dike. Once the water swamps it, the low quarter will flood in a matter of minutes. I want everyone to go home right now and pack up some essentials: food, warm clothing, the like. Be sure to bring tents and blankets, the weather could turn cold quickly. I want everyone to bring their things up to one of the hills. If you live in the low quarter, bring your families to High Hill and make camp. Everyone else, take your things up to the east side of the fort behind the High Tavern. No one sleeps down here tonight. If it floods, it will happen fast."

He hoped for a few stern nods, perhaps a 'here here,' but as soon as his speech was over, the square devolved into bedlam. Not a riot though, he was pleased to note. They were panicked but not outraged. Folks began to leave the square, some running headlong, others shoving each other out of the way.

Someone tugged at the hem of his coat. Henrik looked down to see the scowling prefect waving him down from the wagon. He hopped onto the cobblestones and turned to face Brasca Quoll. All around them, townsfolk shouted fearful questions and shoved each other, trying to leave or get closer to the action. Brasca grabbed Henrik by the vest and pulled him close.

The prefect took off his hat so that he could whisper in Henrik's ear. "You need to be very careful from now on. Decisions like that require my blessing."

The prefect pulled back far enough to look Henrik in the eye, his grip twisting Henrik's shirt until it choked him.

Chapter 22

"The human soul has no special dignity to protect it from binding. I will show you, sweet Izavel. We shall never part again."

-Black Book of Aelus

The outlaws had lost half of their number, and no one was in a forgiving mood. Anders left his hiding spot just as the last of the surviving federals threw down their swords and begged for mercy. Gareth's boy, Nels, was among the dead. He lay face down in a mud puddle with a crossbow bolt buried in his spine. Anders noted with pleasure that the death of his son had put a little iron in Gareth's belly. The Hemmishman hacked clean through the outstretched hand of a federal pleading for his pathetic life. The others followed his lead, cutting down the legionaries who had been foolish enough to surrender.

But seeing Brohr on the ground snuffed his cruel cheer. Anders ran to his grandson and knelt beside him. Brohr looked up with desperate eyes. Blood leaked from his mouth. A gash split his forehead. A chest wound had drenched his shirt in blood. His face was pale, his mouth moving but silent save a whimper.

Anders whipped his head around, scouring the encampment for the barmaid. She was Breylin's pupil. If anyone could help, it would be her. The old man discovered her standing over a fallen legionary, wiping blood off her knife onto her pant leg. She winked at an outlaw on the ground at her feet and held out her hand to help him up.

"Girl!" Anders called. He waved her over. "Come quick. Brohr's hurt."

The smirk vanished from her face, and she ran to them, kneeling on the other side of Brohr. She redrew her knife and cut down the middle of the sweater. His chest was sticky with blood, a gushing wound in his chest.

"Bring me my pack," she shouted.

When Anders didn't move quickly enough, she shoved him. He ignored the insult and hurried across the clearing to where she pointed, returning with her leather pack. She snatched it out of his hands and tore through its contents until she found the vial she was looking for. Lyssa uncorked it and forced the acrid potion down Brohr's throat. He gagged and spat out blood, trying to sit up and crying out in pain.

Brohr was dying. The old skald could no longer ignore the truth. It was right before his eyes. This was a mortal wound. His bloodline was ending. Here and now.

No! He had been promised. After everything he had done. It couldn't all be for nothing.

"Do something!" he demanded.

The look of contempt Lyssa flashed quieted him. A few of the outlaws had gathered around, looking down at Brohr drowning in his own blood. She grabbed one by the leg and pointed to a campfire beside the mess hall. The girl handed him her knife and said, "Heat this until it's glowing. Go!"

Blood trickled from the corners of Brohr's mouth. He rocked side to side as if he might roll away from the pain.

"Can you hear it?" Anders asked. Brohr looked up at him, angry and baffled. "Listen," Anders said.

The boy paid him no heed, instead looking down at the blood welling from his chest wound.

Behind them, someone wailed long and loud, the sound followed by an undignified, breathless cry. Anders turned back to see Gareth cradling the body of his son, head thrown back, sobbing out the strange chant that Hems sang for their fallen. He looked back to Brohr just as the outlaw returned with the glowing dagger and carefully handed it to the barmaid.

"Hold him down," she addressed the man who'd brought her the knife. "You too."

Anders grabbed Brohr's forearm and pinned it to the dirt just as the man opposite him did the same. He worried the pain might rouse Olek. So be it. If the boy died, what was the point of all of this?

The barmaid held the glowing blade before Brohr's eyes. "Oh," she said, wadding up the front of his ruined sweater and shoving it in his mouth. "Bite down on this."

She had no idea what she was doing. *This little fool might kill him right now,* Anders thought. But before he could stop her, she pressed the burning blade to Brohr's chest. A puff of steam that smelled like roasted elk wafted up. The boy struggled as she mercilessly cauterized the outside of the wound. She removed the knife. Seared skin stuck to it. Brohr's eyes rolled into the back of his head, and he passed out. A moment of quiet followed. The girl locked eyes with Anders. She set the knife down in the mud by her pack and rummaged it again, this time finding a needle and some thread.

"I should stitch his face, too," she said.

Anders looked back to his unconscious grandson. "Will he live?"

She studied the boy, a little frown appearing. "I don't think so. Maybe." She dabbed some of the blood from his chin. "It's not a good sign. To cough up blood, I mean. His lung is punctured. I can stave off a fever. Give him a chance. But really, I can't do much."

"Listen girl." He grabbed her wrist and jerked on it.

She pulled away. "Stop calling me 'girl.'"

"Would you prefer I call you 'boy'?" He shook his head. "What use are you if you can't help him?"

★★★★★

The night's first tremor struck a few minutes after the evacuation began. Henrik stood in the square, trading heated whispers with the prefect when it happened. The commotion broke up the argument in an instant, and the two men steadied themselves, watching the cobblestones writhe and buck. A

212

fearsome tearing sound arose as the east side of the Pilgrim's Inn sagged and then collapsed in a cloud of dust and clattering boards. Shouts erupted in the sudden quiet. Frightened villagers peeked out of doorways, lanterns in hand.

Henrik assessed what he could see of the town. The cobblestones in the square had split down the east side, leaving a foot-wide crack. Folk were already flocking to the Pilgrim's Inn to see the aftermath of its collapse.

"We need to help search the Inn," said Henrik. "There will be injuries."

The prefect thumbed his chin at the young mayor. "Go right ahead. We have plenty to do carting the supplies up to the fort."

Henrik ignored the gesture. "Surely at least some of your men can help."

A pair of Norn were already digging through the rubble, chucking bits of wood and stone into the street in hopes of uncovering survivors. One of the shuttered windows on the intact side of the inn burst open, and the young reveler he'd interviewed earlier in the day climbed out and dropped from the second story to the ground. The whole building lurched downward a foot and emitted a long, low groan.

"For pity's sake," said Henrik, moving toward the inn. "Will you really not help?"

The prefect turned to the soldiers loading the wagons full of Ivar's wares. They had stopped to witness the inn's plight.

"Back to work," he ordered.

Disgusted, Henrik turned his back on the federals and sprinted across the square, leaping over the widening crack without breaking stride. The reveler called up to the open window where his father leaned out, too afraid to jump to the stones below. Brom, the innkeeper, kicked open the front door and staggered out. The bald, portly barman still had a rag thrown over one shoulder. When he turned to inspect his inn, he cursed Breyga's ghost, tore the rag from his shoulder, and flung it at the wreckage.

"Brom," Henrik called. When the innkeeper turned around, he pointed to the men digging through the rubble at the east edge. "Brom! Was anyone in those rooms?"

He hustled over, nodding. "Aye," he said. "The temperate one. That's what we was calling him. The old pilgrim."

"Help these men get him out," Henrik ordered. "Who else is inside still?"

"Well," said Brom. "There is that fellow." He pointed up at the pilgrim in the window. "Then there's Tonja. But I fear she's gone. I saw one of the beams come down on her noggin." He made a hollow sound with his tongue as he rapped his knuckles on the crown of his head.

"Look for the old man then." Henrik walked over to the window.

"What's the use? We're all doomed." Brom sat down crosslegged and buried his face in his hands.

Henrik ignored the innkeeper, shouting instead at the pilgrim in the window. "Better get out before it's too late!"

"Jump, Dad!" The boy called up.

His father looked down at the cobblestones dubiously. "It's too high, lad."

"Can't you use the stairs?" Henrik asked.

The boy shook his head. "They're a mess. Jump, Dad!"

The building shrieked like a tortured rat. It was so loud that everyone covered their ears and backed away. The top floor of the inn settled to the east, twisting and sagging, its collapse slow and ominous.

The noise subsided. A second later, the man, Henrik remembered his name was Gurnsie, reappeared at the window.

"It's now or never," Henrik shouted.

Guernsie threw one leg over the windowsill, making ready to climb out. Looking up, Henrik realized that the wind had pushed the clouds south over the water, revealing the fractured remains of Quaya. Through the haze, speckled with motes of ruin that must be as big as the town, Henrik spied three distinct masses drifting inexorably toward them.

The remaining beams of the inn began to whine and buckle under the stress of the foundering building. Everyone backed away from the Pilgrim's Inn, shouting for Guernsie to jump, but he was too afraid. With a series of pops, the floor joists holding up the second story gave way, and the inn crumpled inward, the open window devouring poor Guernsie like the ravenous maw of a wolf. When the cloud of dust kicked up by the collapse began to settle, they could see the pilgrim's severed leg laying atop the rubble.

The boy began to panic at once, crying and running up to where his father had disappeared. He held up his father's leg for a moment. Somehow it seemed to calm him. He quietly set it aside and continued digging. Henrik turned around and headed back to the square. A few others had poked their heads out to watch the commotion, but they returned to their business when they saw Henrik coming.

He walked around the square, hollering up each street that led off into the town for people to gather their things and head for one of the hills. He stopped short of where Brasca oversaw the last goods being loaded onto a wagon. He feared that if he spoke to him now they would come to blows—worse, likely.

Gunnar stood in the doorway of the jail, looking toward the low quarter where steps descended from the town square to the hovels and fish stalls by the waterfront. Henrik saw Gunnar squinting and turned to see what he was looking at. Henrik nearly missed it, but a telltale hint of smoke curled off the far side of a thatched roof in the low quarter.

It was too much. He held the town together by a thread, and every moment seemed to heap more calamity on him. He stood doing nothing as the tongues of flame reached over the apex of the roof. He smelled the smoke now. Some fool must've toppled an oil lamp.

The prefect pointed to the low quarter and then cupped his hands to his mouth, calling across Skolja's town square. "Mayor," he said. "Your town is burning."

Part of him wanted to dash across the square and knock the look off of the federal's face. Part of him wanted to let the low quarter burn. It was probably doomed anyway. When the dam broke, it would quench the flames, unless, of course, it spread to the town proper first.

"Buckets!" Henrik shouted. He ran around the square screaming this as loudly as he could. He clapped his hands. "Let's go, men."

Some appeared on their doorsteps with buckets in hand, but they stood motionless, staring off toward the waterfront, wondering what the point of fighting a fire was while they ran from a flood.

Henrik's voice grew hoarse. "Even if the low quarter floods, the fire may spread up here first. Quickly now. Move it!" No one budged. "You." Henrik called out one of the fishermen coming up the steps into the square. "Turn around and get a bucket. You." He pointed at Gunnar, running over to him and shoving him toward the fire. He kicked him in the backside. "Get going!"

A few of the menfolk finally headed down toward the waterfront, Gunnar among them.

The prefect issued orders to his own men, and the wagons rolled north toward the fort. Henrik couldn't hide his contempt as the prefect marched past. The man stared back, unperturbed by Henrik's low opinion.

"Let's go! Let's go!" Henrik ran a lap around the square, singling out a few men to head toward the fire. When he completed his circuit, he started down the steps toward the water, a sparse line of men stretching before him. Luckily the fire hadn't spread yet, though the house blazed in the night, well on its way to collapsing. If it did, the embers would explode in every direction.

A flaming man streaked from the smoking doorway of the building. His screams echoed through the square, and the stunned townsfolk stopped to witness the spectacle. He stumbled, picked himself up, and ran halfway to the waterfront before collapsing in a smouldering pile. As the shocked townsfolk stared

216

at the man's charred remains, a noise rose up like laundry flapping on the line. Henrik looked around for the source just in time to watch the dark wave crash over the dike. It struck as the fist of a hateful sea god, scattering the sandbags from the dam like sparks leaping from a smith's hammer. A wall of white caps erupted, a chorus of screams. In the time it took to throw his hands up in front of his face, the wave devoured the low quarter, toppling buildings and snuffing men's torches like doused candles.

Henrik backpedaled toward the square as the men he'd ordered to fight the fire vanished in the ocean's fury. The wave knocked his legs out from under him, and his head struck the steps hard enough to knock out a molar and dazzle him with painful light. He put out his arm to brace his fall, and it broke under his own awkward weight. The surging tide swept him all the way across the square, depositing him in a heap against the jail house.

★★★★★

The door of the smeltery was locked. A half-hearted grin spread across Lyssa's face, glad to have a challenge to take her mind off Brohr. But the smile faded as her thoughts drifted back to him, lying in the barracks, coughing up blood. It was her fault he lay there dying. If she hadn't talked him into diverting to the outlaws after they had intercepted the federal courier, Brohr might be in Pederskald by now, starting a new life. As confused as she was about everything in her life, she had hoped for more, he was her only friend, really, and now he wouldn't even be that.

Lyssa plucked two pins from her hair and stuck one in her mouth and the other in the keyhole of the padlock, probing until she felt the tumblers start to give. Focusing on the task before her, she inserted the other into the lock and gave it a gentle twist, hearing a satisfying click. Lyssa took the padlock off and unlatched the door.

The mining camp was too small to break-in without someone noticing. She had waited until nightfall, hoping that the spectacle in the sky and the brandy the men had looted would prove enough of a distraction, but, in fact, a small crowd of bedraggled ex-slaves and battle-weary outlaws had gathered around to watch her. One of the Norn whistled at the speed with which she picked the lock.

Lyssa pushed the creaky door inward, and the crowd pressed in around her, eager for a look at the bounty within. She poked her head into the little stone building. The cloying, suffocating stench of roasting ore filled the room. Tall burlap sacks stuffed to overflowing with charcoal bricks lined the far wall. Opposite them, bags of quicklime leaned against the other. A furnace surrounded by blackened walls still smoldered, hastily abandoned during the attack. A set of small, long-handled crucibles leaned in the corner beside it.

Behind her, one of the outlaws, a greasy-haired, unshaven red-head, tried to shove past her.

"Hey!" She elbowed the intruder in the groin, doubling him over. His friends roared with laughter. When the man gathered himself to retaliate, one of his compatriots, a burly Norn with a hatchet in one hand set the other on his shoulder, emitting a faint growl.

Lyssa's heart raced. A sheen of sweat glistened on her brow. The man who had defended her looked just like the man her mother had run off with. But he was too young. It couldn't be him. Lyssa forced a smile and turned back into the smeltery. Her eyes roamed the room until she found what she was looking for: a strong box made from varnished oak and banded in iron. It stood about two feet high and four wide, locked with a padlock identical to the one she had just picked. She took a deep breath, trying to ignore all the thoughts stirred about about her mother and father.

"What's going on here?" Anders shoved a few men aside and loomed in the doorway, a belligerent frown darkening his face.

Lyssa kicked the strong box. "We're getting rich."

"Leave that filth where it is." The skald grated.

"I'm not going to keep it all."

Anders stomped his foot. "Leave it! It's cold iron. What do you think drew the pigs here in the first place? It made us slaves. We don't need it. It's tainted. Leave it where it is."

"Ten Cocks! You know how much it's worth?" Lyssa surveyed the other outlaws peeking in the doorway. They looked just as incredulous as she felt. With even one bar of cold iron she could go wherever she wanted, be whoever she wanted. Maybe even buy her own ship. "Are you nuts?" She turned back to the lock and popped it open with her hairpins.

Anders closed his eyes and began to hum.

Lyssa opened the strong box to reveal the dull bars of cold iron laying at the bottom. She snatched one of the frigid bars and stuffed it in her backpack then grabbed another and tossed it to the burly outlaw who'd kept the man she'd elbowed in check. He pushed the skald aside to catch the treasure and laughed, holding it up to the light in the doorway to marvel at the unspectacular-looking ingot.

"It really is cold," he said. A murmur passed through the gathered throng as he shoved everyone aside, disappearing through the doorway back into the mining camp.

Anders's song died in his throat as more Norn jostled past him to accept the spoils that Lyssa handed out. When the last of the bars of cold iron were gone and the onlookers had cleared out, Anders bent over her. His hair fell in front of his face, and he tucked the gray lock behind his ear before he fixed her with an icy glare. "That metal is cursed. Like a lodestone for misery. It's brought our people nothing but suffering. You should have listened, you greedy little bitch."

★★★★★

The wave had quenched the fire in the low quarter, collapsing the burning building, while the other rooftops still peeked above the waterline. Quaya reflected in the black sea, the angry fragments doubled, casting the submerged town in

219

sanguine light. Dangerous eddies tugged the bodies in an intricate convolution of the waterfront, collecting them in a clump beside the tavern.

Henrik tested his nose with his good hand then popped it into place. He stood against the jailhouse door. Water pooled around his knees. A fish swam by. Gunnar floated toward him. Henrik's arm was broken, but it didn't hurt as much as he would have expected, given the angle. He wanted to wade out into the square to get a better look at the low quarter, perhaps help if anyone had lived, but he was afraid the riptide would suck him out to sea. Already unsteady from his knock on the head, he stood petrified.

Eventually, Henrik realized that someone was shouting his name. Ivar trudged out from the porch of his storefront and made his way toward Henrik, who looked down the road leading from the square where other figures called out to one another, wading north toward higher ground. Rogan emerged from the front door of the smithy and locked it behind him. He headed over to Henrik too. Ivar arrived first, noticing the way he held his arm.

"You look hurt," he said. "Is it broken?"

Henrik tried to move and winced. He nodded, slipping his good hand to one of the stones in the pouch on his belt then changed his mind. If he used the binding before the bone was set, it would heal badly.

"We should get up the hill," he said. "There may be another wave."

Ivar agreed, looking over his shoulder as Arius splashed out of their store onto the porch. He waved him over and turned back to Henrik.

"Here," he said. "Let me help you."

Henrik shrugged him off. "I'm fine. See if someone else needs help." Gunnar's new red coat caught his eye; he floated face down over by the well house. "Just get up by the fort as soon as you can."

Ivar followed his gaze to the constable and nodded. Wasting no time to help anyone else, he took one last look at his son and waded out of the square.

Rogan reached Henrik. The smith tried to fuss over Henrik's arm, but he shooed him away and asked, "What about *The Muse?*" nodding toward the smithy.

Rogan looked back. "Well," he said. "She's waterproof, sure enough. Sealed up as tight as a spinster's legs. If the whole town doesn't wash away, your father's ship will be fine."

That would have to be good enough. He felt a twinge of shame at the thought of abandoning Skolja. He'd only been mayor for a couple of days, but at this rate, there'd be nothing to defend in a couple more. In the meantime, he needed to stay alive.

"We should go," he said.

Rogan nodded, offering his arm to support Henrik, but Henrik declined. They headed north out of the square, listening to the keening of some far-off woman as they joined the herd of townsfolk retreating to higher ground. Some folk splashed past frantically, scurrying up the hill, others seemed loathe to leave their homes behind, turning back time and again to survey the surreal devastation. A few of them carried baskets or bundles or knapsacks, but many were empty-handed. They hadn't had enough warning to prepare properly. Henrik blamed himself. That should have begun at the same time as the dike. If he had stopped and taken enough time to think things through, this could've been avoided. He could have devised a contingent for this scenario, which wasn't so remote once he realized that the water was rising. Fool! He'd gone chasing looters instead of looking after his town.

By the time he reached the steps at the base of Federal Hill, a line of weary townspeople ascended ahead of him. Finally submitting to Rogan's help, he climbed the steps and, at the top, looked back over the scene. Henrik trembled. Like the three gory eyes of some cosmic witch, Quaya stared down at the doomed town of Skolja. It was difficult, at this distance, to distinguish the bodies from the rest of the flotsam, but down by

221

the tavern he spied the tangled mass where some dread current collected the low quarter's drowned residents.

Chapter 23

"Before you set one foot aboard a void craft, first—and this is of absolute priority—dislodge any and all superstition from between your ears. Take it from this girl, the vast abyss is fairly littered with the popsicle corpses of men with hunches and believers in fairytale."

-Captain Marishna Volgue,
A Practical Guide to Celestial Navigation

Lyssa watched the rise and fall of his labored breath. Brohr lay on one of the barracks cots, covered in a woolen blanket. The cut on his forehead was stitched. The corners of his mouth were scabbed with blood. His eyelids fluttered, dreaming, and his right foot tapped a steady rhythm on the bedpost. She had dressed his wound and poured a draft of wyrmwillow down his throat, but the quarrel seemed to have injured his lung. Breylin may have been able to do more for him, but Lyssa felt like a pretender. All she could do was wait.

Despite the long trek and the brutal fight, most of the outlaws were outside. She was alone with the wounded. Lar squirmed on the cot in the far corner of the room. She'd done what she could for him too, for all of them, but she could smell the reek of his bowels through his wound, and she knew he wouldn't survive. Already he had gone pale and complained viciously of the cold despite the blankets she'd heaped on him. He'd ceased his screaming about an hour ago and now only writhed and moaned. She tried to give him some hemlock to end his suffering, but Lar had balked, ignoring her diagnosis. After that he wouldn't even accept a draft to make him sleep. To a man who fears death, even suffering is precious.

Lyssa stood up and stretched, walking over to where the other injured men lay snoring. Unlike Lar, they had the good sense to let her minister to them. She sniffed their bandages and checked their heartbeats, satisfied that they would all three recover.

Behind her, Brohr groaned. She spun around and rushed to his side, sitting back down on the wooden stool she had just vacated.

His face contorted, and he groaned again, his hands fumbling at the bandage on his chest. Gently, she restrained him so that he wouldn't reinjure himself. Brohr's eyes shot open and darted all over the room, taking in his strange surroundings until finally they rested on Lyssa. He tried to sit up.

"Aagh," Brohr cried out. "Breyga's Ghost!" He closed his eyes and was quiet for a while. Lyssa thought he had fallen asleep again, but, eyes still closed, he asked, "What happened?"

She couldn't help herself. "You ruined my favorite sweater. That's what." He opened one eye, saw her smiling, and did his best to follow suit, not daring to laugh. "Sorry," she said. "You took a crossbow bolt in the chest. Do you remember?"

"Feels about right," said Brohr.

She didn't want to push him, so she just waited while he dozed for a few minutes, but it wasn't long before the pain roused him again.

"You okay?" she asked. "I can give you something for the pain. It'll knock you out."

He shook his head. "I take it we won?"

"Yep," Lyssa said. "All this is ours." She gestured around the barracks.

Brohr carefully turned his head to note the other wounded men. "Where is everyone else?"

She drew in a deep breath and exhaled before continuing. "They're outside. Watching."

"Watching?"

"Quaya."

His brow wrinkled, and a moment passed before understanding dawned on his face.

224

"Is it bad?" She nodded. Brohr reached over and grabbed her hand. "Thanks for staying with me."

Lyssa blushed and snatched her hand free. "Your wound is serious," she said, instantly regretting the change of subject.

"I'm sorry," said Brohr. "I didn't mean to..." His pale cheeks colored. "I didn't mean it like that."

She could tell he was lying. Or at least she thought he was. "It's fine. Don't... It's fine." Lyssa cursed herself. She liked Brohr, but he couldn't understand her. Who would?

"I made you something," Brohr said. "It's here." He rolled to one side, grimacing as he dug in his pocket. Hand trembling, he held out his gift to her. Lyssa took the little carving: the upper half of a man, about the size of her palm, whittled from driftwood. "It's your father."

Lyssa dried her eyes on her sleeve and smiled down at him. "I love it."

"That's supposed to be an ale horn he's holding, but I guess I won't get to finish it."

The door of the barracks creaked open. She looked over her shoulder to discover the old skald standing in the doorway, glowering at them.

"I'd like to speak with my grandson in private, barmaid."

Lyssa bit back a nasty response.

Brohr spoke up. "Have you always been such a prick?"

Brohr's defense brought a smile to her lips, but by the time she turned to face Anders, it was a scowl. "I'll go."

Anders delivered a withering glare, his eyes following her as she gathered up her pack and walked past him on her way out of the barracks.

The smell of campfire wafted through the night air. It was cool and clear, the clouds at either horizon framing the horrific majesty of the falling moon. Quaya had tripled in size these last nights. A ruddy nimbus that stretched halfway across the sky veiled the three great shards, but they lurked like ill-omened travelers, approaching Heimir with dreadful but certain steps.

Terror threatened to overwhelm her. She ground her teeth, fighting a wave of dizziness. How could any of them

225

escape that? She prayed to her father that when her doom came, she would not feel as she did now, like a rat caught in one of Ivar's traps, alive, but wishing it would end. Lyssa started to walk away as if there was somewhere she could go to escape this. But there was nowhere. She prayed to Freyan that she might be stronger, that she might best her fear and live the time she had. Lyssa pinched herself, hard, digging her thumbnail into the skin until the pain broke through her anxiety and the urge to flee became bearable.

Someone cackled over by one of the cook fires. Lyssa peered around in the crimson dark. A murmur from within the barracks caught her ear. She drew in a deep breath and let it out between her teeth. Then Lyssa dropped to her knees and pressed her ear to the crack beneath the door, thanking her elders for the distraction.

"…matter if you kill one." This was old Nilstrom's voice.

Lyssa turned her head to peer under the door, wanting to be certain he wasn't close enough to surprise her on his way out. The flickering firelight betrayed little, but she could tell he had at least moved away from the door. Lyssa put her ear to the crack again.

Brohr said something. She strained to make out his words, but the fire crackled.

"Your blood is strong," said Anders. "You have only to listen." Brohr replied, but again he spoke too softly for her to understand. "If you had run away, would that be better? Have I raised a coward?"

"Are you crazy?" Brohr's voice carried well enough when he was angry. "What do you expect me to do? Whatever you want from me, do it your damn self. I'm dying. I wanted to be far away from here, but at least I can be far away from you. Get out!"

Lyssa flinched, imagining how painful it must be to shout in Brohr's condition.

"Pitiful!" Anders's rage was so vehement and sudden that Lyssa almost burst in to defend Brohr, convinced his grandfather would attack him in his sickbed. "Just a shade after all! I guess

226

half pig is enough to make you all weak. After everything I've done for you."

"Goodbye," said Brohr.

"When you hear it..." This time Lyssa had to strain to make out the old man's icy voice. "Listen. I've paid far too much to have raised a martyr."

With that, Anders stood up, stool legs scraping against the floor. Lyssa scrambled around the corner of the barracks. Nilstrom cursed and slammed the door behind him. Despite her galloping heart, Lyssa heard the irregularity of his breath. The old man was crying.

Anders screamed like a mountain cat. He kicked the wall of the barracks, wiped his nose, and blasphemed the Ten Fathers. She wanted to look but dared not, knowing that anyone Anders Nilstrom laid eyes on at that moment was in trouble. So she cowered in the shadows until his rage was spent and he stormed off into the scarlet shadows of the slave camp.

★★★★★

Brasca surveyed the bedlam from atop the ramparts. Provincials milled outside the fort, tending their wounded and congregating in pathetic, shivering clusters. Someone had already managed to start a campfire, and Skolja's children huddled around, crowding one another for its meager warmth.

An aftershock shook the walls of the fort, the logs grinding against each other, the platform that Brasca and Carthalo stood upon groaning. It lasted only a few seconds. Heartbeats of silence were followed by panicked shouts from the villagers below. The prefect let go of the wall, sharing an exhausted look with his adjutant.

"Perhaps we should go down," said Carthalo.

Brasca nodded, and they hurried down the wooden steps to the interior of the fort. Standing in the interval of open ground between the wall and the camp buildings, the prefect set his hand on his officer's shoulder.

"I want you to recall the men. Don't close the gate yet. I don't want to provoke the Norns if possible. But if they become unruly, I want everyone within the fort so we can seal the gate at a moment's notice."

"Yes, sir."

Brasca eyed the walls of the fort. "I also want the engineers to inspect the walls. The last thing we need is one of the quakes toppling them on our heads."

"Yes, sir."

"And have the extra provisions moved away from the walls, just in case."

"Yes, sir."

A legionary trotted up to where they stood and hailed him.

"Report," said the prefect.

"A group of men from the village are asking to speak with you, sir."

The prefect clasped his hands behind his back and thought for a moment. He nodded to himself. Better to concede a little, he decided.

"Very well," he said. "Inform them that I will be along soon."

"Yes, sir." The legionary hailed him and ran off toward the gate.

"They'll be wanting the storekeeper's foodstuffs," Carthalo said.

Brasca nodded, folding his arms and pacing as he mulled it over. "We'll give them a token. As little as possible. A ration may well help control them, but I'm more worried about us. Food is going to be scarce now."

The adjutant nodded.

"One last thing," the prefect said. "I want each of the men to make an offering. I'm concerned about morale." He looked up at the shards of Quaya crowding the southern sky.

"And you, sir?"

Brasca clenched his jaw. "You know I won't."

"With respect, sir. It isn't really for you."

228

"I'll think on it," Brasca said. "In the meantime, see that the men make their offerings. But nothing that will rot goes in the well. And no food. Coin, blood, or service. Is that clear?"

Carthalo hailed him. "Perfectly, sir."

Brasca nodded. "On your way then."

The prefect headed toward the front gate, his adjutant already barking orders to the soldiers. Six of his men guarded the entrance, two holding torches. He made a note to himself to double the contingent as soon as he finished talking to the villagers.

Brasca had assumed that the delegation would be led by Henrik, but the mayor was nowhere to be seen. Instead, the group consisted of Ivar and his son along with the thatcher and another man he did not recognize.

"Prefect Quoll!" Ivar hailed him.

Brasca ignored the inappropriate gesture and asked, "Where is Mayor Torvald?"

Ivar puffed up. "He was injured in the flood. A broken arm. He retired to his room at the High Tavern to tend to it." Ivar placed a hand on his own chest and bowed. "As deputy mayor, I'm here in his stead."

Brasca resisted the urge to laugh at him; it would not help the situation. "I have important duties to attend to. We'll have to make this quick."

Ivar glanced around at the other men. "Of course, Prefect. Hmm, many of the townsfolk are without food or water or wood for fires. We were hoping to use the well, and I want to reclaim my goods. Which, of course, I am grateful to you for having the wisdom to save. And firewood if you could spare some. We're wet and cold." He sighed. "And frankly, we're dead on our feet."

The prefect considered Ivar's request. The storekeep squirmed, looking to the other men for assistance. Finally, Ivar amended his request. "I don't need all of my wares now, of course. Perhaps one of the wagons." He clutched his hands to his chest, worry creeping onto his face.

229

"We can allow one woman at a time into the fort to carry water. As for firewood, I'm sure someone has an ax. I suggest you chop down a tree. Now, your supplies are safe here. My men are inventorying them as we speak. In the meantime, as you recall, Mayor Torvald is hoarding a cache of food in his room at the inn. Go and speak to him."

Arius stepped forward, pointing his finger. "This is an outrage! How dare you steal so blatantly. You are supposed to—"

Ivar grabbed his son by the wrist and jerked on it. "Arius!" he hissed. "Let me handle this."

"No," Arius tore free of his father's grasp. "He's a thief."

The prefect flicked his wrist, signaling his soldiers who drew their short swords in unison. The effect silenced Arius.

"Rest assured," Brasca said. "You will be generously compensated for your goods. They are yours to sell. But you will sell them to us. If the situation becomes grave, we will see to your needs. Until then, you had best learn to share."

★★★★★

Brohr lay awake. The hour was late, and he shivered from the cold. Lyssa had given him an extra blanket and a bowl to spit blood into, but it was nearly full. He chuckled, careful to do it gently, the pain already making him squirm. His last thoughts would be what to do with this stupid bowl. He couldn't bend down to set it on the floor; he'd already tried to call for help, but everyone else in the barracks kept on snoring. They were all either injured or drunk.

He didn't remember Lyssa leaving his side, but she was gone. He'd never imagined his life would end like this, wounded, dying slowly in a strange bed. He tried to recall the battle, but the day was a jumble. He remembered plucking the bolt from his chest, skewering the bowman with it, searing the wound closed, arguing with grandfather. He had said something to Lyssa, something that made her uncomfortable. She left. But what had he said?

He coughed, pain racking his body. Blood sloshed over the edge of the bowl onto the top blanket. He settled back, writhing into just the right position until the pain diminished. She had come back though. Hadn't she? He pushed the bowl off of his stomach, and it crashed upon the floor, flooding a circle around his bed. He turned his head to the side to spit, but the blood just ran down his cheek. He was dizzy. He closed his eyes. It was so bone chillingly cold.

He could feel his brother's curiosity, faint and muted. This change was no terror to him. He seemed expectant. It was a comfort, after all, to have his brother with him at the end. As the veil between them grew thinner, Brohr felt Olek reaching out to him, frustrated, pushing an image before him. It was his grandfather, reaching down. He was younger, tearful, grim. The picture made no sense, but Olek would not relent.

"I don't understand," Brohr whispered. "What does it mean?"

But it seemed that Olek had finally given up on him and slipped back into his macabre slumber. What a meaningless end. After everything, he couldn't even understand this simple message. The only thing his brother had ever tried to tell him.

What a shame, Brohr thought. What a useless life. Empty of purpose. Dull. All in the little village of Skolja. He tried not to cry. Then, once he began, he tried not to shake. It hurt too much. In the end, he had never made it to Pederskald. Even that simple ambition had proven too much. He could've left anytime, but he'd always been afraid. There'd always been something to keep him home. There had always been a feast or a blizzard or a girl. But if he was honest with himself, he had always been afraid. Afraid to abandon his grandfather, and afraid of what his grandfather would do if he did. Now his tale would end here, a no one without kin to remember his name or carve his idol.

"Father Freyan," he whispered. "I beg..." The words left him breathless, the room spinning. "I beg..."

Brohr felt the weight like a brick of ice on his chest. He forced his eyes open.

It lurked, an ill augur in his dimming eyes. The hand resting above his wound was not his own. He looked up at the form of darkness, cut out of the embers' light in the shape of a man.

"They can't hear you now," it cooed in his ear. "The Fathers have gone where your prayers cannot find them. Hush... better to listen."

Brohr froze as the creature leaned down, radiating terror and cold. Brohr's heart beat wildly. He feared his wound would gush the last of his life.

"Do you hear?" it whispered in his ear.

Brohr wrestled against the horror of its nearness. "Nothing," he managed to say.

"That is one road," it said. "Listen. What do you hear?"

"Just my heart." Brohr blurted.

The Hidden patted him on the chest. "It is your song. Your gift. It has such potential too. Just as you prayed. Greater by far than your grandfather's. He is but a trickster."

Brohr hacked scarlet phlegm onto the floor. He could feel the fluid in his lungs, the hole.

"It doesn't have to end here," it said.

Brohr tried to lean forward. His dizziness made it hard to sit still. He felt like he was treading against an undertow in icy seas. "How?" he gasped.

"A pact." The Hidden rose to its full height. "Just as I whispered secrets to your grandfather, I have much to show you. We can cheat death. After all, does he not cheat us? It would be a shame to see everything your grandfather has slaved for squandered upon this deathbed. There is so much more for you to see, so many paths to travel. I could give you that chance."

Brohr gathered some iron. "For what? What price?" He held onto the edges of the cot so he would not roll out as the room spun.

"Only what you desire anyway." The thing held up its hand, one finger silhouetted against the fire. "A journey. That is all. It begins in Skolja. And so you must return. I know that the

232

compass of your heart points in every other direction, but to go on, you must go back."

Brohr drifted to the very edge. The veil parted. His brother reached out, darkly luminous, mirroring his outstretched hand.

The ancient shook him back to life. "Time is short. Choose."

"Yes," Brohr whispered.

The Hidden dragged its thumbnail across the pad of its first finger. It held Brohr down by the forehead and hung the pricked finger above his pleading mouth.

"Brohr Nilstrom," it intoned. "Son of Torin. I bind you."

The drop fell from its finger, bitter and thick upon Brohr's tongue. Nausea overwhelmed him; he rolled away from the ancient one, dry heaving on the floor until at last a spinning darkness dragged him under.

Chapter 24

*"The runes are not immutable aspects of nature. Each was etched
upon the stuff of the universe by the will of a great binder."*

-Caden, *Axioms of Spirit Binding*

The room stunk of burnt fur, it was late, and Henrik was
utterly exhausted, again. Despite his renewed sense of purpose,
he had already overlooked an important element in his new plan
and retired to his room without soliciting anyone to help set his
arm. He would have to go back down to the tap room and enlist
an assistant.

Someone pounded on the door.

"Henrik!" Ivar shouted from the other side. "I need to
speak with you at once."

More trouble. Henrik stood up and limped over to the
door. He slid open the bolt, looking out into the hallway to
discover that Ivar was not alone. He had Arius in tow along with
Tor, the town's thatcher, and his brother Leif.

"Gentlemen." Henrik stepped back, allowing them into
the room. "To what do I owe the pleasure of your visit?"

As they entered, Henrik noted the look of distaste as they
smelled the room. Tor and Leif both traced a line down their
cheeks like a tear from the corners of their right eyes. Henrik
ignored their superstition.

"Well?" he asked.

It was Arius who stepped forward, motioning for Leif to
shut the door before he spoke. "The pigs are hoarding food."

"Arius." Ivar sounded scandalized.

"It's true, isn't it?"

Ivar set a restraining hand on his son's forearm and turned to Henrik. "You made me a promise tonight."

Henrik puffed out his cheeks and exhaled. "What's happened?"

"Well..." Ivar laced his fingers together and stared down at his doe skin boots. "Some of the men from the village came to me complaining that they had no food for supper. You were gone here already." He held up his hands. "Not that I blame you. But the men came to me."

Henrik rolled his eyes. "Ivar, get on with it."

"I asked for my goods back, and the prefect refused. He made a pretense about paying me back but was quite firm about not returning my property. He also reminded me of the cache of provisions you so wisely set aside."

"Ah," said Henrik. "I see."

The other men eyed the crates and barrels pushed up against the wall. If the prefect sent them here, there was probably no salvaging things with the federals. He was clearly trying to turn them against one another.

"I'm sorry it's come to this, Ivar," he said. "I'll admit I was a little afraid that this could happen."

Arius threw up his hands in disgust. "Then you lied to us!"

"Arius, calm down," said his father.

"Don't you see?" said Arius. "You've ruined us. They've taken everything. We'll starve. We'll all starve!"

"Ten Fathers," said Henrik. "Calm down. Perhaps I shouldn't have gone along with the prefect. But what could we do? They would just have taken everything anyway."

Arius sneered at him, but Henrik saw that he recognized the truth of it.

"And, of course, I'll share my supplies," Henrik added. "This is precisely why I purchased them."

Arius and Ivar glanced at each other.

"We need to stick together," Henrik pressed on. "If things get desperate, we need to keep the town working

235

together. We can't trust the federals anymore. Not after they've taken everything from you like this."

Arius pounded his fist into the palm of his hand. "We can't just give up like that. Come with us to talk to the prefect."

Henrik walked over to his bed and sat down, shaking his head. "It's too late for that, I'm afraid. The prefect sent you here to drive a wedge between us. He thought I'd try to hoard all of this for myself." Henrik unwrapped his arm, wincing as he laid it in his lap. "Arius, will you help me? I still need to set this."

Arius backed away. "I've never done that sort of thing before."

"Neither have I. Please?"

Arius gulped. "What should I do?"

"It's broken here," Henrik touched his forearm. "You'll have to pull my wrist away from my elbow. Gently. And twist just a little this way." He twirled his finger.

Arius paled and stepped further back. "Tor, you do it." He looked back at Henrik. "I don't want to hurt you."

"Just do it, Arius," Henrik said. "I'm already hurt. Let's get it over with."

"Fine." Arius pantomimed the procedure. "Like this?"

Henrik nodded. With his good hand, he slipped his fingers into his belt pouch and pulled out a binding stone. "Ready," he said, taking a few deep breaths, hoping the care to feed and comfort the rat before he bound it would be enough to knit the bone.

For an instant, it felt like a wagon wheel had rolled over his arm. He cried out. But the spike of pain was followed by an almost ecstatic relief. Henrik's muscles had cramped, and the movement stretched them, restored them to the right shape. Henrik had been afraid that Arius would pull too hard or twist too far, but he'd done it deftly.

"Hold there." Henrik focused on releasing the spirit. He hummed his cant, his voice energizing the runes which crackled to life around the stone. A faint glow in the shape of a rat emanated from the binding rock, never quite taking form before Henrik's will guided its energy into his wounded arm.

236

Arius' resolve failed, and he jumped back. But the magic had done its work, the bone fused together again. Henrik probed it with the fingers of his opposite hand. It was still flimsy. He needed a heartier spirit. A dog or sheep or even a cow.

To be safe, he rewrapped his arm to his chest. When he finally looked up, the others averted their eyes and made a show of inspecting the provisions.

"How many townsfolk are trapped on High Hill?" Henrik asked.

The other men looked at each other, abashed at having forgotten the people trapped there.

Ivar said, "It's an island now. Who knows? Maybe twenty or thirty."

"When you hand out rations for dinner, see if anyone has a boat. We should try to send someone over to see what kind of shape they're in."

"Yes, Mayor Torvald," said Ivar.

"Are there any livestock around?" Henrik asked. "I don't need the meat." He held up the spent binding stone. "But I need to be there for the slaughter."

★★★★★

Anders held his finger under the boy's nose to check if he was still breathing. He was, faintly. The blood on the floor stuck to his boots, the hem of his cloak, the legs of the stool as he sat beside the cot. But blood did not bother him. One of Brohr's arms dangled over the side of the bed, the other rested atop his belly. Gore caked his neck and chin.

Anders whispered a prayer but couldn't finish it. He knew somehow that Brohr would survive this wound, the prayer useless. With a quiet gasp, he realized that he had long since put his faith in the Hidden. How far he had come.

His bloodline would not end, and he would claim his fate, complete his pact. But the thought did not comfort him. For all of its promises, he knew that the Hidden was a liar. Or, at least its words were twisted. The truth lurking like the ancient one

237

himself: unseen, misunderstood. Had it not once promised him two grandsons? That was the poisoned truth it offered.

He felt Brohr's forehead. No fever. Anders opened the bloodstained sweater that the girl had cut down the middle to inspect his wound, but the boy stirred, feebly pushing his hand away. How could this dying child fulfill what was promised?

"Brohr," he asked. "Brohr, can you hear me?" His grandson's eyelids twitched, his face contorted. The boy grimaced and turned his head away. "Wake up," Anders said. He shook Brohr by the shoulders, careful not to jostle him too much. Still, Brohr cried out. His eyes shot open. He lay there, panting, gaze locked with his grandfather. Finally, he mustered the energy to speak.

"Go away," he said.

Anders considered his words. "You and I are bound together. Just as much as you and your brother."

"No."

"Deny all you want, boy. One blood. One doom."

Brohr laughed at him then winced at the pain. "Nonsense."

Anger flashed in the old man's eyes. He clutched the blanket covering Brohr, imagined digging his thumb into the wound. He exhaled, forcing the rage out between his teeth.

"Mock if you wish," he said. "You should be dead."

Anders saw his grandson wither, his defiance gutted by these words. The skald stood up, his foot slipping in the congealed blood on the floor. He braced himself on the edge of Brohr's cot, then leaned over the boy. Brohr cringed at his breath.

"What have you done?" Anders asked.

Brohr's eyes grew stony. "I lived," he said.

Anders knew. In his bowels, he knew. This is how he had survived the night. He would be well soon. But what had it cost? No mean price to purchase a second chance at life. The boy was like him now. A prostitute. A plaything of the old one.

After everything. After everything. He had traded his soul for a legacy of slavery.

"Damn you, boy."

Brohr made no pretense to hide his crime. Somehow the boy understood that Anders had bargained too.

"What should I have done?" Brohr asked. "Bled out? Here? For what?" He cleared his throat, making a disgusted face. "I don't know what you want from me, but I want a life for myself. I don't care what you want. I want to be free of you."

"Ingrate brat," said the old skald. "I did it all for us. Our blood. Our people. I damned myself for you."

Brohr sat up. "What did you do? Why don't you say it? Is that why you hate me so?"

Anders straightened. "You could never understand. You were never even free. You don't know what we've lost. What I gave to get it back. There could be no higher price. Don't you dare to judge me. What price did you pay to sit there looking down?"

"Whatever you've done it hangs around your neck like a noose. Everyone sees it."

"That is what it means to sacrifice." Anders studied his guilty hands. "And what did you bargain? If you're so pure."

"A journey." Brohr lost a little of his ferocity. "That's all. I have to go back to Skolja."

Anders smiled coldly. "And you think it's so simple. Believe me, boy, it will cost you more."

Brohr ignored his jibe. "He said I had to return to Skolja first. Doesn't that make you happy? Isn't that what you wanted all along?"

Anders realized that the boy had no trouble sitting up. He was breathing normally.

"How do you feel?" He asked.

Brohr threw off the blanket and swung his feet to the ground. He closed his eyes as if fighting dizziness, but in a moment, he drew in a breath and pushed himself to his feet. The sight saddened Anders somehow. He could only imagine the road ahead, but he'd always expected Brohr to rise above it like a hero from the sagas. And yet the boy had not risen; he had sunk.

He was tangled in dark promises, in the secret burdens of his pact, for he too was a part of Moriigo's game now.

Chapter 25

"Ten they were, men of iron heart and grim virtue, sent by the ancient lights to conquer a wilderness. With axe and fire they tamed the savage land, and sowed a song of kinship, a line of sons, that stretches still, toward the twilight hour."

-The Tale of the Ten Fathers

An ache awoke him just before dawn. Henrik lay for a few minutes in his featherbed, probing his injured forearm with his good hand. The bone was knit, at least. He wiggled his fingers experimentally. They were stiff and sluggish, but they worked.

Henrik threw off the covers and swung his legs to the floor. He considered having the innkeeper draw him a bath but dismissed it as impractical. Instead, he leaned over and grabbed his boots. Henrik rose and walked over to the window, opening the shutters and looking out over the town. If anything, the water had risen another foot or so. Only the peaks of the rooftops could be seen in the low quarter. In the square, the waterline had reached about half way up the first story of the buildings. It would be over a man's waist. He needed a boat.

Downstairs, he found Luthar Ingstrom, the young innkeeper, eating a bowl of porridge at the bar. Luthar looked up from his meal, not bothering to stand or lift a finger to help. Dark circles hung beneath his eyes.

"The pot's over there if you're hungry," the innkeeper whispered.

Henrik followed his gaze to the porridge. His belly grumbled. As he served himself, someone sat up on the floor nearby. Henrik realized the taproom was full of exhausted men and women, stirring to the scent of hot food.

He shoveled a spoonful of oats with a raisin into his mouth. *Freyan's Ghost!* His missing tooth ached again after he accidently bit down, but the pain was nothing beside finally getting some food in his belly. He closed his eyes, sucking on the sweet morsel until his stomach insisted he send it down. When he'd finished, Henrik set the bowl on the counter and asked, "Did Ivar take a room last night? Is he upstairs?"

Luthar nodded. Holding his bowl up to his face, he slurped the milk and wiped his mouth on his sleeve. "He's in the room across the hall from you."

Henrik started up the stairs, nearly stumbling on the first step as the ground trembled and the timbers of the inn groaned in the tremor. It passed after only a few seconds, but it was enough to rouse everyone sleeping in the taproom. Worried voices erupted, and Henrik looked back to see Luthar still seated at the bar, holding up his bowl so that he wouldn't spill.

Arius bolted down the staircase, eyes wide and darting.

Henrik held up his hands. "Easy! It's just an aftershock. It'll pass."

Ivar appeared behind him in the stairwell, looking just as panicked, but Henrik held up his hands, shouted for calm, and ushered everyone to sit down for breakfast. Ivar and his son gathered their composure and joined the other villagers.

Henrik waited for them, mollifying a few of the townsfolk as Ivar and his son wolfed down some porridge. The trio discussed what needed to be done, carefully skirting the ominous shift in tone that the prefect had taken.

They squabbled for a few minutes, trying to decide on the best course of action. Ivar wanted to send as many folk as possible to their families in the hinterland in order to mitigate the food shortage. Eventually, unable to convince Ivar without saying so, Henrik finally brought up what he had hoped would go unsaid.

"And what if there is a fight? With the federals, I mean."

Ivar stepped back from Henrik, shaking his head. "What sort of insanity is that? I don't want any part of it." He looked around to be sure no one had heard, but the nearest villagers were slurping down porridge at the bar.

"We can't dismiss the possibility, Ivar. They've already stolen everything you own. These quakes and floods are not over, I'm afraid. It may get worse."

"He's right, Father," Arius said. "The pigs are going to leave us out here to starve. We can't trust them anymore."

Henrik patted Arius on the shoulder. "Listen to your son. I'm not advising anything rash, but these aren't ordinary times. If it comes to a fight, we'll want every man we can get."

Ivar covered his mouth, aghast at the very idea. "I can't believe I'm hearing this. And from the two of you. If it comes to a fight, we should just disappear into the woods. What chance do we have against the federal legion? It's crazy." Ivar looked around the High Tavern and jerked his thumb toward the door. He led the trio outside where they could talk without being overheard.

They stood at the crest of Federal Hill, a frigid breeze blowing in from the sea, and stared down at the flooded hamlet. Henrik had set up his easel once on this very spot. To the east, he looked across toward High Hill, backlit by the sunrise, and counted five cows grazing by the ruins of his old home. How the landscape had changed. Water now surrounded the hilltop on all sides, locking the survivors upon the newly formed island.

"It's not crazy," Henrik finally said. "If we organize, we'll outnumber them. And we have a binder. The federals do not."

Ivar looked skeptical, but his son concurred. "I've seen him in action." He nodded to Henrik. "If he can kill the prefect, it might swing things."

"This is getting out of hand," said Ivar. "You two need to think long term. Like it or not, we've thrown in with the Tyrianites. We're tied together. Besides, what if we won? What if we wipe them out? They would just send another prefect out here and in six months we'd be working the mine -if we were lucky."

243

"I'm not sure how to make you understand, but this," Henrik swept his hand across the flooded vista, "this is just the beginning. Quaya is not done with her death throes. She may drag us all with her." He pointed down the hill where a fishing boat was lodged in a tree near the edge of the water line. "Look, a little luck. We need to get over to the other hill. Those cattle can feed us for weeks. And I can bind them."

Ivar's shoulders slumped. "Are we really considering rebellion?"

★★★★★

Two of the outlaws swung Lar's body onto the pyre. He was the last of them. As the men gathered around, Anders stepped out of the ring of onlookers to deliver the ritual. They'd been without a skald all of their lives; still, their grandfathers had imitated the rites, remembered the Fathers, and kept their ways alive. It was only natural that they looked to him now to take his place. He drew his belt knife and cut his palm, stopping at each body to flick a few drops of blood.

"Honored brothers," he intoned. "Go boldly into the dead place. Your kin will remember you. Do not forget those you have left behind, and give our thanks to those who went before. Enter the Fathers' halls with pride, for you died well. *Immra blosch altes binde*," Anders said in the old tongue. "Blood shall bind us always."

The mourners echoed his mantra. "Blood shall bind us always."

Anders motioned toward the unlit pyre and one of the outlaws stepped forward with a torch, tossing it on the pile of chopped wood and fallen Norn. It took a moment to catch, then its dark smoke rose into the afternoon sky, carried toward the hills by a gentle wind.

Those with close kin among the dead stepped forward, tossing tokens onto the pyre. Normally, they would be figurines carved in the likeness of the fallen, which would be retrieved and buried after the pyre burnt itself out, but they had no time to linger, so the outlaws settled for stones or slices of wood with clan markings drawn in soot from the breakfast cook fires. Someday, if they survived, the Norn could carve a new pair of idols for each of the fallen, burying one near the family hearth, and adding the other to the altar.

Anders watched his grandson standing next to the girl as the flames crackled, the heat pushing them back a step. Brohr looked sickly, but he was on his feet.

Gareth stepped forward and threw a clan marker made from limestone where his son lay, the flames just catching the fallen outlaw's clothes. Gareth knelt beside the fire, oblivious to the heat, and began to recite something in Hemmish. *Fool.* It only served to remind everyone he was a foreigner.

Once the men had placed their markers, and stood awhile in contemplation, some clasped hands and murmured condolences. By tradition, they should hold a feast next, with mead toasts and song, but there was no time for any of that. They needed to return to Skolja.

He had hoped to find the slaves in better condition. They were a tough lot, outlaws to a man, but underfed and overworked. He supposed they could carry axes as well as they could carry picks. If the wind didn't blow them away. There were twenty-six of them that could be considered close enough to fighting shape. The rest didn't seem like they'd make the journey back to Skolja. It was hard to imagine them getting much work done, but facing death, they had found a way.

They scavenged swords, armor, and crossbows from the federals before hurling their bodies down the old mine shaft. The freed slaves whispered that a Raag dwelled at the bottom. Though he didn't believe in such things, it pleased the old man to imagine their desecration. Tyrianites burned their dead too, believing their essence floated up into the void. Their souls would be forever trapped in the confines of that pit. Raag or not. It was a fitting end for the swine.

Gareth finally finished his absurd, whining ritual, and stood up, the pyre blazing in the background. Wilted, emasculated by his loss, it was time for Gareth to go. How could this Hem lead? *Pathetic.*

Anders followed him into the ordinal's quarters as the rest of the group gathered their gear to leave. Inside, Gareth turned just as Anders closed the door behind him.

"Leave me be," Gareth said.

Anders shook his head. "Gareth," he said. "It is good that your son is not alive to see how truly worthless you are."

Gareth sat on the ordinal's cot. "Go away you old snake. I am mourning."

Anders spat at his feet. "I think I finally understand why these men let you lead them. A Hem. A coward. I've always wondered."

"Such a noise you make. Like a braying ass."

"They let you rule them… because she ruled you."

Gareth looked up, glaring. "No one rules me! Marta was my wife. Just because I wasn't afraid to listen to her, just because I'm not a tyrant like you. You Norn; so bloody ignorant. So proud. She would have been a great leader. Better than you."

"She deserved a real man. I'm sorry she had to settle for you."

"Get out!" Gareth slapped the cot he sat on. "Out! Let me grieve in peace, you wretch."

"We have no time for your simpering. You finally get the nerve to fight after decades of hiding, and after one battle, you're spent."

"I shouldn't have listened to you. We shouldn't be here. Now my son is dead. While that piglet of yours is still breathing. How is that possible? More of your black magic?"

Anders snickered at him. "What a squeamish thing you are. Nels was weak, and Brohr is strong. Never mind how." Anders shook his head, pulling the knife from his belt. "This isn't your fight."

Gareth saw the blade in the old man's hand and sprang to his feet. He grabbed for his sword, which leaned against the bed, but Anders slid the dagger under his ribs and up into his chest.

246

They stood eye to eye; the sword fell from Gareth's hand, and Anders smiled, kissing him on the cheek.

"Goodbye, old friend."

Anders shoved the Hemmishman's body onto the cot. He sung softly to himself, reaching down and cupping his hand to Gareth's wound. He smeared the blood on his own forehead and around his crown, losing the twinge of guilt he felt in the rhythm of his magic.

★★★★★

Brasca laid down on the cot in the stuffy communications room. Carthalo had been inside trying to raise Arabo on the helm all morning. The prefect dismissed his subordinate and donned the helmet, squirming back and forth until he was comfortable. A candelabra flickered beside him on the end table, casting shadows of his reclining figure on the wall.

Once he settled in, Brasca closed his eyes and began to concentrate on the first tier of runes. He searched the circle, listening to each constellation until he found Absalon. Then, superimposing the figure of the war leader atop the lines of power, he anchored himself there and sought the next tier. He'd never really understood the archetypes. His tutors had vomited stories about them ad nauseam, but they had never answered the fundamental questions of how and why they worked. Sometimes he wondered if he was thick or if they were. As long as he could use the helm, he supposed it was moot.

Holding Absalon, a faint impression of a man wielding his sword above his head, Brasca matched its pitch and ascended to the second tier, feeling a flutter of vertigo as he hopped the starry void between the rings. One by one, he passed the Wife, Prince Hopeless, Eshzidon the Boor, and the Spirit Bound until he reached Darmuz, the corners of the rune like the arms of a dancer exulting. Brasca linked Darmuz to Absalon and climbed to the final tier. There he found Ashtara, the Angel of Accord. He hummed all three notes of the sequence, and his mind reached out across the void to the waiting presence.

"Brasca?" Arabo's luminous form coalesced from the void.

"Damnation, Arabo, it's good to hear your voice. I haven't been able to reach you or anyone from Bishop Adrychaeus's staff in two days. What is going on in Trond?"

"Adrychaeus is dead. His porch collapsed on him while he was drinking tea. One of the quakes. Have you felt them too?"

"Yes," Brasca said. "Adrychaeus is dead? Who is in charge then?"

"You have to understand, this city is a madhouse. No one expected this much trouble. We weren't ready. The aqueduct collapsed in the first quake. There were fires. Pontiff's balls, Brasca, half the city burned."

"Who is in charge?"

"Well," Arabo said. "That's the thing. I am."

"What? There must be ten officers outranking you."

"I know," said Arabo. "Trust me, I know. One of the helms was lost. The command staff was slaughtered in a riot. You can't imagine what these provincials are like now. Brasca, I need your help, my friend."

"Then send me a ship, Arabo. There's nothing worth saving out here. Send me a ship, and I'll come."

"Thank you. You don't know how much I need this. I'll send it right away. It should be there tonight."

"I'll be ready."

"Thank you, Brasca. I need someone I can count on. One last thing."

"Yes?"

"The astronomers are all contradicting each other. All saying that what happened to Quaya was impossible. They're all pointing fingers at each other, saying it's not their fault we weren't ready for this. That it would take a hundred comets to do that much damage. But they all agree on one thing. Quaya is going to rain hell tonight. Not sure how to be ready for that. But I thought you should know."

"Thanks, Arabo."

"You'd better start calling me 'sir.'" Arabo's form flickered out, leaving Brasca alone in the starlit expanse.

Henrik bribed the thatcher's son and his friends to wade out to the tree and get the boat down. The canoe stretched twice a man's length but wasn't quite big enough to ferry cattle back and forth between the hilltops. At least it floated. They could go reconnoiter and figure things out from there.

The water grew choppy as Arius steered them out into the shallow waters flowing through the streets. A swarm of butterflies, black with blue-spotted wings, had settled on the thatch of a sunken home they rowed past. Somewhere in the drowned village, a dog barked.

Henrik tried to paddle, but with one arm, he wasn't much help. They hugged the new shoreline as much as possible, fearful of the eddies and riptides lurking in Skolja's alleys. Over by one of the houses on the northwest side of the square, they spotted a body jerking ominously as some sea creature fed upon it.

Henrik stared back at the distant figures huddled in groups around the fort. He looked west toward the smithy, mired in floodwaters, but the intervening houses afforded a scant view. He wanted to detour to inspect *The Muse*, but something told him to keep the ship a secret. The last thing he needed was for the townsfolk to suspect he was considering abandoning them.

They passed a flooded house with the door open. Henrik looked in to see a table set for dinner, a seagull pecking at an uneaten plate of chicken. Something beneath the water swam out of the doorway, passing beneath the boat. It was big, two or three hands wide and as long as a man was tall.

A white shark.

Henrik looked over at Arius who gripped the sides of the boat, the oar across his lap.

"Don't stop," Henrik said.

Arius paddled on, the pair soon emerging from a cluster of half-submerged houses near the foot of High Hill. A few folks trapped on the hill spotted them and were waiting as they arrived. The owner of the Pilgrim's Inn took Henrik by his good hand and helped haul him out of the boat. The villagers crowded around. They were cold and unwashed, tired and eager for news.

"I know that you've had a trying night." A few of the villagers grumbled at the understatement, but Henrik quieted them with a wave of his hand. "Some of you have lost members of your family. You're all probably tired and cold and miserable. What we need to remember most right now is to stick together. Everyone around you will still be your neighbor in a few days or a week when things go back to normal. Remember that. And take care of each other. I think we should try to get everyone off of this hill today. We'll keep ferrying people across, and you keep working on the other boat. Don't try to wade across town though. There are strong currents, and we saw a white shark on the way. It's probably safer to wait for a boat. So let's get to it. Okay?"

One of the villagers stepped forward. "Brig and Oren Ulsten waded over last night. We couldn't see them. Did they make it?"

Henrik looked to Arius, who shrugged. "I didn't see them. I'm sorry. It's possible they made it, and we didn't hear."

The crowd broke up, gathering their things, settling back in to wait. Jan Hagstrom, the farmer who owned the cattle, approached him. He was a middle-aged man with a pitted face who shaved his head to hide his baldness. "I can't take my herd across on a boat. The well here is fouled. Now everyone's leaving. What am I supposed to do?"

Henrik stroked his chin as if he had not been thinking about this already. "Um," said Henrik. "Well, we could use more food over there. I suppose we could purchase the herd from you?"

Jan's eyes bulged, and he covered his gaping mouth. "The whole herd? What would I do then? They're my livelihood."

"Well then let us purchase a few. We can take the meat over in the boat. You stay here with the rest. I can make sure we bring you water."

"Isn't there another way?" Jan asked.

"The water should come down soon. We can help you drive the herd across once the tide rolls back a little. Once it's too low for white sharks. I'm afraid it's the best I can do."

Jan finally nodded. "Very well. I appreciate the help."

Henrik held out his hand, and they shook. "I'm glad to help," he said. "I do have an odd request."

"Oh?"

Henrik draped his arm around Jan and lowered his voice. "We need to kill a few of the cattle in a particular way. I need them for a binding."

Jan swallowed and looked around to see if anyone else had heard. "What?"

"I'm going to bind them. And you're going to help me."

Jan scratched his scalp. "You bring plenty of water, okay? Enough for the cattle? That's ten buckets, easy. Every day."

"As I said."

"Okay," Jan conceded. "What do I have to do?"

It took a little convincing, but Henrik organized a small delegation to assist him. They moved the rest of the herd to the back side of the shrine and walked one of the heifers far enough away not to scare the rest. While Jan comforted the creature and fed it oats, Henrik formulated a binding sequence. For an archetype, he chose *the Mother,* hoping that the life-giving connotations would synergize with his purpose. The essence would of course be life, and the intent would be repair.

When he was ready, he nodded to the fisherman whom he had enlisted. The man brought his axe down on the back of the beast's neck, dropping it like a felled tree. Henrik concentrated on *the Mother's* rune, intoning the first note to snare the beast's soul. As soon as the transfixation was finished, he pictured the rune of *life*, faintly evocative of a tree, and the essential note brought it shimmering to light. The other essences bled away, and the heifer's animus was distilled to pure vitalizing force. Then Henrik focused on his arm, on mending the bone, bringing down the swelling. He incanted the final note, fueling the intention he had selected: *repair.* The runes danced around the stone, their warm light ebbing as the sparks of animus were

251

drawn into the waiting stone. As soon as he felt the binding take, Henrik repeated the sequence, loosing the spirit to do his bidding. A radiant echo of the cow floated up from the stone in miniature, dispersing like smoke in the wind. A surge of warmth flowed into him as he drew the last glowing motes into his arm, and the fibers of bone and tendon were infused with new strength.

Henrik opened his eyes. His assistants had all retreated twenty paces. Most of the folk trapped on the hill looked on in horror. Several of them ran their fingers from the corners of their eyes.

"Good work." Henrik tested his arm. He couldn't help smiling. It seemed like the first thing to go right in days. "Go fetch another. A bull this time. This one doesn't need to be gentle."

Jan swallowed, back-peddled toward the rest of the herd, and finally gathered his composure enough to obey. He returned soon enough leading another cow. This time Henrik struck the killing blow himself and kept the spirit bound. He sent Jan for a third, but before he returned, a commotion broke out. Henrik and Arius ran over to get a better view. They looked northwest toward the back side of Federal Hill, where a large group of horsemen had circled around from the west and were searching for a way up the hill. Henrik's stomach lurched. Arius cursed beside him.

Clan Kriega had arrived.

Chapter 26

"The Federal Inquisition is inundated with an endless flood of petty accusations, yet true unorthodoxy is vanishingly rare. Only in the most backwards of provinces, and those dark quarters beyond federal control, is there any real evidence of the black arcana. Still, rumors of proscribed magic cling to prominent citizens like barnacles to the hull of a ship. Perhaps these heresies truly persist in back alley cabals and courtly whispers. We may never know."

-Quentus Mori, A Volume of the Bizarre

When the funeral rite was over, Brohr sat down on an old stump next to the barracks. One of the outlaws started to boil a pot of yams and offered him some. While they cooked, he watched his grandfather follow Gareth into the ordinal's house. He'd grown weary of their bickering and bitterness. With a little luck, they'd kill one another and leave Brohr in peace.

Lyssa sat on a rock a few feet away, keeping a wary eye on him. He'd seen the shock on her face when he walked out of the barracks for the funeral. He doubted that anyone else knew how deadly his wound should've been.

"You're alive." She stood. "You're walking around."

Brohr nodded to each of her statements, not wanting to volunteer anything about his sudden recovery. When it became clear he wasn't going to explain, she asked, "How? Brohr you were dying. Even if you survived, you would still be bedridden."

He didn't want to lie to her, but the prospect of explaining daunted him.

"Say something," she demanded. Lyssa's face twisted into a frown.

Brohr drew in a deep breath and began his admission. "Do you remember that thing on the dock?"

Lyssa took a step back as if he'd slapped her. "What have you done?"

Brohr pushed on. "It came to me last night. I was so close to dying. I tried, but I couldn't say no."

"To what?"

Brohr looked away. "Just that I would go back to Skolja. Except…"

"Except that thing is evil. And you're an idiot!"

Brohr nodded. He looked up at Lyssa, searching for mercy in her face. Behind her, Anders emerged from the ordinal's house. Blood covered his face. He hummed a tune full of noise and power.

Brohr stood up. "Ten Fathers."

"What?" Lyssa asked.

Brohr pointed at his grandfather.

Lyssa looked and turned back to Brohr, puzzled. "What?" she repeated.

Brohr glanced back and forth between Lyssa and his grandfather. She didn't see.

Anders cupped his hands to his mouth and shouted over the cook fires and idle chatter. "Everyone, listen up," he said. "I have bad news. Gareth has killed himself. He was distraught over the death of his son."

The explanation seemed sufficient to everyone. They looked at each other, shaking their heads at the tragedy, but no one even bothered to investigate the body.

Brohr studied Lyssa. She was shaking her head too.

"What an ass," she said. "All that caution, and then he kills himself. It's almost funny."

"Do you see anything unusual about my grandfather?" Brohr asked.

She examined him for a moment and shrugged. "No," she said. "Why?"

"I'll be right back," he told her.

Anders watched him come, gore dripping from his ears and chin. "You see it. Don't you?"

Brohr leaned in, speaking softly so no one would hear him. "You murdered him."

His grandfather looked back at the ordinal's house, as if he could see through the wall to where Gareth's body lay. He nodded. "You have to admit you're a little relieved, aren't you?"

"Relieved?" Brohr stepped back a pace. "You're unbelievable. Gareth may have been spineless, but he was one of us."

Anders turned his head and spat. "He was not. He was a Hem and a coward."

"You used this trick on the constable. You've used it before haven't you?"

Anders shrugged. "Don't you wonder why you can see through it? You're getting closer. Picking out the first notes of your song." Anders smiled up at Brohr, his teeth and the whites of his eyes brilliant against his red mask. "You're becoming a skald."

★★★★★

Henrik crouched on the balls of his feet as the canoe coasted to shore. The second the nose touched ground, he leapt out of the bow and sprinted up the incline. The new arrivals clustered at the crest of the hill on the northern side of the fort. It was hard to tell, but Henrik estimated perhaps thirty fighting men. Once they had secured the ascent, their womenfolk and children emerged from the wood, slogging over the marshy ground.

Henrik ran through the makeshift camp, leaping over cook fires and dodging past a woman with an armload of firewood. As he came around the back corner of the fort, he saw Ivar watching from behind one of the villager's tents. *Idiot!* If he had just taken charge of the situation and managed it, they could probably blame it all on the federals. Who knew what the Kriegans had found out now? If they discovered that Henrik had

255

killed Erk Grafstrom and turned his wife in to the prefect, the situation could get ugly.

Clan Kriega gathered between the entrance to the fort and the path that led into the hinterlands from the backside of Federal Hill. They milled around in a disorganized mob, shouting at the wary Tyrianites by the gate, bragging and goading one another to stir their courage. The townsfolk watched the spectacle, keeping their distance from the Kriegans. But for how long? Eventually someone would mention that he'd been the one sent to hunt the looters. That he had killed Grafstrom and turned his wife over to the pigs.

Henrik stooped over and picked up a stone. He threw it at Ivar, and it struck the tent, startling him. Henrik waved him over.

"What are you doing?" he demanded.

"We're dead," Ivar whined. "The Kriegans are here. What was I supposed to do?"

Henrik shoved him toward the crowd. "You're supposed to take charge. We've got to get in there and make sure they blame the prefect for everything. I know I don't have to say for you to keep your mouth shut about Grafstrom."

"Of course," said Ivar. "Are you sure this is wise, Henrik?"

Arius ran up, out of breath. "This is bad. What do we do?"

"Ivar, go and find the Grafstrom baby but keep it out of sight. Arius, keep your mouth shut and follow my lead."

Ivar split off, and Henrik and Arius jogged up to the mob of Kriegans, pushing through the villagers until they emerged in the center of the group. The clan was led by an old woman with hair dyed bright red, holding a leash tied around the neck of a young boy of nine or ten. She wore ragged clothes and a patchwork cloak. Her eyes were rheumy, but as soon as Henrik emerged, her gaze swung toward him. She sniffed the air, smiling with rotten teeth. Scars ringed her mouth. The crone stooped over and whispered in the boy's ear.

256

He turned to Henrik and, with scarred lips of his own, pronounced, "Freylka asks if the outworlder's dog has kept the child safe?" She whispered something else to the boy. He looked back at her, and she gave him a little shove. "Give back Freylka's grandniece and she will not kill you for being a traitor."

"What are you talking about?" Henrik asked.

The boy spoke on his mistress's behalf. "Freylka knows. She sees. Give back the girl so that we can turn to the pigs. We must get inside that gate."

Henrik looked through the open gate, reinforcements were arriving from the interior of the fort, the prefect's plumed hat bobbing amongst them. Brasca shouted orders and mounted the steps up to the rampart. An ordinal remained outside, but the rest fell back within the fort.

"Freylka is it?" Henrik said. "You're right. I know where your grandniece is. A friend is bringing her now."

"What's the matter, Henrik?" Brasca shouted down to them. "Did she ask about Grafstrom?"

Henrik looked from the prefect to the witch. She bent to the boy's ear and spoke to him.

"Freylka knows," he said. "That is her gift. If the dog can serve, she will still be merciful."

Her clouded eyes lingered on him.

"Prefect," Henrik shouted up. "These people are still subjects of the federation. We need help!"

"These people are thieves, Henrik," Brasca said. "Is there no more law in Skolja?"

Arius pushed forward. "You've stolen ten times as much!"

The ordinal who still stood outside the gate cupped his hands to his mouth and shouted toward the crowd of Norn. "Astrid," he called. "Astrid, come with me! I'm sorry." He beckoned to a pretty Norn girl at the edge of the spectators.

"Carthalo!" She started toward him, but her father reached out and grabbed her by the arm.

As the girl struggled to free herself, the prefect leaned over the rampart, looking down at his officer. "Ordinal Carthalo, get in here right now. That's an order!"

The Kriegans inched forward.

"Astrid!" Carthalo ignored the prefect, wavering between the girl and the gate.

Freylka jerked on the boy's leash, and he yelled. "Attack!"

Both sides sprang into action. The last federal besides Carthalo darted inside as the Kriegans dashed forward. Carthalo turned to flee, but the massive wooden gate slammed shut. The Kriegans swarmed around him, knocking him to the ground and throwing their shoulders into the gate. The frenzy of their assault kept the federals from barring it for a moment, but the defenders held.

Freylka stood beside Henrik, watching. She reeked, an unwashed stench of sweat and piss, like she'd never taken a bath in her life. Her boy looked at her expectantly as crossbowmen fired down from the ramparts.

Freylka sang, her voice delicate, lovely, raising the hairs on the back of Henrik's neck. It surprised him that such beauty could come from such an ugly creature. She ended her tune abruptly, hissing something unintelligible to the boy.

"Fall back!" he screamed. "Fall back!"

Freylka tugged his leash again. When he looked up at her, she tapped her fingers on her belt. He nodded, plucked a ram's horn from his own belt, pressed it to his lips, and blew a single rising note.

The clan pulled back, dragging the unfortunate ordinal who had been left outside of the gates with them. The crossbowmen atop the ramparts continued to fire at the retreating Kriegans as they fled out of range. Freylka turned her back on the battle and limped away from the action with Henrik and her boy close behind.

★★★★★

The outlaws gathered, weary from the long march, just within the edge of the forest, looking out at the flooded ruin of Skolja. A few hundred paces from where they stood, the grass

258

and blackberry bushes gave way to the muddy soil and standing water that encircled Federal Hill and covered most of the town.

Brohr tried to imagine what had happened here since he'd fled, still in manacles, a noose strung around his neck. He could see that most of the townsfolk were camped on the little plateau to the east of the fort.

"The gate is barred," his grandfather said, pointing up the hill.

Brohr folded his arms. "How are we going to get up there without being spotted? They'll see us the second we step out of the woods."

Lyssa tapped him on the arm. He hadn't realized she was standing there. "I should go in first," she said. "I can have a look around without raising the kind of trouble that a company of outlaws will."

Anders turned to her, looked her up and down. "Aren't you wanted in Skolja too? You did help Brohr escape, didn't you? They saw you?"

She nodded. "Yes, but I can sneak in. I'm not worried about that." Lyssa bit her lip. "I have a cousin who looks just like me. I can pass for him. I can be ten feet away, and his mother would mix the two of us up. I just need to make a few changes."

Anders scowled. "You get caught, you could lose us the element of surprise."

"Surprise?" She raised an eyebrow. "You think anyone is going to be surprised by the time this bunch gets across that?" She pointed at the marshy expanse encircling Federal Hill. Their ragged band numbered over fifty men, some of them the scrawny slaves recently freed from the mine. She doubted they could even run that far, and there was no way they were sneaking up on anyone.

"She's right," said Brohr. "What do we have to lose? It sounds worth it to me to find out what's going on."

Anders waved his hand at Skolja. "Go then," he said. "But be back in an hour. We don't have time to waste."

Lyssa plopped down on the bed of pine needles cross-legged and opened her pack. She brought out a pair of scissors and looked up at Brohr.

"What are you doing?" he asked.

She separated a lock of her hair from the rest and snipped it short. "If I'm going to pass as my cousin, I have to look the part." Lyssa trimmed another lock and another until her hair looked how a young boy might wear it.

Brohr bit his lip. "Don't you have a hat?"

"Brohr." She reached out and set her hand on his leg. "Don't get upset."

He hadn't realized that he had raised his voice. Anders stared at him too. He wasn't quite sure why he was so upset, but Lyssa rubbed the side of his knee reassuringly.

"Why do you want to look like a boy?"

Lyssa stabbed the scissors into the ground. "What does it matter to you?"

"You know why. You *know* why. Am I crazy? I just want to know…that you feel the same way."

Anders voiced a little note of disgust and the look Brohr gave him forced the old man back a step.

Lyssa bit her lip. "It's how I want to look, okay? If you don't like it, you don't like me. I'm not about to prance around in a dress and spend my life nursing some man's whining babies."

"That's not what I'm saying." Brohr knelt in front of her. "I will like it. I just…do you? I mean… Do…you?"

"Ten cocks, you dope. Yeah, I do."

His grandfather snapped. "Get on with it! We haven't got the time for this sort of nonsense." He clenched his fists at his sides. "Brohr, take a few men and circle around to get a better view from the east."

Brohr noted his grandfather's balled fists. Bits of Gareth's dried blood still clung to his face. "I'm not going anywhere," said Brohr.

Lyssa paused to watch the tension but went back to cutting her hair. Anders gave her a foul look and stormed off to yell at some of the other outlaws.

"Be careful around him," Brohr said. "Especially if I'm not around."

"No offense," she said. "But your grandfather gives me the creeps. I'm not about to turn my back to him."

"He murdered Gareth, you know."

She looked up, scissors poised. "Gareth committed suicide." She wore a funny expression like she was trying to remember something but couldn't.

"No," he said, sitting down beside her. "It was a trick."

"If you say so."

"I do."

Lyssa finished cutting her hair. It looked boyish but cute. She flashed a smile. "What do you think?"

Brohr found himself blushing. "You look good."

Somehow this was not the right thing to say. She scowled at him.

"What?" he asked.

She stood up and produced a baggy black over-shirt that hung to her knees. "What about now?"

He nodded. "Now you look cute, but your clothes don't fit."

"Do I look like a boy?"

"Yes," said Brohr.

She smiled at him, multiplying his confusion. "Good. Okay," she said. "Wish me luck." Lyssa stepped forward and pecked him on the cheek before darting off to leave him bewildered, hand pressed to the spot where she had kissed him.

His smile faded when he heard his grandfather's voice.

"She's a strange one," Anders said. They watched her make her way a few hundred paces west and leave the tree line, headed casually toward Federal Hill. "Don't let her distract you." He turned to face his grandson. "I wouldn't want her to become a liability."

Brohr leveled his glare at the old man. "Don't you dare, old man. Just leave me alone. Let me have a life besides your revenge. Ten Fathers, did you ever see me as more than a dagger

261

to shove in some Tyrianite's back?" Brohr shook his head. "I wish I could get away from you."

Anders swallowed. His chin trembled. "We are blood, boy. The line of Freyan. The future of our people rests with you and me. It doesn't matter what you want."

Brohr stepped up to tower over his grandfather. He leaned down in his face. "You don't get to tell me what to do anymore. That thing you worship wants me here, so I guess I have to be. But as soon as that debt is paid, I'm leaving. I don't want to ever see you again."

"Fine." Anders didn't back down. He scowled up at his grandson, poking his finger into his chest. "But don't you think for a second that you're any better than I am. It came to me just like it did to you, in a moment of weakness. When all was lost. We were broken. Slaves. It promised that we would drive them out. Slaughter every pig in Skolja. It offered so much for so little. How could I say no?" Anders turned his back on Brohr. "All it cost me were the things I would never have had otherwise."

"It turned you into a murderer."

Anders nodded. "If you only knew. But which is worse... to be a murderer, or to be murdered? Try to imagine what it was like, Brohr. I was just a boy when they came in their ships from the sky. We thought they were spirits until the men came out and the killing started. Who do you think taught me to be ruthless?"

"What does it want?" Brohr asked.

Anders tucked a lock of blood-caked hair behind his ear. "You, I think. But I don't know why."

Brohr set his hand on the hilt of his sword, as if that could help. "Well, it can't have me. Whatever it wants, I won't do it. I won't."

Anders stared out over the flood plain. "If you only knew how many times I have said that to myself."

★★★★★

262

Someone knocked on the door of Brasca's office. With a sigh, he set down the sheet of parchment he'd been reading and rubbed his eyes, cursing when he realized he had ink on his fingers.

"Come," he said.

Ordinal Belizar opened the door, stepped in, and hailed him.

Brasca nodded, waiting. "Well," Brasca cocked his head. "What is it?"

"A caller, sir." Belizar folded his hands together.

"From Trond? Is it Arabo?"

"No, sir. It's from Tyria. It's... Elector Quoll, sir."

Brasca stiffened. He looked up at Belizar, who looked away. "Why is my father on the helm, Ordinal?"

Belizar shrugged. "I'm sorry, sir. He didn't say."

"Damnit." Brasca rose, shooing his ordinal out the door. He left his office, entering the main room of the command building, where the clerk on duty had turned around in his chair to gawk. "Back to work!" Brasca snapped.

The prefect entered the communications room alone and shut the door behind him. The helm lay on the bedside table, next to a flickering candelabra. Brasca plunked down on the cot and kicked up his feet. He lay back, staring up at the ceiling in the gloom.

Finally, he reached over, grabbed the helm, and shoved it onto his head. He had to calm himself to attune to the first rune: Eshzidon the Boor, a squarish sigil with a pair of slashes at the right corners. Once he'd matched pitch, Brasca climbed to the next tier, found Tova, the Merry Piper, and hummed his note. Last, he ascended a final time, lashed the first two notes to Magnus, the Tinker, and intoned the triplet.

A starscape whirled around him, strange planets looming within distant clouds of bluish gas, asteroids forever tumbling in their lonely orbits, darkness dotted by winking lights. His mind soared to everywhere, hurtling eons compressed into an eyeblink.

And then he was still and felt a dour presence brooding there on the celestial stage. Brasca waited for his father to speak, but of course he was intractably stubborn, as always, so caught up in his melodrama that he no longer even noticed his petty aggressions. Brasca wondered how long he would have to wait until his father caved and spoke first. It was moot though; the elector might have all day for this sort of foolishness, but Brasca did not.

"Was there something you wanted, Bostar?" It was a childish jab, but his father had always hated it when he called him by name. Perhaps pettiness ran in the family.

"It's Sabina."

Back on the cot where Brasca's body lay, he balled his fists. He had been expecting this though he had never expected his father to play the messenger. Their marriage had always been a practical one, and Sabina blamed him for Silvano's death. It was etched on her face every time she looked at him. When he told her that their son had burned to death, he had expected to see grief in her eyes, but first came the hate. He knew that she would leave him. He was just waiting for the axe to fall.

"So she's appealed for a divorce," said Brasca.

The elector paused to consider his next words. "Perhaps if you had been here this wouldn't have happened. But your self-righteous outburst—"

"Enough!" Brasca shouted. "I will decide for myself what is right and wrong. Thank you very much."

"No matter what it costs the rest of your family? You have another son, Brasca. And he needs you now more than ever."

"Ha!" Brasca scoffed. "You hypocrite. I couldn't possibly be a worse father than you!"

"If you would let me finish, you arrogant little shit—"

"I don't have to listen to—"

"Sabina is dead!" the elector shouted.

Silence filled the starry void. Brasca struggled with the urge to tear off the helm, to march out of the fort, to wander into the wilderness, find a quiet place, and fall on his sword. And then he wondered why? Had he loved her after all? No, he decided, but she had given him his boys. "How?" Brasca asked.

"She killed herself." The Elector's voice had no soft edges, no pity.

"How is Lycus?"

"Too young to understand." The elector sighed. "It gets worse."

"What could be worse?" Brasca asked.

"The note."

Brasca's stomach churned.

His father pressed on. "It was quite the catalog of your shortcomings, your impieties, your outright blasphemies even. Did you really rant to her that the Pontiff was just a man? And a fool at that? How could you be so indiscreet? You're lucky the synod has the disaster on Quaya to worry about. Incredibly lucky. If the federation weren't in the midst of a catastrophe, this would be everywhere. I've managed to get my hands on the note and destroy it but not before the rumors started. You need to conclude this little episode and get back to the home world before your reputation is damaged beyond repair."

"I don't care," said Brasca. "I don't care about that anymore."

"Brasca, my son. You think I'm too thick, too cold, to comprehend the magnitude of your suffering, but you're wrong. You think I felt any different when your brothers died on Shinei?"

Brasca said nothing.

"I think," said the elector, "that you can't forgive yourself that you weren't a better father than I was. If you'd been a nice daddy, Little Silly would still be alive."

"Careful," Brasca said.

"Lycus needs you, Brasca. He's lost his brother, now his mother. His father is in exile. Come home son; he needs you. I might even be able to find you a new wife. If you can show that you haven't lost your nerve."

"You must be joking."

"Not at all," said the elector. "I'm sure it sounds crass to you, but this is no time for idle mourning. I know that it was cruel that you had to put the torch to Crassa so soon after Silvano. But life is cruel sometimes. You've let it get the better of you. The future of our house hinges on your return. I know you resent everything that's happened, that it's troubled your faith. But you needn't be sincere to lead. Merely willing to submit to certain expectations. This is your last chance to be a father. Get yourself together and make a show of good faith. This is it, son. Swallow your accursed pride and get back here."

Chapter 27

"Truth has a habit of marring beautiful things. To understand the greatness of Cassian, one must set aside the idealized creature he became upon his apotheosis and embrace the butcher who cowed the warring houses into anointing him their first Pontiff."

-Orian Quo, An Heretical History of the Divine Office

Lyssa jogged up Federal Hill.

When she reached the top, the sight of the Selvig Sea took her breath away. For a few heartbeats, Lyssa tuned out the clamor of the villagers, the condition of the fort, and stared out at the choppy waters she had so often daydreamed about setting sail upon.

But, after a few blissful moments, the spell was broken by a shouting Tyrianite. The sentry stood on the rampart of the fort, pointing down at her. Lyssa's mouth went dry, thinking they had recognized her, and would come pouring out of the gate to arrest her any moment. But they had closed the gate. Her eyes swept back and forth across the plateau, but she saw no soldiers outside of the walls.

A few Norn stood at the edge of bow range, watching the fort, but they didn't challenge her as she passed. Most of the villagers had gathered on the east side of the plateau, so she headed there. Lyssa spotted Rogan roaming the crowd, and he glanced at her, but there was no recognition in his eyes as he wandered by. A thrill shot through her. She knew it was silly, at a time like this, but she couldn't help it.

Lyssa spotted a sheep farmer from Clan Kriega. The shepherd with carrot red sideburns came to town every year for the spring fair and always drank himself stupid. She'd mopped up his sick more than once. But he didn't give her a second look. Instead, he pressed into a circle of clansmen gathered around some sort of scuffle.

Lyssa pushed through the edge of the crowd to find a pair of Kriegans beating a federal prisoner. Blood dripped from his nose, and he stared up defiantly from his knees. A tall, lean redhead with scarred-up lips brandished his axe in the legionary's face. Beside him, Henrik Torvald looked on, with his hands on his hips, glancing between the soldier and the fort. It surprised her. All things considered, she would have expected him to be locked up in the fort with the federals. A hunched old woman with a cut-up face and a leash tied around a little boy's neck held a baby in one arm, muttering sweet nonsense to it until the beating had run its course. At the edge of the circle, Astrid Olsgaard sobbed, pulling at her hair. Her brother and father flanked her, holding the sleeves of her torn dress to keep her in place. The crone handed the babe to a scrawny teenaged girl with fiery hair and freckles. She whispered something to the boy on the leash and he spoke for her.

"That's enough, Hel."

The tall, wiry Norn shoved the prisoner to the ground and stepped back, waiting for her orders.

Henrik spoke up. "If you want Erk's wife back in one piece, you'd better not hurt him too much, Freylka. We can use him to negotiate."

"No one asked you!" Hel shouted, his voice a hoarse croak. He ran his thumb along the blade of his axe and licked the bead of blood it drew. Hel turned back to Freylka with a hunger in his eyes.

Freylka shook her head.

She tugged on the boy's leash, and he turned to Henrik. "Negotiate?" She whispered more, and he repeated it for her. "That time has passed. My niece is as the dead. Freylka knows. She knows you are accustomed to licking their boots, but now you must pick a side." She whispered something else to the boy, pointedly eyeing the pouch of binding stones on Henrik's belt. "You can be useful, or you can be dead. Choose."

268

Henrik gathered himself up and spoke to the entire crowd. "I'm for the people of Skolja. As I have always been."

The gathered Norn grumbled, folded their arms, and shook their heads. Freylka sniggered. She bent to the boy's ear again. "No," he said. "You have been on the side of Henrik Torvald."

"We should kill him, Auntie!" Hel pointed his axe at Henrik.

The mayor backed a pace away from Hel and looked around at the townsfolk, his eyes coming to rest on Freylka. "You're right," he said. "I have been selfish. But now I see. The federals have used me. They promised to keep us safe. But when we needed them most, they robbed us and locked themselves away. No more. My great-great-uncle Olaf vowed that he would return to drive out the invaders. It's time I fulfill that promise."

Freylka laughed at him, and her boy said, "Enough." She spoke in his ear. "Spare us your pretty words. Freylka knows your selfish heart. Perhaps you see now that our struggle is the same. To be free before we die." She leveled her gaze at her own people and whispered a message to her slave that he repeated. "But Henrik spared Freylka's grand-niece and gave hope to the line of Kriega. For that shred of mercy, no Kriegan shall lay a hand on Henrik Torvald."

"No!" Hel shrilled.

Freylka silenced him with a sharp look then stared him down until he averted his eyes. When it was clear he would obey, the old woman began to sing, her voice sweet and clear. For an instant, Lyssa picked out a note so low it made her dizzy, but it vanished in a heartbeat, leaving her unsure if she'd ever really heard it. Freylka held out her hand, and the little boy pulled the knife from his belt and gave it to her. He looked away. Freylka's song faded to a hum. Eyes closed, she pressed the blade to her lip and cut. The gravel-voiced Kriegan, Hel, reached down and grabbed a fistful of the ordinal's hair, pulling him up to his knees. Hel jerked the Tyrianite's head back and held his knife to the federal's throat.

"Carthalo!" Astrid tore free of her father's grasp, dashing toward her lover. But her brother caught her by the locks of her golden hair and jerked her up short, switching to a chokehold and dragging her back to the edge of the circle.

Freylka stooped over and kissed the Tyrianite. He struggled at first, but Hel's dagger stilled his fight. A shudder ran through him, and his eyes shot open. The hag bit down on his tongue and wrenched her head back, tearing it free. The ordinal screamed, but Hel pushed him to the ground and kicked him mercilessly until he cowered into a ball, blubbering, a froth of bloody drool seeping from his mouth.

Freylka kept her eyes closed, a smile on her scarred face as she hummed to herself, chewing on the man's tongue. The crowd fell utterly silent, listening to her tune, rapt. The crone opened her eyes and spat the federal's flesh in the mud. She gazed around at the stunned onlookers, her eyes coming to rest on Lyssa.

Without breaking eye contact, she bent to the boy's ear, handing him back his knife. "Bind the federal; he may be of use." Her unnerving smile returned. "They will flee Skolja. Tonight."

The revelation sparked an uproar. The crowd erupted into a mixture of anger and exultation. Freylka slapped her boy on the back of the head. "Silence!" he cried. She whispered his next words to him. "If we allow them to escape, we shall all perish. Like rats in a fire!" Freylka grinned madly at Henrik as the boy delivered her pronouncement. "Freylka has seen it."

The news unsettled the crowd. Henrik raised his voice above the murmurs. "What are we supposed to do?" he asked. "Attack the fort? We'll be butchered."

Freylka spoke to the child. "No, we have allies." he said. The slave and his master turned toward Lyssa in unsettling unison. "You. Come forward."

They all looked at her. Henrik's head rocked back in recognition. "You," he said.

Lyssa stepped into the circle.

"You are not alone," said Freylka's boy.

270

Lyssa shook her head. "I'm with Gareth's band."

"Though Gareth is no more," he said.

"We attacked the mine. He—" Lyssa hesitated. "He died there."

Freylka laughed and whispered more. "Nilstrom," the boy said.

Henrik tensed. "Anders Nilstrom? Is he here?"

Freylka hissed at him, whispered to her boy. "Let go your vengeance," the child said. "Or doom us all."

Henrik reddened. "He murdered my mother and father. I won't forget."

Freylka wrapped the leash around her fist, drawing the boy closer. She locked eyes on Henrik as she muttered in her slave's ear. "We must stand together or perish," he said. "But he will not escape justice. Let us deal with the invaders first. That is all Freylka asks. Will you swear it?"

Henrik looked around at the crowd. Hel made a show of twirling his axe, smiled with scarred lips.

"Fine," Henrik said. "After the pigs."

★★★★★

Henrik could see now that he'd been a fool to think he could manage the end of the world. It was superstitious, he knew, to interpret his failure of Skolja as an omen. But he did. Deep down in the unlit corners of his mind. The world was coming to an end. He had failed these people, and they were doomed for it.

His hatred of his father's murderer had blinded him to the prefect's motives. He had underestimated him, falsely assumed that there were two sides to the struggle.

Brasca had seen things more clearly. He had used Henrik to placate the folk while he bled and abandoned them. Though how he would love to see the shock in Brasca's dying eyes, his spasms of vengeful thinking could only draw him into a whirlpool of blind reaction where emotion dragged him down unto death.

271

He must be cold and set aside his petty hatreds if he expected his intellect to save him from the maelstrom approaching.

First, he needed—

The world lurched.

Henrik sprang to his feet, looking around at the equally frightened faces of the Norn beside the campfire with him. He staggered to one knee. Someone off to his left screamed and scrambled out of the campfire into which he'd fallen. To the southeast, a roaring, louder than anything he'd ever heard, drew his eye, and he turned just in time to watch High Hill collapse on the other side of town. The entire thing just seemed to melt, men and cattle swallowed up by the churning earth, the shell of the mansion he'd grown up in, the cobblestones of the courtyard, even the statue of Saint Olaf at the peak, toppled and was enfolded by the landslide that swept into the eastern edge of Skolja. The collapse sent a wave crashing through the streets, knocking over half submerged buildings, burying them under tons of earth and stone or smashing them like eggshells and washing them out to the sea.

The quake stilled for a moment, and he listened to his heart thumping. Then the earth rumbled again. In his panic, he wondered if this might be the end, if the world might finally tear itself apart. When the tremor passed, Henrik stood, aghast, taking in the destruction. He felt queasy. He looked down at his feet, expecting Federal Hill to crumble as High Hill had. Nothing happened.

Skolja was gone. His knees wobbled. Everything his father had striven for. The generations spent as caretakers here. All hope of becoming mayor lost. Every trace of the life his mother had lived. The home she had built. The places Henrik had played as a child. The inns where he had caroused so many nights and curled up by the fires with his father's books. Even the docks, where he had witnessed something he still couldn't explain. It had all vanished. Pummeled into the watery grave before him. Entombed beneath the slide.

Worse, *The Muse* was there. *The Muse* was inside the smithy, gone too, washed across town and buried under a deluge of mud and stone. The countless hours his father had spent, lovingly perfecting every bolt and binding. His father's achievement, the last that remained of him. Gone. His escape. Gone too.

They were all dead now. He felt it in his bones.

Around him, Skoljans cried out to their loved ones. Folk pointed at the slide, wailing, falling to their knees and pulling out their hair, mourning the destruction of their homes, their last shreds of hope buried with the town. He turned to the fort, realizing with a dire sort of faith that the southwest corner sagged inward, though it hadn't quite collapsed. This was their only opening. A dwindling probability that they might butcher the pigs cowering in their sty and somehow wait out the carnage inside the fort.

Henrik wiped away his tears and found Freylka on the northeastern corner of Federal Hill. She had gathered the other Kriegans, and they waited, overlooking the approach of Gareth's band. Nilstrom's band, he supposed. Henrik looked back at the fort, but the gate was still closed, and the Tyrianites made no effort to challenge the arrival of the outlaws. Dread curdled in his stomach as he picked out the old murderer and watched him make his way over the muddy ground to the base of the hill.

Freylka stood beside him, humming to the babe she held. She looked up at Nilstrom's band approaching and said something to her slave, who looked up at Henrik. "Freylka hates him too," he said. "But we will need him and his kin." She studied his reaction as the boy continued. "Can you still your fury long enough to wield him?"

Henrik noticed Lyssa and Brohr among the group. It helped to cool his indignation. He vowed to himself to work with the old butcher, to wield him as Freylka put it, and to stick a knife in his back as soon as it was prudent.

The group crested the hill, paused to take in their surroundings, and headed over to Freylka and Henrik.

"Freylka," the old skald said. "I knew it would take the end of the world for you to scuttle out of that hole you live in." Anders glanced at Henrik, but he said nothing else.

Henrik's heart raced, and his face flushed. He set his hand on the pouch on his belt. The witch's boy replied, but Henrik didn't hear.

"And what about this collaborator?" Anders was looking at Henrik.

"I will tolerate you, for now," Henrik said. "But if you don't stay out of my way, you'll die screaming."

"Hardly," said Anders.

His grandson pushed the old man out of his way. "You're no better, Torvald." He pulled the collar of his shirt down to show the bruise around his neck. "I hanged for your lies, you coward. All you had to do was say you'd seen it."

The Grafstrom baby started to cry. Freylka tugged the leash. "It?" Her boy asked.

It was Anders who replied. "The Hidden, Freylka. Moriigo."

She laughed, her scarred smile failing as she looked at each of them, realizing it was true. She whispered something. "Impossible," the boy declared. "Freylka would've seen it."

Anders smirked. "Perhaps your gift is not as strong as you think. After all, it is called the Hidden for a reason."

She whispered something else and then straightened, licking her lips suggestively. "Give Freylka a kiss." The boy shuddered. "Then she will see everything." Freylka handed the infant off to its new nursemaid.

Old Nilstrom shook his head. "Your beauty has failed more than your magic. You'll just have to trust me."

His grandson pointed at the fort. "Why aren't the federals out here? We are all criminals, aren't we?"

Freylka's boy spoke for her. "They have given up on Skolja. The prefect despises this place. He seeks only to weather the storm. To escape."

"We need to wipe them out," Anders said. "If we're to survive, we must kill them all."

Freylka muttered in her slave's ear. "Freylka is the one gifted to see. How do you know this?"

The old man flinched, but he steeled himself, looking the witch in her cloudy eyes. "The Hidden," he said. "We have a pact."

Freylka spat. Disgust contorted her ugly face. She hummed, closing her eyes, tapped her lips, and stepped toward the other skald.

Anders hesitated, his hand resting on his knife. Freylka opened one eye and beckoned him with a lewd smile. He drew his knife and stepped forward, cutting his own lip. She grabbed him by the hair at the back of his neck and planted a long, slow kiss on him, humming all the while.

Henrik turned to Lyssa and Brohr, who looked as uncomfortable as he felt. At last, Freylka pulled away and coughed a bit. She glared up at Anders and then at Brohr, where her gaze lingered.

★★★★★

Brasca waited in the front room of the command building, examining the map which dominated its western wall. He stood with his hands clasped behind his back, staring at the tiny dot labeled 'Skolja.' Of course, only a map made for the prefect of Skolja would bother to label it. Places like Trond and even little Pederskald dwarfed this village, and those were backwaters in their own right compared to the glittering cities of his homeworld. He wondered if he would ever see Tyria again.

It was time to be done with this dot. For a practical man, it was ridiculous that he had allowed his reputation to be tarnished by his grief and doubt. It was enough if he could be honest with himself. As his father had said, sincerity was less important than appearances. It was time he began to repair his stature. He would mime the rites of office, and in return he could leave this accursed backwater far behind him.

He sighed, turning away from the map. His scribe looked up from his desk.

"Sir?" the young officer asked.

"Go and fetch Belizar," said the prefect. The men were frightened. Facing a disaster of this magnitude, they needed something to stoke their faith.

Brasca followed the scribe out of the command building to await his adjutant. It was late afternoon and warmer than it should have been in autumn. As he emerged, the men on the southern rampart pointed out to sea and called out to the prefect.

"Sir," said the sentry. "You better have a look at this."

The prefect climbed up to the platform on which they stood watch. He expected to see another tidal wave rolling in, but the site before him was far worse. The shattered moon loomed just above the southern horizon, its pale red shards suspended in a glimmering curtain of shooting stars that stretched east to west as far as the eye could see. Larger meteors streaked to the surface of Heimir like falling embers.

Dread twisted Brasca's stomach. Had the astronomers predicted this? How could they survive *this*?

"Steady," he told the sentries. "We'll be evacuated soon." He hoped. But would Trond be any safer? That curtain of ruin must have stretched across the whole continent, perhaps all of Heimir. He realized his men were waiting for him to say something. "As you were," he ordered. "I want a report every hour."

Brasca climbed back down the ladder and found Belizar lumbering up to him.

"Sir," his ordinal hailed him. "Bad news I'm afraid."

Brasca sighed. "Out with it."

"A legionary has committed suicide."

"Who?"

"Legionary Urum, sir. He fell on his sword."

"Go and fetch the prisoner," the prefect said. "I've been stalling because, well, never mind. The men need to see an offering." Brasca ignored the surprise on Belizar's face. Did he think it was an overreaction?

"Yes, sir," the ordinal said. "Right away."

"Have you seen Quaya?"

Belizar's eyes watered. He nodded. The officers stared at one another, sharing a grim, wordless understanding until the prefect finally sent him off. While he waited for Belizar to return with the prisoner, Brasca considered the possibility that their evacuation ship might take one look at the horizon and leave Heimir for the void. *It should be more than halfway here by now*, he thought. It could still beat that curtain of death, he hoped. But would they bother? He considered the likelihood of returning to Trond and shook his head.

"Sorry, Arabo," he whispered.

But his old friend Arabo had probably taken one look at Quaya as it rose and left Heimir in his wake without a second thought for Brasca. Another hope, he supposed.

Chapter 28

"In that year, Lycus of House Tibrus and Adrian of House Crassa were anointed the Judges. Stern Lycus was given the honor of putting order to the squabbling electors while intrepid Adrian set his eyes upon the outlands."

-*Agbal IV, The Judge's War*

Brohr stood transfixed by fragments of the rising moon. He felt his brother's awe, mirroring his own, as they stared at the doom creeping over the horizon. They gazed up, the seconds passing like centuries, waiting for it to come, trapped beneath the nightmare sky. The scope of it dwarfed him, left him trembling. He had thought he could run away to Pederskald. He should have laughed at that, but laughter was impossible in the face of this.

Someone beside him retched, but he could not look away. A child wailed. A voice called his name. He heard it again but did not turn. Brohr feared that if he looked away, when he turned back, it would be upon them. A hand rested on his shoulder. It reached up and caressed his cheek, pulled his head away.

Lyssa looked up at him, her eyes red and puffy. She lay her head on Brohr's chest, and he rested his chin on top of it. He wished the world would go away—his grandfather, the federals, the moon, the screams, the dire vista—but even when he closed his eyes, it was there like a weight pressing on his mind.

Anders stormed up beside them. "Enough!" He grabbed Lyssa by the elbow and pulled her away. "There is no time for this—" the old man bit off whatever he was going to say, revulsion on his face. "If we are to survive, we need to get into that fort."

Lyssa pulled her arm free. "What makes you think it's any safer in there, you old creep?"

"It's not," he said. "But there is a path that leads through it."

"More damned riddles." Brohr grabbed his grandfather's shirt and twisted it tight against his throat. "I'm sick to death of you." He held his fist up to Anders's face, teeth grinding as he fought to keep his anger shackled.

"He's right." Freylka and her boy walked up beside them. "Freylka has seen it too."

Anders wormed free of Brohr's grip. "Besides," he threw up his arms grandly framing the remains of Quaya, "would you rather wait for that?"

Henrik joined their circle. "It's quite possible that the federals have an escape plan. If we can get in there..." He shrugged. "What else can we do?"

"So," Brohr asked. "How do we get in?"

Lyssa rummaged in her pack, holding up a glass bottle filled with milky liquid. "I have witch fire," she said.

The circle froze, watching Henrik go pale as his thoughts turned to the murder of his parents. He regarded Anders with undisguised malice, his jaw clenched, color flooding back to his cheeks. Henrik folded his arms and turned his narrowed eyes at Lyssa. "Is witch fire overkill?" he finally asked.

Anders glanced around at the others, scratching his cheek to hide a smile. "There is a cleared area on the inside of the wall. The fire shouldn't spread to the interior. The problem is that it will be burning for hours. How are we supposed to get in?"

"I can get us inside," Henrik said without looking directly at Brohr's grandfather. A few eyebrows went up while everyone waited for an explanation. "I have a binding that can break down the front gate," Henrik continued. "But even if we get through, can we win?"

Brohr said, "We've got even numbers now."

"Yes," said Henrik. "But they're soldiers, and they're defending a fort. It's hardly a fair contest."

Freylka whispered something to her slave. "It is the only path," he said.

The group nodded to one another.

"I have an idea," said Henrik, his eyes locked on Brohr's grandfather.

★★★★★

A squad of legionaries built the platform from crates stuffed with straw and lashed the widow Grafstrom to the pole fixed at the center. Her hands were tied above her head, the rope looped around her, binding her at the ankles and the waist.

The broken moonrise lent a portentous mood to the grim proceedings as soldiers came and went, tossing flowers and coins at her feet, mumbling prayers for salvation to the divine Pontiff. All could see that the three great shards of shattered Quaya, tumbling through the florid clouds, prefigured a grisly end to Heimir. An unseasonably warm wind blew through the parade grounds, the pleasant doldrum at the verge of an apocalypse. The widow spat on legionaries and cursed their mothers, even daring to condemn them in the old tongue now that her fate was sealed. But for all her bravado, Brasca saw her mounting terror.

He recognized that look of fading defiance. That look had sparked his exile, sapped his faith, and brought him plummeting to this backwater world. Adrocar Crassa had worn just the same expression on the day he'd been burned alive. It had been summer in the capital, unbearably humid, just a few weeks after Brasca's son had died. The city sweltered. And Brasca was hungover. He had spent all morning drinking again to work up the courage to set a man on fire. Crassa had been so sweaty that the soldiers had joked he wouldn't catch. Brasca couldn't muster the energy even to force a laugh.

He should have been elated. He'd known Crassa all of his life. A haughty braggart, a handsome bully, hailing from a rival house. They had courted the same women and vied for the same commissions. Crassa was on track to be elevated to the Electorate. He had once been promoted over Brasca and quickly soared into the upper echelons of command. But Crassa's ambition had drawn the Pontiff's ire. Some chance comment or clever conspiracy had risen to His attention, and the charge of heresy had shortly followed. A month before that, Brasca would have felt unadulterated glee to see Crassa burn. But immolating a man brought dread reminders of his own son's last moments.

And so Brasca had balked.

The torch burned in his hand, the rite unspoken, until his subordinate had pried open his grip and cast the torch at Crassa's feet.

"Prefect!" The widow's cry roused Brasca from his memories. "*Fjeckel Svikke!* You won't outlive me by much, you pigs! We're all dead!" She spat at him, but he was too far away.

Brasca turned, watching Belizar jog up.

The ordinal shot out his arm in salute. Dusk had fallen. "That's it, sir. Every man has had his chance at offerings."

Brasca swallowed, a bead of sweat running into his eye. He wiped it away and held out his hand. "Torch."

A legionary standing beside him handed Brasca the torch. The widow's defiance wilted, and she fought like a wild animal to win free of her bonds.

"No!" she sobbed. "Please."

Brasca wrestled with his imagination, his mind flooding with images of his son burning alive. He forced the picture of his youngest into his thoughts, fixing little Lycus there as a compass needle to guide him through what must be done.

"Children of the Pontiff's light," he recited to the gathering of ordinals and off-duty legionaries. "We gather here to offer the spoils of war. To bring sweet gifts before the divine Pontiff, who holds the keys of heaven and hell, who unlocks the way to the dead place, who was given the light by shining Tyrus. We gather to set fire to the lies of heresy..."

The widow renewed her screaming, but Brasca shouted over her. She turned away from the torch, shaking her head as if she could deny its power.

281

"To light a beacon in the night, to shine the truth where His enemies cower. We give our coin, our blood, everything we have, and when we have nothing left to give, we will take from His enemies."

Brasca turned to the platform where the widow was bound as the assembly repeated his final words. She gasped, a whimper escaping her throat, eyes pleading, her head still shaking in denial of the awful truth. Brasca could not keep the images of Silvano at bay. He saw the boy's tears, heard his cries, his pleas for his mother. Watched him scramble through the barn, looking for a way out. With clarion detail, Brasca saw him cough, the black smoke everywhere, until the flames were all around, until the hem of his shirt caught fire, until his skin cracked and blistered and his mouth belched smoke and his flame merged with the conflagration around him and he lay burning, robbed of his youth, his clever wit, his silly, sweet self gone who knows where.

Brasca tossed the torch at the widow Grafstrom's feet, where a cask of oil anointed the platform. He could not shake free of his macabre thoughts, so he stared at the widow as her pleas turned to shrieks, as the flames lapped at the hem of her dress, hoping the vivid scene might somehow outshine the horror playing over and over in his head. The fire whooshed, the blaze streaking up her leg. Her hair ignited like the head of a match.

A hand grabbed his shoulder and turned him gently away. "The rite," said Belizar. "Finish the rite."

Brasca faced the congregation of soldiers. "All is dim before His glory."

The men echoed his words. "All is dim before His glory."

The cries grew quiet behind him, flames crackling in their absence, the steaming hiss of boiling blood. The widow Grafstrom was dead, gone wherever souls go. "In His light..." Brasca faltered, his breath ragged, his voice trembling as he fought the pictures in his head. "In His light may we reign."

★★★★★

Brohr nodded to the dozen Norn around him. Backlit by the moonfall, the crimson sea behind them, they started toward the gate, a slow trot at first. Each held a rock in their hands, approximating the vial of witch fire that Brohr carried. They spread out, approaching warily, until the first bolt sailed from the rampart, landing twenty paces in front of the nearest Kriegan. Once it struck, they surged forward, trying to close within throwing distance before the quarrels claimed them.

Another bolt whistled past Brohr's ear, close enough that he flinched. To his right, one of the Kriegans pulled ahead, faster than the other men. He tumbled to the ground, clawing at the fletching poking out above his belt.

Brohr tried not to think about him, instead, studying the ground between himself and the gate. There was no cover except a few haphazard tents, and none of them seemed close enough to throw from. *Brother*, he thought, *I could use a little strength.* He sensed Olek, he was always there, but it was as if he hadn't heard. Or as if he couldn't understand. Brohr kept pace with the others. Another Kriegan to his right dropped. He wondered if it was the same crossbowman. Just in case, Brohr veered to his left. Another bolt landed where he had just been. *Brother!* It was no use; he couldn't understand.

He thought about the wound he'd taken at the mine, about one of these bolts doing the same thing to him. He felt Olek stir like he'd rolled over in his sleep, roused by the images, by Brohr's fear. Brohr pictured Torin pinning down his mother as she screamed, imagined hurling a bottle of witch fire, its flames devouring the screaming pigs. Olek lashed out, snapped Brohr's arm forward like a sprung trap, and the bottle arced neatly, tumbling end over end, to shatter in a blue flash at the base of the southern gate.

★★★★★

283

Henrik stared to his left at the lookout's silhouette, waiting for the signal. The boy with the scarred mouth snuck up beside him and tugged at his sleeve, startling Henrik.

"Freylka says it is time."

Henrik jerked his sleeve free of the boy's grasp and looked up at the grinning witch. She disturbed him, her freakish smile, her unsettling insights.

The lookout waved his arms, frantic. Henrik held up his hand and shouted, "Let's go!"

To his annoyance, the Kriegans and even the other Skoljans looked to Freylka, who made a shooing motion with her free hand. They jogged around the eastern perimeter of the plateau, keeping well out of crossbow range. From the other direction, the second half of the Norn ran towards them, beyond them the splintered moon and meteor shower. As they drew closer, a meteorite struck out to sea, still miles off but close enough to watch it hit the water and fizzle out.

Smoke rose from the far side of the fort, but none of the telltale blue tongues of witch fire yet peeked over the wall. The approaching Norn slowed, and one of them pointed to the eastern horizon.

As the two groups came together, Lyssa called out. "Look!"

Everyone turned east. When Henrik saw it, acid lurched up the back of his throat. He swallowed, his mouth falling open. A distant metallic cylinder hung in the air, light spilling from its portholes and the engines running its underside: a void ship. The vessel had just cleared the Jotunspar mountains which isolated them from most of Trondia. The folk beamed at each other, insipid grins spreading through the little war party as if it were on its way to rescue them. Still, there was hope. A little. The Tyrianite pilots would be looking right into the setting sun, and it would be dark by the time they landed.

He turned to Anders, who had arrived with the other group. "All right, you snake." He pointed at the dot on the horizon. "Maybe there is a way out. Time to earn your keep."

★★★★★

For all of its manipulations, the Hidden had not lied about this. Their salvation came from the east. One of the accursed ships which had brought the invaders in the first place. Anders still had so many questions, so much wrath he wished he could vent. He had never imagined a life beyond Skolja. He couldn't. Everything he'd been fighting for was here. But when he looked back at the unfathomable destruction crawling toward them, he knew he could not stop it. How could his town survive that? It could not. His people then. He would fight for them. There was nothing to do but claw their way out.

Anders drew his belt knife and stood before his grandson.

"I know you hate me," he said. "But everything I've done has been for you."

Brohr said nothing. Nostrils flared, he stared back until Anders looked away. The old skald raised the knife to Brohr's cheek and cut him. Then he did the same to the girl, to the other Kriegans, until he came to Henrik.

"Keep your filthy blade away from me."

Anders shrugged. He had what he needed. He pictured their disheveled little band, his raspy baritone and its unnatural echoes giving the deception shape. To the pigs, it would seem as if the whole group were headed with him back to the burning gate. Meanwhile, wrapped in an illusion, they would head north, unseen. The skald held his bloody knife above his head like a torch and set off south as fast as his old bones would carry him.

Chapter 29

"When the last of them had ceased their kicking, and their frothing lips whispered no more curses, the hall grew eerie quiet. She sat in her father's chair, hand on her belly, and looked upon the destruction she had wrought. Let the name of Breyga be forgotten, his accursed descendants too. At least she would never again have to act the doting daughter. Never pretend that she bore no secrets."

–Peder the Skald, A Song of Hateful Cups

"Sir!" the soldier screamed down, hands cupped to his mouth, then pointed to the east. "Sir, the transport. I can see the transport!"

"How long?" Brasca asked.

The legionary turned back to the horizon, trying to judge the distance. "An hour or so."

The prefect nodded and looked around the fort to assess his defense. He sprinted across the open ground in the center of the fort to where Belizar and four squads of ten men each were stationed.

"Sir," Belizar hailed him when he arrived.

"They're headed back to the south gate. I'll leave you one squad. Be sure to keep an eye on us. If the provincials break through, be prepared to reinforce us."

"Yes, sir." Belizar rattled off a new set of orders to his troops.

Brasca jogged back to the south gate with his troops and arrayed them in the interval between the flaming gate in the interior of the camp. The witch fire had nearly consumed the

286

gate, but it would remain impassable for some time. He hoped that the transport would arrive before then.

"Sir." One of his ordinals pointed back to the north end of the fort. Belizar waved both arms at the gate, held both hands above his head, and then waved at the gate again. When he completed the signal, Brasca and the nearest ordinal looked at each other in shock. They had been tricked somehow.

"Take your men to reinforce Belizar!" Brasca turned to another nearby ordinal, fighting to keep the panic out of his voice. "Ordinal, you too. All of you!" He pulled his sword. "Defend the gate!"

★★★★★

Henrik held the stone in his fist, staring at the north gate. He cocked his ear, listening to the power of the bull bound within, envisioning the sequence of runes. *Toru, the Alpha. Force. Destruction.* A quarrel thumped into the ground beside him. He ignored the attack, calling out the three notes, silvery runes spinning around his fist. The bull erupted from the stone. It charged the fort, a scintillating echo of the beast it had been, light and power and stubborn fury. The spirit lowered its head, crashing into the gate, splintering it with a deafening crack, and tearing it from its hinges.

The ragtag Norn contingent charged into a flight of crossbow fire, met by the squad of federals left to protect the gate. Most of the fort's defenders were on the far side, dashing across the open ground to reinforce their beleaguered comrades.

Brohr ran past him, screeching his high-pitched battle cry. The berserker hacked at a legionary, knocking the sword out of the man's hand with the first blow and splitting the side of his face open with the second. Henrik followed more cautiously, entering the fort, but staying just inside the perimeter so that the crossbowmen above wouldn't have a clear shot at him.

He dug into his pouch and found one of the stones into which he'd bound a rat. He didn't want to waste it, but he was no warrior. If one of the legionaries got too close, he'd need it.

Around him, the Norn pushed into the fort, overrunning the Tyrianites stationed at the gate. Beyond the fighting, he saw reinforcements closing in, led by the prefect. He switched the stone to his left hand and dug in his pouch for the other. If he could kill the prefect, that might tilt the battle in their favor, but he wanted to save one of his bindings for Anders Nilstrom.

★★★★★

Brohr stove in the man's skull, delighted by the sensation. He replayed it like a flash of light in his mind. He cocked back to cut down the next legionary, only to find himself looming over Lyssa, a look of terror on her face. Beside him, a Tyrianite who had lost his helm lashed out and Brohr spun, burying his blade in the man's ear. He turned back to look for Lyssa, but the melee had swallowed her up again.

Olek wailed their deadly tune, tearing Brohr from his fleeting worry. He drowned his glimpse of Lyssa's horror in the blood of Tyrianites. Hacking away at it, one federal at a time, losing himself in the rhythm of his sword strokes. Another legionary to his left lunged at him and nicked Brohr's side, a note of bright pain. But the song only grew in his ears.

An aftershock shook the battlefield, and the legionary charging him stumbled back, off-balance. Around him the battle slowed as some paused, stunned by the quake, but Brohr called out, surprised by the balance his tenor struck with the ear-piercing shriek of his brother's rage.

He heard it. Calling from every direction, the percussion of sword clashing against sword renewed, the crescendo of wounded screams. The perfect rest of death. The federal he fought thrust at his face, and Brohr ducked his head to one side, feeling the blade slice across his cheek. As the soldier drew back, Brohr snatched his wrist and lopped his arm in half, tossing the hand away as the man collapsed, clutching the stump. Another bellowed beside him, raised his sword above his head to strike, and Brohr pivoted, sprung, and tackled him.

The tune played on. The man's curses the lyrics of this verse. Their blood mingled as, beat after beat, Brohr drove his forehead into the soldier's nose, measure by measure. The blood drizzling from Brohr's lip fell upon the man's ruined brow like some dread sigil. Brohr threw back his head and sang a long, uncanny note, his bright baritone and his brother's shrill soprano a witchy duet, an ode of becoming.

All around him the fighting stopped. He stood up, singing, his blood and the blood of his enemies defying nature, floating off his face into the air above his head. His voice and his brother's voice harmonized, a fraternal chord, a magic unleashed, a sound beyond sound that jolted every fiber of his conjoined soul. The rising blood unmasked his face, coalescing above his head as a pair of gory antlers.

He dropped his sword, his head lulled back to the ancient tune, the song of discord, the cries of the old world passing away. He looked down at his hands to find vicious, bloody claws. And when he peeled his eyes from those wicked talons, he felt joy in the terror of the swine before him.

★★★★★

Henrik shrunk away from where the farm boy had metamorphosed into... what? A Raag? Brohr brandished claws and antlers of blood, his voice a terrifying cacophony, and he moved with preternatural speed and lethal strength. Even the charging reinforcements had faltered, awed by the horror. He was like some sort of folktale monster, a ravening beast, singing, laughing, butchering the hapless Tyrianites.

But Brasca shouted orders, forming his men up into a tight line. They warily surrounded the Raag. Henrik shouted at the Norn who had forgotten there was a battle going on. For a moment, the savage creature seemed as if he could win all on his own. Even Henrik expected the pigs to break in the face of that thing. He would have. Henrik shook free of the spell, tearing his eyes away from Brohr to where the crossbowmen were reloading above the gate.

289

"You there," Henrik shouted. "With me. We need to flank them while they're worried about that."

Above the gate, two crossbowmen fired down at the attackers from behind. Henrik grabbed the shoulder of a man gawking at the horror Brohr had become. Across the fray, he picked out Lyssa, darting in to backstab an unwary federal.

"You," he said to the Kriegan. "Take those three and go up that ladder to the rampart. We need to get those crossbowmen before they kill us all."

Henrik ran over to the lanky redhead with the scarred lips, Hel. The Kriegan swayed back and forth, entranced by Brohr's song.

"Snap out of it. Ten Fathers! There's a battle to fight."

The Kriegan seemed to notice him then, sneering. He looked back to the gate, where Freylka and her slave waited for the fighting to subside.

"Let's go!" Henrik shouted. "Gather your men."

Hel nodded. He looked around, seeing that men from both sides stood transfixed. He shook his head as if fighting dizziness, and raised his axe high.

"Blood and blade!" Hel shouted.

Finally, the other Kriegans broke free of their trance and took up the cry, hefting their axes and echoing the clan motto.

With a binding stone clenched in each fist, Henrik led Hel and a few other Kriegans around the left flank of the federals who were trying to surround Brohr. To his surprise, he saw Arius in the thick of the fighting, covered in blood, wielding his axe like a madman.

They charged into the side of the pigs' formation, screaming, but the federals' discipline held. The legionaries pivoted, forming a new front to face the Norn.

Henrik himself hung back, gauging the flow of the battle, looking for the prefect. He found him again in the crook of the L that they had formed, shouting orders to the stragglers arriving from the other side of the fort.

"Brasca!" Henrik called, but the din drowned out his voice. "Brasca!" Still the Tyrianite didn't turn. Henrik edged around the outside of the fighting, trying to judge the interval between them, the distance that his binding could traverse before it dissipated.

The federals finally managed to envelop Brohr, though they kept a wary distance from the snarling skald. His bizarre antlers bobbed above the fray, darting at anyone who came too close.

Henrik circled wide around the federal formation, coming up behind the Tyrianite lines. He skulked as close to Brasca as he could before the prefect turned, sensing the movement behind him.

"I sort of hoped I'd get to kill you," Brasca shouted. He glanced down at the binding stones Henrik clutched in his fists, detached from the rear of the formation, and took a couple of practice swings with his sword. "I'll give you one last chance though. Get this rabble to surrender, Henrik. I'll take you with me when the transport arrives. Even that thing..." Brasca looked back over his shoulder where his troops surrounded Brohr. He shook his head. "Even that won't help you."

"I think it's time I went my own way, Prefect," said Henrik. "It seems you federals aren't to be trusted."

"Look at the sky for the Pontiff's sake!" Brasca pointed behind Henrik with his short sword. "How do you expect to escape that?"

Henrik turned his head to behold the ghastly spectacle, and when he did, Brasca broke into a sprint, trying to close the distance between them before Henrik could loose a spirit. Henrik jerked his head back around, fixing his eye on the prefect. He began his cant, the first rune flashing to light before him, but Brasca had gained the initiative, covering a few extra feet while Henrik was distracted. Realizing that he didn't have enough time to get his spell off, Henrik panicked and simply threw the rock. It sailed through the air and struck Brasca on the chin, drawing blood, and breaking his stride.

Henrik restarted the incantation only to realize midstream that the stone in his other hand didn't use the same runes. Brasca renewed his charge. Henrik fumbled the second stone and flinched out of the way as Brasca swung his sword. The mayor dropped to one knee to pick up the binding stone, but the prefect was upon him. Brasca slashed in an upward arc, trying to behead Henrik, but Henrik ducked out of the way just as the sword whooshed past his skull. The prefect crashed into him, driving his knee into Henrik's ribs as he fell over the top of him.

Henrik rolled on his side, the wind driven from his lungs. He reached for the stone and turned to Brasca to loose the binding, but Henrik couldn't breathe to sound the notes. Around them the din of clashing steel and screaming men swelled. The thing Brohr had become hurled a body which landed nearby. The clot of soldiers shrunk away from the horror. A Tyrianite at the back of the pack threw down his weapon and fled, only to be cut down by a Norn axe as he ran.

Brasca sprung to his feet and raised his sword, poised to hack down at his prone adversary, but Henrik kicked him in the groin and tripped the federal to the ground. The prefect dropped his sword and clutched between his legs, his eyes clenched shut and his lips mouthing curses. Henrik scrambled back on all fours, gasping for breath, putting as much distance between himself and Brasca as he could without crawling into the thick of the battle. The prefect opened one eye that roved his surroundings until it fell on Henrik. A crossbow bolt thumped into the ground between them. Brasca grabbed his short sword, pushed himself to his feet, and staggered toward Henrik.

The young mayor held his stomach, frantic to catch his breath. As Brasca loomed toward him, Henrik flopped on his side, throwing his head back and arching his spine to escape the cramp and get some air in his lungs. He sucked in a sharp breath. *The Scavenger. Fire. Destruction.* Henrik lit the runes with his voice, and the haunt tore free from the stone just as Brasca's overhand sword stroke reached its apex. The hateful little spirit streaked into Brasca's eye. The force spun the prefect in a circle, and by the time he came back around the hole in his socket flared, a plume of oily smoke jetting from his seared brain. An astonished expression passed Brasca's face, but before he could even get his hands up to cover his eye, the prefect collapsed, his wound steaming, a foul smell blossoming from his corpse.

Henrik stared at the dead man, oblivious to the battle, until, amidst the clamor of swords, he discerned the sound of clapping.

"Well done, Henrik." Hel stood above him, a nasty grin splitting his scarred face. "I had thought the federal would rob me of my vengeance," the Kriegan said, his voice manic. "I don't want the world to end until I slide this axe across your throat."

Henrik held out his hand. "Wait," he screamed. "Freylka promised my safety."

Hel turned in a circle as if scouring the battlefield for her. "But where is she now?"

"She'll know."

Hel hefted his axe. "Good."

Henrik sprang to his feet and juked backwards, out of the way of Hel's first playful slash.

"This is going to be so much fun," said Hel. "This is how I want to die."

Henrik bolted across the parade ground. Behind him, Hel's taunting voice hurled insults as he fled into the interior of the fort. Like a fool, he'd panicked and retreated in the wrong direction, toward the flaming southern wall. He needed to double back toward the fighting; perhaps someone would help him fend off the attack. No, he had failed his people. They would only scorn him.

With a strident crack, the southeast corner of the fort collapsed, throwing fiery splinters and a cloud of acrid smoke toward Henrik and his pursuer. Behind him, Hel cursed, and Henrik looked back to see him pull off his flaming shirt and throw it aside.

Henrik turned back to the south, and without stopping, surveyed the shattered wall for an escape route. Just east of the gate, he spotted a section where the witch fire had burned itself out and mundane orange flames smoldered across the charred logs. To either side, tongues of indigo flickered, threatening a

293

screaming death if he failed to choose the right path through the wreckage. Henrik pushed the imploring wail of his mother from his mind, the bright flash of his father consumed in witch fire. He was out of binding stones, and Hel stood between him and the rest of the battle. Either he crossed through the flames or Hel would hack him into pieces.

Henrik darted toward the collapsed section of wall where it looked like the witch fire had spent itself. He leapt atop the first log, a puff of cinders erupting where he landed. From there, he stepped down to the ground and then up onto another log. Behind him Hel shouted, "I will follow you even to the dead place, Henrik Torvald. Did you know that Erk was my brother? My only brother."

Henrik knew that nothing he said would placate the Kriegan. So he ignored him. Henrik held his arms out to his sides as he balanced, moving at a determined pace down the length of the fallen palisade log. Ahead, a flare crackled, barring his path. Henrik looked around for a way through the haphazard forest of fiery, fallen logs. He hopped down to the ground and ducked beneath a burning pole. It singed the hair on the back of his head, and he swatted at his scalp, smothering it before it could spread.

He was nearly clear of the flaming wall, just one more clump of logs, perpendicular to his path, left to vault. He tried to bound atop them, but the part of the log he landed on disintegrated to ash, and he fell, seeing a flash of blue just before his eyes as he rolled past the last of the blazing wall.

Hel called out again. "Wait for me Henrik. We'll cross over together." He laughed.

Henrik reached the crest of the hill, the moonfall's red palette painting the waters below—a tableau of splintered boards and tangled rope and drifting bodies—a town drenched in blood. He shuddered to look upon the desolation of Skolja. The tide had receded again, taking with it most of the mud and debris from the landslide, though waist high water still pooled in the streets.

Henrik held his breath. Just west of where Rogan's smithy had once stood, the iron hull of *The Muse* protruded from a tangle of beams, roots, and clumps of sodden thatch. Henrik scrambled down the steps from Federal Hill to Skolja's ruins. By the time he reached the water at the bottom, Hel's footfalls echoed behind him. Henrik plunged into the murky shallows, wading west toward the smithy, his wake as dark as wine. Hel splashed along behind him, gaining on him as meteors streaked through the sky and a curtain of annihilation loomed in the south.

A man's body floated face down ahead of him. He recognized that it was Gunnar. His fingers had been gnawed away—in fact much of him was gone—but Henrik recognized his red coat. The body jigged as something beneath the surface fed on the constable's remains. Henrik redoubled his pace, giving the corpse a wide berth. Hel waded along, only ten paces behind him. At this rate, he'd catch him before Henrik reached *The Muse*.

Henrik was out of bindings. He was no fighter. Logic could not save him. Hel could not be reasoned with. This would end in blood. And in Henrik's calculation, it would be his own.

"Damn you, Kriegan!" Henrik swore over his shoulder.

Hel cackled. "Damn us both!"

Henrik's desperation mounted. After everything, he would die here in the ruins of Skolja. Perhaps it was a fitting end, given his failure. He splashed on, Hel gaining with every step, his catcalls growing louder behind Henrik. Meteors streaked into the sea before him, the flotsam of his devastated town drifted everywhere he looked. Framed by the monstrous beauty of the debris cloud, the three careening hulks of Quaya tumbled torturously nearer. But from the corner of his eye, Henrik saw the telltale wake of a white shark break away from Gunnar's corpse. Then a second wake, and a third, converging on them as they trudged through what was left of Skolja. With a mixture of terror and hope, he veered toward the nearest wreck of a building. The back corner of the structure had collapsed entirely, and it leaned at an angle, guaranteeing that it couldn't support his weight. But it was the only option left. Henrik jumped up to grab a rafter poking out from the paltry remains of the thatch. Henrik hauled himself up to the waist and threw one leg up onto the roof. Hel was too intent on Henrik to see the white sharks closing in. He grabbed Henrik's dangling ankle, and Henrik lashed out, kicking with his free leg back at the Kriegan's face. The blow caught Hel on the cheek and broke his grip on Henrik's ankle. Henrik rolled onto the roof, and with a mighty crack, it gave way and dropped a few feet, pinning Hel's foot below the waterline. Hel had just enough time to curse before the first white shark took a tentative bite out of his thigh. He screamed, startled by the attack. He struggled to free his leg and fend off the shark at the same time, but one of the others darted in, tearing a meaty chunk from his submerged calf.

Henrik rolled off the other side of the roof into the water and plunged across the flooded town, Hel's horrified screams echoing through the deserted streets behind him.

★★★★★

The swine panicked!

Brohr bit the throat from one legionary, tore the bowels from another. Light flashed from the corner of his eye. He saw the prefect die, and he howled, the crisp note sending those around him into flight. But there was no escape. He sang! It was all so beautiful. Brohr bounded across the open ground, pouncing on another soldier and clawing the back of his head off.

Another pig swung down at him, but he rolled to the side and sprang up, slashing across the man's neck. This! This was the song. This was the magic he was born to. It was the power. He felt godlike. Unstoppable. He killed and killed and killed and killed. The screams a sweet chorus, a dire hymn.

The brothers gloried. Together they made such music. Such a perfect arrangement. Forgotten was the broken moon, the Hidden's games, everything was merely a prelude to this anthem of death.

Soon the federal formation was scattered. His mind distant but just present enough to discern the difference between the fleeing pigs and the horrified Norn. He chased a soldier here, found one cowering there. He loped across the interval and gored one with his antlers.

And then... with a note of despair, the song began to recede, and he chased it, finding a sentry shivering by the mess hall. He found another by the well. The music dimmed. *No!* There were more. It could go on.

The Norn watched, trembling together. Distantly, he knew they feared he would not stop when the pigs were bled. And how could he? This was the blood. This was the magic. This was his right. His destiny. So pure. So perfect. He wanted screams! To feel gristle pop and veins gush!

He tackled another pig. Rolled him over, looking down into the horror-wide eyes of the prefect. Savor this. This swine. His kind raped your mother. Brutalized the whole world, the stars even. Brohr wrapped his talons around the man's throat. Brasca said something, but the words were blurred, indistinct. *Something wrong here*, he thought. It was a distant echo, drowned out by the last phrases of his glorious tune. Still.

He looked down at the man's panic-stricken eyes. Felt his slender neck. So feminine after all. It was discordant. Out of tempo.

He remembered the world around him and looked up, seeing the watching faces like notes out of tune. He groped inwardly to regain that righteous wrath, that song so bright and clear and red a moment ago. But his rhythm was broken. The battle was won. Henrik and Freylka and his grandfather stared down at him, waiting for him to strike the last blow, to rip out the heart of the pig who would rule them.

The prefect said something else, her words still jumbled. Something was wrong about that. The others spoke too. *Wait.* Brohr cocked his ear, the strain so faint he almost thought he was imagining the other tune, so soft, so subtle.

His brother screeched against his sudden restraint, wrestled for control of Brohr's gory hands.

297

"No!" Brohr wailed.

She spoke again, begging for her life.

What is this? Him. The prefect was a him. Brohr raked his hand across his own face as if he were tearing a spider web from his eyes. He looked back up at the Norn watching him grapple with his rage. They should be greedy for this man's death. But their faces were wrong.

Henrik shook his head.

Wait. Just wait.

A fragment of the Prefect falling, fire flaring in his eye. A flash of memory. Far away but calling desperately. Hadn't he seen it? He looked down at the man beneath him, her chest heaving.

This was a lie.

Anders' glamer faltered, shifted.

Brohr snatched his hand away from Lyssa's throat. It was her. *Oh Fathers, oh, what have I done?* She was so afraid. Brohr stood up. Backed away. He looked around. They watched him. Fearful of what he would become, what he had become already. His song was silent.

"Grandfather!" he bellowed. Freylka looked at him, and her eyes slid over to Henrik. A sly look. An accusation. She knew. Grandfather hid behind Henrik's face.

No more. Kill him and be free. It wasn't Henrik at all. Another illusion. Slow, like creeping death, he went to the image of Henrik. *Be free of him.*

Henrik's dog barked. He had not noticed it before. Henrik jerked the dog's leash, bent to the dog's ear, and it barked again.

He knew who that was, not his grandfather at all. Lies atop lies. He had seen Henrik run off, chased by Hel. Brohr turned back to Freylka, who had tried to point him to Henrik.

"Where's your boy?" he asked.

"He died in the fighting," she said. The words came from her own lips.

"No," Brohr said. "I know it's you."

298

Freylka took a step back. "Brohr," she said. "We've won. There is no more need for killing."

Brohr lashed out, batting his grandfather to the ground. Olek howled, desperately reminding Brohr of the image he had shown him as he lay dying. The picture flashed in his mind again. His grandfather reaching down to him, weeping. Guilty. Brohr leapt on him.

"Please." The illusion of Freylka faded, revealing Anders' bruised and wizened face. "I'm your kin. We're blood. Please." He looked away. "I'm sorry, Brohr. I'm sorry!"

The music was gone. The magic was gone. But Brohr's hatred remained. His brother's too, burning now more than ever. The bruise around Brohr's neck chafed. Dim memories flitted through his mind, the umbilical cord looped around his neck, strangled beside the fire. Olek's hate stoked ever hotter.

Brohr reached down, his hands no longer talons, his antlers dissolving, dripping on the two of them like a hot rain. Anders had murdered Olek; he saw it now. He had tried to trick Brohr into killing Lyssa, into becoming like he was, a murderer. "I won't!" Brohr screamed in his grandfather's face, gore and drool dripping down. He squeezed Anders's throat, hesitated, and then gave in, strangling.

Anders clawed at the hands around his neck, but he was old, and Brohr was much stronger. "I won't!" Brohr shouted. "I won't!"

Anders beat his fists feebly against Brohr's ribs. His mouth opened and closed like a fish washed ashore. He was trying to say something. Trying to tell him something. Old secrets, or apologies—it didn't matter. Brohr could stomach no more lies. He tightened his grip, watching the old skald's eyes change from rage to remorse and finally an emptiness to mirror the void growing inside of Brohr.

When his grandfather was dead, Brohr stayed atop him, staring down at his own red hands, listening to the battlefield sounds that filled the eerie quiet: flames crackling to the south, gentle weeping, the moaning of the wounded. If he could have kept his eyes forever averted, he gladly would have, for he knew in his guts what was waiting when at last his eyes met another's. But the shame and horror and revulsion were there whether he could face them or not. So at last he mustered the courage to look up at the gawking crowd, and there he saw himself, and he wept.

Chapter 30

"A man need only look behind him to discover a land full of strangers."

-Brom Gelfstrom, Breyga's Dirge

Lyssa rubbed her throat, shuddering at Brohr's transformation. She knelt, watching him strangle his grandfather. They all watched. She knew it had to be done. Anders was a murderer, a snake, but she couldn't help edging away as Brohr choked him to death.

When it was done and the old man had stopped kicking, stopped hitting and clawing at his grandson, Brohr froze, not looking up or saying a word. The tension in the crowd built until finally Brohr stood, looking around at them as if he were waking from a dream. Tears welled in his eyes, running through the mask of blood that covered his face. He blubbered for a minute but soon mastered himself. She wringed her hands. He was so beautiful, in his brutal way. But like a wild animal, not a man. She shivered at the thought of his touch, his bloody talons around her throat.

Brohr looked up at her, and she averted her eyes. He stepped towards her, and she stepped back, instinctively running her finger down her cheek to ward against him.

"Lyssa," he said. "I'm so sorry. He made me think you were one of them. It was a trick." He stepped toward her.

"Stop." Her hand trembled as she held it up. "You did what you had to, but..." She shook her head.

"No," he said. "Please Lyssa. I'm sorry. It was a trick."

She could see his rage had faltered; his shoulders slumped, and he was out of breath—but the thought of those claws disgusted her. He was... She didn't know what. A skald, surely, but something else too, something to be feared.

"Please," she asked. "Don't touch me. Please."

The shame on his face as he cast his eyes down brought out a flicker of pity, but it was dashed by the memory of his antlers, his keening cries, the murder of his grandfather, his pact with the thing from the dock. She knew he had done it to save her, at least a little. But she also knew that he might have killed them all if things had ended just a little differently.

Freylka whispered to her boy, and he said, "The federal ship is coming soon. We need a plan."

To the east, the sun had passed below the wall of the fort, casting them all in gloom. The red light from the pieces of Quaya loomed over the burning ruins of the southern gate. Sapphire flames crackled, crawling around the corners of the fort. It wouldn't be long until they were ringed in witch fire, trapped within.

"Their armor," Lyssa said. "We need to gather their armor."

★★★★★

Brohr sat beside his grandfather's corpse, looking down into its staring eyes. A ring of blood encircled its neck where his hands had been, its mouth gaping in a silent accusation. Brohr closed the old man's eyes then closed his own, hoping to escape the reproach he'd glimpsed. But the look was no less vivid in his mind than it had been on his grandfather's face.

He had never felt like this, not even when he'd beaten Vili half to death. Brohr wanted to vomit, but the shame would not come up. The way the others looked at him was unbearable. They saw him.

Brohr lay there, strangled by the creature he had become. He put his head back, and a whine escaped. He felt his brother's concern and curiosity, but it was no consolation, just the opposite. It only reminded him that he was a stranger, an alien to those around him. And there was no going back.

He thought he should be crying, but he realized then that he didn't miss his grandfather. He tried to conjure up a happy memory, a tribute of sorts, but nothing came.

It was not his grandfather he mourned.

"Waking up is never easy," said a little boy's voice behind him—Freylka's slave. "Freylka remembers when she found her song."

They waited for him to say something, but speaking required more strength than he could gather. Brohr just stared up at the pieces of Quaya burning in the sky.

"Freylka was kissing a boy named Grunnir. They were only twelve summers. He had a sore on his tongue from eating too much salt beef. When Freylka tasted his blood, she knew. He was thinking about an older girl, one he'd seen in the village, with blonde hair. Freylka saw her in a blue dress wearing a red kerchief to hold her hair back while she cleaned a fish. Freylka asked him about the girl. And she watched him change. She watched herself transformed in his eyes."

Brohr could almost see the girl cleaning the fish. And he had no trouble imagining the look in the boy's eyes. It was little Freylka he couldn't quite picture. Had she become an old hag that very instant? In a way, he knew she had.

"The lullaby is over, Brohr," the little boy said. "You're a skald now, and skald songs are sad songs. Freylka's song is a burden she bears for our people. To know the hour of our sacrifice approaches." The witch set her hand on her slave boy's shoulder. He struggled not to cry. "But the music is yours to play, Brohr. Make of it what you wish. These people cannot bind you. Their horror is their own."

Brohr nodded. He said, "Freylka knows."

The crone tittered. Her boy agreed, smiling. "Freylka knows."

Brohr rose to his feet. He looked back at the witch, her lips painted with scars.

"What happened to Grunnir?"

The boy started to speak, but Freylka gave his leash a jerk. She stooped to his ear to tell him what to say. "Dead."

303

Brohr turned back to the body of his grandfather. He had no clan marker, no pyre. Instead, he pulled his belt knife and cut his palm.

"*Immra blosch altes binde.*" Brohr held his bleeding fist over his grandfather's corpse, letting it trickle onto his face. "Blood shall bind us always."

★★★★★

Lyssa put her foot into the man's armpit and pulled his leather skirt down. It was crusted with drying blood, and it tangled around his feet, but she managed to tear it off after a brief struggle. She unbuckled her boots and kicked them off one at a time, looking around at the fort. The fire had spread halfway from the collapsed southern gate up the eastern wall. It burned a pallid orange, the witch fire almost spent, but the blaze it left was deadly enough. The wind blew west to east, sparing them the worst of the fumes, but still her eyes watered from the smoke. A shooting star streaked from the sky, striking the sea a few miles out. Seconds later a sharp crack resounded across the plateau.

She turned back to her task, ignoring her embarrassment as she peeled off her trousers and pulled on the studded skirt. It was too big for her, but she cinched the belt, and it stayed on. No one cared about her bare legs, she told herself. Standing up, Lyssa leaned over the dead soldier and rolled him onto his face to get the clasps on his breastplate. She undid one and tried to open it, realizing it had another clasp by his hip. She undid that one too and opened up the armor like a clamshell. Lyssa pulled him out of the breastplate and rolled the corpse onto its back again, revealing a deep gash across his belt line where his guts spilled out.

She turned away and donned the breastplate, struggling to pin the clasps while wearing the heavy armor that was much too big for her.

"Arius." She hurried over to where he sat cross-legged beside a corpse of his own, trying to get its armor off. It was the

304

prefect's body, its eye still steaming, the reek of cooked meat and shit wafting from it. "Help with this clasp."

"I have my own armor to worry about," he said.

She ground her teeth. "Help me, and then I can help you. It'll go faster that way."

He nodded, a leer growing on his face. "You look like a boy wearing his father's clothes, you know. Better legs though."

She ignored him, waiting for Arius to fasten the second clasp for her before she helped him into his own armor. "We have to be convincing."

"What else can we do?" He tore the broken feather out of the prefect's tricorn and put it on.

"They'd be organized. In formation," she said.

"Where is Henrik?" Arius asked. "Shouldn't the mayor be in charge?"

"One of the Kriegans chased him through that." She pointed at the smoldering wreck of the southern wall. "I didn't see them come back. I guess it's up to us. What about the wagons?"

Arius sneered at her, and, without another word, trotted off to organize a team to pull the wagons. Lyssa shrugged, shook her head, and turned to the northern gate. Brohr stood in her path, eyes blinking through a mask of blood, a short sword in his hand. With a deep breath, she jogged toward the gate, avoiding his eyes as she neared him. He was like one of the spiders behind the kegs back in her father's bar. She knew he wouldn't touch her, but she shuddered to be so close. He started to say something as she approached, but she tucked her head down and ran right past.

"Lyssa, wait!"

She knew it was cruel. Brohr's grandfather had worked his dire charms; Brohr had never meant to hurt her. She knew this. She knew, too, that Brohr had needed to kill Anders. That he would never have let Brohr go. She knew this, but knowing it was not enough.

"Lyssa, please! I didn't know it was you. Lyssa!"

★★★★★

Ash tumbled like snow through the unseasonably humid air. To the south, fire rained from the sky, and the ocean swelled, swamping what remained of the town below. The fort burned blue and red, its dense plume sucked high in the air, a pillar formed by strange currents.

The void ship drew near enough for Lyssa to make out the individual lights running along the underside. Loud enough to be heard amidst the cries of panic, the roaring flames, and the rumbling planet, the transport thrummed in the air. She watched the last ray of sunlight dip below the horizon, plunging them into a crimson twilight as Quaya began her collision with Heimir.

"Stand in formation," Lyssa shouted. "The ship will arrive in time. Don't panic. When I say, hail them like the federals do. Just a little game of pretend, and we'll be on board."

Ivar strode up beside her, puffed out his chest, and put his hands on his hips. He looked uncomfortable in his tight-fitting Tyrianite armor. His bare legs shivered, pale and flabby. "Listen up! I'm deputy mayor, which means I'm in charge." He turned a reproving glare on Lyssa. "Everyone wait for *my* signal. Men go to the ship first. Stay calm."

The rasping engine drowned out his last words as the Tyrianite transport began its approach. The moment before it landed stretched unbearably. The men stood rigid in their stolen armor. Someone had pissed themselves and the stench mixed with the toxic smoke of the sizzling witch fire. They'd assembled on the eastern edge of Federal Hill, the only place still free of devastation. To the north, a forest fire raged in the hills, adding to Quaya's eerie light.

The children and womenfolk huddled in a separate group from them, hopefully seeming like prisoners. Two wagons laden with the last bounty of Skolja were parked beside them. The federal ship slowed to land. A bank of portholes glowed around the length of its cylindrical hull. Running along the underside, two rows of runes crackled with mystic power, holding the vessel aloft.

Lyssa's stomach fluttered. Was it turning away? No, the ship swung around and began to descend. Ash swirled around its lights like moths around a lantern. As the transport dropped, she saw row upon row of eldritch markings, each no bigger than her hand, the graven notes of ancient bindings. Lyssa glimpsed a face in one of the portholes. She hailed the landing ship and the others imitated her, all in all, a slovenly gesture, unlike what she had imagined. Lyssa turned her head away as the ship threw up ash and dirt, its arcane engines emitting razor sharp chirps as it came to rest upon the plateau.

"Steady!" Ivar shouted.

Lyssa realized she had no idea which end they were supposed to enter through. A little redhead boy darted toward the ship. All discipline collapsed. The women and children broke first, scrambling after him toward the nearest end of the ship. Seeing their families panic, the men followed, all semblance of a formation lost.

Lyssa ran too, terrified of being left behind. To her relief, the side of the ship to which they flocked unfolded mechanically, forming a ramp. A squad of legionaries rushed out, beating back the women and children too frightened to wait for the ambush. At first the soldiers shoved them back, struck with the flats of their blades, but the frenzy overwhelmed any clemency they might have offered, and within seconds the fight turned lethal.

The Norn men pushed through the folk, shoving their own panic-stricken wives and children aside to get at the federals. The first legionary to fall looked relieved to see his murderer charge up the ramp, but the Kriegan surprised him with a belly full of iron, and the ruse collapsed into a fierce and fleeting melee. The Norn overwhelmed the federals in a span of heartbeats as the desperate pretenders hacked their way through the outnumbered soldiers and onto the ship.

Lyssa shoved through the crowd of Skoljans, pushing up the ramp. It rose about ten feet up and then leveled off with the main deck of the ship. When she reached the top, she saw the massacre inside. Most of the area was a cargo bay about fifty feet wide and three times as long, with crates and bunks along the lower walls and down the center. A metal catwalk wrapped around the outside. Startled soldiers leaned over the rail, strange navigational instruments twinkling behind them.

Kriegans were already pushing up the staircase toward the outnumbered crew. A new terror gripped her. The moment was too bloody, too chaotic, for any hope of order or restraint. If the Norn slaughtered the crew, who would pilot the ship? They would be trapped here as Quaya crashed down upon them. She called out, but her voice was nothing compared with the pandemonium inside the ship. She watched in horror as Arius mounted the steps to the catwalk and gutted the nearest Tyrianite. Lyssa looked around her for some way to signal a truce, but there was nothing. It was happening too fast.

Behind her, the throng of desperate townsfolk parted, shying away from Freylka as she mounted the ramp. She held her niece on her hip, and when she reached the mouth of the cargo bay, Freylka pressed her scarred lips to the girl's forehead for a kiss and handed the child to the redhead who'd become her nursemaid.

Freylka turned back to the chaos inside the ship. Her boy handed her the knife, and she smiled down at him. Freylka opened her mouth and unleashed a single, ear-splitting note, high and bright and unnaturally loud. She met Lyssa's gaze and gave her a little nod as she knelt before her boy and wiped a tear from the corner of his eye. Freylka's voice plunged into a virtuoso run, notes leaping high and low, a dynamic, haunting plea. As the last note resounded through the ship, she grabbed a fistful of hair from the back of the boy's head and planted a desperate kiss on the child, her blade lacerating his jugular. Lyssa watched in horror as Freylka gouged her own neck, her final, arcane note somehow still resonating through the cargo bay.

It began as a twitch, a spasm in every single eye aboard. The vision hit like a shock of cold water, a wave that crashed over all of them—Norn and Tyrianite alike. Their eyes rolled back in their heads and the swords dropped from their hands. A sudden and horrifying certainty spread amongst them as they witnessed the terrible price of seeing this battle through. The Norn would corner and butcher every pig on the ship. The Tyrianites would battle valiantly against the provincials but die to a man. The moon would fall; this paltry craft crushed as Quaya's shards rent the face of Heimir. The total annihilation of a world. The Norn extinct. The federation in disarray. A multitude of souls snuffed as the last grains of sands ran through the hourglass of this world. It was a doom fled now or never escaped.

And then it was over.

They blinked, looked down at their fallen swords. Looked at each other.

"Everyone!" Lyssa shouted. "Stop fighting and get us out of here!" Her words echoed through the cargo bay.

A beat of silence ensued. Freylka dropped the boy, the sound of his body crumpling resounded in the quiet. She struggled to get up from her knees but couldn't. She gurgled blood, her gaze roaming the ship. A macabre smiled passed Freylka's scarred lips as her eyes settled on her niece. The crone tottered, staring, her eyelids drooping, until she collapsed atop her little slave's body, and the spell was broken.

Chapter 31

"The lies we tell our children collect the everyday wisdom of good intentions. They are believed, and compounded, steeping in our dreams and dreads until, at last, they are the lies we tell ourselves."

—Umbrian Hasdrubal, A Litany of Sins

Brohr stood alone on the darkened plateau, watching the Tyrianite ship swing around and land beside the cowering townsfolk. Beyond, the apocalypse drew nearer, streaks of flame crashing into the sea, the three great pieces of the moon tumbling toward him. A heard of elk bounded across the field to the west, sped by their terror, their flight hopeless.

The end couldn't come soon enough. He relished the thought of Quaya smashing into him, vaporizing him in a flash of incalculable power.

A chill crept into the balmy night. "Pity," said the Hidden.

Brohr turned to the creature, silhouetted by the wildfire in the hills. He said nothing.

"You recoil at what you have become," it said. "But it's a fool's pride, this shame you feel."

Brohr turned back to the ship, watching the desperate bloodbath on the ramp. "Let me die in peace," he said.

"Peace?" It laughed, a sound like grating iron and wounded dogs. "Are you at peace?" Brohr did not answer him. "You see yourself as they see you. A horror. But you are nothing like that. I have seen the horrors, and they would make you tremble and weep." It paused, a silence laden with calculation. "What if I told you that you could save her?"

Brohr looked back out of the corner of his eye.

"Oh yes," it said. "Your friend is doomed."

"More lies," Brohr turned away.

"Not this time. She will die soon, with certainty. And only you can save her. Perhaps she will see you then as I see you."

"Why should I believe you?" Brohr asked.

"The answer is there." Brohr turned back to see the Hidden pointing up at the stars. "The blue giant. Omnir, your people call it. It was my home once. Long ago. Only there can you find your salvation."

"Everyone dies."

"Yes," it said. "The great enemy of us all. But the dead place will be most cruel to her. She will be damned."

Brohr turned back to it. "Why? What has she done?"

"She? Nothing. It is *you* who have displeased me."

Brohr looked back at the ship, the distant figures crowded on the ramp. He turned to the Hidden, but it was gone.

"No!" Brohr cried. He hammered the crown of his head. "No! No! No!"

Brohr ceased his useless assault. He opened his eyes and took stock of the townsfolk packing into the ship. A mechanical whine echoed across the plateau as the ramp began to rise.

He set off at a gallop, fear and shame driving him like a spooked buck toward the ship. Olek screeched, and he sang at frantic tempo, the tune slingshotting him, his feet churning up the soil with supernatural haste. The ramp groaned upward as high as his waist and still far off. He ran, a blur of hulking fear across Federal Hill. The ramp climbed higher, over his head as he approached, and Brohr and Olek belted a note of singular regret in unison which launched him up over the ramp and into the federal ship.

★★★★★

The waters around Henrik's ankles rippled as a meteor streaked into a distant hilltop. *The Muse* lay half submerged in

311

mud and debris, the saucer jutting out at a 45-degree angle. In the ruddy light of the mangled moon, he at first thought it had flipped upside down, blocking the top hatch and dooming him to Skolja's fiery fate. But as he neared, his fear proved unfounded; *The Muse* was right-side up and seemed to be intact.

Testing some of the clutter wedged beneath the ship to see if it would hold his weight, Henrik pushed off and got his hands around the rim of the saucer. His fingers found a pair of rivets to cling to, and pushing off the wreckage of the house, he got a leg over the side so that he could lever himself atop *The Muse*.

With a bubbling squelch of mud, the void craft settled a few feet, flattening out and causing Henrik to hold his breath. When the ship stilled, he scrambled over to the hatch and cranked it open.

Inside, *The Muse* was dark and cold as a tomb. He lowered himself into the cockpit, glanced around, and sealed himself into the gloomy cabin. A central chair commanded the small enclosure upon which rested a void helm ringed with rune-gouged stones. *The Muse* had just enough room for him to stand inside of it, the circular walls just wide enough for him to touch opposite sides if he leaned one way and then the other. A ring of enchanted glass portholes surrounded the navigator's seat, though they were caked in mud and difficult to see through. Control plates covered the walls, sheets of copper inset with cold iron pathways conducting the spiritual energies which powered the vessel.

Henrik picked the helm up off of the command chair, and a chill ran through him. How many times, he wondered, had his father sat here, dreaming of the heavens? Had he ever brooded in this seat, safely away from prying eyes, and pondered why his son had turned out such a selfish, drunken disappointment? Henrik's mouth went dry. He pushed away the image of his father's startled horror as the witch fire devoured him. By an act of will, Henrik replaced the picture with one of his father sitting before his telescope, puffing on his pipe, an absently contented look on his face. Henrik looked at the helm he carried. He remembered something his father had once said, that "what we lack in courage we must make up for in wisdom, and vice versa." He saw his father's thoughtful smile and discovered one of his own. Henrik sat in the command chair and donned his helm. Much like the first time he touched her, the sheer complexity of *The Muse's* bindings dizzied him. He closed his eyes until the sensation passed.

Henrik concentrated on the energies radiating from the helm until he found the pitch he was looking for. He hummed the note, blending it with the vibration of the device itself, until quite suddenly, he peered through the lens of the helm's magic. His vision saw in every direction all at once, from a spot just above the half-buried ship. To the south, a wall of dazzling chaos swept toward the remains of Skolja, promising to obliterate even the ruins of his town.

Henrik took a moment to cast his awareness around for one last look at his home. The waterfront was gone, the docks, the dike. Replaced by the dregs of the sea, kelp, and drowned townsfolk, the flotsam of his own wrecked mansion intermingled with the simplest of the fishermen's huts. Not one building was left standing except within the burning fort atop Federal Hill. There was nothing left for Henrik to do for Skolja or its people. He was an exile now, and there would be no homeland to which he might one day return. His mouth fell open, momentarily overcome by the totality of his isolation. His chin quivered, his eyes teared, and his nose ran.

"Courage," he said.

As if to urge his journey, the ground trembled. The disjointed relationship between his helmet sight and his other senses nauseated him. Henrik choked down the acid at the back of his throat and quested for the ignition binding, goading it with his will until *The Muse's* engines fired.

The void craft lurched into the air, dislodging rubble and muck as it rose. Henrik calmed himself, steeled himself, and began the flight procedures, spurring the bindings that governed his father's marvel in their proper sequence. When all was ready, he paused, wrestling a strange thought, his head tilting to the side until the weight of the helm became awkward.

"Father," he said. "I know it's stupid, but I could use the company. So if you're listening, let's take her up. You and me."

Henrik focused on a distant point in the sky to the north and tethered his mind there. Then, with gritted teeth, he dragged the ship toward the spot, sluggishly at first, but soon conquering the task, mastering the manifold bindings. The speed pinned his body in the navigator's chair, the force dimming his vision, turning his stomach, but soon he mastered that too, and looked around to behold the sea of shooting stars, the churning banks of fiery clouds, and the vanishing world of forest and sea below. *The Muse* soared into the heavens, ascending to heights where his father had never dared to tread. And a sudden joy seized him. A feeling beyond doom or devastation or the petty squabbles of men, beyond death and fear and disappointment. He was elated, light, free of all burdens for one precious moment.

"We're flying!" Henrik cried out. "We're flying!"

★★★★★

Lyssa climbed the catwalk stairs to get a better view of the ship's interior. The federals had surrendered after Freylka's final spell, and now they frantically set to work, readying the ship for takeoff, securing cargo, and directing the Norn refugees to hold on or lash themselves to the bunks lining the walls. The loading door was nearly closed when Brohr leapt over the side and rolled into the cargo bay. Fear and relief warred in Lyssa at the sight of him, but there was no time to spare for her confused affections.

The Tyrianites shouted orders back and forth as they scrambled around the ship. There weren't many of them left. On the front side of the catwalk, three of them plunked down into chairs and strapped themselves in, donning strange helmets ringed with glowing stones.

Something clanged against the hull of the ship, and panic registered on every face. Her stomach revolted as the vessel lurched into the air, but Lyssa fought down the nausea and

314

gripped the railing with all of her might. A strange tinkling sound, as if the ship passed through a cloud of pebbles, was soon drowned out by the thrust of the engines. Lyssa closed her eyes, trying not to be sick. All around her the townsfolk wept and screamed. The crowded ship reeked of sweat and something metallic she had never smelled before. Another meteor struck the hull, startling her. She lost her grip on the rail, realizing with a fright that the catwalk was tilting. She slid a few feet and grabbed the next post in the rail. The ship pitched violently, and she almost lost her grip again.

A rhythmic whooshing sound filled the cargo bay, and the ship accelerated at breakneck speed. It was all she could do to hang on. She watched, helpless, as old Axl lost his hold on the rail and fell sideways across the interior of the ship. His head split against the handle of the rear door where his body was pinned by the force of their ascent. The ship rolled to its right, and she whipped over the rail like the hand of a clock, nearly losing her hold. Someone further down was not so lucky, and their aborted scream, as much as the movement in the corner of her eye, told Lyssa the crash was fatal. The ship twisted back, long metallic scrapes sounding on the other side of it.

Her stomach fluttered as the pull of Heimir fell away and she floated into the air, still clutching the handrail. She looked around in wonder to see others rise from the floor, hovering in the air like ghosts. Her mind struggled to make sense of what she saw, but she was mystified. A blue light shone from somewhere below, and a whispering sound filled the cargo bay. She crashed back to the catwalk, the wind knocked out of her. A fresh volley of screams echoed through the ship as people fell back to the ground. Debris tinkled against the hull again, but the ride was suddenly and eerily calm.

One of the Tyrianites unstrapped himself from his chair and scrambled over to a porthole to see out. This was not a sight Lyssa was going to miss. She pushed herself to her feet and staggered to the nearest porthole. Through the enchanted glass, Lyssa marveled at a blue orb suspended over a sea of blackness—Heimir. All across its surface, fires raged and clouds of black smoke churned. The shattered pieces of Quaya careened into the planet like hot coals bursting in the fireplace.

She watched as the greatest of the shards impacted her home, sending a wave of smoke that enwrapped the world in a final shroud. The seconds ticked by as it spread across the blue and green face of Heimir until it was cloaked all in gray, embers flickering beneath the veil.

Chapter 32

"Ere Tyrus, last of the old ones, passed unto the dead place, he gave the keys of heaven to Cassian, and raised him up to rule the starry void. As his light faded, shining Tyrus, taught divine Cassian the sacred majesties, so that the elect might rule forever after."

—The Federal Scriptures
Book I Canto XXVI (Cambian Era Revision)

The Bright Guards bowed at right angles, one to either side of the great portal as the Pontiff led the slave into the holy of holies. Overawed, the sacrifice slacked his pace to take in the marvels, their beauty magnified by the herbs that pacified him. The Pontiff jerked his leash, and he stumbled after. Behind them, the shrine guardians shut the massive golden doors with a heavy clank.

The slave gasped. "It's... It's wonderful."

"Shut up," said the divine Pontiff.

He led the long black-haired, red-skinned man into the ruins of the old place. Beneath the great dome, grass grew under their bare feet, a benefit of the specially enchanted wall sconces that lit the site. Tumbled walls of ancient stone littered the enclosure, which stretched a thousand feet from side to side. Ivy and holly climbed the ruins, and toward the middle, golden light spilled out of an arched doorway from a long crumbled building atop a hill.

The slave looked to him, wonder on his face. The fool held up his hand, marveling at the way the light scintillated off his fingertips. He slowed his pace, luxuriating in the way it felt to slide the backs of his knuckles across his own cheek.

"Move." The Pontiff shoved him.

A path worn by the countless steps of the many Pontiffs, this daily pilgrimage, led through the holy ground and up the little hill into the doorway leaking light. He prodded the slave onward, annoyed at the Shinei man's awe for every blade of grass and trick of light.

At last they reached the doorway, and the slave pressed through, eager to discover what awaited him. They entered a large room, its walls little more intact than the rest of this place. Across from the doorway sat a shining figure atop a throne of golden skulls.

The Pontiff tensed, forever wary of the ancient thing. He knew in his bones why the scriptures lied and said that Tyrus had died so long ago. The people would inevitably reject such a creature. It was a brilliant horror: tall and lithe, its head oblong, humming through the toothy orifice beneath its great black eyes.

The slave yelped and threw himself to his knees. Laughing, he pressed his forehead to the grass. Between them lay a stone altar, sized for a man to lay upon. Half-naked, the slave shivered at the cold it radiated.

"Welcome, my chosen." The old one's melodic voice filled the rooms with radiant warmth.

The slave quailed. Pontiff Cambian bowed to Tyrus, awaiting instruction before he raised his head.

"The Wound is hungry, child," it said.

Cambian reached down and grabbed the slave by the hair, pulling him to his feet. He guided the drugged slave onto the altar, laying him down firmly, then looked back to the raised throne. Ever so slowly, Tyrus rose to his full height and descended to the altar. The very spot where he had pulled his brother back from the dead place, all those countless years ago. Cambian took a step back, forever unnerved by the ritual.

The thing said nothing, looking down on the enraptured slave. The man tried to sit up, and Tyrus pushed him gently back to the frigid stone slab. The slave's smile faltered, the first inklings of doom penetrating his addled mind.

318

Ancient Tyrus began to sing, its voice so rich in magic that Cambian could almost swear he heard the trill of fife and the braying of horn. The song built, so frightfully beautiful that tears welled in the Pontiff's eyes, so potent that Cambian's jaw hung slack and he tottered on his feet. At the height of the tune's crescendo, Tyrus shoved down on the slave's chest, pushing him, impossibly, into the stone.

And just like that the slave was gone. No screams—a good thing, for the old one found them distasteful. The altar's cold abated, the Wound satisfied another day. Cambian raised his head. He never knew if Tyrus would impart wisdom or send him away, never knew if it would dismiss him or not.

"Moriigo's champion has fled doomed Heimir."

Cambian was afraid to speak. He waited, beginning to sweat as the silence lingered. Just as he was turning to leave, it spoke again, an entrancing sing-song of impossible timbre.

"I have foreseen your death. The end of our long war approaches, Cambian, but you will not live to see it. You must prepare the way for my own champion, for you are not he."

Cambian felt dizzy. He reached out to steady himself, recoiling as his hand touched the cold stone of the altar. His heartburn flared, but he choked it down, surprised to feel a sense of relief that it would finally be over soon. "What must I do, Great One?"

"Nothing, child. You must do nothing."

Cambian bowed his head and waited for more. After a few minutes, he mustered the courage to turn away and flee the holy place.

★★★★★

Lyssa tore her eyes from the porthole, her vigil for Heimir ended. She stepped back from the window, an ungainly lurch, and reached out for the handrail of the catwalk to keep herself from falling. Clinging to it, she began to weep: ragged, wretched sobs that, try as she might, Lyssa could not contain.

When she had regained control, Lyssa looked around the ship. Below her, fighting had broken out again. Outnumbered, the last few Tyrianites backed into a corner of the cargo bay, constricted by the clot of Norn surrounding them. At the end of the catwalk to her left, a pair of federals guarded the platform at the front of the ship where a trio of Tyrianites sat in three chairs, crowned with ornate helms, seemingly unconscious. Lyssa decided that they must be the pilots.

She leaned over the railing and looked around until she spotted Arius over by the surrounded federals. She shouted his name, but her voice was lost amongst the other cries. Lyssa drew the short sword that was part of her costume and banged the flat of the blade against the handrail. She screamed for Arius until she finally got his attention. When he looked up, she pointed with her sword at the three helmed federals at the bow of the ship.

It took him a minute to register, but she assumed he knew more than she did because his posture jerked erect. He froze for a few seconds then turned to the men around him and spoke, his words lost in the din. Arius raised his sword, and the group charged across the cargo bay toward the stairs up to the catwalk.

Lyssa approached the pair of federals guarding the corner and sheathed her sword. She stood before them and folded her arms.

"You'd better have surrendered by the time they get here." She tilted her head to the group of Norn shoving toward the stairs. "We're going to need you to survive; you'll be fine hostages, but they're too riled up to bother right now. They'll hack you to pieces."

The guards looked down the stairs at the bloody, bearded men wearing the uniforms and armor of murdered soldiers. They turned to each other for a tense moment, and then one of them handed Lyssa his sword, followed quickly by the other.

Lyssa wiped sweat from her eye. "Good," she said. "Kneel down and put your hands behind your heads so they can see you've surrendered."

The federals looked at each other again, uncertain, but as Arius and a half dozen Norn charged up the stairs, they held up their hands and knelt.

"Get out of the way," Arius shouted at her as he mounted the last step. "We need to get to the caller before he tells someone what's happened."

Lyssa darted ahead, rounding the corner to the niche where the Tyrianite officers sat, oblivious to the chaos within the ship.

"Wake up!" She slapped the nearest of the three seated federals, who lay with his head back, eyes closed. He wore a curly black beard, trimmed. His eyes shot open, the whites stark against his dark skin. He held up trembling hands.

"Peace, woman." He looked around at the other Norn and the swords they brandished. "We give up. I am Captain Antillus of *Cassian's Mule.*"

Arius shoved forward and prodded one of the other entranced federals.

"Wake up!"

The man's eyes snapped open and he sat forward.

His captain shouted, "No! He's the navigator. Let him fly the ship or we'll crash. It's not safe yet."

Arius paused, relishing the control for a second before he nodded. "That makes this one the caller."

Captain Antillus nodded.

Arius stepped forward and drove his sword into the sleeping man's chest. His eyes bulged open, and he gasped, a stream of blood pouring from his nose and mouth. He looked to his captain, eyes wide. He reached out to him and then slumped over dead.

The captain and navigator screamed, struggling to unbuckle themselves from their seats and fight for their lives. Lyssa cuffed Arius on the ear, and the other Norn, unsure whose lead to follow, cowed the federals back into their seats with raised swords.

"What the hell was that?" Arius wheeled on Lyssa, holding the bloody tip of his blade in her face.

She leaned forward, letting the edge of the sword touch her cheek. "That was stupid, Arius," she said. "We can't afford to kill these men."

"I was just being sure he wouldn't send out a message. You're the stupid one, getting in my way." He adjusted his grip on the sword.

Lyssa looked around at the men with Arius. She knew them all, except a pair of Kriegans. There was Tor the thatcher, Soren, and Rogan the blacksmith.

"I suppose we should listen to you, eh Arius?"

He nodded warily. "Why not? Should we listen to you? You can't even pay your rent on time, much less command a void ship."

"All of that is gone now," Lyssa said. "All of your money is gone. All the respect you thought it earned you."

Arius puffed out his chest. "No one's going to listen to you, you little—"

"You ass." Lyssa made a show of looking around the ship. "No one here owes you anything anymore. You couldn't even manage to get the wagons aboard, could you?"

Arius gagged. His hand shot up to cover his mouth as the magnitude of his blunder hit him. He whipped his head around toward the cargo bay and rushed to the railing, looking down, hoping that the wagons laden with the last of his wealth had somehow made it onto the ship.

He whimpered, beat his fist against his forehead, and cursed. "Idiot! Idiot! No!"

"You panicked, Arius," Lyssa said. "No one can blame you for that. I've never been so scared. But you also killed that Tyrianite, and he may have been of use to us." She gazed around the circle of Norn, eyeing them one by one. "That's two mistakes one right after another. We can't afford that. Not now."

The men grumbled and nodded to each other.

Arius stammered. "This is ridiculous. You're not going to listen to her. My father is deputy mayor."

Tor scowled at Arius, leaned in toward him, and without breaking eye contact, spat at his feet. That summed up the group's opinion well enough, and to a man, they turned from Arius to Lyssa, awaiting orders.

"What about this lot?" Rogan winked at her. "Captain?"

Lyssa struggled to contain a little twist of a smile on her face. She turned back to the federals. "Captain Antillus," she said. "Do you surrender?"

He hung his head, sucked in a deep breath, and said, "Yes, I surrender."

"I'm sorry about your man." She glanced at the body slumped in the caller's chair. "Did he send a message out? Does anyone know that we've taken this ship?"

"No." Captain Antillus shook his head. "It was too chaotic. Too many people trying to call. He couldn't get through. No one knows."

Lyssa nodded. "You're going to take us somewhere safe, as far away from federals as you can. If you get us to safety, I'll let you go. If we're captured, no matter what, no matter how, you and your men are dead. Do you understand?"

He struggled to look her in the eye. "Yes."

"Where should we go?" Lyssa looked around at the Norn with her. "Where can we start over?"

They frowned at each other.

Captain Antillus shrugged. "Perhaps to the outer giants? Not safe exactly, but it's outside the federation."

Lyssa looked around at the other men. They waited for her to say something. "To the giants then. Captain Antillus, set a course. And I have oh so many questions for you."

Chapter 33

"Born of shame, Breyga's bastard desecrated the idols of his Fathers, and in despising them, he despised himself and became a stranger to his own gods."

-Ols Grafsten, The Wayward Son

The world was its own pyre.

Lyssa finally managed to pry herself away from the porthole again. It was the most beautiful thing she had ever witnessed. The most terrible. Had anyone ever seen the like? She tried to grasp the scale of it. How many Skoljas, Pederskalds, and Tronds had perished? Hemmings gone, the far country. Everything. Never to be seen again.

The tavern, with its kegs of oak, its spidery nooks, its countless nights of toil and laughter. Forever gone. Her father. Entombed somewhere on the smoke-shrouded wreck of Heimir. She fought to keep her composure, ashamed that she had not stayed behind in Skolja to observe the proper rites. But no, she had chosen to try to help, however desperate and fruitless it had been.

Rogan climbed back up the steps to the catwalk, a weary limp slowing him down. He looked up at her and forced a smile. When he reached the top, Rogan took a deep breath and gestured back toward the folk huddled in the cargo bay. His mouth opened and closed as he paused to search for what to say, his eyes roaming to the back corner of the room, where Brohr lay on one of the bunks, facing the wall.

"The folk are upset. They're frightened," Rogan said. "They've been asking."

"For what?" Lyssa asked.

"It's Brohr. You seem to be his only friend."

"I doubt that." She looked away, her fingers tapping faster.

"I know you're frightened of him." Rogan forced a laugh. "Damn, we all are. But he seems to listen to you."

"What of it?"

"Talk to him, Lyssa. The folk want him to say something. They want a funeral for... for everything. He's the last skald."

Lyssa put her hands to her mouth and bit her knuckle. She looked down to where he lay. What was he feeling? She had hurt him, she knew. But goosebumps broke out on her forearms.

"Lyssa," said Rogan. "The folk need this. We're going to be on the ship for weeks. If you want to take charge, then do it."

"I don't!" Lyssa snapped. "I don't want to take charge at all. I just don't want the wrong sort doing it."

Rogan shrugged. "You have to talk to him sooner or later."

She closed her eyes and steeled herself. "Okay," she said. "Okay. Fine. I'll talk to him."

With a sigh, she walked past Rogan to the staircase. As she descended, every eye followed her, every face a mixture of fear and pleading. A hopeless lot, grasping for some way to make sense of the insanity that surrounded them. Lyssa walked through the crowd, many of them wounded, some whispering entreaties and thanks as she passed.

She sat on the edge of Brohr's bed, closing her eyes. She wanted to flee. She wanted to curl up beside him and apologize. But she did neither. Instead, she leaned close and whispered. "Hi Brohr." He said nothing. "I'm sorry if I was cruel to you," she said. "You frightened me." He murmured something. "What?" Lyssa asked.

"I said I'm sorry!"

She flinched, quickly recovering her composure, but she knew he'd felt the cot shake. "It's okay. I know the old man used one of his tricks."

Brohr rolled onto his back, looking at her from the corner of his eye. "Not just for that. I'm sorry... I'm sorry for all the blood on my hands. I wish I was not like I am."

She nodded. "I know."

"Freylka told me that skald songs were sad songs. She was right, of course. I don't want to be like them, like Freylka and my grandfather, sad freaks that live off of blood and lies."

"Maybe you don't have to. Things are different now." She looked over at the cargo door as if she could see through it to the remains of their world. "Everything is different." Again, he said nothing. Lyssa pressed on. "They want you to say something. The folk do. They're terrified. With everything gone, having a skald again feels like a way to get back a little of what was lost. They need you."

He rolled away. Lyssa looked back at the expectant faces of the townsfolk. She wasn't sure what to say; it seemed as if he would not reply. But a moment later he exhaled, nodding to himself. "Give me a minute."

"Sure," Lyssa said, standing. "When you're ready."

★★★★★

The Norn pressed up against the walls to leave a place for him. They were filthy, wounded, hungry, frightened. Fewer than a hundred remained, a mix of Kriegans and townsfolk. All bedraggled, all without a home. Brohr regarded the bodies laid out at the rear of the ship, the Norn separated from the Tyrianites in two rows. Around him the remnants of Skolja waited solemnly, a few moans from the wounded and stifled coughs breaking the silence.

"The old ways are dead," he said. "As Skolja is dead. As Nornlund is dead. As Heimir."

Brohr took the dagger from his belt and held it up for all to see. He looked up to the catwalk where the remaining crew gazed down, where Arius stood with his arms folded, looking impatient. Brohr walked over to the row of bodies at the back of the ship. Freylka with her dyed hair and scarred lips. Her boy,

326

pale, his eyes still staring. Amongst the familiar faces, he was startled to discover his old friend Vili, lying on his side, his face cut along the jawline, his golden curls dark with blood. Brohr searched the other bodies to see if Birgit was there too, but he didn't see her, couldn't find her face in the watching crowd.

Brohr cut his hand, shaking a few drops of blood onto each corpse in turn.

"The song of our people has not yet ended. But we are a new clan now, a new tribe." He paced around the room, flicking a spatter on the face of each he passed. As he went down the line, Brohr came to the Tyrianite ordinal, Carthalo. The federal straightened at his approach, giving the him slightest nod. Brohr paused to study him. He was not atop the catwalk with the others of his kind. Dried gore caked his chin. He held Astrid Olsgaard's hand. The couple froze, only their eyes following him. Brohr looked around for her brother and her father, but they were gone, piled beside the rest of the dead. Brohr tipped his head to Astrid and Carthalo, flicked his blood in their faces, and continued down the line. "The land that the Ten Fathers conquered is gone. Our home is gone."

He paused. For whatever reason, he thought of his dog, Grendie, and a sad smile played across his lips. It reminded him of the day his grandfather had brought her home from town. They fed her scraps of venison, and the old man had let Brohr name her. He forced himself to remember the time his grandfather had kicked her after he'd stepped in Grendie's shit. He could see his grandfather's face, red with anger, red when Brohr choked the life from him. A tear slid down the corner of his eye, and Brohr wiped it away. He looked up, seeing many of the folk mirror the ward.

★★★★★

Brohr stood at the porthole looking out at the star-flecked expanse. He was thinking about the Hidden. About what it wanted from him. About what it had said about Lyssa.

She hadn't spoken to him again. No one had. He walked among them like a ghost, and they parted reverently, fearfully. He was like an elder now, the voice of the tribe. They would listen when he spoke, show him respect, keep their distance.

Cassian's Mule had set course for the outer giants. Perhaps there they could find a new home, carve out a new place where the folk could start again. He knew it was a lie though. Was that another of the skalds' burdens? To lie. They would dwindle or go out in a rage. Whatever shape their doom took, the damage was done, their way of life annihilated.

And Lyssa would die too. He believed that creature, the lies spilled from its lips with every breath. But he believed it. Knew it. Some dark fate awaited them. The Norn were broken, bracing for the deathblow.

But out there, way out, the blue giant waited too. No doubt that thing wanted him to go to Omnir for its own purposes; no illusion could hide that simple truth. But what other roads could they tread? Though his pact was concluded, he remained a servant, a plaything of that ancient creature.

The end of Heimir was long since out of sight. Left behind. A grave for all the things that were. From his vantage, all he saw was darkness broken only by a countless sea of tiny lights. Long he stayed at the window, peering out, looking for that blue glimmer as the last of the Norn ventured deeper into the waiting arms of the abyss.

Please rate and review this book on Amazon and Goodreads!

Online sales algorithms factor your ratings and reviews, one of the most important keys to a book's success. Please take a moment to leave a simple review. It makes a huge difference. Thank you!

Jordan Loyal Short is a debut author of epic fantasy. He graduated from the University of Washington with a degree in Creative Writing and has worked in a variety of industries, as a waiter, bartender, copywriter and more. Jordan loves travel, music, and playing games. He lives in Washington state with his wife where he is currently daydreaming about the end of the world.

Visit:
WWW.JORDANLOYALSHORT.COM
For free fiction and updates about new releases!

Follow me on social media @
Twitter: www.twitter.com/Jordanloyalshor
Facebook: www.facebook.com/jordanloyalshort

Binder – A practitioner of spirit binding magic, a studious form of magic that empowers runes with the sacrificed animus of living creatures.

Bishop – A commanding rank in the Federal theocracy, typically commanding large garrisons and provincial cities.

Elector – The highest rank of federal officer below the divine Pontiff, Electors vote in the Synod, passing system-wide legislation, and appointing the succession of Pontiffs.

Hemmish – A culture of the southern end of Heimir's major continent.

Moriigo – Also known as the Hidden One, this Shining Ones is cloaked in darkness, an ancient curse from his brother. Raised from the dead by Tyrus, Moriigo plots to return the rest of his brood from the dead place.

Norn – The people of northern Heimir, who were conquered generations ago by an off-world force from Tyria.

Ordinal – The lowest rank of priest-officer in the Tyrianite Federal Legion.

Otho – Heimir's small moon.

Prefect – A commanding officer in the Tyrianite Federal Legion.

Quaya – Heimir's large red moon.

Rune – A mystic symbol imbued with meaning by a powerful magician and subsequently used by binders in the capture, refinement, and repurposing of spiritual energies.

Skald – A traditional Norn spiritual leader who practices a hereditary form of blood magic.

Ten Fathers – The original patriarchs of the Norn clans, now deified in the local practice of ancestor worship.

Tyrianites – The people hailing from the city and world of Tyria. The successor state of the Shining Ones, and conquerors of the majority of the solar system.

Tyrus – The leader of the Shining Ones, thought dead by modern Tyrianite society, but secretly still leading the Federation.

Wanderer – A comet.

Made in the USA
Middletown, DE
28 July 2022